The Bitter War of Always

THE BITTER WAR OF ALWAYS

IMMORTALITY SHATTERED BOOK TWO

Christian Warren Freed

Copyright © 2020 by Christian Warren Freed

Excerpt from *The Land of Wicked Shadows* 2021 Christian Warren Freed
Cover design by BRoseDesignz
Cover copyright 2021 by Warfighter Books
Author Photograph by Anicie Freed
Map by Jamie Noble

Warfighter Books
Holly Springs, North Carolina 27540
https://www.christianwfreed.com

Second Edition: August 2021

Library of Congress Cataloging-in-Publication Data
Name: Freed, Christian Warren, 1973- author.
Title: The Bitter War of Always/ Christian Warren Freed
Description: Second Edition | Holly Springs, NC: Warfighter Books, 2021. Identifiers: LCCN 2021900398 | ISBN 9781957326276 (hardcover) | ISBN 9781734907599 (trade paperback) Subjects: Epic fantasy | Military fantasy | Paranormal

Printed in the United States of America

ACCLAIM FOR CHRISTIAN WARREN FREED

HAMMERS IN THE WIND: BOOK I OF THE NORTHERN CRUSADE

"I love this book. This book hooked my attention on the first page and it was hard to put down. There is darkness in this book, you know something is going to happen so you keep reading to find out what. The author writes it so good, it's like you are there experiencing what the characters are. And I love it."

"I purchased this book to read to see if it would be suitable for my daughter to read. She is advanced in reading, but some books for kids older than her can be a little to much content wise. I think this one will work out great for her and she would enjoy it as much as I did. I'm glad I came across this book and can't wait to read the rest of the series."

WHERE HAVE ALL THE ELVES GONE?

"This story is fresh and a little tongue-in-cheek, a nice fantasy change of pace with twists here and there that make you have to keep on turning the pages."

"Christian Warren Freed is a very gifted, well-spoken author and his story took me in from page 1. His descriptions of situations, momentary happenings and his vivid characters of the world within the story made my fantasy run wild. As a reader, I felt like being part of the carefully woven net of this book."

THE DRAGON HUNTERS

"Excellently written. The author is able to really capture the stress, fear, and panic of life and death situations such as combat. Greatly looking forward to the next installment in the series!"

"Mr. Freed weaves the parts of this tale together smoothly, keeping the story moving at a good pace. He uses his own military background to paint powerful battle images and then he moves on. With only a little background, he makes the reader care about the members of the band – to worry about them and want them to do the 'right thing'. He adds depth to the characters through their actions and his dialogue is very realistic."

ARMIES OF THE SILVER MAGE

"Armies of the Silver Mage was a great read...any fan of Lord of the Rings or Game of Thrones will love this book. I'm looking forward to next book."

"The book is almost an homage to the great classics like Sword of Shanara and the Lord of the Rings. The author has cleverly used his past military and combat experience to make the battle scenes more realistic."

Other Books by Christian Warren Freed

The Northern Crusade
Hammers in the Wind
Tides of Blood and Steel
A Whisper After Midnight
Empire of Bones
The Madness of Gods and Kings
Even Gods Must Fall

The Histories of Malweir
Armies of the Silver Mage
The Dragon Hunters
Beyond the Edge of Dawn

Forgotten Gods
Dreams of Winter
The Madman on the Rocks
Anguish Once Possessed
Through Darkness Besieged
Under Tattered Banners

Where Have All the Elves Gone?
Tomorrow's Demise: The Extinction Campaign
Tomorrow's Demise: Salvation
Coward's Truth: A Novel of the Heart Eternal
The Lazarus Men
Repercussions: A Lazarus Men Agenda

A Long Way From Home: Memories and
Observations From Iraq and Afghanistan+

Immortality Shattered
Law of the Heretic
The Bitter War of Always
Land of Wicked Shadows
Storm Upon the Dawn

<u>War Priests of Andrak Saga</u>
The Children of Never

SO, You Want to Write a Book? +
SO, You Wrote a Book. Now What? +

Forthcoming   + Nonfiction

For Taylor

Dream Haven
Crimson Fields
Krim Salat
GALDEA
ARAGOTH
Mount Dominion
The Twins
Hyrast
Daltoran
Galdarath
Drim
ALMARIN
Steel River
Greyhawk Keep
Kitenurem
SUROC TOL
Dol'ir
Prossin
Macifin
Camarena
Drear Hills
CORONAN
TRIMLON
Wood of Ilis
THE WILDERLANDS
Urichar
Lilsen Mountains
Lilhaven
Savarin
Moistholm
Goretsch Plateau
Grim Mountain
VALADON
Arlen River
Port of Grespan
Broken Mountain
Jerincon
Grun
JEMMAN SEA
Barren Town
GOBLIN LANDS
THE ISLE OF ILLUSIONS
EITERLAND
Nonicks
Grimstone Mountains
Fallon Run
Towers of Perdition
Plains of Darkpool
Eieran
XIL-AN LAKE
SADITH OOM
Tower of Souls
THE FREE LANDS
Morthus
Mordrun Hath

12

THE BITTER WAR OF ALWAYS

The Bitter War of Always

PROLOGUE

Dawn bestowed unparalleled grace upon the lands, yet no bird rose to greet it, nor did beast nor insect stir. Instead of peace only nature could provide, a battle raged. A battle so great and intense that none could recall a time in history to match it. Columns of smoke billowed up into the clouds, carrying with it the stench of charred flesh and worse. Bolts of supernatural power flared across the battlefield, killing scores with every strike. Catapult rounds accompanied the blasts, chewing up ground and smashing armored bodies.

The battle had raged for three days and was finally coming to the inevitable conclusion. Stacks of bodies filled the tree lines to make room for the current batch of combatants. Ranks were dangerously thin. Exhaustion spread across the field. It was all each individual could do just to suit up and march toward their enemy. Vultures crowded the treetops as eager spectators. Soon they would feast.

Ils Kincannon stood atop a lonesome hill and somberly watched as the remnants of his once proud army took the field for what was destined to be the final time. They had been cut down to a mere seven thousand men and were outnumbered five to one. This would be the final march of the knights of the Seven Manacles. Arrayed against them were the loyal order of the Golden Warriors, sworn protectors of the Hierarchy and the wizards who ran it, as well as the kingdoms of the Free Lands. They were a most impressive sight, especially for a man who had once been their commander.

Kincannon knew them to be the very best the Free Lands had to offer. He'd been proud to lead them, until greed and corruption seduced his soul. It was greed that veered him away from order and decency, thus plunging the world into the worst war in history. Kincannon broke away from the Hierarchy with the mind to steal the newly created Staff of Life, a divine rod capable of linking the user to the land, virtually turning him into a god. Only now, after years of violent conflict, was he aware of the wrongness in his judgment. He was at last prepared to accept that and atone.

His colorless eyes took in the waning moments of the battle below and wondered what had gone wrong. He'd aimed to seize the Staff and set the world to what he viewed as right. The Hierarchy immediately labelled him a heretic, yet people continued to flock to his banner. Despite the accusations heaped upon his name, Ils Kincannon remained a hero to the general population.

Swords clashed as the front ranks collided in a massive press of men and iron. Pikes ran through armor and into the soft flesh beneath. Both knights and soldiers fell by the score. Screams of the dying echoed with thunderous intensity. It was a sound Kincannon was all too familiar with. He had served the Hierarchy for almost forty years and knew many of those pitted against him. *Friend should not have to kill friend.* Perhaps that was what pained him the most.

"My lord?"

Kincannon turned to face his most trusted friend and advisor. "Yes, General Issius?"

The war lord, a tired old mercenary with more scars than hair on his head, strode up to him with battered helm under an arm. "The army is on the verge of annihilation. You must use the Staff or call for retreat, else all is lost."

Kincannon shook his head in sorrow. "I cannot. Only now, after all this senseless slaughter, do I understand what this Staff really is. They were foolish to create it. I cannot use it or it will be my hand that condemns the world to death. Summon the squire to bring my horse. I will ride into battle and seek at least a small measure of redemption for my soul. Any man who is not a coward, nor afraid to face his death, is free to ride with me. Perhaps we may make an end worthy of legend."

"But the Staff!" Issius protested.

"Will be found by another, but when the world is ready for it. I have already dispatched men, with the aid of that wizard, to see that it is properly disposed of. I fear for the world should the day of rediscovery arrive. Now, summon my squire!"

General Issius turned to walk away, furious with the deceptions of his leader and friend.

"Will you ride with me, old friend?" Kincannon called out to him.

The words scorched his heart. After countless battles and nearly twenty years, the end of his life was finally here. It was not the end Issius had envisioned. He replied without stopping. "Aye, but I fear the end shall lack the glory you so dream of."

Close to five hundred men were mounted and waiting for commands. They were Kincannon's personal guard and battle staff. A retinue of his finest fighters not already spent in combat. He looked into each man's eyes and felt his heart break as minor details of each came to him. Rolfnir with his four children. Adgal who had lost his wife during the past winter. Sixteen year old Olaf who joined because his father had, and his father before that. On and on. They were all a part of him. It was a difficult thing to do, asking men and boys to die in his name. Difficult but necessary.

"Each of you has fought for me and sworn your loyalty to a cause greater than your own. Your brothers are in the vale fighting for you and me. Will you fight with them? Give your blood for theirs?" he addressed them.

A small cheer went up from some of them. He knew it was mostly bluster, for no sane man truly wanted to die in battle. Not even the crazed were anxious to pass on to the next world. His veterans had been through much more than the youths, so eager to prove themselves, and they knew that what was being asked was tantamount to suicide.

"I ask you all, will you follow me into the gates of death and find victory for our cause?"

Another cheer, louder, rippled through them. General Issius turned his head away rather than let Kincannon see his utter disgust. Kincannon was too wrapped up with his five hundred. He nodded approvingly. *They have spirit, if only they had numbers as well.* He looked down into the vale again and couldn't help but feel distressed that his army, the one he was purposefully sacrificing for the greater good of the rest of the world, was surrounded and dwindling. With a grunt, Kincannon spurred the side of his mount and started down the hill. The last glory of the Seven Manacles had begun.

To the soldiers lost in the swirl of battle, life had grown precariously short. Fear took root and started to overcome many. No matter how many of the enemy they killed, a hundred more seemed to surge forth to take their places. Young men, not yet old enough to marry in their homelands, fought with amazing tenacity. But the cold darkness of reality was catching up to them. Talk of their leader deserting them reverberated harshly through the rank and file. The only thing keeping many from breaking away was the ring of steel hemming them in.

A shout suddenly arose from the beleaguered men of the Seven Manacles.

"Lord Kincannon fights among us!"

The Golden Warriors blanched at the name, even as the defenders roared. There was new hope. The very sight of the Lord of the Seven Manacles inspired his ranks into new fits of rage. The bedraggled men doubled the fever pitch of battle and fought to the last. Kincannon and his five hundred broke into the enemy lines, cleaving great holes with every sword swing. Everyone, except those nearest, understood the desperation. There was no possible way the Seven Manacles could find victory, not even with the near legendary Ils Kincannon at the head.

Kincannon paused long enough to see Issius pulled from his saddle and killed. His own horse buckled a moment later before throwing him to the ground. Kincannon struggled to rise but it was too late. Dozens of men in stained golden armor set upon him.

Late that night, when the dust settled and the smoke began to clear, the entire host of the army of the Seven Manacles lay dead or dying. The Hierarchy leadership had instructed the army to take but one prisoner. Teams of men scoured the battlefield in search of the heretic Ils Kincannon. Healers ignored those orders and treated wounded from both sides. The rebellion was crushed and it was time to restore the semblance of humanity. After all, it was all they had left.

It wasn't until midday of the following that they managed to find the heretic. Blood continued to flow from wounds too numerous to count. Arrows pierced him.

Broken swords lay around his dying body in tribute. He was dehydrated and bordering on death.

"Captain!" shouted the young soldier standing over the body.

The commander strode calmly over to the small knot of warriors. His head was bandaged, entire body bruised. He looked down on the prize but couldn't force himself to smile. There was no satisfaction in this victory. This was not the way he imagined the end of the war. With a sigh he said, "Go and inform the general, lad. Let them know they can call off the search."

"Yes, sir!"

The once proud Ils Kincannon tried to laugh at the exuberance the soldier displayed, but only managed to cough up blood. He raised a weak arm to grab the captain by the bottom of his cape. Pulling the man so close that only he could hear the heretic's dying words, Kincannon whispered the prophecy that would forever dominate the fate of the world.

ONE
Out of Galdarath

The thunder of some fifty odd horses roared across the open plains of northern Galdea. Snow kicked up in a small blizzard. The wind was freezing, numbing the riders to the point of frostbite. Despite the hardships already endured, the drain of strength from the horses, all the sores and pains that came from a forced ride, they could not allow themselves to stop. Pursuit followed close behind.

Enemy forces had been lying in wait for the column not far from Galdarath proper. A brief battle ensued and resulted in several darklings slain and none of the Golden Warriors. The minor victory felt good after many long months of pursuit and too many setbacks. Since then, the column successfully managed to evade the darklings and stay one step ahead.

All night they rode, racing to reach the valley of the Twins. They didn't rein in for a brief halt until the first fingers of light were stretching across the sky. Aron Kryte was forced to make unsavory decisions. The eastern plains stretched farther than his eyes could see, rolling softly under blankets of snow and interspersed with light forests and glades of silver bark birch trees. Normally this part of the Free Lands was serene, peaceful beyond reproach. But war had come, threatening to render everything into terms of despair. Making matters worse for Aron, the Lord of the Golden Warriors and heir to the mad Ils Kincannon's legacy, it was still a three-day ride to where Field Marshal Dlorn waited with the main body of Galdea's army. The horses would tire long before they ever reached the Twins if he maintained the breakneck pace. The rebel armies of the Black Imelin weren't far behind.

He turned from the landscape. His men sat clumped around a handful of campfires, just large enough to warm them and cook a meager breakfast. He decided to take council at his private fire.

"We could be worse off, if we had split up," Amean Repage, his second in command and most trusted advisor, said. He liked the idea less and less as the minutes dragged on. "The terrain is unfamiliar and the Black is hard on our scent. Splitting up now will only make it easier for that bastard turncoat to catch and kill us."

Aron sipped on a lukewarm cup of coffee, relishing the minor amount of heat entering his system. "We don't have much of a choice. I seriously doubt that we can fend off hordes of darklings for another three days. They're smarter than we give them credit for and driven by the Black's magic. We must do what is best."

He was still coming to terms with being named the heir to Ils Kincannon. Combined with the Black being a direct descendant of the man who had taken and hidden the Staff of Life from that fateful battle of Sadith Oom so many years ago, he couldn't help but feel trapped in a game far beyond his ability to conceptualize. Making matters odder, both he and the Black Imelin, once the great wizard-warrior of the Free Lands and member of the Hierarchy High Council, had reversed the roles of their ancestors.

"They seek the power of the Staff," Karin Ilth broke in. "My visions haven't returned but I can see the obvious. That and what the Black wants me to."

Venom singed her voice. Since having the vision that took her into Aron's path, she had been stymied at every turn. Her one solace came from her developing relationship with Aron. Theirs was an odd love affair, born in the fires of a fledgling war.

"There is a way," Andolus announced. "And we should be able to take a few of the enemy down in the process"

All eyes but Long Shadow's turned to the elf prince. The silent warrior left the warmth of the fire for an open area away from the others. He already knew what the elf counseled. Shrugging his heavy travel cloak off, Long Shadow drew both of his mighty broadswords. Using a skill few in these lands had mastered, he went about a daily training ritual that would exhaust most. Steel flashed and hacked with the grace of angel wings. Long years of discipline honed his skills to the sharpness of a blade.

Elsyn, once princess of Galdea, now turned queen-regent in the wake of her father's assassination but a few days earlier, broke her saddened gaze from the fire to watch him in awe. She had seen him go through his drills just once, but from a distance. She was impressed with his rugged stiffness. His body was heavily muscled and honed to a deep shade of bronze. Save for a small knot on the back of his head, he was always freshly shaved. She couldn't remember ever seeing such a man. Almost by accident, she picked up the conversation around her.

"North of here is a place mortal man has long forgotten," the elf began as he resumed his seat. "It was once called Dreamhaven, the barrows of the elven kings. Our people have not buried a king in two hundred years. Not since our struggles with the goblins, where Cerelin was killed from atop his mount. It will take another day's ride to reach them, but the enemy will be confused with the redirection and fall off the trail. By splitting up, we can regain the advantage. Otherwise, they will have us not long after nightfall."

Aron looked to each of those assembled. No matter how hard he tried, he couldn't help but recall how Elsyn reacted when she accepted her father's death. She turned stony, more terrible than he had ever seen in a woman of her tender age. She had spoken little thus far, breaking the silence only long enough to make a small statement.

"My father is dead," she told him.

Hatred and sorrow mixed together. Hatred for those responsible and sorrow for the loss of her only family she held dear. She was intent now, intent on returning Galdea to the great kingdom it once was. Intent on driving the hordes of darklings back into their foul land of Suroc Tol and sealing the way forever. She was becoming a force to be feared.

He also knew that with such drive came the slim chance of budding insanity. Would it be too much for her to handle as she compartmentalized her grief? He didn't know. Karin had gone to her when they stopped in the middle of that first night. What they said remained private and would stay that way until the princess decided otherwise. Both understood what it meant to lose a father.

"They shouldn't bother with the main body as much as they will with us. I imagine they have eyes on us as we speak," Andolus surmised.

"Can we make it?" Karin asked.

The elf shrugged. "We stand a very good chance of it. Since we can't hide our tracks, the enemy will be in no hurry to run us down, even with the Staff of Life in our possession. The Black knows we won't risk stopping in any village."

"He should also be wondering about Dlorn and his army. They would have already acted if they were still in

Galdarath," Amean reasoned. "If he catches us in the open …"

"The barrows will give us protection. Dreamhaven lets no evil pass within," Andolus said. "The only problem is reaching them. Long Shadow and I know a few tricks. We should be able to shake the darklings just enough. Other than that, I offer no reassurances."

Amean shook his head firmly. "I don't like it."

"There is nothing to like about any of this, old friend," Aron said, having already made up his mind. "Jou Amn will lead the main body on to the Twins and Lord Felbar. The rest of us will head for Dreamhaven. Jou, tell Marshal Dlorn about us. Get the army ready to march. Once we return, I imagine our first battle won't be far off. The Black will stop at nothing to get the Staff from us. With Dlorn and the legions of Galdea, we might be able to hold out long enough for the Hierarchy to field their army.

"If we don't?" Amean asked.

"Aldar have mercy on our souls," the elf answered.

"Then it's settled," Aron said. "The time has come to be on our way."

The tired band broke camp and remounted. Each knew the enemy was close behind and time was slipping away. The burly Jou Amn led the column east, while Aron and his small band stayed and watched until the golden mass was out of sight. Aron gave those remaining an odd look. A more curious collection of people he couldn't imagine. An elf prince with his silent warrior friend from across the shore, an old veteran ready to retire, a seer and now love interest, and a princess bent on revenge. With a grim nod, he spurred them on.

Jent Tariens stood atop the wall, pained with fatigue. Bodies lay strewn all around. Some were men, others darkling. The battle began shortly after the discovery of King Elian's corpse. A host of darklings then emerged from the cover of the outlying forests and laid siege to Galdarath. The defenders barely had time to close the gates before the black wave crashed upon the wood and stone.

Darklings were already climbing the walls when Harrin Slinmyer rallied those already on duty and sounded the alarm, virtually saving the city by doing so. The fight was well underway by the time archers manned their towers and began firing their deadly bolts into the mass of enemies. Despite this effort, darklings continued to gain the upper hand.

The wall was almost lost by the time Tariens and the main force arrived. Harrin and his company fought bravely, but they knew they wouldn't be able to hold long. The battle continued for two hours. Weary men fought for their lives, their city, and their kingdom. Fatigue bit into them as they carried on. Each knew that should the gates fall, so too would Galdarath.

Thoughts of sending a mounted counterattack out into the darklings were quickly discarded. Even with their senior leadership off to the Twins, those left in power were reluctant to waste manpower on a whim. Tariens managed to seize control of the battle, sending fresh troops to plug holes in the line. Kill teams were dispatched to hunt down those darklings that had managed to break through. Enemy fighters died by the score and still they came on.

Jent Tariens studied the battlefield for signs of a plan. His horror emerged when he realized what the darklings were doing. The battle at the gates was a feint. Darklings were trying to draw attention away from something else, something important. A portion of the battlements crumbled, allowing dozens of darklings into the city. Harrin Slinmyer and his valiant few were there immediately, keeping the defense from collapsing. Several men and all the darklings died in the fever pitched struggle. Harrin suffered from injuries to his right leg and had to be removed, against his will.

The newly titled Steward of Galdea posted lookouts to watch for another airborne incursion. Thankfully, none came. Tariens still wasn't comfortable with his new position but was also equally determined to perform at the highest level. Anything to keep his people alive. Another battalion of fresh soldiers poured up the ramparts. The darklings broke off their attack, despite having most of the advantages. They filed away without a word, leaving their dead and wounded before folding back into the forest.

A great cheer arose from the defenders, for it was their second victory over the tide of darkness. Hope was not lost. Only Jent Tariens wasn't so sure. The darklings knew exactly what they were doing. They had the numerical advantages and were threatening to break through with each attempt. Tariens turned to face his beloved city and wondered. What were they protecting?

"Arison!" he bellowed, sheathing his sword.

The young, blood-stained lieutenant approached.

"I want the city put on lock down. Everyone is to remain in their homes until further notice. All soldiers not involved in wall defense will break down into squad-sized elements and scour the city. I want the Black Imelin and his entourage found and detained, preferably alive. You have your orders," he barked.

Arison saluted and began shouting at his subordinates. Wind driving his hair back, Tariens faced the forest and waited for the next attack he was certain was coming. *As long as that damned wizard remains within the walls, we'll be under siege.*

The Black Imelin rode free of Galdarath with mixed emotions. His deception with the darklings went exceedingly well, even if it cost him too many lives. Hundreds of darklings died, but it was a small price to pay. He regretted the loss of Artle Colinger, but that, too, had been necessary. There was no way the king killer would have been accepted as the new ruler. Artle was a worm and could not be trusted. Still, the man had served his purpose and was properly disposed of.

The death of his men, loyal soldiers and mercenaries who had followed him from Meisthelm far to the south, at the hands of those meddlesome priests of the Red Brotherhood was inexcusable, however. They deserved a better end. That too, he reluctantly admitted, was necessary. If the world were to die this very day, it would bother him little. So long as all ended by his decree.

The relief on his face quickly faded as images of the young lordling Aron Kryte came to him. The very name filled him with such intense rage, he felt the urge to kill. Gulnick Baach, his renegade general and second in command, rode behind in silence. Matters were spiraling too far out of control for the tempered man's liking. This was not what he had bargained for when he betrayed the Hierarchy and blindly followed Imelin across the face of the world. The way matters were progressing, Gulnick was certain they were barreling towards the fiery pits of the underworld. Yet together they continued north. To the only place the Black could think of. The valley of the Twins and dragon that was Field Marshal Dlorn and his waiting army.

Fear drove them. Night fell and so too did the gripping fangs of the darklings. The attack happened shortly after Aron and his companions stopped to rest their horses and snatch a quick bite to eat. Frantic moments of struggle ensued, resulting in the death of a handful of darklings and minor cuts and bruises for the heroes.

Hours had passed since the first darkling had broken through the startled defenders' camp and Aron pushed them harder. He practically felt the enemy's breaths upon him. The terror of their icy fingers clawing down his back. Sweat lathered the horses. Pure adrenaline pushed him on, for every second meant one in which they might be caught.

They ran on through the night, until at last Aron felt the tension was eased. He brought them back to a slow walk and took in what he could see of the surrounding terrain. What he saw disturbed him. They had been driven into a small ravine. A death trap for sure. It was Andolus' warning that broke his thoughts. The elf prince smelled the trap and tried to warn the others. It was too late. Long Shadow drew his sword, as the others looked about in confusion. The ravine walls had come alive in the night with the piercing red glare of eyes. The darklings had never left them after all.

TWO

Dreamhaven

Aron swung his sword with all the force he could muster. The darkling fell, neatly clove in two. Howls went up from the dozens more watching along the steep banks. Rage pounded them, the hunger of a promised kill. A horse snickered in fear, trying desperately to bolt, only to be held fast by the rider.

"We have to get out of here!" Karin shouted above the roar.

Thus far, only three darklings had bothered attacking. It was almost as if they were trying to force the trapped humans into making a miscalculated move. A crash sounded behind those trapped. Aron wheeled his horse around in time to watch a giant tree slam to the ground in a blizzard of broken branches, kicking up snow and dirt. Their escape route was cut off.

"Aron!" Karin cried out in grief.

The split-second plans to which he had grown so accustomed, abandoned him. Aron could do nothing but sit back and watch as the glaring red eyes edged closer, drawing the noose tighter. The stranglehold was about to succeed. All the dreams of saving the Free Lands evaporated.

Unseen by anyone, Long Shadow growled with preemptive satisfaction. Taking the reins between his teeth, his twin broadswords were poised to strike. The forged steel danced like wild magic in the pale moonlight. Andolus motioned to Karin and both simultaneously nocked arrows. The old, but dependable Amean drew Elsyn's horse close to his and confided that all was going to be fine, though he was ignorant as to what was about to happen.

Andolus caught Long Shadow's attention and nodded slowly. Darkling howls subsided in the night, as if they were suddenly eager to bear witness to what followed. Another nod to Karin and arrows flew, whistling through the air and echoing dully within the soft flesh of a pair of darklings. The chaos began anew, but this time, the tiny band of heroes was prepared.

In the split second they shot their arrows, Long Shadow charged into the darklings. The others were hard pressed to keep up as the silent warrior went into battle rage. There was but one way to quench his need. The blood of darklings. Speed of horse and skill with steel, sent him plunging into the massed ranks. Long Shadow was upon them before the darklings were able to establish a cordon. Swords swung with blinding speed. Aron and the others smashed into the darklings moments later. The darkling line broke, what few remained alive or uninjured.

"Quickly!" Andolus urged, "Before they reorganize. We have to get clear of the ravine."

Amean snatched Elsyn's reins, as she clung for dear life. He looked up in astonishment as the elf prince somehow managed to spin around in his saddle and draw a bead on a tree halfway up the slope. A thick rag had been wrapped around his arrow shaft. Andolus slowed his horse and took aim. A darkling sprung from hiding, barreling towards the much hated elfling. Aron swept in to intercept the darkling, splitting it open from neck to hip. Andolus fired as the corpse struck the ground.

The arrow sped, fast and true, exploding upon contact. Several darklings too near the tree caught fire and ran shrieking into the night. Others fell dead. The tiny band struggled on.

"Keep riding!" Andolus shouted to them. "Press hard and we'll make it."

Long Shadow was already blazing a path through the press of bodies. The sloping ground was littered with corpses. Snow turned dark with blood. The stench of death choked them all. Horses jerked, threatening to break away. Swords rose and fell. Claws raked exposed flesh. The battle became fluid, moving from one end of the ravine to the other as the band of heroes struggled ahead.

Bringing up the rear, Aron Kryte did his best to buy time for the others. The Staff of Life bounced along his horse's flank, bring much attention to itself. The darklings caught sight of it and the primitive parts of their brains registered it as the object their master desired. They howled with perverse delight. The master would be pleased, or perhaps they might take the Staff to Duoth N'nclogbar so that the darklings might rule for eternity. Decisions like that, while complex for the monsters, could come after the Staff was secure.

Aron felt the incline as horse and rider started to climb. Hope drove him forward. Once clear of the murderous ravine, his group stood a much better chance of outrunning the darklings. To his surprise, none of the vile creatures were waiting as he began the ascent. He also grew concerned at how far behind he was falling. What little he could see, prevented despair from sinking in. Long Shadow was in the lead, already clearing a small patch of earth, while the others sprinted to him.

"Look! Aron's being trapped!" Elsyn called, pointing back, as throngs of darklings swarmed in from the sides to cut off the Golden Warrior's escape.

Long Shadow reacted as if he'd been expecting such. Dismounting, he stalked toward the mass of darklings and to what Amean was convinced, certain death. Archers nocked and fired in support. Swords cut and slashed. Bodies piled. Long Shadow was immersed in his element. A natural force of nature, unstoppable and volatile beyond compare.

Amean watched, helplessly, as Aron struggled to climb out of the ravine. Claws raked Aron's horse. It kicked back in reflex, crushing the chest of the darkling responsible. The move allowed Aron to win free of the trap. With a final burst of speed, the wounded horse surged past Long Shadow and on into the safety of the group. Darklings on the ravine floor snarled in rage. They pushed ahead.

Seven clambered over their fallen to encircle Long Shadow. The bald, mountain of a man was clearly the greatest threat. Man and monster squared off. Long Shadow's eyes took in each detail of the darklings. Their body language. Their poise. One sword raised, the other low, he darted forward. Two darklings fell dead. Fresh blood dripped from his blades. Another pair fell, feathered with arrows. Long Shadow pressed.

A darkling leapt high, seeking to come down on his head, and was skewered for the effort. Long Shadow threw the body away and crouched low with a backhand swing that decapitated a second darkling. The last, suddenly losing courage, sought to run but was killed by an arrow in the throat. Long Shadow rose slowly, arms out to his sides in silent challenge. No enemy within eyesight, he moved slowly and deliberately back up the slope to his waiting horse. The grim smile on his blood streaked face left Elsyn in fear.

"Come on!" Karin shouted. The weariness of their flight showing in the strain of her voice. "We have to go before others show up."

"She'll never make it, not with my weight on her," Aron announced after inspecting his wounded horse. "Andolus, how much further to Dreamhaven?"

"Mayhap six hours. It's hard to tell without the sun. Much of this terrain is unfamiliar to me. The night and snow only make it worse."

"Here, take my horse. Maybe I can at least slow those beasts down enough for the rest of you to escape," Amean volunteered. Dark resolve oozed from his words.

Aron looked at him with shock. "What are you saying? No one is staying behind. Suicide serves no purpose. Least of all for you, old man."

"I'm too old to go running all over the creation on some damn fool quest," Amean shook his head.

"You don't know what you're saying," Karin said. She'd come to think of him almost as a father figure. "What about your daughter? And her child? Are you going to abandon them to the wolves as well?"

He said nothing.

"We need you, my friend," Aron said with the finality of a commanding officer. "No one stays. If we can't make it together, we don't make it at all."

"And your horse?"

Aron shrugged. "Will go as far as she can."

"Wait," Karin offered. "You can double up with me. I don't weight that much and it should give her enough time to heal."

He caught her sharp smile, so well disguised behind a stern face, threatening to crack. She was going to enjoy this more than he. A howl went up from the opposite end of the ravine. It wouldn't take long for the darklings to get around that fallen tree. Aron, reluctantly, climbed behind Karin and tied his wounded steed to hers. Once again, the little company struck out for promised safety. Andolus led. The doom bringer Long Shadow bringing up the rear. In a burst of rage, darklings swept past their dead and continued the hunt.

To the burly Jou Amn, it was just another day in a kingdom that looked the same, no matter where he went. Since splitting with Kryte and the others, they had seen no contact. Indeed, there was little of anything alive out in the cold winter plains. The Black and his foul army seemed unconcerned with the main body, as if they knew Aron Kryte had the Staff.

They'd been riding for almost two days and still hadn't seen a sign of pursuit. Jou Amn was uneasy. Years of service told him extended periods of inactivity often led to violent surprise. Complacency threated to set in the longer they rode. Men such as those around him needed battle to remain sharp, occupied. Though they'd fled for their lives, no enemy pursued. He didn't particularly mind that part, but the hairs on the back of his neck continued to stand. An eerie feeling haunted him.

By the dawn of the third day, they began to smell the ice-covered tendrils of the first of the Twins. Both massive enough to be rivers of their own, the twins ran several hundred leagues south before combining to form the strength that was the Simca River. The main stem of the river eventually poured out into the oceans at the Port of Grespon.

Life suddenly reappeared, uncontaminated by the foul presence troubling the lands west. Winter birds, raptors and carrion eaters perched scattered throughout the sparse groves of birch and elm dotting the valley. A sharp crest rose another two leagues distant, marking the heart of Lord Felbar's territory. Still, Jou Amn couldn't find it in himself to relax.

A shrill whistle filled the afternoon sky, followed by another in the distance. Great raptors with green and black feathers erupted from their perches, disturbed by something Jou Amn couldn't see. Those hairs threatened to leap off his neck. His hand dropped to his sword. The comfort of being within reach of his weapon allowed him to think clearly.

Jou Amn halted and turned to issue orders, as a single arrow struck the ground at his feet. Fate tempted, the grizzled veteran drew his sword and brought up his small shield. The instant his blade touched the chill air, a hundred elven bowmen slipped from the shadows and aimed. An even smaller armored force emerged from seemingly nowhere, lances with honed, barbed tips leveled and ready to charge.

One rider made his way down to the front of the Golden Warrior column, stopping well short, yet within speaking distance. The wind blew his long, raven black hair away from his shoulders, adding to his already ominous authority. Cold eyes stared at each of those he could make out. He finished his impassive scan and returned his gaze on Jou Amn. The wind stopped as he opened his mouth.

"I wouldn't do that, if I were you."

The looming hulks of massive barrows marked the edge of Dreamhaven territory. Yet, there was no sense of relief among the weary band. It wouldn't take the darklings long to figure out where Andolus was leading them and when that happened… The lure of the Staff was powerful, almost aphrodisiac-like. The enemy would sweep down upon the tiny group like the hounds of death itself. Time, despite being so close to their destination, was a growing enemy. Aron almost despised his job.

The keen eyes of the elf prince guided them through the great barrows of past elf kings. Once marvelous statues of marble and bronze decorated the surrounding grounds, now worn and broken by years of harsh neglect. Stains streaked the face of a proud elf king, standing with his sword raised high in a killing blow, giving the image of tears streaming from his sad eyes. The crystal and marble head of his war stallion lay broken in a patch of ivy, lifeless eyes and mouth gaping.

The barrows themselves sustained little damage through the years, though all had turned pale shades of grey and brown. The splendor that once gave life to Dreamhaven had fled. Decay wormed from grave to grave. Droves of gardens once teeming with rainbows of flowers were now overrun with weeds. Dreamhaven, the past glory of an ancient elven empire, was ignored to the point of doom.

Each new step of horse brought another vivid terror to the young Galdean princess, despite the sense of calm struggling to sooth her nerves. Elsyn couldn't tear her eyes from the ghostly figures standing in snow and weed. Originally intended to depict the splendor of an entire people, the tombs gave an ill-boding that reminded her of a graveyard. Shadows danced within shadows. She felt as if she was being watched. Vile eyes marking her every movement. Paranoia washed through her frail body.

Elsyn fought off the mounting fright and rested her gaze on the dashing young warrior in golden armor. She caught herself sighing and silently reprimanded herself. What would her father think of her indecent behavior? A royal princess and heir to the throne pining over a soldier. Memories of her father stole into her and she felt her heart sink further. *Father! How cruel the world is to take you from me!*

"What's wrong?" Amean asked, in a low voice with genuine concern.

Elsyn shifted uneasily in the saddle, startled by the unexpected interruption. "I was just thinking of my father."

He knew it. Grief and loss were difficult to accept and then discard. "He was a brave man, princess. Wise and strong. He …"

"Please. You don't have to patronize him on my account. He knew he was going to die. I told him months ago. It's strange, but I almost feel as if his death has an integral part in the way the rest of this is being played out."

She fell silent, once again becoming enshrouded in her personal mystery. Amean turned back to Aron, who had heard the entire conversation. He shrugged his shoulders and continued to ride behind Karin, oblivious to Elsyn's infatuation.

They came at last to a grove of mighty trees nestled atop a small knoll. They stretched over a hundred feet into the air, shining with silver bark. Branches spread as if the world was theirs, none of them touching. Small, yellow birds peered out from behind leaves that kept them secluded from prying eyes. They sprang to life upon sensing the elf, giving those new arrivals the gift of their song.

"Behold! The Druinna Calar!" Andolus cried in adulation. Joy and relief spread, the first any but Long Shadow had seen in him.

Elsyn immediately lost her fear of shadows and those things that go bump in the night. The trees were the most beautiful sight she'd ever witnessed, far surpassing the castle fortress of Galdarath. They almost appeared surreal, as if made from the paint of a god's eye. Vivid colors spiraled in her head. Each passing moment saw her hopes rise, her spirit strengthened.

"Here we shall camp. No darkling will dare attack us so long as the Druinna Calar protect. Nothing evil can exist close to their eternal boughs," Andolus explained, as he dismounted and hurried to the nearest tree.

Andolus took a deep breath as he reached a tentative hand out to the smooth bark. Flesh and bark combined, sending ripples of ancient emotion through his tired body. With a sigh, he faced his friends and said, "Be at ease. We are well protected in the warmth of the trees. We are safe."

For the time being.

THREE
Changing of the Guard

Laughter, happiness, joy and peace died along with the beloved king. Mirth and love turned sour to the grim tunes of the funeral dirge echoing through the city streets. Mixed emotions divided the population. Most wept openly, lost in the grief of their departed king. Elian was well loved by young and old alike. Anger and rage filled their once complacent, gentle hearts.

A call to arms was raised by patriots and self-proclaimed vigilantes. Small riots in protest broke out, inflicting minor damage to the already beleaguered city. Jent Tariens sent in units of the royal guard and army reserves to quell the unrest and restore order before madness claimed them all. In the three short days since the death of King Elian, Galdarath had become a living nightmare.

Jent Tariens stared into the vastness of wilderness surrounding Galdarath with his empty eyes. Reflections of watch fires danced across his face, adding age where none should be. He was tired, mentally and physically pushed far beyond normal constraints. Sleep had become a rarity. Every hour it seemed a new problem arose, another riot in the streets erupted. Just the day before, he received word that vandals had unearthed the carefully hidden and disguised grave of Artle Colinger and cut his body to shreds. The head was found on the doorstep of another suspected of being one of the Black's puppets. Soldiers swarmed in and managed to successfully recover most of the body before stray dogs got the rest.

Jent heard Harrin Slinmyer come up from behind and smiled. They had become fast friends over the past few weeks and his company was usually able to take Jent's mind from the continual pains of the day.

"There are times when I truly believe the Black has already won," Jent said in a shallow voice, so that none of the others nearby overheard. "I'm not ready to rule a kingdom."

"There is no better man in all of Galdarath," Harrin said. The words bothered him, for now was the time for stern and good leadership, not dithering rumination.

"Field Marshal Dlorn should be where I now stand. Even the princess," Jent continued.

"Dlorn wages war against the enemy far to the north and Elsyn rides for her life." Harrin's voice turned serious. "You were handpicked by the king. Not a fledgling lord or boy prince, but a soldier. A soldier in whom the confidence of an entire kingdom has been placed. Will you let the people suffer more than they already have?"

Dark thoughts floated through Jent's brooding mind. *Steward of Galdea.* He snorted. *Handpicked by the king.* He found it all hard to accept. There must be others more qualified to lead. A season ago, he'd been a mere captain of the guard. Now... There must have been over a hundred minor nobles and others with royal blood clamoring to get to the empty throne. He snorted again. They were all scared away by that bastard wizard.

"Has any news returned from Dlorn's army?" he asked.

"None, as of yet. You must remember that an entire army separates us, somewhere between the mountains and the Twins. It could take weeks for a messenger to circle around and find a way through," Harrin answered with a shrug.

Jent growled at that last. The main body of the army could already have been annihilated and we'd have no way of knowing. The whole world crumbled a little more each day and he was helpless to prevent it.

"We need positive proof that they haven't engaged the darklings yet. Events are moving entirely too fast and beyond our sphere of influence," Jent said. "Time. We need more time."

Harrin laid a caring hand on his friend's shoulder. "You try too hard. Dlorn knows what must be done. He has close to twenty thousand men and elves at his command. They will be enough until the other kingdoms can be mustered."

"Will they? I am fearful to deploy any additional forces. What should happen to this city if we become defenseless? The elves speak of vast armies of darklings, numbering in the hundreds of thousands. No one knows exactly how many devils from Suroc Tol the Drehenzia created. I cannot leave Galdea unprotected. I will not."

The former captain of the guard moved to the next fire. He took small comfort in the simple warming of hands. It reminded him of better times.

"With our guard and reserves, we can mobilize at least another ten thousand men. A formidable force on any field," Harrin reminded.

Jent waggled a finger at him. "Against a mortal army. These devils drop from the very skies to tear us apart. How can we defend against an enemy with flight capability?"

Harrin had no answer.

Jent shook his head. "I need to speak with Felbar. Either him or Dlorn."

Harrin's eyes widened in shock. "You cannot jeopardize this kingdom on the folly of one man! What happens when you die? Who becomes king?"

"Does it matter? Does anything matter anymore?" He threw his arms up in futility. "The wizard and his host are more powerful than anything we have ever encountered. The Hierarchy has yet to dispatch a relief force other than Aron Kryte and his few. Nothing we do here in Galdea will avail. Why not take the glory of our force and meet an end worthy of legend?"

"Have you any idea what you are saying?" Harrin asked in horror. The conversation was quickly getting out of control. "How can you sacrifice everything we have done to make this land strong, just because? You were chosen for a reason, Jent. A madness is in your brain. You must fight it!"

"I must get word to the main army."

Jent made to move on down the wall but Harrin blocked him.

"I won't let you pass," he growled.

"Get out of my way, Harrin," Jent warned. "I have business to attend."

He took another step and was met by the sharp song of steel being brandished.

"Any means necessary," Harrin said. "The lives of every man, woman, and child are more important than a man stricken with weakness. Do not let the dark wizard win this early in the game. You were chosen. You must rule. Who are you to defy the wish of a king?"

Young Jent Tariens edged his breast against the tip of the blade. He wanted to break and run. To let Harrin run him through, if only to end the insanity. End it all now, before the devils of Suroc Tol swarmed over the walls one final time. Tears welled before bursting free to stream down his face. He sagged against the unbending strength of steel, crumbling to the floor an emotional wreck. He held his face in his hands and cried out in sorrow.

"I can't do it," he whispered amidst sobs. "I'm not strong enough. Not strong enough at all."

Harrin's first instinct was to ensure none of the men on duty could see their commander in such a state. Once done, he shoved his sword away and sat opposite of his friend. "No better king than Elian was there. Strong and wise. Those who were not in awe of the man, feared him. No one questioned his decisions, leastwise not openly. Jent, he made you his successor. No one will question his last command."

Palace guards marched in step down Galdarath's main avenue in search of brewing trouble. The city was slowly devolving into a military state. Other guards followed, though in far different attire. They wore gowns of deep blue, their polished armor glittered with jewels bright enough to rival the sun. Many of them had never had the opportunity to wear such before. Today was a special day, one in which all citizens could vent their grief and bid farewell to a well-loved man. Today was the funeral march of King Elian.

Grim faced, the guards marched with crisp, exaggerated movements. Their polished boots echoed like thunder down the crowded corridors of the aged city. Proud standards of the House of Elian waved like beacons amidst the despair. A pair of drummers beat a powerful dirge that reminded all of what had happened. A hundred men marched in front of the wagon-borne king. Another hundred followed behind.

Men and women crowded the streets in throngs. Most wept openly for both their departed king and the future. Small children pointed from between parents' legs as the casket rambled past. Six men in silver robes flanked the open wagon. The plumes on their helmets waved slightly with each step. None of the guardians so much as glanced at the crowds. Flowers were thrown before the wagon. Prayers and oaths uttered.

This day all forgot the cold and accepted the warmth of sorrow and futility. Many vividly recalled images of their king sitting high atop his grey steed, strong and proud, erect with the confidence of the world as he waved and greeted them at every convenience. That was how they wished to remember the king. Not as merely a corpse stolen from them before his time.

Who now would lead them against the dark tide already running rampant across the kingdom?

As if in answer, Jent Tariens stood in the most elegant dress uniform. Pressed and creased, his blouse and trousers were rivalled by the high shine of boots worn only on the most important occasions. A thin rapier was belted at his hip. Once the formality and ceremony were finished, he would return to the more familiar and comfortable war attire.

He greeted Elian's body at the gates of the small royal cemetery, head bowed low in respect. Harrin Slinmyer was there as well, off to the side, along with several minor nobles trapped in the city by fear. The gates were opened as the wagon rolled to a stop. An honor guard stepped forward to line the road. On command, swords were drawn and raised in a bridge over the path. The funeral procession halted. In unison, the six men faced the casket and gently lifted. The wagon was led away.

Jent did a precise about-face and marched the pall bearers to their destination. Throngs of citizens crowded in after, though only kin and royalty was allowed within the hallowed walls. Among the hundreds of anxious faces stood one tiny and insignificant woman. She watched all with growing interest, mixed with concern. She tried searching through the crowds for the one she needed to see but was met by disappointment. Curiosity peaked, Anni Sickali slipped through the crowds and set about the plans she once hoped wouldn't become necessary.

The broken, battered, and burned form of Halvor finally dug out from under the debris that was once sacred ground. His first sights abhorred him. Bile choked his throat. He swallowed it back down and crawled to the first body. A quick inspection showed that virtually all his brothers were dead, murdered by the Black. Two sat upright against the far wall with mouths open from the agony of being burned alive. Fragments of crimson robes clung to their charred flesh. Halvor himself was naked. His robes having been torn away by the wizard's magic.

Bruises and cuts blanketed his frail body. Most of his hair was burned away and his right leg felt like it was broken. He smiled grimly. The others had always considered him the lucky one. The Red Brotherhood wasn't finished, however. Other cells were scattered throughout the kingdoms. Halvor lacked any knowledge of how to contact them though. He sighed. Halvor the elf, priest of the Red Brotherhood, was left alone to carry on the quest of stopping the Black Imelin from gaining the Staff of Life.

He looked in disgust at the dead soldiers. Imelin's men. Their deaths hadn't been pleasant either, from all appearances. The big man impaled to the wall was curious, for he didn't fit in with the others. He wasn't a soldier. Halvor decided he was just an unfortunate caught up in the illusion of power. He took a closer look and reeled back. Those eyes! He'd never seen such horror permanently etched within a man's eyes. Halvor felt honest fear for the second time.

Night dropped on the grieving city with merciful swiftness. Life slowly attempted to return to normalcy. Patrols continued to strengthen and the violence, which had never been particularly intense, gradually subsided. Curfew was enforced, more for the citizens' protection, than the need to impose martial law. Handfuls of miscreants took to the shadows to continue their brand of mayhem but they were ineffectual.

Harrin Slinmyer drew his cloak tight around him and warmed his hands over the watch fire. It was particularly cold this night, much more so than any other this winter. He cursed the thankless job keeping him exposed to the elements so cruelly. The burdens of leadership. The good of the people depended on his ability to perform under duress. It was a position proudly served.

His men performed much the same. Stationary pickets kept watch for two-hour shifts. Roving guards marched segments of the perimeter as a secondary measure. Sergeants of the guard checked their men at intervals, each ensuring that all were alert. Harrin was convinced the enemy wasn't gone and conveyed that to his chain of command. Complacency threatened the defenders of Galdea. Experience taught him that singular act was responsible for killing more soldiers than actual combat.

He left the fire when his nerves tingled. Harrin immediately glanced skyward, praying that none of those fearsome winged beasts were overhead. No wraith-like terrors loomed. No guards cried out in alarm. The outlying forests were quiet, seemingly asleep, though he remained positive those vile red eyes were watching him.

Harrin needed to speak with his men, hoping to calm his frayed nerves. He stopped randomly and made small talk, while trying to find the source of his suspicions. All was calm, quiet on the surface, yet the nagging feeling intensified. Clouds rolled in to occlude the pale moonlight. By the time Harrin returned to the main guard house, he was exhausted.

He slipped out of his cloak and collapsed in an empty chair. The warmth of the building crept into his frozen arms and legs. It was only after rubbing his eyes that he realized he was alone. No less than ten men should have occupied the room, a ready reserve, just in case. The bunks and small kitchen area were empty. Only the tender cackling of burning wood accompanied him.

Harrin rose and drew his sword. "Show yourself."

An old, bent and broken woman stepped from behind the divider in the back of the room. Reluctantly, he lowered his sword and stepped forward. Her eyes held him in their power, locked onto his own, searching.

"You have no need for weapons against me, Captain," she said, her voice plush with the song of a winter bird.

"Who are you? What have you done with my men?" he demanded.

She smiled, an awkward, childish giggle escaping her lips. "Your men are safe. They are merely hidden beneath a spell of my casting. It was necessary for me to do so. I must make sure you are the right one. I am the mage Anni Sickali, confidant to the crown princess and friend of this city. I may have a way of helping your situation and… your army."

Harrin's mouth dropped open as she explained.

FOUR

A Spy Thought Lost

Five hundred Wylin milled about the gates of the desert city of Jerincon, armed and ready for war. Defenders welcomed them with cheers and open arms. Camden Hern viewed them with suspicion, knowing too well how the first encounter with a Wylin ended. The amphibious creatures were generally regarded as non-violent and rarely strayed far from the rivers of the Wilderlands. Jerincon must be in grave peril, for them to risk so much.

He and Sylin Marth slipped through the throngs of onlookers come to see the latest addition to the city defense force and eventually found Drimmen Giles. The dwarf couldn't have been happier, though their position was still desperate. A few thousand more and the goblins would be stopped in their tracks.

Sylin caught the familiar glitter of the pains of leadership in the dwarf's eyes but said nothing. He'd seen enough during his tenure as a member of the Hierarchy's High Council to know the worries never stopped. Besides which, it wasn't his place to advise another leader, when his own situation was growing increasingly precarious. Garin Stonebreaker intercepted them before they managed to reach Dremmin.

"Dremmin Giles has a long night ahead of him," the dwarf warrior explained. "Wylins are most secretive and must be dealt with carefully. If he says anything they don't like or approve, they will turn and leave without so much as a word. We need every sword we can get."

Camden wondered if it had occurred to anyone that if they disarmed the city's population and sent the soldiers off to join the main army, the goblins might pass Jerincon entirely. Rather than making anyone look the fool, he held his tongue and instead suggested a bite to eat. All three were starving, so there was no discussion. Between bites, Garin explained more on the fractured history of dwarf and goblin. The two had warred for as long as history remembered. Rumors said they were once the same race until a great conflict arose, producing a major schism. One faction went north to the mountains, while the other left for the hard forests to the east.

Of course, such things were largely absurd. Though, as with all rumors, there were certain elements of truth that remained debated to this day. Ask any dwarf, Garin argued, and they would fiercely deny it. Not even the Drehenzia, in all their diabolical ways, could be so cruel as to do the twisted things of nature suggested.

The meal ended, Garin decided to return to Dremmin Giles and hash out the remaining details. Wylins were inside the walls of Jerincon, in force, for the first time anyone could recall, moving through the different parts of the city to their temporary barracks. Sylin and Camden made an effort to look each in the face in passing, hoping not to find the familiar, traitorous face of Oo Ynlon.

The dwarf war leader greeted them with stern nod, the façade of elation already passed. He was back to being his natural untrusting, taciturn self. The addition of the Wylin battalion was a great help, but nowhere near enough to what he was going to need to properly defend Jerincon and the surrounding lands.

"I have studied your requests quite in depth, Councilman Marth. It's no secret that every sword and axe I can get a hold of is needed, direly. Your request, however, I deem slightly more important than the continued security of my city."

Garin rocked back, shock etched upon his weathered face.

"We are all lost if this wizard seizes the token of power. Either way, it appears I am destined to lose. I am granting you ten men, all volunteers. Garin and his brother Talrn shall lead them. We can provide you with a map and two weeks' worth of provisions. When you leave is entirely up to you. I imagine you will wait until your shoulder is properly healed and strength returned in full?"

Even as he said it, Dremmin knew it was the opposite.

"There are small towns farther east, but I wouldn't trust a soul in them. No decent, law abiding man would live so deep in *their* lands without good reason. I wish you all success and that there was more I could do to aid you, but my present dilemma is equally perilous. As I said earlier, the goblin offensive in the north is stalling. Casualties are high on both sides, but those foul bastards have suffered considerably more. There is growing fear, despite our victories, that the enemy is massing to strike south. We will be naught but a roadblock should that happen."

This also surprised Garin Stonebreaker. Only days before, he had spoken as if the walls of Jerincon would hold forever. The younger dwarf wondered what had happened to make that untrue. Being a mere scout, Garin wasn't afforded the opportunity to voice his concerns. Dremmin dismissed them and went back to planning the defense.

The three left in a chatter, each offering their views on how events should unfold. All agreed that Garin was best to round up those ten volunteers. Gul Killingstone had already offered his axe and according to Garin, was a most welcome addition. In fact, the dwarf explained as they broke free of the crowds and out into the city proper, Gul was already preparing for the coming journey, as well as any dangers they might meet.

Gul, it turned out, was highly proficient. By the time Sylin and the others reached the small barracks on the opposite side of Jerincon they saw a rugged company ready to ride. Sylin found it hard not to be impressed and was suspicious at the same time. Things were getting well beyond the point of control, as the situation within the walls continued to devolve rapidly. He wanted to know how the dwarf hunter knew what to do without being told, unless of course, Dremmin Giles had already issued orders before seeing Sylin and Camden. The dwarf leader was highly intelligent and more cunning than most back in Meisthelm, leaving the option entirely possible.

Gul Killingstone went about his self-appointed tasks without looking up. Horses needed to be readied. Provisions packed. Extra water bags were filled and assembled. Weapons sharpened that final time. Sylin found it interesting how none of them bothered speaking. There was none of the typical pre-deployment banter soldiers often shared to calm their nerves. Each and every one of those assembled was stone faced, resigned almost.

"You know Ynlon could be among those wylins?" Sylin ventured.

Camden grunted as he swallowed a chunk of desert pheasant. "I wouldn't worry about it. He could have drowned for all we know. If he is here, he won't be much of a hassle."

"Unless he brought his horde with him to start the invasion," Sylin countered.

The dwarves dropped what they were doing and glared at him. The conversation being spoken had already run through their minds and none were in the mood to be reminded of that foul possibility. For an outsider to utter such suspicions made the hair, rather thick and gnarly, stand on the back of their necks. Preparations were further interrupted by a handful of the amphibian warriors lurching their way. Gul and Garin snuck passive glances to Sylin, hands slowly dropping to their axes. They relaxed only after he failed to recognize any of the wylins.

The dwarves relaxed, if just, and the wylins set about making a small place to enjoy their meal, while ignoring the dwarves. None noticed the shifting reptilian eyes of the reddish-purple Wylin concealed a short distance away as he watched both groups with equal interest. His scaled muscles rippled beneath his loose-fitting tunic. His gills flared angrily. Oo Ynlon focused his gaze on the men from Meisthelm and watched.

"How is your shoulder?" Garin asked, seeking to ease some of the tension filling the formerly unoccupied square.

Sylin rotated it gently. *Still stiff and sore.* "It will be all right by the time we get to our destination."

"We leave early?" Gul Killingstone growled.

The former councilman nodded. "Tonight, just before dawn. I want to be away from here with the least amount of attention."

"Shouldn't appear more than another patrol heading out," the dwarf agreed. "Good thinking. Can't trust too many these days. You might work out."

Sylin didn't know why, but the dwarf's words of encouragement held meaning. In a time where hope dwindled, each shining voice inspired him to continue.

Sunrise was still well off, giving the small band time to slip through the walls without too many eyes upon them. They wove their way through the sleeping city, making as little noise as possible. Sylin was impressed with the natural stealth the dwarves demonstrated. Dremmin Giles had already coordinated an unexplained disappearance of guards, thus allowing Garin to lead the group out into the uninviting desert. Sylin took one last look at the front-line defense of Jerincon and shook his head. The gates, strong as they were, would hold for only a few hours should the goblin army attack in force, or get close enough to use battering rams or catapults.

The dwarves closed the gates behind them and scurried off into the dwindling darkness. It was bound to be a very long road in the hunt for the missing wizard Elxander. They'd been on the road for six hours by the time Garin called a halt for the morning meal. Surprisingly, not a word was spoken for the entire time. Sylin drank in the silence, knowing it wouldn't last. Peace seldom did.

He honestly couldn't remember the last time he had been given the time to reflect and sort through his thoughts, to reorganize his agenda. Those thoughts took him back to Meisthelm, to the day when Shali Kolm was killed and the treachery of the Black was revealed. Those pompous idiots on the High Council thought him a fool, especially Zye Terrio. Sylin left them to their crumbling world and went in search of the one man capable of restoring order and stopping the Black. Elxander was a forgotten salvation, but one Sylin couldn't ignore.

His musings were interrupted when they pulled into a small oasis and took their break. The dwarves were as efficient as they were silent. A small fire was burning within moments. The delicious smell of roasting meat filled the air. Sylin found himself salivating, as Gul relished the idea of being a quality chef.

Garin produced the map while the food cooked. Other dwarves went out to form a perimeter and stood watch, while the leaders debated on which route best served their intent. Camden offered little, for the Goblin Lands were fairly new territory for him. He'd been as far as the western edge of the Grimstone Mountains but no farther.

"There is a place," Garin ventured, after washing down the last bite of biscuit with a swig of fresh coffee. "One of unimaginable power, rumored of course, lying southeast of the mountains. Men in these parts call it the Tower of Souls. Few have ever seen it, fewer still have ever returned. I think it is a good place to begin the hunt for your lost wizard."

"How many days ride?" Camden asked. He still harbored doubts about trying to find a man who didn't want to be found.

The dwarf studied the map. "Hard to tell. Could take up to a month. We'll have to pass through the heart of the goblins to get there. Less than a league separates the mountains from the forests. It's too perilous. We may run right into their army."

"We could always go around the mountains," Sylin ventured.

"No," Garin said. "That would take too long. Besides, there are strange happenings going on that far south. Folk have been disappearing without reason. Damnedest thing I've heard in a long time. We must go around the Grimstones to the north. It's the only way."

An obscure noise in the distant palm trees drew Sylin's attention. He searched, not fully trusting the dwarves on guard, but failed to spy anything out of the ordinary. "Isn't there a pass through the mountains we can use? Some way to avoid both perils?"

Garin chuckled softly. "Nay, Councilman. There are no easy ways through this cruel land. The Hyber Pass does run through the Grimstones. Unfortunately, it's guarded quite closely by a rogue dragon; the Red Tragalon. We've sent two raids out to displace him over the past fifty years. None returned."

"Reds are the worst," Gul grumbled in affirmation.

Garin took it as a sign to continue. "No one knows why the dragon left the Mountains of the Fang. Some believe the roost became too crowded, but we of the east know little of the west. Elves guard her borders, the chosen of the gods themselves."

Garin fell silent as he felt the stares of all eyes upon him. None of his peers had known him to be a deep thinker, much less to waste time in pointless speculation. He was a superb tracker and survivalist. Indeed, none better dwelled within the borders of Jerincon. His sudden revelations were a most pleasant change.

"Have you seen elves?" he asked Sylin.

Sylin shook his head. "I've been from one part of the Free Lands to the next but have never laid eyes on one of the fair folk. They keep to their woodland fortresses and have little to do with the world of men. Perhaps we should all take heed of their examples. The world might become a better place."

"This world is what we have made of it. Our fathers' fathers and the ones before. The next few years will decide the end of a story they set in motion. We pray it to be a good enough end to tell our children with pride. Garin fell silent and signaled for them to begin packing up. They'd wasted enough time.

No one heard the soft clicking noise coming from the bushes. They also failed to spy the naturally camouflaged skin of Oo Ynlon lurking just out of sight. Nor did they see the wicked, spiked-tooth grin spread across his face as they rode away. He laughed in victory.

Word of the approaching riders reached the main camp just before noon. The outer picket lines let them pass, as both mission and identity were confirmed. The riders pushed their horses hard, driving on to reach the end goal. Weeks on the road in constant fear, spurred them. When at last they ventured into the main camp, they found men waiting.

Soldiers throughout the camp hardly spared them a second thought as they busied with daily routines. Horses were wiped down and fed, as were two of the three riders. The third was escorted to the center of the nearly league long army camp under the watchful glares of two untrusting guards. To his credit, the rider ignored the mock custody. His mission was paramount over mortal pride.

A dozen tents, each massive in stature, comprised the army's operations center. Haggard faced officers and senior enlisted shuffled from tent to tent. Whispers of something big about to happen circulated. A pair of gnome trackers walked by, both speaking their native tongue. The rider hadn't seen a gnome in years. People across the Free Lands revered them as the best trackers in the business, though most saw them as little better than pickpockets and thieves.

The rider was stopped at the middle tent. He watched as his escort departed, only to be replaced by another set posted beside the tent flap. They uncrossed their pikes long enough to let a dour faced lieutenant appear. He immediately extended a hand in introduction.

"I'm Zin Doluth, adjutant to General Conn," he said.

"Rhea Ailwin, commander of messengers of Meisthelm," said the other. "I have urgent business with the general."

Zin smiled, breaking the harsh lines on his worn face. "We've been expecting you. Follow me, please."

They entered the tent, with Rhea more than a little suspicious. Obviously, his scouts had been watched on their approach, but for how long? Did Conn have spies within Meisthelm separate from the Hierarchy? His first view of the assortment of people standing around an old maple field table made his heart skip.

Man, elf, dwarf, gnome, and Wylin mulled over maps and upcoming battle plans. Most he'd only caught fleeting glimpses of as they strolled about the golden halls of Meisthelm. Myths and faerie tales came to life before his eyes. At the head of the table was the wily, experienced General Conn. He was a man who needed no introduction. His legend was famous across the breadth of the Free Lands.

To Rhea he appeared a giant, tall and proud. Conn was renowned as a difficult task master, driven by the urge to defeat the oppressors of righteousness. Dozens of battles were heaped upon his shoulders, great victories and minor ones alike. He was the hero of the Hierarchy. There was none greater.

"General," Zin announced. "The messenger from Meisthelm has arrived. Rhea Ailwin."

Conn's intense green eyes stared hard at the young man standing awkwardly before him. "I've been waiting for you for almost four weeks. What kept you?"

Rhea swallowed his nerves. "I … I was held up by the darklings and a winter storm. The roads around Meisthelm are no longer safe. We came as fast as we could. I don't remember how many times we were forced to hide from …"

Conn held up his hand. He had heard enough. "I already know the situation in the north. What you're telling me has been known for weeks."

"The Council wants you to return at once, General." Rhea winced as he said it.

The General shook his head. "I cannot. There are pressing matters that need to be taken care of down here.

Pirates have seized the Port of Grespon. In doing so, they managed to kidnap the heir to the throne of Guerselleorn. I've pledged to return him to his father's custody. The army marches on the morrow."

"But the Council …" Rhea tried to say, surprised at the blatant disrespect Conn displayed.

"Can wait!" Conn fumed. "I've given my word, and that is one matter on which I will not bend. My army marches tomorrow. Nothing you or anyone else says will make a difference. Meisthelm is in no immediate danger."

The dwarf, dour faced and bitter, was known as Haf Forager, scoped Rhea and scowled. "Decisions have been made long before your arrival. Matters of allegiance, that may well improve our chances against the Black when the time comes, are at stake here."

"What of Galdea?" Rhea argued, forgetting his reservations. "King Elian has need of us as well. Will you ignore their needs as his kingdom is overrun by the darklings?"

"They are in no danger. I know Elian and Field Marshal Dlorn. Both are strong men who know the arts of war."

"But when the Black gets the Staff …" Rhea was confused.

"He will leave," Genessen said, as he stepped forward. The elf was a head taller than Conn. From the Wilderlands, he knew what the army of Galdea faced. "It will take time for Imelin to amass his armies and supplies to mount a major offensive on Meisthelm. That will undoubtedly be his primary target. With the Hierarchy removed, the kingdoms will fall into chaos. There will be no leadership and many may well join the cause of darkness. What we do here, now, may cement the loyalty of a much needed ally."

Rhea found himself almost mesmerized by the natural song of the elf's voice. He didn't think anything could sound so … pure. Mystified by the goings on in the Hierarchy's army, Rhea Ailwin stood quietly and watched as the masters of the battlefield resumed their task and continued planning the next chapter in the history of the world.

FIVE

Battle of Dreamhaven

They truly felt safe for the first time since fleeing Galdarath. The oath of the elf prince and the very trees themselves compelled an intense feeling of security as they set about making camp and for the first time, a fire to cook and warm themselves with. Right before nightfall, Andolus and Long Shadow struck out in search of fresh meat and water. Protesting at first, Elsyn soon found herself overcome with undreamed of calm. The trees whispered reassurances only she could hear.

The hunters returned swiftly, gone for less than an hour. Watch was established as they cleaned and quartered three rabbits and a put on a pot of fresh potatoes and carrots. They ate in relative silence, drinking cold spring water and enjoying a good, hot meal. The darkling threat, of which they'd been so engrossed in the last few weeks, was forgotten, set aside.

Andolus warned the enemy would still come, for Dreamhaven was no longer regarded as a threat. The Druinna Calar, he explained, were as old as the world but steadily losing their power. The elves first brought them to these shores at the dawn of recorded time. Like their caretakers, the silver trees gave the impression of immortality. That truth was flawed, for when one of the mighty trees died, it simply vanished and was immediately replaced by another.

They possessed a power few outside the elven people could explain. The trees were old when Gelum Drol, the mighty dwarfholt, stood where Galdarath now occupied. Those who knew of Dreamhaven feared the magical powers associated with the sacred ground. Even dragons flew clear. Only the select among the elves knew the truth of the trees, a secret they gladly took to their graves.

Shortly after midnight, Long Shadow snuck back from his post to stir the others awake. Soldiers all, save the princess, they flushed the sleep from their eyes and took up arms. The group was small but excessively deadly.

Elsyn stared in surprise at the lethal intent displayed in mere moments. "What is it?"

Battle was still a relatively new experience for her. She failed to rationalize how a man could kill without feeling and keep on doing it. Even with her father a king, and having grown up around soldiery, she'd never witnessed the cold act of killing until the darklings came.

"Darklings," Amean whispered. "They've found us."

The squat, hairy creatures stole through the broken monuments and barrows with undaunted arrogance. Their very presence was an act of defilement, desecrating the tombs of elven legends along their path. The fear of Dreamhaven was gone. Some remained cautious in their approach. They remembered what once was and were still deathly afraid of the elves. Many remembered the long years of oppression at the hands of Dol'ir. Now was the time for retribution. It was fear of the Black that drove them onward.

The first darklings caught the flicker of flame as it died out. They tensed with wicked anticipation. The stench of their enemy reached them. It was laced with fear. Before them stood the hulks of the Druinna Calar. Unwillingness to advance spread through the darklings. Only the promise of obtaining the Staff of Life unlocked their aggression. It called to them, luring them closer, so they could partake in the power and glory. Madness called upon by the Black pushed the darklings to new levels of insanity. If not for the rogue wizard, they would still be oppressed in the bitter pits of Suroc Tol.

Andolus used his superior night vision to discern the front ranks. Taking careful aim with his bow, he drew a deep breath. A quiet voice in his head whispered for him to wait. To not fire. The elf prince turned to tell the others and was surprised to find they had already stood down. The trees! He looked to Aron and the Golden Warrior nodded understanding, though he failed to understand the governing principles of magic.

The darklings arrived with alarming rapidity, seemingly oblivious to the inert threat the trees possessed. The defenders found it most difficult to do nothing as a wave of enemy advanced on them. Praying salvation was close at hand, they hunkered down and waited. A sudden wind swept through the glade. Change danced upon the air. The Druinna Calar came to life. Their branches swayed and moved, angry at the intrusion of the demon spawn.

The first darkling stepped foot onto that most sacred ground, eyes fixing on his prey. Frozen breath stole from the creature's gaping maw. Strings of hot saliva, acidic to the touch, splashed on freshly fallen snow. That his prey wasn't moving didn't matter. He took another step forward, claws extended for the kill.

Elsyn screamed when she noticed seven sets of red eyes bearing down on her. The group was surrounded and still no one moved. Horses snickered. Should the darklings kill the horses … Her heart fell, even as it pumped furiously. She stepped back, bumping into the hard bark of an unforgiving tree. Rather than screaming again, Elsyn took comfort from the energy streaming from the tree. Then the world erupted in chaos.

The ground trembled, as the darklings halted in stride. Elven magic, ancient and largely forgotten, awoke. The Druinna Calar bent down with remarkable flexibility no natural tree had. Branches snatched the nearest darkling and crushed the life from him. Bodies were flung to the cold earth, dead before striking. Silver leaves fell from the trees as those small, yellow birds erupted in a very different, more volatile song.

Darklings tried to flee but were snatched up within a few steps. The mayhem lasted but a few harsh minutes before the last of the darkling invaders was dead. Roots burst free from their eternal prison and dragged the bodies underground, until not a sign remained. Eventually, the trees returned to normal. It was as if the battle never happened.

Long Shadow and Amean immediately scouted the surrounding terrain, should there be a secondary force lurking. Not even a fool would dare resume the attack after witnessing what just happened. The elf prince went to kneel before the closest tree. He spoke softly, almost imperceptibly, in ancient elvish. Though the trees showed no outward indication toward their caretaker or his companions, they conveyed respect through the power of the earth now filling his soul with hope.

When finished, Andolus rose with a smile. Long Shadow and Amean returned a short time later with good news. The area was clear. They had escaped one more time but were far from being safe. Darklings proved most relentless. It was just a matter of time before they came again. The journey to the Twins was still many days. Days in which anything could happen.

Aron decided to let them sleep for a few more hours, once the excitement faded. Only Elsyn took him up on that. She still wasn't accustomed to the hard life. Three days on horseback was more than she'd ever endured. The others conferred quietly around the rebuilt fire. A change of course was necessary before leaving.

"What now?" Aron asked. "The darklings haven't given up on us. We can't go back the way we came and they will more than likely be waiting for us somewhere ahead."

Andolus agreed. "It will be very hard to sneak between their lines. The night is theirs, despite my ability to see in the dark. They know we can't remain here for long. Even if we tried, the Black would soon arrive. I think his magic is a threat, even to the old elves."

"How far to the nearest river?" Amean asked.

The veteran was as anxious as any to reach the security of the army. The cold tore through his battered frame, down deep into his core. He was past ready to end the quest. Days of heroism had come and gone. It was days like this that made him wish he'd retired long ago.

"A day and a half at a good pace. But we can't just ride straight for it. The darklings will complicate our movements. Might take two, three days," the elf guessed.

"What would you do, if you were the Black?" Aron asked out of nowhere. The others jerked their heads up, questioning his motivations. "If I were in his position, I'd focus on attacking Dlorn's main army. That is, after all, our ultimate destination. He's going to keep a small force pushing us. They should be in a place to strike long before we gain the army. What we must do is find a way through the flankers. We're not a large force. That gives us the advantage."

"Sounds easy," Karin said sarcastically. "What are we waiting for?"

"Did you know that when we started this quest, I had the utmost confidence in the world that we would succeed?"

She backed away from the brutal tone in his voice.

"And now?" she asked, reluctantly.

He hung his head. "Now I wonder how we're going to make it from day to day. And the Staff! I set out to stop a traitor, not become the caretaker of a token so powerful it destroys the minds of those who wield it! This is madness, the whole damned thing."

Karin laid a consoling hand on his arm and stared hard into his fierce gaze. Even the tiger backs down when looked upon with love. He saw in her something he'd been fighting since the night in Prossin. Never having known it before, he was perplexed by what men called love. Aron reached up and gently stroked her cheek with the back of his hand.

"What are we going to do?" she asked.

His smile was gentle, strong in her warmth. "We are going to give them the ride of their lives. I don't intend to rest until we are safe within the strength of Dlorn's perimeter. Wake the princess up. We're leaving."

Field Marshal Dlorn and Jou Amn finished their morning meal and made their rounds of the camp. Company level weapons masters kept soldiers in constant drill, anticipating the battles ahead. Day in and out, thousands of soldiers worked to hone their already lethal martial skills. Earlier battles with the darklings provoked a collective rage. Their appetites became whetted and they were eager for the main course.

The company of Golden Warriors was welcomed with open arms. Only fifty strong, they were well worth over six times their number. They were given tents, hot food, and most importantly, privacy. They trained alone, ate alone, making it a point to keep to themselves. The rest of the army understood them and did little to get in the way, aside from gawking awkwardly as the knights passed.

Growing concern among the army focused attention elsewhere. Two days past reports came in of the approaching darkling army. There was no legitimate way to halt the advance, only delay. Field Marshal Dlorn decided to lead a raiding party of five thousand to attempt to stall the darkling army. Though many contested the hasty decision, none denied that Dlorn had never lost a battle.

"Still no news of the princess," Dlorn muttered from atop a small rise at the edge of camp. From here he had clear sight of the entire army, all the way to both rivers.

The army was nestled in the middle of the two-thirds of a league valley between rivers. Offensive and defensive positions were constructed on all sides. Though the darkling army was clearly coming from the west, they might attack from any angle. Leagues on both sides of the bridges were rigged to burn should the need arise, or after the raiding party returned. The darklings would be forced to either swim or construct new bridges. If they swam, they would make easy targets for the archers.

Ten catapults had been constructed from fresh cut pine by Lord Felbar's engineers. Felbar visited frequently, offering what he could, always explaining that his castle stood at the island as well and that he regrettably couldn't commit his entire force to the coming battle. How could he be expected to defend his lands and people if everyone was stationed north?

Felbar was one of Elian's strongest supporters, but no fool. The throne was not up for contention, but lesser lords squabbled for position in the hopes of gaining the throne. Dlorn grunted as those thoughts continued to interrupt his thinking process. The old general despised the backstabbing nature exhibited by the nobility. They had all the finest possessions in life and never had to fight for any belief. It was that superior attitude that earned his disdain. He put up with it by carrying on with his job.

"I wonder if evil has befallen them?" he asked, a thick, bushy eyebrow raised.

Jou Amn shook his head. "They have the Staff of Life and are small in number. Aron Kryte will make it, if any can."

"Would you use the Staff if for no other reason than possession? It is the antithesis of evil. Made in an ungodly time when the night ruled the world. If they yet live, they may well be trapped by this darkling army. Northern Galdea is vast and un-traversable during deep winter. Getting lost out there is the same as committing suicide"

"They will come. I can't explain it, but I know they will," Jou repeated. The Golden Warrior fell silent and resumed his vigil, the same one he conducted daily since arriving. A nagging feeling in his bones told him all would be fine, that Kryte would never use the Staff other than to strike down their enemies and deliver light back to the Free Lands.

Each pounding step brought them that much closer to the final destination. The darklings had yet to reemerge. Dreamhaven was far behind. Fear aside, the horses sprinted into their run. A thin film of sweat coated their flesh, keeping them warm through the blinding cold. Their riders, however, found their positions less fortunate. Ice crystals pelted their exposed flesh, froze in their hair and eye lashes. Even the thick pelts they wore provided little protection. Winter was just as aggressive and relentless as those in pursuit.

A fresh storm blew in shortly after dawn on their way out of Dreamhaven. It wasn't as severe as the initial storm but was harsh enough to keep pushing the riders to the edge of endurance. Drifts as tall as a man began icing up, making it treacherous for both horse and rider. Caution became priority. They had to find a way to beat the storm and darklings simultaneously.

Aron halted them by an ice-covered stream where they refilled canteens and relieved themselves in the nearby bushes. Andolus struck out almost at once to scout the lands ahead, for he had a terrible feeling the enemy had managed to circle around them. Aron chewed on a half-frozen piece of jerky and spoke with Amean. Long Shadow watched their trail, while the two women sat atop their horses and made small talk.

Days of escape and pursuit were pushing Elsyn much harder than she expected and she wasn't handling it well. Karin did her best to sympathize, but she found it difficult. She mused at the strange twist of fate that had brought them together. The daughter of the man who killed the other's father. Now both were orphans. For them to break through that level of despair would take much more than pushing beyond idyllic hatreds and secrets.

Andolus returned shortly, a perplexed look on his face. "We should start heading south. The river isn't more than two or three leagues ahead. We ought to be able to reach it by sundown, if we set a good pace and there is no outside intervention."

"Good," Aron said. "I am tired of running."

Long Shadow crept from a stand of pines. The expression on his face was one of distress.

"We have to move now," Andolus warned. He squinted to catch all of Long Shadow's hand signs. "The darklings are less than a league behind us. Hundreds of them. I am afraid it will take more than what we have to escape this time."

A howl shattered the still. Their enemy had discovered their tracks. Now fugitives, they dug their heels into their steeds and ran for dear life. Kilometers flashed by, each moment another stage in the deadly game. The darklings were steadily gaining ground. Andolus led the six of them through a pair of hills, successfully eluding their pursuit. Ominous peaks in the distance jutted into the sky, casting shadow upon the lands.

Once free of the pass, they saw vast forests of conifers blanketing the valley from the base of the mountains to the closest banks of the river. So long as the darklings were all behind, they didn't expect to meet much resistance. Andolus edged into the trees, confident in the lead. Some of the trees were so massive, it would take all six of the fugitives to encircle. The rush of the river pounded through the forest. A sense of accomplishment threatened to take them. Each fought it, for this was the most dangerous time.

Any illusion of hope dashed as the band exited the forest to find there was no bridge across the river in the immediate area. Aron made the call to strike south, knowing that was where the main army was camped. Midnight passed and still they found nothing. The river was too wide and deep for any natural crossing. The elf in the lead, they hurried south in search of an escape route.

Five thousand lightly armored warriors stole through the outer picket lines. Dawn was but an hour away, giving them enough time, just, to get in position before the front wave of the darkling army arrived. Dlorn rode at the head of the column. His hard eyes focused on the terrain ahead. This was his true calling. The cold hand of destiny molded into the perfect warrior. Through his sword, would the future be wrought.

Jou Amn and ten of his men road with the Field Marshal. They chose to leave their golden armor behind, instead wearing lighter, more suitable leather armor for the strike-and-move series of attacks Dlorn had in mind. Sword and battle axe suited for mounted combat filled their hands. Tired of running, the Golden Warriors looked forward to confronting their foes.

The mounted force found and swarmed over the darkling advance party, hardly slowing as they slaughtered the enemy. Dlorn, after ensuring that none of the darkling escaped through the confusion, decided to claim the area for his ambush sight. Any farther forward and they ran the risk of being smashed by the main darkling force. Dlorn and his commanders went up and down the lines, drawing units in tight and developing the trap. A smile cracked the old man's face when all was in place.

"Any suggestions?" Karin asked, as she double checked her quiver. There were less than twenty arrows. Nowhere near enough to face what awaited.

Over a hundred darklings, and something bigger, more dangerous, guarded the bridge. The small band hadn't been spotted yet, giving them the option of continuing south or stopping to fight through it.

"Long Shadow and I will swim across the river. I think we can set the bridge on fire from both ends. This should confuse those devils enough for them to scatter, thus giving you enough time to charge across. By no means are you to stop and engage the grohl. Leave him to us. The measure of your strength combined would not be enough, for they are dark creatures made from twisted magic. My people are well acquainted with them. Worry about the darklings," Andolus said.

"You'll freeze in that water," Aron countered, ignoring how the elf knew what the monster behind the darklings was. None of them had never heard of such a creature and were loath to confront it.

Andolus offered a tight shrug, as if to say there was no other way, and both he and Long Shadow shed their cloaks, tightened weapons belts, and handed over their reins. Without waiting, the duo edged through the night to the frozen waters of the Simca River. The others waited in tense anticipation as soon their companions all but disappeared in the water. Hundreds of darklings were drawing closer, forcing the group between rock and anvil.

Aron resisted the urge to pace his nervousness. He hated not being in control, especially in a life and death situation. Time slowed the longer they waited. To keep his mind fresh, he went through various battle drills and potential scenarios they were about to encounter once the signal was given. If given. The waters were so cold and moving fast enough to drown a man in mere moments. He didn't think the elf stood much chance of success.

The high-pitched cry slashing the night from across the river startled him. Aron rode forward to the forest edge and frowned. Darklings, having discovered the subterfuge, were hurrying to the far side of the bridge. There were no flames.

"Come on. If we don't try now, we're not going to make it," Aron commanded. He drew his sword.

The others gave concerned looks, but none objected. With the darkling force barreling down from behind, this was their only chance. Extra horses tethered to their own, Aron led them down the gentle slope of the bank and into chaos before they had time to rethink the situation. The princess was his main concern. She was their weakest link. Though trained in battle, Elsyn had never been tested. Much to his surprise, she'd already drawn her short sword.

Conclusions of personal courage yet undiscovered, Elsyn found herself speeding toward maddening death alongside the others. It took every ounce of strength she possessed not to break and run, but Aron had led her this far. She had full confidence that he could get her the rest of the way. She briefly thought of those days when he rode with her. The warmth of body heat they shared was … inspiring. Now that the Druinna Calar had healed his horse, she was left alone. And heading for a massing of creatures desperate to kill her.

The time for speculation ended when Aron's horse set foot on the bridge.

They emerged from the frozen waters, skin turned pale shades of blue. Teeth chattered as Andolus pushed his clinging hair away from his face. His sharp eyes blinked rapidly to clear away the small ice crystals formed in the lashes. A quick look showed the immediate area clear. He and Long Shadow drew their weapons, the weight almost too much in their frozen hands, and crept through the snow and ice. Fragile branches snapped underfoot.

The killers eased into light underbrush with hearts pounding as they always did in those precious moments when anticipation dominated the senses. The unseen squad of darklings hiding in the bushes startled them. Long Shadow's reactions proved quickest. Three darklings were dead before either they or Andolus fully registered what was happening.

A cry went up from the bridge. It was brutal, and high-pitched. The grohl. Andolus plunged his sword into the last darkling's chest and looked to Long Shadow. To his credit, the silent killer didn't hesitate. He charged toward the advancing grohl. Andolus was hard pressed to keep up.

His nerves blanched upon seeing the monster for the first time. Almost as large as a troll, it had no equal. The grohl stood seven feet and was packed with bulging muscles. Long, silver hair ran down its back, giving the look of a killer. Black, lidless, eyes stared down on them. Andolus sensed that the grohl had been created to kill elves.

Flexing those massive shoulders, the beast roared so deep, the very ground trembled. Long Shadow snarled, for he was born for such a challenge. He thrust a hand out, beckoning the beast. The challenge was accepted. The grohl charged. Predator versus predator, they circled each other. Darklings fell back to give them room. They cheered their champion. Andolus balked. Even should Long Shadow manage to kill the grohl, there were still far too many darklings to defeat.

Long Shadow swung hard, opting for a single sword rather than both. The grohl easily deflected the blow, nearly knocking him to the ground in the process. Swift and decisive movements were exhibited by both. Claws raked flesh. Five small tears opened across Long Shadow's chest. The grohl laughed.

Anger sparked in Long Shadow and his discipline nearly broke. He stepped back, took a calming breath, and raised his sword. When all looked as if he were destined to fail, an arrow whistled through the fractured night and pierced the monster in the throat. Blue-black blood spurted from entry and exit wounds. The grohl reeled in disbelief, one clawed hand reaching futilely to staunch the blood flow. Long Shadow attacked. His heavy sword struck the grohl's head with a single swipe.

Darklings wailed at the loss but were set upon from behind unexpectedly. Four humans broke through their ranks, spreading fire and death. Several in the back ranks burst into flame from carefully hidden torches. The grohl's body fell atop a handful of darklings too stunned to move, crushing them. Andolus and Long Shadow seized the opportunity and made a mad dash for their friends and horses. Bodies dropped as they passed, hacked down. The darkling mass waivered before breaking altogether. By the time they regained composure, the six riders were already across the bridge and heading toward the safety of the army ahead. Flames licked higher as the bridge caught.

Duoth N'nclogbar stepped away from the bridge in dismay. The riders were gone, lost to the night. He had failed. He looked hatefully at the fallen grohl and the host of his dead. The darkling, wisely, feared the consequences of when the Black discovered what had transpired.

"How did this happen?" he asked the nearest warrior.

The darkling shifted, uncomfortable with being noticed. "Surprise! Many on horse!"

Duoth drew the short-blackened blade from his belt and stabbed the warrior in the heart. "They were handful."

The king of the darklings stalked away from the others and stared into the waning night with the knowledge that his enemies would soon be safe among a considerably larger force. Getting the Staff became infinitely more difficult.

SIX

Reunion

Aron drank long from the flask of cold ale. Bitter to the tongue, the golden liquid burned going down his throat. Even as harsh as it tasted, the ale reminded him of better days in the barracks. He tried hard to forget that he was one of the senior commanders in the midst of a winter warzone. To forget that tens of thousands of grotesque creatures, rumored to be legend until last fall, marched toward him under a traitor's banner. He wondered what Sevron and the rest of the men back in Saverin were doing. Were they prepared?

He paused when Karin entered the tent. She offered a knowing smile and sat down. They'd arrived at the main Galdean army camp two days past and were still trying to recover. Andolus and Long Shadow both sustained multiple wounds during their ill-advised battle with the darklings. Fortunately, none were severe enough to garner medical attention. They, like the others, were worn down and sore for so many days of hard riding.

Aron passed her the flask, which she greedily accepted, and said, "A year ago, if you would have told me that I'd be here in the deep winter, I would have thought you mad and walked off laughing."

"And now?"

He shrugged. "I'm not so sure."

She propped her boots up on the table but said nothing. She chose to finish the flask and hand it back with a wry grin.

"Any news from Dlorn or the others?" he asked, tucking the flask away.

"Not yet. His commanders say they should be back some time this afternoon. Unless they've been overrun," she answered.

"Five thousand men couldn't be destroyed in a handful of day. He'll be back. The only way he couldn't make it is if the Black were involved, but I don't see that happening."

"Why not?" she asked, confused.

"He wants Meisthelm, more importantly, the Staff. The Black won't commit himself and risk the chance of being killed without reassurances that he's going to get what he wants."

A messenger entered. The anxious look on his face made Aron's stomach clench. "Field Marshal Dlorn has returned, my lord."

Aron could have slapped the man for taking too long to deliver the word. Both he and Karin were on their feet, headed out the door before the messenger finished speaking. Matters were already starting to look better. The prowess and time proven skill of Dlorn brought him and most of his strike force back in one piece, a feat many of those assembled hadn't thought possible, even if they were reluctant to admit so.

Aron found the haggard marshal slumped on a bench near the hospital tents. A field medic bandaged a nasty slash on Dlorn's left arm. Loss of blood and near fatigue made Dlorn look much older than his seventy odd years. He was flushed and out of breath. Only when he spied Elsyn, approaching from the opposite direction of Aron, did he perk up.

"Ah, Princess! Gods, but I'm glad to see you safe," he said, as she all but crashed into his embrace. "We feared the worst when news of your father reached me."

Thought of her father choked her up, but Elsyn managed to overcome any emotional outbreak by introducing her companions and reacquainting Dlorn with those he knew. It did his old heart good to see the elf again. There was an odd reassurance in finding both Andolus and Long Shadow guarding Elsyn. He felt as if the kingdom had hope.

Aron cut through the niceties. Even though they'd reached the safety of the army, he still had the problem the Staff of Life created. "Marshal, how long do we have before the army arrives?"

The old man sagged. "Not much longer. We made contact with the darklings' advance body only a half day across the river. We emplaced and waited. Their scout units ran into us and we managed to kill most of them. They don't fight very well, once you understand their tactics and take the offensive."

He paused to rub his lower jaw. "The main body surged into us shortly before dawn. I think they were as surprised as we were. They could have, should have used the cover of night to mask their movements and flank us but they didn't. Once they managed to disengage, the darklings waited for sunrise. I'd ordered a withdrawal to a secondary location. The darklings took offense and charged. It's hard to say how many we slew, thousands at least."

The medic cinched down the bandage, drawing a foul look.

"I didn't become distressed until cresting a rise where I could view the vast strength of their army. It was… a dark wave stretching for leagues, possibly back to Galdarath. Never once, in decades of service, have I known fear so strong. Not even as a new private in my first engagement. I wonder how men might hold back the dark tide approaching."

He drank deep from a canteen. "How fares the city?"

"We don't know. Aron and the Golden Warriors left after… my father died. We've had no contact with Galdarath since," she said.

"It stands to reason the enemy will continue putting pressure on Galdea until the Black gets what he wants," Aron added.

"Jent Tariens is more than capable. The city is in good hands with him as steward," Elsyn offered.

"Tariens is still a boy," Dlorn snapped. "He knows as much as I do about running a kingdom. My lady, if Galdea is to survive, I must take the army back."

"How do you propose to get there?" Aron asked. "Ride right through the darkling lines? You must know that they have already secured the bridges north of here. We barely forced our way through. If the enemy is as strong as you suggest, your army will be slaughtered."

"Shall I sit here while our city burns? While my family is murdered by monsters who shouldn't exist?" The fire raged within. It was an old hate he used to prepare for battle.

Aron squared on him. "Galdarath is in no immediate jeopardy. I assure you."

"False promises of a self-proclaimed prophet! You blind yourself with illusions. I'm willing to guess that none of our problems would have happened if not for the arrival of you and that damned Black wizard."

"How dare you say such a thing?" Elsyn cried out. Aron had saved her life too many times in the last week to allow Dlorn the opportunity to besmirch his honor.

Dlorn rose with swiftness an old man shouldn't possess. "Open your eyes, girl! Magicians created the devils of the world, this one and his High Council. The

Hierarchy is to blame for all our troubles. When I finish with the darklings, I march on Meisthelm!"

"You don't know what you're saying," Aron calmly said.

"But I do. I know exactly what I say. My king is dead, kingdom in turmoil. My city is under siege and my army stands on the brink of annihilation. You and your meddlesome bigots created all of this and you have the nerve to try and tell me I don't know of what I speak?" Dlorn spat.

Aron ground his teeth, lest he speak unwisely. "I tell you again, Galdarath is in minimal danger. The real danger stands before you."

Dlorn froze. His eyes narrowed dangerously thin. "What do you mean?"

Aron brought forth what Dlorn had assumed was a mere walking stick. "This is the Staff of Life, created by wizards long before our forefathers were born. This is what the Black seeks and so long as I have it, he will come for me."

"We all die for a piece of wood?"

Aron offered a smile. "I don't control the flow of events. The Staff was hidden beneath Galdarath. It has fallen to me to find a way to destroy the Black and end this war. Like you, I am a mere puppet."

"Now that you have this stick, what do you intend to do with it? Can it unlock the mysteries of life? Save us all from those beasts?" Dlorn's anger threatened to erupt.

Good question. I don't know what it does or how to use it. Logic told him he had but one option. "I need to get the Staff to Meisthelm. The High Council will know what to do with it."

"Can you trust them? The Black has already turned. What's to say the others won't follow him?" Dlorn asked, plans already formed.

"I don't know but I have faith. If the Black beats me there, I will take the Staff to its place of creation and destroy it." The words came so easily, he knew they weren't his thoughts. Voices of long dead ancestors whispered to him, quietly urging him in the right direction necessary to save the world.

"Men haven't set foot in Sadith Oom for many years. No one even knows if the forge of wizards is still intact," Dlorn countered.

Mordrun Hath. Aron shook his head. He didn't know where the name came from, for it was one he'd never heard.

"I have never run from a fight," Dlorn vented, some of his anger dissipating. "I will not do so now. If the darklings are already on this side of the river, I need to adjust the defenses. Find me Captain Calri. I think we will be going back out tonight."

His aide, who'd been standing patiently a few steps away, saluted and hurried away.

"I will do everything I can to help you in your quest, though there are additional matters transpiring I fear you don't know. All I ask is that you keep Galdarath safe," Dlorn said.

"Agreed. What matters?" Aron answered without pause.

"The Rovers are mobilized and moving in force. Scouts report them in Trimlon now, but they have turned south toward the Unchar Pass."

"We have a garrison in Unchar. Almost three hundred men," Aron said.

Dlorn mused. "And if the Black has already thought of this? He is a warrior first. Your three hundred won't be much more than a delay against an army of Rovers with darkling aid. We need to stop the enemy here, even if only for a week or two. By doing so, we buy the rest of the world a little precious time to prepare. It's a three hour ride to Felbar's castle. He had close to five thousand men defending his immediate holdings and estates. He may be able to help you. I was going there tonight, if you would like to accompany me."

Aron and Amean exchanged approving looks. "That works, if you'll be back in time to lead your foray."

"Don't worry about me. If you will excuse me, I have much to accomplish and a short time in which to do so."

Field Marshal Dlorn walked off, strapping his well-used broadsword to his waist. Aron admired the warrior, despite their tempered conversation. A man like Dlorn knew and understood who and what he fought for. Dlorn was one of the most respected veterans in the Free Lands. An invaluable asset necessary in the dark days to come. Any differences they had now needed to be quashed before they could proceed.

The soft chirps and howls of a pair of snow owls sang across the lightly forested river basin, an eerie tune accompanying the small, dark shapes writhing across the land. The black mass moved like a great serpent. The darklings, intent on their mission, paused as the sound of distant thunder rumbled over their ranks. Odd, for not a cloud adorned the sky. Suddenly, the sound became clear. Darklings cringed, hissing that turned to menacing chatter.

Several hundred cavalrymen thundered out of the night, barreling into the front darkling ranks. Lances were lowered. Dozens of darklings were skewered, impaled in the first moments of the battle. Screams soon followed, some from the darklings, others from wounded horses. Riders were torn from their saddles and stabbed to death before they had the chance to defend.

Captain Calri rode through the center of the charge, while trying to maintain at least a measure of control. He'd caught the enemy by surprise but they reacted much quicker than even Dlorn anticipated. The deeper his cavalry wedge penetrated, the more chance the darkling flanks could respond and counter. If his unit slowed even a fraction, they might become trapped and slaughtered.

Calri barked orders and miraculously, one in three riders managed to disengage and surge off in a new attack direction. The darklings broke under this added strain. Those who could, retreated in disarray. Those who couldn't, were run down ruthlessly. Calri knew that pausing the assault would erode momentum and give the enemy much needed time to recover. The wedge of armor and horse wheeled and drove toward the closest bridge. Darklings were trampled along the way. He knew, as did most of his command, that every darkling killed now was one less they had to deal with in the latter stages of the war.

He dropped back in the column, settling in with his rearguard of fifty elven archers. Their sole purpose was to set the bridge on fire, while his cavalry provided cover. Elves were precious and few. He'd been given instructions not to let a single hair on their heads get singed. Unwilling to face the consequences of failure, Calri intended to do just that. Elven bows were a deep strike asset the Galdeans lacked.

Squad sergeants and young officers issued orders as they rode. Darklings dropped back in knots of three or four but failed to make any significant impact. The horsemen barreled ahead and were upon the bridge much sooner than expected. A trail of cooling bodies marked their passing. From his observation point along the riverbank, Calri just made out the last of the darklings cross the far side of the bridge. He tried, unsuccessfully, to search the far bank but night was too complete. Inherent dangers of fighting at night plagued the speed and veracity with which he liked to fight, but caution was paramount to success. Those darklings he did make out were massed together, paralytic with evident confusion.

"Archers," Calri ordered. His voice was soft to avoid drawing unwanted attention. Should the darklings gain composure before the bridge was alight, he wasn't positive his force could extract in time.

The elves lined up three deep, while several foot soldiers moved through the ranks with torches. Jerns Palic, the stern elf captain, raised an arm once the last torch was lit. His angular face reflected the shimmer of water. Narrow eyes studied the darklings, recalling the atrocities committed when Dol'ir fell. Naught but contempt boiled through his veins. Poised to give the final command, sudden commotion in the trees to their right flank drew his attention.

Darklings sprung forth, felling several men and elves before the Galdean task force recovered enough to shore their defenses. Calri quickly reinforced the flank, while staving off an ill-fated frontal assault back over the bridge. The thunder of a thousand feet crunching over snow and ice came from yet a third direction as a fast approaching darkling force aimed to end the battle and preserve their route of march into the valley of the Twins.

The bridge in danger of falling, Calri drew his sword and led a company onto the weathered planks. "Consolidate ranks! Let no darkling near the archers!"

Jerns Palic took in the flow of battle and knew there wouldn't be a more opportune time. His arm fell. "Fire!"

Fifty flaming missiles scorched trails across the night sky. They struck hard, deep in wood and flesh.

Darkling screams were rivaled by the intensity of awakening flames. Those not struck by the first salvo were hit by the second and third. Calri's raiders succeeded in clearing the bridge long enough for the entire length to catch flame.

Fighting raged on for another hour until the darklings were steadily beaten into submission. Unfortunately for the Galdeans, their fervor for attack heightened once the bridge became impassable. Cutoff from their army, those darklings on the wrong side of the river made the Galdeans pay for each life taken. There was no real contest, however, Calri and his force overwhelmed and eliminated the darklings. The sickening stench of charred flesh and hair accompanied the defenders on the cold ride back to camp.

SEVEN
Lord Felbar

They rode like ghosts through the sleeping village surrounding Grayhawk Keep. Dlorn guided them through three picket lines, taking time to point out the hastily built bulwarks and entrenched defenses Lord Felbar felt would prevent the darklings from taking his castle. Spike filled trenches stretched in each direction off the main road, while cauldrons of oil were mounted strategically atop old buildings and natural rock formations. Alert guards patrolled the trenches. Dlorn was glad to see Felbar's men had learned from Galdarath's mistakes and were prepared to deal with an airborne assault as well.

The town itself was largely insignificant, so small, in fact, it had no name. Nor did many live there. A few of Felbar's minor relatives and most of his home army made it their home, but without an ingrained logistical center, the Twins was forced to rely on outside trade in order to function properly. And Lord Felbar had no trouble obtaining that support. He was the logical choice to succeed Elian, provided Elsyn was unfit for rule or got killed before the war ended, even if he had no actual desire to languish under the burden of crown.

Dlorn rode in the lead, for he'd been to Grayhawk Keep more times than he could easily count. The others were content with following. Aron most of all. There'd be more than enough time, too much in his modest opinion, for the anguish of command. Any respite was greatly appreciated.

"Felbar is as strong as royalty comes," Dlorn explained, as the rusted gates of Grayhawk Keep closed with a groan. "But he's also brash and likely to fly off the handle on a whim."

"More reserved, I'd say," Aron commented.

The Field Marshal scowled. "He's no fool. Loyalty is a tender thing to have. One not given easily. These people here have placed their trust in him to do the right thing. Felbar won't abandon them, not when it means stealing from the defenses and leaving their families unprotected. This town wouldn't hold up for an hour if the army pulled out."

Stable hands rushed out from side doors and took the horses after Aron's party dismounted. Dlorn gave instructions that they were to be saddled and ready to ride within two hours. An escort was offered to take the party to Felbar and was politely refused. The page did go on ahead to alert Felbar his guests had arrived. Soldiers and various visiting merchants and dignitaries watched as the unlikely group of, now seven, westerners and southerners awkwardly made their way through the outer courtyard.

Few others were about. The hour was already late and there was need of rest, if the reports coming from the river were true. How any army could be as large as the scouts' reported was beyond belief. At some point, numbers stopped rising and simply became pure death. A pair of wolfhounds, their long grey fur scruffy and unkempt, sat beneath a torch-lit porch. Their piercing eyes watched the strangers closely; their noses sniffing deep. To Aron's surprise, the dogs fell in, almost too obediently, behind them.

Felbar's private chambers were open and inviting as the page ushered them in. Aron took in the surroundings with melancholy. Despite the shelves containing rare books and, even rarer, bottles of liquor from across the Free Lands, it felt akin to Marshal Sevron's chambers back in Saverin. Familiarity meant more than raw titles. His gaze fell on Felbar, the portly lord seated on his favorite cushioned chair before a quiet fire and enjoying a goblet of wine. He rose with the grace of a much smaller man and gestured them to sit. Elsyn smiled upon seeing him but said nothing.

"Princess, it is good to see you again," Felbar wasted no time. "Dlorn, you as well." Who are your new friends?"

"You remember Prince Andolus and Long Shadow. The others come from the Hierarchy garrison in Saverin. This is Lord Aron Kryte and Amean Repage of the Golden Warriors. Last is Karin Ilth. She has the ability to *see*."

"Greetings to all, though they fall in bitter days," Felbar said sincerely.

Aron picked up the hidden agenda buried in his tone. *No doubt every lord and noble from here down to Meisthelm has special concessions in mind while dealing with the Black. How much will this cost the High Council before they decide to put life above all else?*

"I am intrigued by this unexpected visit, though I can surmise a goodly amount of it. I have already spoken at great lengths with Dlorn and King Elian. Those forces I could spare are already in the army ranks. All else I have need of on my own borders. Elian understands this."

"King Elian is dead," Aron growled in a voice betraying his urge to shut the other up before matters became too muddled. "The Black Imelin and his army march on the Twins in numbers too vast to accurately count."

The pompous lord fell back into his chair, mouth agape in shock at the revelation. Just a few days ago he and Elian said their farewells and set about defending the kingdom.

Aron pressed before Felbar tried to find a way out of his commitments. "I speak for the Hierarchy in this matter. We do not ask for additional troop support. Darkling units may well be across the river and operating in your domain. We cannot send aid to your lands either. The die has been cast and we both must play the hands dealt. Instead, I need detailed maps of Trimlon and Almarin. I also have need of a network of scouts in both kingdoms, primarily Trimlon. There are reports of a Rover army moving in the south. These scouts will report directly to me or Field Marshal Dlorn, if I am unavailable. No exceptions. "

Felbar shifted uncomfortably. He was proud, almost too much so to take orders from a man not representing a kingdom.

"Lord Felbar, we are done retreating. Done hiding in the shadows while this mockery of humanity plays out his schemes. The Hierarchy was cohesively taken off guard but I've been given the opportunity to make amends and reclaim the advantage. All I require is your faith and complete support."

Aron leveled his gaze, a measure of sanity returning, and extended a hand. He saw the turmoil in Felbar's eyes. That cloudy struggle to figure out what was happening. The Lord of the Twins bordered on losing composure.

"Felbar," Dlorn gently prodded. "We need to cooperate if victory is to be accomplished. The darkling army is vast, just as he says. Listen to him."

Reason seldom carried weight when dealing with matters of state. Felbar was a man used to getting his way, usually handed to him with smiles. Now he was confronted with a series of nightmares from which there was no evident escape. Secretly, he knew he wasn't as ready to assume control as others thought. Both of his parents had been killed earlier in the year in a freak wagon accident, thrusting the burden of leadership more heavily down upon his already sagging shoulders. Long moments stretched on before his internal deliberation ceased. He accepted Aron's hand. "Very well. I give you the entirety of my lands and forces for as long as you have need."

A thin smile broke Aron's serious façade. *Add another small victory to the list.*

"Do you think that was the proper approach?" Amean asked.

They walked down the halls in search of the delightful smells of the kitchens. Andolus came with them, faking his hunger. Men knew so little of elves, including their reduced need for sleep or nourishment. Besides, he dearly wanted to know what was going through the young lord's mind. Any conversation this night involved what remained of his people as well. Decisions had yet to be made, ones on which the fate of the world rested.

"He lacks guidance," Andolus said, making public his otherwise private observations. "A man like that might easily be swayed to join the wrong factions. Felbar needed to be herded in the right direction. Otherwise, we stood to lose him to indecision."

Aron pushed what had to have been the same wooden door in every castle kitchen aside and strolled in. Wondrous smells entertained their senses. Roasting meats. Fresh baked breads and pastries. Wine and ale. Cheese wheels and winter vegetables lined one of the walls. It reminded him of home. Or what home he enjoyed as a commander of the Golden Warriors. He perused the cauldrons of homemade soups and stews and his stomach growled.

A kindly old woman saw them enter and ushered them to an empty table without delay. Her pleasant nature was almost as warming as the food. She smiled as she prepared large plates of venison, still hot bread, and bowls of soup. Each was served a very large mug of foaming wheat beer to wash it all down and offered a pipe of exceptional southern tobacco. Andolus passed on the latter, though Amean graciously accepted under the reasoning that so few comfort features were going to be available the moment they departed Grayhawk Keep.

"It's hard to convince me that the world is teetering on the brink of collapse," Amean said, after a mouthful of beer. "Damned fine, this brew is!"

Aron agreed, but his mind was centered on other matters. "Felbar has a good heart, or so I deem. He has the potential to rise in station the longer this war draws on."

"Or fall like so many others are sure to," Amean countered.

Andolus frowned and asked, "What do we do now? He's given his support, unconditionally, I might add. That's a healthy chore for any race."

Aron swallowed a bite of deer. "I think it's about time we headed back to the army. We'll certainly think clearer away from these pleasant, and most appreciated, distractions. The darklings will no doubt be getting closer and I am curious to see how effective Captain Calri's unit was at night fighting."

"Not much of a plan."

Aron's smile was painfully thin. "I'm open to suggestions. Karin's bringing the maps. Dlorn and Long Shadow are off inspecting the defenses, and I'm pretty sure our Lord Felbar has taken a shine to the princess. I'm not one to broker people's lives, but that last might be an added bonus to our plight."

"Cold, but I agree," Andolus said.

Karin entered a short time later, followed closely by Dlorn and Long Shadow. Her arms were overflowing with an assortment of maps, scrolls, and the odd book. Aron immediately felt secure. She had a calming effect on him, one he was so desperately craving the longer they spent in the field. He caught himself before smiling like a love-struck fool and glanced at the materials. The old books would serve little purpose given how the boundaries between kingdoms had shifted so radically over the generations. The maps however...

"Where's Elsyn?" Dlorn asked.

"With her unsuspecting lover," Karin chided. "What's for supper?"

They were given plates before the small company poured over the maps. Ones older than a year were set aside and forgotten. They needed up to date information, if they hoped to escape the darkling army and continue south toward the Rovers. What they desperately needed was a way through to Meisthelm without detection. Aron hoped the answers were in the disorganized mess before him.

The Black Imelin stepped lightly across the freshly fallen snow, practically walking on air in his passing. What amounted to a near permanent scowl was affixed to his face. One severe enough to keep most away. All knew, save perhaps the darklings in their savage, primitive thought processes, the source of his vehemence. What they didn't know was how he failed to understand how so small a band was capable of stealing the Staff of Life and eluding his pursuit at every turn.

Detaching from his thoughts, he turned to see Barathis heading his way. The young soldier, once pure and almost innocent in his approach to life, was now a bloodied warrior, sworn to the Black. Imelin needed more like that, if his vision of tomorrow was to become reality.

"Ah, Barathis. Good news, I trust?" A lie. A false hope that matters were improving.

Barathis shook his head. "They have beaten the northern detachment and burned the bridge. The grohl we deployed was killed by the giant with two swords."

"Enemy casualties?"

"A hundred at most. Certainly not enough, considering the amount we sustained." Disappointment collided with frustration, blending into a most foul mixture.

To his surprise, Imelin waved a nonchalant hand. "A hundred here, a thousand there. Each man we kill is one less to face when open conflict is joined. Worry not over our losses. They are insignificant compared to the size of the army the darklings bring."

"What of the hundreds killed by the Staff bearer?" Barathis asked. Bittersweet thoughts of revenge clouded his judgment.

Imelin chose to keep his old hatreds tucked away. "Let me handle him. Barathis, summon Gulnick Baach and Duoth N'nclogbar. There are issues requiring my personal attention before I can focus on the Staff bearer."

He left at once, forgetting what he'd planned on saying. The Black clasped hands behind his back and watched his chosen successor, should Barathis prove worthy, go about his task. A chill went down his back. Not even the magic of a wizard was enough to keep the cold away. He regretted, for an instant only, the timing of his offensive, but the dreams had been most adamant. And it proved they were correct, for the young lordling Aron Kryte was already proving a worthy opponent.

Stalking like a spider across the snow, Imelin parted the heavy wool curtains of his command tent.

Fashioned similarly to his comforts back in Meisthelm, before he destroyed them, of course, he found peace of mind in the almost Spartan conditions. Odd, considering how traumatic his life had become. A small fire burned in the middle, providing just enough warmth to keep his mind off the deepening winter. Taking a seat on the one crudely constructed chair, he leaned back and closed his eyes.

The obscene scent of a darkling creeping into the tent not soon after stirred him. Although expected, the darkling's stealthy ability caught him slightly off guard. Snarling, Imelin said, "The promises made under the Drehenzia at Mount Dominion are not being fulfilled. Please tell me why."

Duoth snapped his jaws shut. Ropes of saliva flew. "We do what is asked, black wizard."

"Are the mighty hordes of Duoth N'nclogbar so afraid of a tiny band of men, that after a three day chase they fail to kill a single one? More importantly, fail to secure the Staff? Perhaps I've chosen poorly in your race, *darkling*."

Normally ice colored eyes flared hot red, as if the pits of the underworld burned in his soul. Steam rose from the squat darkling in response. Both knew that any confrontations would get them nowhere, save dead.

"We kill humans and get staff," Duoth snarled.

Imelin laughed, a terrible howl sweeping across his armies far and wide. "You'd better. Fail me and I will personally remove every last one of your foul kind from the face of the world. Destruction so fierce, you can only dream."

He paused when Gulnick Baach stepped in. From the look on his haggard face, he'd been listening outside. "Do join us, General."

"I feel as if I already have," Gulnick said, caution lacing his tone.

No surprises there. Imelin had noticed that Gulnick was steadily declining in his will and ability to perform to standard. His attitude worsened and he was drifting. Something was going to be done before too long.

Imelin wet his lips, staring thoughtfully at his chosen companions. "Events have forced me to change my plans for the coming campaign. These," he paused, "foolish little people have stolen the Staff and bear a strange power I failed to anticipate. An all-out offensive against Galdea will accomplish nothing aside from unsubstantiated deaths. The Staff will disappear and it might take years before we find it again.

"Tomorrow night, under the cover of darkness, half of the army will strike south at the point where the twin rivers meet. There they will cross into Trimlon. Duoth, you will lead. I want you to link up with Denes Dron and his Rovers. Dron will then assume command of the entire army."

Duoth, to his credit, stormed from the tent without a sound.

"I don't know why you tolerate those worms," Gulnick sighed, once they were alone. "He'll turn on you the first chance he gets."

"And you, my dear general? What will you do when I give control of the northern army over to you?"

The Black's eyes regained their natural color.

"I will do my job," Gulnick replied, with a hint of insult.

"I wonder," Imelin mused, while warming his hands over the tender flames. "I leave tonight, to go south and meet with Dron. If this new plan is to succeed, the Rovers must be in place with their objectives secured on time. Our numbers, combined with the Rover army, are vast enough that those fools in the Twins won't notice how many are actually missing."

"Is that wise? The Staff is here."

"I shouldn't be gone for more than a day. You need to be at the riverbank and in position to begin the assault upon my return. Take control of the army, you'll have the rest of the men from Meisthelm to maintain order. Break the Galdeans, Gulnick."

Gulnick accepted his charge. His face was passive, emotionless, despite the enormity of what he was being asked. "Just like the wars in Aragoth."

Imelin gave a cruel smile in remembrance of the bitter string of battles between Dal Toran and the Hierarchy's ultimate victory at Krim Salat. Thousands of men, and women, too, died for dreams never realized. It was there, in the ashes of conflict, that Imelin discovered the potential in his magic and was awakened to his true path.

The general left him. Imelin didn't notice.

EIGHT

Ambushed

Less than two days ride from their current location stood the ominous Grimstone Mountains. A vast expanse of rugged foothills lay at their base, barely visible through the midafternoon haze. Sylin had never seen a more majestic or impressive range. Not even the Mountains of the Fang, legendary roost of dragons, compared. Only the stain surrounding Suroc Tol were said to be more oppressive.

He'd found himself deep in thought about minor factors of life. Until now, he hadn't realized how many simple pleasures missed or tender moments not shared the life of a councilman endured. Time, he mused, the one thing there was so little of. Ironic and tragic at once.

Gul Killingstone eased beside the westerner. "He's back there again. I can't say how far, but he's definitely one of them."

Camden Hern kept riding, though his gaze shifted to the taciturn dwarf. "Anyone with him?"

The dwarf shook his head. "Hard to say. I'd guess no, but he's too far back. A clever one, this fellow. I think he'll catch up to us once we make the foothills. We can either kill him or lose him, your call."

"I could kill him now. Won't take but a half a day to circle around," Camden said.

"No. I've got a better idea," Sylin snapped.

Mutual plans of murder were abandoned, as both men were willing to hear what the diplomat had in mind.

"Dremmin Giles is worried over the imminent goblin invasion. We have the enemy on our trail already. If we can draw him and whatever force he commands into the mountains, we might delay a major piece of the goblin force," Sylin theorized.

"We need to scout the area ahead. Unless we know exactly how many are hunting us, we could well be killed for our efforts," Camden said.

"Precisely the reason you shouldn't double back. I'll not have another unnecessary death on my conscience." *Not while I can avoid it.*

Gul said, "He talks sense, but precautions are needed. I have no desire to awaken to a slit throat because we failed to take into account this watcher might not be alone."

"There are no goblins from here to the mountains," Garin added. "Those behind us are not goblin either."

"Oo Ynlon," Camden confirmed with disgust.

Sylin offered his best political face. "We cannot be sure. They may only be a scouting party. We are faced with too many uncertainties."

Disapproving, Camden snarled. "You can be sure of one fact. We are going to be attacked before we make it to the foothills."

All fell silent and continued the trek.

A freak thunderstorm rolled in from the east. Dwarves, being naturally superstitious, assumed it was the works of the gods abandoning them. Lightning hurled down from the skies to strike the daunting peaks of the Grimstones. Showers of rock and sparks cascaded down the slopes. The noise was infuriating. Horse and pony pranced nervously. It was all their riders could do to keep them under control.

Still far enough away to be physically untouched, the little band overcame their difficulties and entered a small grove of acacia trees. The rains soon followed.

Wave after wave of waist high plains grass was flattened by the storm's intensity. Even the trees seemed to bend. Garin ordered tarps strung between the trees to give them all adequate shelter from what was a worsening storm.

"I've not seen a storm so fierce since I was but a lad in the Drear Hills," Garin grumbled between thunderclaps. His legs were drawn up, thick arms wrapped around his knees. Water dripped from his poncho. "Old Grim hisself stalks us this night."

"Ill to speak of him like that," Gul said.

"Ill or not, his grey blade is swinging tonight."

"To reap the world as it lays before him," Sylin whispered. All eyes fell on him, causing him to blush slightly. "It's a poem I learned when I was young. I've often wondered what the whole thing meant, though I must admit it's all becoming much clearer the older I get."

"What's the name of it?" Garin asked.

The sword master/statesman said, "A Mother's Love."

A tear slid down his face. "It's taken me this long to fully comprehend the truth strung out in the words."

Sylin's thoughts drifted away from the camp to a time when life was… easier. He saw his mother standing in their kitchen. She was long dead now, but not a day went by where he failed to regret not being able to tell her how much he loved her one last time. Word of her passing reached him during a minor border war in Guerselleorn during the heat of summer. Not a council member at the time, his commanding officer reluctantly approved his leave. To this day, he didn't know what kept him in the south. He had every right and reason to ride north and attend to her affairs of state.

She'd been alone for so long. His father passed twenty years earlier from the blood cough. An iron shod woman, his mother raised the family and provided as best she could. He was the result of that strength and was immeasurably grateful. Another blast of thunder tore him from the past. The sympathetic faces of his companions resonated in his heart.

"Go to sleep now, Sylin Marth," Garin said gently. "Nothing is going to happen tonight."

Even before he could manage a reply, Sylin felt the first fingers of sleeping stretching forth to claim him. The storm rumbled on.

Though the storm had passed, they moved with less speed and efficiency than before. Most of the dwarves were trackers, after a fashion and warned that their pursuit would easily take up the trail. The sheer amount of rainfall made their tracks easily discernable to even the untrained eye. Foul moods hung like palls over them as they carried forth. It was well after noon before anyone spoke.

"Not much longer," Maric said in a vain attempt to lighten the mood. "We should make the foothills by morning. Midday at the latest."

"Barring uninvited interruptions. What do we do when we get there? It's either a nation of goblins to avoid or a rogue dragon. Which shall we contend with?" Sylin asked. No matter what was discussed, he maintained his reservations about the safety of their quest.

Taciturn, yet remarkably resourceful, Gul Killingstone's coal black eyes stared hard into the darkness. The company kept no fire. No cackling flames to illuminate his position. Dwarves had been positioned around the perimeter in the hopes of discovering their pursuers in time to sound an alarm. Thus far, the night proved highly disappointing. Gul wished the Wylin, or goblins — he still wasn't convinced of Camden's suspicions — would make his move. He was tired of skulking about the prairie. What he needed was to swing his axe and be rewarded with a mug of warm ale. Those simple pleasures inspired him.

"Anything yet?" Garin asked, as he slid silently beside his friend.

"Nothing. It's almost too quiet. An ill wind blows from the east. It won't be much longer before I fall asleep or they strike."

"I wish we knew how many. Twelve against the world isn't exactly the sort of odds we need. We might as well be marching into Eleran."

Gul shivered, involuntarily, at the thought of entering the heart of the goblin empire. It made as much sense as a small company of goblins charging into the Drear Hills. Only death or worse could come of it.

"I suspect they will oblige us before dawn," Gul said.

Garin agreed, though he wished it were otherwise. "Get some sleep. I've got the watch."

Never one to pass on the amenities of not being in command, Gul burrowed down into the sand-dirt mixture and pulled his cloak over his head.

Sylin awoke to the gentle shaking by Garin Stonebreaker. Sleep clogging his eyes, he was disturbed to notice he'd been the last roused. The dwarves were already armed and moving by the time he propped himself up on an elbow. Even Camden had his sword drawn.

"What's all this?" Sylin whispered.

Camden lowered his sword. "Battle. We're about to get hit."

"Is there time to get out of here? If we can ride out and arou…"

"There's no time. Here we stand and fight. Better strap on your sword and calm those nerves. The fun is about to begin."

The dwarves drew together in a tight circle, close yet far enough apart to wield their weapons without fear of striking each other. One guarded the mounts corralled in the center, though Sylin couldn't see the dwarf's face, he knew it must be etched with contempt for being excluded from the battle.

Crickets and nocturnal birds sang their eerie songs, oblivious to the ministrations of those below. Sylin took it for a good sign. True enough, he'd seen limited action on the battlefield, but he did have a degree of experience in the arts of war. So long as the wildlife surrounding them continued unchecked, there was no enemy moving. Just to prove the gods had a sense of humor, the noise quieted the moment he became comfortable.

Palms began to sweat, much to his disliking. Sylin felt his throat dry, constrict. Why now, of all times? He'd never felt such before. An ill feeling crawled over his flesh. The horses snickered in fear. Sylin turned in time to see the first grey body barrel into their camp. Steel clashed with sparks and deadly screeches. Dwarf and goblin, ancient enemies from the dawn of time, parried blows, surging back and forth in a fluid circle.

Sylin overcame his issues and joined the fray. If the goblin managed to kill the dwarf holding the horses, the entire party was threatened by continuing the journey on foot. But as he did so, the entire night erupted with the clamor of pitched battle. The entire strength of goblins struck the dwarf perimeter in force. A scream was chopped short as one of the dwarves fell with the lower half of his right leg amputated. Another swipe cut his throat.

Goblins poured in through the breech, heading directly for Sylin and the horses. A hulking goblin struck the ground not far away. The haft of Gul Killingstone's axe jutting out. The dwarf pounced on him, tearing the blade free with a sickening crunch. The battle was much fiercer than Sylin anticipated, though he failed to notice that none of the goblins made a move against him directly. He watched as Gul was tackled by a trio of goblins. Saw Camden reel back from a cut on his upper arm and replied in kind by smashing his sword in the goblin's mouth. Teeth and blood dribbled out before Camden took his head.

Sylin watched the beleaguered dwarf guarding the horses sag to one knee while fending off the blows of two attackers. He wasn't going to last much longer. Sylin moved. He caught the goblins unaware, severing the sword arm of the nearest. Thankful, the dwarf utilized that to his advantage and drove his axe deep into the second goblin's chest. Sylin finished killing the first and helped the dwarf to his feet before rushing off to another part of the fight. All the old lessons instilled by the sword masters of Dal Toran returned to him now.

The dust kicked up by bodies locked in struggle started settling. As far as Sylin could tell, the battle was over. Three dwarves were dead, killed by an enemy force over three times their number. He didn't bother counting how many goblins lay dead. The loss of a third of his already meager force was grievous. He watched with mute silence, and no small measure of respect, as the dwarves went about the gruesome task of taking care of their dead. Personal injuries waited. Sylin found it inspiring how the dwarves changed their attitudes so thoroughly in the span of moments.

Wiping the gore from his sword, Sylin went to help his new friends.

"That was but the first attack," Gul announced, wiping his hands free of dirt and grime.

They'd finished burying the last of the dead in time with the rising sun and moved on. The disaster of the night before was already forgotten. Hard as it was to accept the deaths of their friends, the dwarves concentrated on their objective with uncanny focus. The foothills were upon them before long.

"There's always the chance we lose all pursuit in the mountains," Sylin replied as he looked up at the daunting peaks of the Grimstone Mountains.

All of the answers he sought lay somewhere ahead.

NINE

The War in the South

Winter storms blew fiercely across the plains of Trimlon. Denes Dron wondered when that fury was going to let up. His Rovers had been hit relentlessly since they crossed the Simca River several weeks ago. Dozens, probably more, but there was no way for him to verify those suspicions, had already died in the night from the cold. No matter how many blankets they pillaged or fires they built, Denes knew more would pass. Hundreds more had already caught frostbite in their fingers and toes. Morale was low. Even lower than the defeat at Krim Salat decades ago.

The life of a soldier was a hard, miserable experience. They endured hardships no sane man should have to, did more than most thought possible. To be a soldier meant doing what others wouldn't attempt. It meant watching friends die, without being able to prevent it. There were regrets and hopes, shattered dreams and extreme violence. It was the ultimate test of manhood.

Denes Dron sat in his decidedly fragile tent, trying to warm up with a fire that did little good. Fortunately, the flask of ale kept him warm on the inside. It wasn't very good, in reflection, but it managed to please his unrefined palate. The map laid out on the ground, anchored by stones dug from the snow, showed his army was halfway to the Unchar Mountains. He grimaced at that. If the storm continued to magnify, the Rovers would never make it through the pass.

The wind howled like a monster prowling for blood. *Damnable weather this. There must be a better way.* He searched the map for another, a better route past the mountains without being funneled into the Hierarchy garrison. There wasn't one. Weeks would pass trying to circle the mountains. The Black wouldn't stand for that. It didn't take much imagination for Denes to find the darklings attacking him rather than the rest of the Free Lands. His frustrations mounted.

Perhaps a little sleep would help. On the same token, he couldn't sleep when a world of troubles continued to lie in wait. He took another swig of ale and exhaled the bitter aftertaste. Now, even the ale failed to do much good. Angered by his worsening predicament, Denes collapsed in his chair and stared at the mesmerizing dance of flames.

His tent flap opened and closed so fast, snow barely had time to blow in. Denes looked upon a nightmare. Ten feet tall and dark as the foulest pits of the underworld, the figure was enshrouded in black robes. Or maybe it was the alcohol distorting his vision, turning what might have been a mere man into a winged monstrosity, threatening to steal his life. Old Grim come to pay a visit.

"I have come for you, Denes Dron."

He dropped the flask and fumbled for his sword.

A skeletal hand reached forth. "You'll have no need of that with me, or have you forgotten what I am capable of?"

The Rover commander let his hand slide down. Alcohol riddled eyes narrowed, desperate to see through the illusion filling his tent. Regardless, he felt … evil. Old Grim devolved into a man. One terrifying figure of a man. Denes slumped back in his chair and fumbled for the flask.

"Gods, wizard!" he barked. "Do you need to sneak upon men so?"

"I come and go as I please. Pathetic creatures such as yourself are of little concern to me. Time is mine alone," Imelin said, as calm as the morning sun rising.

Undaunted only by the vast amounts of ale already consumed, Denes leveled his fierce gaze. "Why are you here? Especially now? Our campaign is still weeks from evolving into combat. Unchar Pass is plugged with snow. It will take forever to dig our way through. By then, the enemy will know we are coming. Not even my strength here will be a match against a reinforced Golden Warrior battalion. All they need do is fall back to their entrenchments and let us break upon the stone. I am in a losing situation, wizard."

Imelin's eyebrow peaked. "Are you quite through?"

"Why?"

Warming his hands, Imelin continued. "Much has changed since last we met. A new factor is working against us. I am sending half of the darkling army to your support."

Denes scoffed, even as his stomach clenched. "What of the snows? Can these demons of yours tunnel through several feet of snow for near a league?"

Imelin decided the Rover leader was quickly outliving his usefulness. "Men have died for less. Do not think to insult me again. The snows of Unchar Pass are of little concern to me at this juncture. The pass will be clear by the time you reach the mountains. Magic is a tool of necessity and it is very necessary for you to seize the objective and hold it within the next three weeks. When deep winter hits, you should be in possession of the high road down to Meisthelm."

"If you can clear the pass, my men can hold it," Denes said confidently.

"Good. Your change of mission goes as follows: deploy several units of riders out into the surrounding fields of Unchar. They should be sufficient to draw out enough of the defenders. I am familiar with the garrison commander. Like most of his breed, he is young and overanxious to make a name for himself. There are few left with the true warrior soul."

Imelin sat in the opposite chair. "A siege will be fruitless. The enemy has enough supplies and weapons to withstand any prolonged assault. Not to mention direct access back to Hierarchy command. Lure the Golden Warriors back into the pass. By the time they give pursuit, a legion of darklings will already be deployed in the surrounding forests. Denes Dron, it is imperative that you hold Unchar until the main army arrives. Capture the townsfolk and hold them in the fortress. Let a few escape to spread word of our coming. Fear will take care of the rest."

In the blink of an eye the wizard was on his feet and gone, leaving a much confused Denes staring back at his fire in confused reflection. What a strange breed wizards were. No wonder most of the world didn't trust them. Weary from too much too soon, the Rover commander finished his flask and drifted off to sleep. Executing his new orders could wait until morning. After all, what was a few hours?

Guerselleorn was a vast kingdom west of Valadon and the capital city of Meisthelm. The Jemman Sea formed the far western border with Coronan in the north and Sadith Oom far to the south. It was one of the largest kingdoms in the Free Lands and was filled with grassy plains, the southern tributary of the Simca River and the largest port on the continent. Trade with Guerselleorn was vital to the continued economic growth of the Free Lands as well as keeping the Hierarchy funded.

Those plains became the breeding ground for warriors in extreme situations. Such as now, thousands of soldiers, both afoot and mounted, marched down the dusty roads. Supply wagons and hospital crews trailed for a league behind the main combat power. Logistical support used to keep the army moving was far more organized, and developed, than any campaign in Hierarchy history to date.

General Conn and his inner council of advisors and senior military commanders rode at the head of the great beast snaking across the kingdom. His strong eyes took in the sights of the land stretching out before him. The land he'd come to save. Content with his role, Conn had always considered himself above a nobleman. He was a knight born for the quest. A driven man in search of the ultimate quest.

Elf, dwarf, and Wylin rode in his entourage. A pair of gnomes rode the far point. They were, for the moment, one of his most valuable assets while on the move. Their skills in tracking and hunting left him wishing for a thousand more. As it was, two would have to be enough.

Young Rhea Ailwin also rode at his side. Where once he rode to deliver an urgent message from Meisthelm, he was now immersed in what might well amount to the direst, and important, campaign since the war against Ils Kincannon. Being so near General Conn helped him forget the worries of the High Council. It was easier to focus only on his own desires and needs. Glory awaited. Or death.

This was what life was meant to be. Rhea became one with the campaign and the will of the strongest man he'd ever met. He'd tried explaining, to anyone who would listen, the depth of his inexperience. He hadn't wielded a sword since basic training, as all new recruits were required to do. Even so, the messenger rode proudly at the head of a vast army. The tales he'd be able to tell his grandchildren inspired him. I was there, he'd say with bluster, the day General Conn liberated the Port of Grespon and saved the young prince.

"We should gain the port within the next two days," Conn mused.

Rhea was surprised at the sudden change in Conn's mood. The general had barely spoken since breaking camp. Lost within himself, Conn focused on what needed to be done to successfully accomplish his goals. A stern look hardened his already weathered face when he thought about what it would take to sack the city while keeping civilian casualties to bare minimums and remove the pirate captors. Numbers flowed across his vision. Casualty figures. Dead and wounded, both friend and foe. Men sworn to defend the freedom of the kingdoms, while obeying his word, were going to fall. Some screaming from help. Some emerging from the fray missing limbs, crippled for life.

"Good," Haf Forager grunted. "It's been too long since my axe was wet."

The dwarf was as hearty as they came, slightly robust and honed to a razor's sharpness. He was as lethal as a dragon. Like most in his position, his best years were behind him.

Genessen laughed, his voice golden with merriment. "Why is it, for as long as I've interacted with your kind, dwarves are so intent on death and gore? Do you ever take the time to enjoy the fragile smell of a flower? Or the way the sun beautifies the land after a summer rain shower? Enjoy life while you can, for tomorrow may never come."

Haf grunted again. "Elves. I can't for the life of me figure out why our two peoples have stood in alliance for so long. Exact opposites, if you ask me. Flowers and sunshine. Give me an axe and the rush of battle and I'll be happy to meet the makers."

"We balance each other."

The dwarf had trouble disputing that. "We are from the same lands, my friend. I credit you much for the roads we have travelled together. Now let us go down this one before returning home. I would exercise my muscles once. Call it a warmup, if you will."

Genessen sighed. "Too sad, and much too true. The Wilderlands are engulfed in war with goblins and there is little hope of it ending soon. It seems our quest of obtaining aid from the western nations has failed. Though not through our doing."

"Then we make do with what we have. It will be a cold day in the underworld before a dwarf runs from a fight, be it here or home," Haf said. The resulting silence afforded them the opportunity to brood over his words.

It was, even to the most optimistic thinker, a dire prospect.

Flankers and outriders guarded the army with watchful eyes. Lieutenant Zin Doluth led a company of scouts spread out along a league wide line. Their purpose was to give warning should the pirates move on the main army and discover the best approaches to Grespon. Each man was hand-selected and bore Conn's complete trust. Their orders were not to engage unless they had superiority.

A dust cloud hovered over the sky on the horizon. Genessen's elf eyes spotted it first, though he failed to make out the source. Whatever it was, was well within the scout screen. His hurried looked spurred Conn forward.

"I don't believe it, he's the general of the army!" Rhea whispered to the color bearer at his side.

"See all those standards?" the younger man asked, with a jerk of his head.

Rhea turned and was instantly impressed at the fifty flags of every color waving in the slight breeze.

The soldier continued. "Each one is a reminder of a battle won. I think I'd be confident as well, if I'd managed to do half as much."

Rebuked, Rhea fell silent and smarted at his wounds. The dust cloud ahead was getting closer at an alarming speed. What new tortures did the day hold?

Conn held up a hand and the army ground to a halt. Easier said than done, however, for units in the middle and rear bounced off each other. Genessen announced the source of the cloud as a scout returning from the Port. Much anticipation bustled through the front ranks. Rumors spread, as they did in every army, quickly to the rear. Perhaps battle was about to be joined much soon than thought.

Conn's eyes narrowed to bare slits when he saw who the scout was. Zin Doluth. His uniform was the color of dirt.

"Sir," he panted. "The enemy is dug in much better than we anticipated. They've been waiting for us." Concern painted his voice.

Conn nodded, grim with the knowledge. "Spies can be anywhere. Perhaps within our own ranks. These are days when nothing is what it appears. We cannot afford to take anything for granted. Have any of your scouts been able to infiltrate yet?"

"No, sir. As I said, they are well coordinated and seemingly waiting for an attack," Zin said.

Haf Forager let out a deep, bellowing laugh. "Of course, they are! Pirates are a cautious breed, lad. They check and double check everything, leaving nothing to chance. When they took the city and the bastard prince, they knew they started a small war. Wouldn't you expect to be counterattacked?"

"I suppose I would, but this is too odd. Most of their defenses are geared toward fending off heavy cavalry and pointed directly at us. I have an ill feeling."

"Relax, young lieutenant," Conn's voice boomed. There was no denial of his authority. "War is always a tricky sport. I recall my first battle. Wasn't but a mere foot soldier. We took on a force three times our own. By the gods, it was a fight. They surrounded us and squeezed until less than a hundred of my brothers remained. We struck out in one final, determined attack, knowing that if we failed, it would be our heads on the pike. Men perform better when desperation is all that remains."

An odd glimmer caught in his eyes, cold and fierce, as memories forced their way free. "We fought like demons that day and were rewarded with victory. The enemy was shattered and driven back into their forests. When the dust settled and the pains of our wounds became reality, less than ten of us stood. I… fear these days are returning."

Conn fell silent. None spoke for a long while, allowing the general the respect of revisiting old wounds. Listening to each word on the edge of his saddle, Rhea absorbed both glories and doom clashing in the eternal struggle of right over wrong. Though, he was quickly coming to understand, there was no glory in war. He wanted to weep for the old man, for all those simple pleasures in life Conn had never, and would never, experience.

Undaunted by the ghosts of the past, Conn called his army back to the road. There was a battle ahead waiting to be met. Nostalgia aside, he planned on marching his army down the pirate's throats and retake the Port of Grespon. There was no other choice. The rest of the Free Lands was falling apart and would soon have need of his force.

TEN

The Darklings Attack

Dawn wormed slowly across the night sky. For the men of the Galdean army, it came far too soon. As eager as many were to extract revenge on the darkling hordes of Suroc Tol, they liked less the idea of watching more of their friends and countrymen fall. Today marked the first day in what promised to be the long war against the rising darkness, though the first blows had already fallen many weeks before inside the walls of their home city.

Aron Kryte rolled over and stretched the sleep away, oblivious to the nervousness setting in among the defenders. His bed was crudely constructed but did the job. With a smile, he leaned down and kissed Karin's cheek. She smiled in her sleep and awoke with a tender, warm feeling. Forgotten for the moment was the dilemma of the day and the near freezing temperature. This was the simple morning that she decided made life worth living.

"How did you sleep?" he asked.

Her smile widened. "Mmm. Like a baby. I wonder if this is but a dream. If maybe one day I'll wake up and nothing ever happened."

She stopped abruptly, her eyes glazing over as they did when a vision came to her. Her body writhed and constricted under the bear skin blanket. Sweat covered her face and hands. Horror gripped her face. Spittle drooled from the corners of her mouth. Aron fell out of the bed and watched helplessly.

"Gods, Aron!" she whispered as warmth returned to her body. "It's Imelin! He knows. He was inside my mind. Laughing. We're all going to die."

The combat veteran and future of the world, reluctantly, eyed her with fright. How did that devil get in her mind? Her very soul? The toll of a hundred drums suddenly stole his thoughts. War drums beating out their death knell. Paining him to do so, Aron released his love and hurriedly got dressed. There was but one reason for the drums. The armies of the Black had been sighted. War was upon them.

Field Marshal Dlorn stood atop the highest point in the battlements, back stiff as calculating eyes watched the front ranks of the darkling vanguard slither across the snow-covered fields. The enemy front was close to a third of a league across. No surprises there, for he had come to overestimate the size of their army. What caught him off guard was the handful of men riding at the head of the force. This was discouraging, to an extent, but nothing he wasn't prepared to deal with. Men he knew how to kill. Returning from their own forward lines, Captain Calri and Andolus assumed positions on either side of Dlorn. Optimism yet shone in their eyes, though his were much more skeptical.

"They got here much faster than I thought they would," Calri said in his typical flat tone. He still ached from wounds suffered during the raid several nights past.

Dlorn clasped his hands behind his back. "We still have time. It will be past midday before they can mount a direct assault. The main army won't arrive for a while yet, maybe not until tomorrow, if we're fortunate. They may be creatures of darkness but a cold-blooded man commands them."

"A traitorous serpent of humanity," Andolus cautioned. "That man is none other than General Gulnick Baach, former commander of the armies of Valadon and hero of Meisthelm."

"There seems no limits to treachery," Dlorn muttered.

"Your orders, sir?" Calri asked. He had never heard of Baach, thus leaving the respect the others showed flat.

"Bring up the catapults. Have the archers on standby. All reserve and reinforcement units need to maximize downtime. Ensure they get enough rest to keep them going for at least three days. This is not going to be an easy fight. Secondary units need to gear up and be prepared to plug any holes," Dlorn said.

As much as he wanted to direct his army in battle, micromanaging his commanders served no purpose. He trusted each of them and would allow them to react as necessary, while he still retained overall operational control. The battle promised to be fluid and he needed to stay far enough back to observe the entire battlefield. History was littered with tales of lesser armies failing to do so.

With a monstrous sound, great teams of work oxen lurched forward, pulling forward the catapults supplied by Lord Felbar. They had fifty of the machines with plenty of ammunition dug out from the far river. Soldiers in the trenches cast fleeting glances at the war machines and took hope. The promise of smashed darklings helped take away the sting of what was sure to come.

Metal clashed against metal in deadly song. Jou Amn fended off yet another blow and dropped back. Out of breath and feeling his age, he plunged the tip of his sword into the snow and drank deeply from his canteen. He looked disdainfully at his opponent, even while knowing the old man was scarcely breathing hard.

Amean Repage, on the other hand, was quite pleased. It had been too long since he'd last carried on single combat like that. The reassurance in his psyche was immediately noticeable, yet there still lurked the nagging vision of his death. Only through great strength of will was he able to force that thought aside and carry on. Sometimes he was successful, others not.

"I didn't think a man as old as yourself could run with the youth," Jou taunted.

Amean scowled. "You can't be talking about yourself. If I recall correctly, you're only a few years younger than me."

"Age is only what you fe…"

The rhythmic beating of drums across the plains cut him off. Time for training was ended.

When the entire command structure under Dlorn was at last assembled, they began hashing out final plans. Long Shadow sat in the corner nearest the exit of the massive tent. While watching and listening to the various lords and commanders proved insightful on how mainland armies fought, he felt awkward. They were so different from his own people. At best, deep down, he was a barbarian, though coated with political savvy. The silent killer's blood surged with the aspirations of battle that had yet to unfold. Instead, he simmered and listened.

"I want catapults firing as soon as they get within range. No arrows," Dlorn said, his eyes sharp as a wolf. "We'll have need of every last shaft once the darklings get under the catapult cover. What is the status of the forward units?"

"Our infantry is well entrenched. Some of the battalions managed to provide overhead cover on their main positions. Rows of spikes are implanted for twenty meters on the approach to the first line. They will slow the darklings to an extent but not long," Calri said.

Dlorn nodded approvingly. Young Calri was proving himself a worthy successor to the fallen Irrius.

"Our only question now is how long the Black is going to take to attack. Will he commit now and risk the lives of thousands of his vile army or wait, taking us apart piecemeal?"

Aron cleared his throat. "He will not commit. Though his army is vast as the sunrise, there is a limit to their number. We are but a stepping stone on his dark path. He will have need of their strength once he gets past this army. Baach will use the vanguard to probe us, searching out weaknesses in the defenses. Crossing the river is not a primary concern, but we do have a contingency in place for the inevitable airborne assault."

"Thus far," Andolus broke in, "We have managed to score several minor victories against smaller components of his army. The bridge Captain Calri burned may well have been rebuilt by now. We also have no idea how many of those beasts are already across the river. Troops could be ferrying down from leagues upstream. Remember, a man leads them."

"The elements have hampered us considerably but our engineers still have a few surprises emplaced along the way to slow the darklings." Pride rang in Calri's voice. Youthful ignorance left him filled with confidence. That and the unfaltering faith in the capabilities of his men.

A runner burst into the tent, out of breath and three shades of pale. "They're here! Trying to ford the river!"

The glorious sounds of the first catapult firing accented the situation. The battle they long awaited and feared was begun. Dlorn looked at his friends and compatriots one final time. "Well then. Our day has come at last. All I ask from any of you is to do your best. With the grace of the old gods, we may make a bid for our lives and return to the arms of our loved ones. Luck in battle, my friends."

The commanders of the Galdean army saluted and took to their posts.

Catapults fired continuously. Each boulder and flame covered round tore massive holes in the darkling lines. Screams from the dead and dying sang out in hideous, inhuman wails. Gulnick Baach's horse reared back on hind legs. He had expected a fierce battle, and thus far was not disappointed. Hundreds of darklings were already dead, twice that wounded, and they still hadn't closed with the Galdeans. The stench of burning hair and flesh choked his lungs. His advance was rapidly devolving into an unorganized quagmire of bodies. In all, he expected nothing less from Dlorn.

Darklings, already too close for the catapults to be effective, began to crawl from the icy waters of the Simca, only to be run through by sharpened pikes. Gulnick was most impressed with the vibrant young commander on the far side as he ran up and down the lines in great efforts to inspire morale. The men of Galdea were indeed valiant, if foolish.

The defenses had been chosen well, for here the river was at its narrowest. A slight rise on the opposite bank gave the Galdeans the upper hand. Bermed up with hardened snow and frozen earth, Gulnick realized the enemy could feasibly hold out for days, while he tried to marshal his army in a different direction.

Half of that army was already gone, moving down south to their rendezvous with Denes Dron. The rest were still leagues away and in no hurry to get here. Gulnick had no qualms about sacrificing the almost hundred thousand darklings he had under him. The world was far better off without them, in his estimation. But losing sat ill on his mind. Combined with what the Black would do to him in the aftermath, Gulnick needed to find an advantage and end this. All he needed was a beachhead.

The first wave of darklings died in vain. While they were being skewered on pikes and spears, a second wave swan across the river, towing makeshift bridges. Preoccupied with the devils already before them, the Galdeans failed to notice the foundations of their demise being laid. The death toll of the catapults continued to rise behind them.

Gulnick reached out to the nearest soldier, a cutthroat mercenary picked up in Prossin, and barked, "I want the army moving as soon as that first bridge is emplaced. Keep shuffling more bridges. We need numbers to break that trench!"

It was difficult working with beasts that had only rudimentary control of the common tongue. Worse, Gulnick knew the darklings had a hidden agenda, whether the Black controlled them or not. What they lacked in trust of each other, they made up for with tenacity. And they continued to die in the hundreds because of it.

Calri Alsimmons ran up and down the lines, rallying his men. This was his first important combat action and he was determined to give a good showing. Bitter satisfaction etched upon his face as he watched his men fight. The first squat darkling bodies emerged from the frozen waters of the Simca River. Mats of hair clung to their grotesque bodies, lending an even more devilish appearance. The murderous intent in their eyes almost made Calri blanch, despite having confronted them before. Being on the offensive was one thing, waiting for an entire army to crash upon the trenches, another altogether.

"Pikemen!" Calri barked, forced to shout above the roar of the catapults. "At the ready!"

Galdeans rose from the trenches and formed ranks. They roared almost as loud as the darklings, as pikes were lowered in a blanket of polished iron. Snow drifted from the tips. They caught the tidal wave of darklings and surprisingly, held without buckling. Darklings were impaled. Sometimes two or more to a pike. Calri expected such. It was the subsequent drive that concerned him more. Engaged, the pikemen were unable to clear before other darklings swarmed between them.

Calri brandished his sword and bellowed at the top of his lungs. Hundreds of armored swordsmen plugged the holes and slaughtered the darklings. Trapped in confined space, the enemy made easy targets. Primitive, they failed to suspect the counter move, and were cut down by the score for their ignorance. Men fell as well, though in greatly reduced numbers.

With the immediate threat all but taken care of, Calri pulled back to survey the battlefield. What he saw sickened him. Darklings were starting to cross the river, and in numbers. He squinted but made out the amount of rickety bridges that were laid down. Darklings could cross by the hundreds. A blood-spattered helmet rolled past his feet. If he didn't act fast, there would be many more. Too many.

He grabbed the man nearest him and spat out, "Go to Dlorn. Get the second battery of catapults to direct their fire on those bridges!"

The freshly appointed courier ran as fast as his armor allowed, leaving Calri to seek out his lieutenants. Five minutes later, his plan was ready to be executed. Several hundred swordsmen, a full battalion worth, surged over the berm, with Calri at their head, and down the embankment into the darkling mass. Even Gulnick Baach was caught off guard.

Battle was fast, furious. Bodies from both sides fell in a bloody mess. Calri crushed in the head of one darkling and swung hard enough to pierce the lung and heart of a second in a back swing. Gradually the tide shifted and the defenders outnumbered the living darklings. Any victory of numbers was short lived. Increased pockets of darklings broke free of the icy waters, while even more streamed across the ramshackle bridges.

Young Calri, already exhausted and fighting the urge to take a knee, was at the end of hope. Then the first catapult round smashed into a near bridge. Flesh and flames exploded. Darklings snapped their heads in surprise.

Field Marshal Dlorn stood with clenched jaw as the initial assault crested his outer defenses. The fighting was fearsome, with many falling on each side, but the enemy was gradually beaten back. Smoke from a hundred fires choked the air and obscured a good portion of the field. *Damned luck. I need to see into the enemy camp if I'm going to stop them.* He scratched a finger, absently, at the corner of his mouth.

Dlorn had originally questioned the decision to send his soldiers down into the riverbed. He didn't see how any would survive, being so close to the darkling power base. Such thoughts weighing heavily on his mind, Dlorn failed to notice the message runner, a boy who couldn't have been more than fifteen summers, run up to him. Message delivered, Dlorn immediately acted.

"Master gunner!" he shouted, while striding toward the catapults. A weathered, beaten face looked up.

"Adjust your fire into the river. We need to give the line more support or the whole damned army will be forced to fallback."

"Sir!"

The master gunner resumed his control of the Galdean artillery. "Number Two battery, sight in on the river and fire at will! Give them everything you've got!"

Crew chiefs adjusted their weapons to compensate for the shorter range while the front battery continued spewing death into the darklings across the river. Heart beats passed before the first round thundered out and over the battle. Geysers of frigid water fountained. The gunners were too far back to see the devastation they caused.

Frozen water soaked him. An arm struck his chest, nearly knocking him down. Round after round struck the river, destroying the bridge network and ending life. Calri watched the wholesale destruction with the wide eyes of enlightenment. He knew, or rather thought he did, the price of battle before wading into it, but this was so much worse than any construct him mind was capable of imagining.

A fierce cry arose from his men, suddenly buoyed by the ravaging suppressing fire of their catapults. Darklings on the other side stopped trying to swim across. The suicide of the slaughter was more than they were willing to risk, despite orders from Gulnick Baach to continue the assault. Calri sidestepped a rushing foe, slashing a crippling cut across the back of the darkling's neck. His follow-on swing ripped out the guts of another. Blood stained his armor breastplate. A foul stench covered him. The smell of slaughter. He ignored it as best he could, but ultimately couldn't keep from voiding his already empty belly.

The intensity of the struggle subsided, if only just. No darkling reinforcements came across the river and the numbers of those already across dwindled rapidly. Calri knew he had to press the attack. Never having been confronted with retreat before, the darklings died to the last. Pikemen, now finished with their defense, cried out and swept down the slope, pushing the enemy back to the water. Catapults ceased firing into the river, readjusting their aim to the main darkling camp less than a kilometer away.

Only when the cheer went up announcing the last of the enemy had been purged from the trenches did Calri realize he'd won his first victory. Exhausted beyond measure, the young captain struggled to crest the rise of the embankment. Weary survivors, far fewer than he would have liked, limped and hobbled back to their lines and kept going to the surgeons tents as fresh reserves took their place on the line. As much as he wanted to turn away from the grizzly scene, Calri refused to look away as the dead were carried past.

The instant the first catapult round struck the river was the instant Gulnick Baach realized it was going to get far worse. He signaled to the bugler to sound retreat when a burst of rock, dirt, and snow threw him from his mount. Brushing the grime from his eyes, Gulnick saw his horse fall dead with a sharp piece of granite in his throat. Blood splashed the front of his Hierarchy uniform, a reminder of his past that he couldn't bring himself to abandon.

Gulnick rose and marched back to escape the range of those dreaded catapults. He looked into his camp and saw utter disarray. The old general was disgusted. Painful memories of the men he once led drifted back from the nothing of the past. A piece of him wished to be on the opposite side of the river, celebrating victory and buckling down for the next iteration. He longed for the feeling of brotherhood strengthening among the Galdeans. Brotherhood that was decidedly lacking among his forces. He knew those same enemies would be stronger in the morning. Fortified.

Those thoughts soon fled and a bitter anger lingered in his soul. Defeat was not an easy thing to accept, yet he did so with a grain of salt. All the while, new plans developed. Gulnick stiffened. Ignoring the screams and shock of explosions coming from his camp, he marched with shoulders thrown back. Tomorrow was a new day. He would not be defeated. Not like this.

Alone and forgotten by the throngs of men surrounding her, Elsyn sat in her tent listening to the furious sounds coming from the river. Shouts and screams mingled with the crash of armor and the distinct sounds of catapult fire. With each new scream she knew another life ended. Each life had become precious to her.

She wrapped her arms around her drawn up legs and cried before realizing the foolishness of her actions. She was a princess of Galdea, the heir to the throne. This was no way for her to behave. Rising, she straightened her travel clothes and strapped the short sword Andolus had given her to her waist. Elsyn left the sanctuary of her tent and strode out into the army. The men deserved no less.

Those not involved in the struggle on the river stopped what they were doing to stare at her. Some longingly, others with admiration. She gave them hope, where none was to be found. Already outnumbered, the Galdean army knew this was but the beginning. An entire army swarmed against them. Elsyn stopped when she reached a rise high enough to survey the entire battlefield.

Her throat trembled. Never had she been witness to such acts of brutal violence. Her stomach churned, palms clenched reflexively. Elsyn's mind begged her to turn away, to not look a moment longer, but her body refused to budge. It was, after all, oddly fascinating.

Her limited exposure to violence back in Galdarath wasn't enough to provide an accurate description. She had no idea war was so… graphic. Warriors often spoke to her of elegant tales spun around half-truths and blatant lies. They whispered of glories she knew she'd never see. Now, finally exposed to it all, she knew it was all a lie. There was no glory in war. Only pain and suffering. When at last she couldn't stand to watch any more, she headed back to the sanctity of her tent. She'd seen enough.

Alone, forgotten by the throngs of soldiers surrounding her, Elsyn sat on her cot trying to ignore the estranged sounds assailing her as night rolled in. Mercifully, a messenger arrived with summons to the army council. She happily followed and was surprised to hear laughter and a generally spirited mood coming from the soldiers. Elsyn wondered how anyone could laugh in the face of such adversity.

"Ah, princess," Dlorn said. "I am glad you are well."

"Thank you, General, but these men are certainly more important than I." How true her words were.

Aron looked up from the map table containing unit positions. "I would beg to differ. Soldiers fight and die, that is why we are here, but you are the life blood of Galdea. The last living heir to the house of Elian. Your safety is paramount."

She blushed, feeling warmth spread through her. Embarrassed by her thoughts, she took her seat amongst the various battle lords.

"Though we pulled out a minor victory, the facts haven't changed. We are still outnumbered at least three to one and the Black has suspiciously disappeared," Dlorn argued. "We need to fight a delaying tactic. Turn back and assault here, retreat a little, and fight again. Heads up confrontation will result in nothing less than our annihilation."

A flaxen haired man of middle age and rounded belly rose. "How long and how far do you intend to retreat? We have already been expelled from our homelands. How far, General?"

Dlorn eyed him respectfully. Daril Perryman was a fine man, and an even better strategist who was well respected and revered throughout the army.

"For as long as we must, Commander. We are not only fighting for our homes but that of the entire Free Lands. Will you forfeit the lives of millions for selfishness?'

Perryman stood his ground. "I will forfeit my own to keep my men and their families alive. We don't even know what this damned wizard wants. I say leave him be and let us return home."

"He comes for me."

All eyes shifted to the partially shadowed face of Aron Kryte. Their collective gaze left him feeling cold, shallow. After all, he was but a single man. Why should the world die to keep him safe?

"What makes you so damned important?" Perryman asked.

"To be truthful, it's not exactly me. I have a thing he very much desires and will stop at nothing to obtain. The Black has been blinded by the prophecy of Ils Kincannon. He follows the law of the heretic, seeking to become a god."

"Nonsense," Perryman defended. "Kincannon is barely a memory."

Aron continued, working out his thoughts for personal reasons rather than explain everything, again, to those few faces he didn't know. "To most men, the Staff of Life is naught but a myth, forged in the illusions of drunken stupor. To me, and those who ride with me, it is a token as real as the air we breathe. This Staff, not me, is important. It needs to be taken back to Meisthelm. The High Council will do what needs doing."

Perryman laughed, despite failing to notice he was the only doubter. "And all of our troubles will magically wither away? Your Hierarchy doesn't seem to be doing much good for the Free Lands now, does it?"

Eager to quell his anger, Aron said, "No. The problems which you so proudly stake claim to as your own will not go away. The madness of the Black will grow, even thrive, until he has the Staff in his possession. What we fight for is much more than the insignificance of self."

He fell silent and moved to the center of the tent, staring with empty eyes into the roaring flames of the fire pit. Karin cast a wicked glare at Perryman before going to her lover's side in support.

"Now you see, Commander Perryman, why I cannot give way to the dark hordes. The value of the future is too much for me to abandon," Dlorn echoed.

Defeated, Perryman sat. He'd been a loyal son of the crown all his life and would remain so. Doom or not. Dlorn would have his full support. "I know nothing of wizards or tokens of power. Sometimes I know not the hearts of men, but to this I swear. You have the full support of my men in your quest, Lord Kryte. General, forgive my outbursts. They were uncalled for and unbecoming of an officer in the Galdean army."

Dlorn nodded in consent, silently wondering if he would have done the same if the situation was reversed.

"What we need," sang the golden voice of Andolus, "is a diversion. We need to find a way to keep the darklings from attacking. For if we continue as we are now, they will soon be able to cross the river on the backs of their dead."

"What are you suggesting?" Calri asked. He'd been able to clean some of the blood and gore before answering the summons.

"Darklings are brutal, efficient killers, but they've never been exceptional. Much like conventional armies, they have a body of leadership. If we can cross the river and cut off the head, so to speak, their army will devolve, making them far easier to deal with. I would suggest that your Gulnick Baach is in command. Kill him and we stand a chance."

"An admirable plan," Dlorn noted, "But who is suicidal enough to lead the raid?"

Long Shadow, last of the Lords of Teranian, stood. His grim façade spoke for him.

A horrible clamor arose from the northern flank of the army before any could question Long Shadow. The darklings had plans of their own.

ELEVEN
Redirection

Gulnick Baach was once considered among the very best of the Hierarchy commanders. A fact the Galdeans had forgotten. Using the cover of darkness, he sent battalions of darklings farther north to cross the river and attack south. Five thousand killers waited in the shadows in utter silence. This was a campaign of probes. Gulnick absorbed the losses of the initial battle while developing a counter plan.

Wrapped in a thick cloak, he went as close to the riverbank as he dared and listened to the night sounds. The waters of the mighty Simca River lapped against the rocks and chunks of ice, tempting one to slip in. Cloud cover blocked the moon, giving Gulnick cause to wonder if the wizard had had a hand in it.

He watched the illuminated sentinels on the far riverbank, scant meters away. Common sense told him the last units on duty had already been replaced with fresh troops eager to be blooded. Again came the dreams of being in their camp, if only to feel the exuberance of victory. He missed the days of enjoying a cask of wine with his men.

Minutes danced away, turning into hours. He toyed with the idea of sending another assault across in diversion for the main assault. Gulnick watched as units continued to emplace a wall of spikes and spears, making any frontal assault all but impossible. His mind was focused on finding any weakness in the defenses and exploiting them, not turning his army into worm food.

The sounds of battle erupted from the north. He sighed. *So begins another round of slaughter. It's going to be a long night.* He went back to his tent. Sleep was needed if he was going to maintain the pace of battle. Hopefully, his tactic would be successful enough to keep his enemies away from the tender embrace of sleep. Either way, he'd find out in the morning.

Ignoring the protests of his men, Field Marshal Dlorn took his command staff into the fray. Axe and sword rose and fell. A large body of darklings was already deep into their lines, driving the defenders back on a path of mutilated bodies. Some died in their sleep, a terrible price paid for dozing off. The rush came unexpectedly, catching the weary soldiers off guard. Reinforcements were slow in coming, leaving the brave men on the flank alone. Until Dlorn arrived.

Long Shadow ran with blinding speed through the steel ranks. His might crashed into the darklings, wielding death as a powerful friend. Those unfortunate enough to come across him fell without much of a struggle. Elven hunters joined the battle behind the example of their prince. Arrows whistled through the air, decimating the darklings. The elf prince checked their fire enough to allow the surging knot of Dlorn's men room to attack. It was a bitter fight. Heads were lopped from shoulders. Bodies cut in half. A man of weak stomach wouldn't have lasted.

Seizing the initiative, Dlorn and Calri Alsimmons led one hundred men into the flank, driving the confused darklings back toward the river. The old man fought like a caged beast. His sword was an extension of his flesh, his very spirit. Parry. Thrust. Slash. The foul bodies of his foe fell again and again under the onslaught of his fury.

Yet even his remarkable strength ebbed. A darkling barreled into him, knocking him to the ground. Another swept in, threatening to tear his head off. The darkling doubled over in air, entrails spilling down onto Dlorn's chest. With the second darkling distracted, Dlorn pulled out his dagger and stabbed. Blade sank through flesh and sinew in the back of the darkling's knee. The creature howled, giving Dlorn the opportunity to drive his weapon into the darkling's exposed throat.

Daril Perryman helped his general to his feet and surged past with the flow of battle. A great cheer arose from the opposite side of the fight. Terror sparked in the darklings near and far as a fist of golden armor plunged into them. Fifty of the best warriors in the Free Lands exercised their pent-up aggressions. Over three times their number fell as the darklings were entirely overrun. The Golden Warriors provided the Galdeans that spark they needed to rally.

They worked as one, the culmination of Hierarchy training standards and instilled discipline. Yet even the renowned Golden Warriors weren't enough to make the darklings retreat. They redoubled their attack but the Galdeans had rallied. Unable to break through or wrap around the edges of the defense, the darklings were forced to pack tight and rely on numbers. Back ranks, oblivious to what was happening in the front, continued to surge ahead, trampling many of their own out of sheer bloodlust.

Snow started falling in gentle amounts. Bodies slipped and fell, grappling to the death. Back and forth the battle rage, neither side gaining or losing. Dlorn read the situation and despaired. Darkness prevented him from ascertaining the darkling numbers. Confronting the unknown, he needed to develop a counter strike before his entire northern flank collapsed.

He was stepping through bodies when searing pain lanced across the back of his calf. Dlorn slashed down instinctively and killed the darkling. Scowling, he searched for more pretending to be dead. Then he caught a glimpse of Calri and a handful of others. They were surrounded, fighting for dear life. Several darklings fell, pierced with arrows, before Dlorn could head that way. The elves surprise assault was enough to enable Calri and his men the opportunity to break free and back to the safety of the line.

Dlorn eventually made his way to Calri and grabbed him by the collar. "Send a runner to Lestrin. I want the heavy cavalry here now! That should be enough to break their backs."

Slowly, but gradually, the defense lines began to break. Pockets of resistance were swarmed over and killed. The Galdeans made the darklings pay for every foot of ground. It was a price the enemy was willing to pay. Dlorn fought with his men but knew the futility of the situation. Unable to summon reinforcements from the river, he prayed his men could hold long enough for the cavalry to arrive.

Killing with vengeance, Aron Kryte smote all enemies as they presented themselves. His men were equally vengeful. They made him proud to be their commander. Darklings shied away, knowing this threat was the most dangerous. Golden Warriors were trained to fight like no other man. But the darklings had never known fear and refused to back down, even as the men in golden armor slaughtered all.

Fighting with incredible intensity, the demons of Suroc Tol raged with berserker strength. Meter by meter, the alliance of men and elves were forced back. Aron Kryte and his band did their best to quell the tide. Firelight reflections danced from the fist of gold, delivering hope where none was to be found.

Each Golden Warrior was a master at arms. Each had been under the knife at various points in their lives and were well versed in battle. Some grinned savagely behind the anonymity of their faceplates. They killed with ruthless efficiency. Soon the bodies piled beyond count. Despite this, Aron saw the hopelessness of their predicament. They were locked in a no-win scenario.

"Fall back!" he ordered.

A staggering Amean bumped into him, blood stained and exhausted. He'd lost his helmet along the way. His hair was pasted to his scalp. A sharp cut above his right eye dribbled blood down his face.

"There are too many," he gasped through waves of pain.

"Take the men back to that rise. Form a line and wait for help. We've got thirty thousand men here and less than two in the fight. This is a foul night," Aron scowled.

"What about you?" Amean asked.

"I've got to get to Dlorn and the others. If we're to stand a chance at all, we need all the help we can get. Now go!"

A thunder unlike any they had heard in a long time resonated across the river valley and over the darkling ranks. Timorous madness sparked and grew among them. The rumble grew louder, until darklings begged for deliverance. And deliverance arrived, on horses girded in iron. Teeth gnashing. Hooves crushing. Two thousand cavalrymen burst from the cloak of darkness and smashed into the darkling horde.

Enemy ranks held for a moment only. Notions of valor were short lived as hundreds died as the opposing forces met. The darkling attack broke. Those still unaffected ran for their lives. It was a vain effort.

Dlorn was down on one knee. Disbelief registered on his face. Never had he been suckered into such a debacle. His men, on the brink of utter collapse, endeavored to retreat in orderly fashion. A fighting withdrawal. Many were already dead. Many more wounded. Broken pennants and guide-ons lay buried under corpses. Some continued to wave in the stale breeze. The sad realization that this was just the beginning crept into his mind.

Beaten back by considerable strength, the tireless might of Long Shadow, the silent killer, now stood next to the general. Several minor cuts and scratches decorated his steel-like body. He didn't show the pain he felt. Instead, he stood like a rock. An immovable object against an ocean of hatred. Dlorn found courage in him. If only he had a hundred more. Buoyed by what may well be a fleeting vision of false confidence, Dlorn rose and planted a broken standard in the snow.

"I will not let these damned beasts pass. Who will strike with me through the heart of darkness? For crown and kingdom!" he bellowed, with sword raised high.

A cheer rose from those nearby. Charging into the darklings was suicidal, but all had sworn oaths to the crown.

"Long Shadow, will you stand beside me as well?" Dlorn asked, knowing he couldn't command the foreigner.

The silent killer nodded once. This was what he was born for.

"Men of Galdea! Rally to me!"

Five hundred strong, they doubled their efforts and crashed into the darklings with unmatched brutality. Men and beast continued to fall as the death toll increased. Lives and dreams were shattered in a ghastly contest of primal instincts. Dlorn had never been prouder of his men, though he knew the act was doomed to fail. They lacked the numbers and it was but a matter of time before the darklings realized it.

The thunder echoed. Dlorn shoved a lunging darkling back and stabbed it through the chest. The cavalry was upon them. Monster after monster fell as a tidal wave of horse flesh bore into them. Soon, much faster than he anticipated, the battle was well beyond him and already beyond the original defensive positions.

A rider reined to a halt and saluted. "My apologies, General, but we had some difficulty on the other side of camp. It appears the darklings are much more coordinated than we expected."

Dlorn had feared as much. "No demon commands this army, but a man of Valadon. My thanks for arriving in time, Lestrin." He paused to drink deeply from his canteen. "What is the status of the river flank?"

"It still holds, though not by much. They hit us hard and only minutes after the attack from the north. I'm a bit surprised they didn't continue the assault," Lestrin said.

He was a thin man, much younger than the other senior commanders in the army. Sweat coated his exposed flesh, lending him the look of a man unmistakably lethal. His frame was thin and lightly muscled, covered splendidly by leather armor many others frowned upon.

"They yet may," Dlorn growled. "When this mess is cleaned up, I want all commanders in the command tent. I'll be damned if they catch us with our trousers down again."

"Sir," Lestrin said as he remounted and hurried back into the fray.

Dlorn and those few around him limped their way through the hundreds of bodies and limbs. Surgeons and medics raced across both ends of the battlefield. The groans of the wounded wailed long into the early morning hours, far longer than the clash of steel had. Soldiers not involved with the mopping up actions, helped move the wounded. The dead stayed where they fell, for the moment.

Three hours later, Dlorn's council began.

"We are playing right into the Black's hands," Aron said, his voice thick with sleep. "Baach is going to keep us off balance long enough for Imelin to get here and find a way to steal the Staff."

His words echoed the thoughts of those assembled. Calri sat at the corner of the war table, head down and fast asleep despite his best efforts. Lestrin and Perryman spoke quietly in front of the fire. Karin rested her head against Aron's shoulder. She'd fought alongside the elven archers and was beyond exhausted. Andolus, Long Shadow, and Amean were present as well, battered but alive. Jou Amn rounded out the last of the council. His shoulder was heavily bandaged. Like a true warrior, he sat through the pain.

"Precisely the reason we need to strike now," Perryman looked up and said. "Andolus gave us the plan. All we have to do is implement it. To do otherwise is to invite our doom."

Aron disagreed. "Suicide isn't going to win the day. There has to be another way."

"What of the wondrous Staff of Life? If the Black wants it, there must be power undreamed of locked within," Perryman said. Like the others, he found no valid point in arguing until dawn.

"Because I have no idea what to do with it. I'm no wizard, nor do I profess any wealth of knowledge regarding it."

Dlorn rose, his legs shaky. "I think perhaps we are avoiding the purpose of this battle. We stand against the armies of the dead. A last hope for the world. For that hope to retain significance, young Lord Kryte must escort the Staff of Life to the wizards of Meisthelm. This is why we fight. We may not find victory, but if we can delay the enemy long enough for the Golden Warriors to gain a large enough lead, there might still be hope."

"Thank you, General, but we can't leave just yet," Aron replied with a forced smile. "The Black needs to see that I am here. I imagine he can sense it already. When he sees me, and I will ensure he does, he will settle down for the long fight. I know a little about him and he is considered a man of infinite patience. The night he arrives, my companions and I will slip away, probably toward the town of Drim. With us gone, the Black will likely only leave a token force behind to delay you."

"Drim is too small to hide for long. What is your secondary destination?" Dlorn asked.

"The mountain stronghold of Hyrast."

"You go east rather than south?"

Aron said, "The Black will have all roads south watched, expecting us to head directly for Meisthelm. Why would he suspect we'd go elsewhere first?"

"What becomes of us?" Lestrin asked. Playing bait for the monster sat ill with him.

"Galdea needs to be cleansed and the ways to Suroc Tol closed again," Andolus interrupted.

The Galdean war lords were pleased with the admission.

"When do we kill that traitorous bastard across the river?" Lestrin asked.

Gulnick Baach awoke refreshed and ready for the next phase of the war. Word had come down that the bulk of the army was due to arrive soon and at full strength, he could unleash nightmares unchecked upon the enemy across the river. Any elation was cut short by an inexplicable sense of defeat. He set out to find the commander of the night operations and discover the truth behind his malaise.

Darklings barely looked up as he passed. They'd gone into battle knowing that their mission was to decoy and harass, but the memories of the night burned harshly. Most glared through the morning mists at an enemy they couldn't see. Gulnick ignored them. His march was one of imperviousness. Those in his line of march scurried away. He was, after all, a man and no man was to be trusted.

Duoth N'nclogbar and a young mercenary named Hurst sat beside the dying embers of a fire. Their glares were mutually hateful. Both blamed the other for the cruel results of the ill-fated assault. Questionable at best, Gulnick had quickly come to learn that they were both cut from the same cloth. Both would sell their souls for the right price and neither was trustworthy enough to place any value in. Gulnick figured out what had happened before either said a word.

Crouching down beside what remained of the fire, Gulnick asked, "What happened last night, Hurst?"

The one-eyed mercenary continued staring at the embers. "Armored mounts. Don't care how strong a unit is. Dismounts will break under a couple thousand heavy horse."

"How many casualties?"

Hurst shook his head bitterly. "Almost all. No way of telling for sure. Had 'em on the run for a good spell. When the horse come in, we got swept under worst defeat I've ever been part of. What's next for the mighty general?"

Taking the sarcasm with a grain of salt, Gulnick took in the cinereous skies. Snow came down in trickles. A sudden urge to strike both Hurst and Duoth down overcame him, though better judgment stayed his hand.

"We do the same thing. Hammer into them again and again until they break. We still outnumber them substantially. When the main army arrives, we'll only need attack once. Break them, Hurst. Keep them exhausted to the point where they can't raise a sword."

"And the casualties?" Hurst snapped. "We keep losing like we did and they'll soon have the numbers. All-out blitz. That's what we need ta do."

"I have my orders. Now you do as well."

Hurst wasn't satisfied. "I bet you do."

Gulnick stormed off, doing his best to ignore what would have been a crime punishable by death in the Hierarchy. The words, however, had already done their damage. He was tired of being a puppet. Tired of doing what everyone else wanted. And most of all, he was tired of this pointless war. None of it was going to bring his son back.

TWELVE
Best Laid Plans

Day turned to night and there was no sign of another darkling attack. The defenders of the Twins, now referred to as the Crimson Fields by those fortunate enough to survive, wondered if they were stronger, better equipped than the darkling army. Any wonderment was hampered by the sense of exhaustion spread through the ranks. Motivation and momentum hung precariously. Too many of the reserves had been used already, leaving Dlorn in a poor position. Worse, men began to doubt the strength in their hearts.

Long Shadow stalked through the steadily demoralizing ranks of Galdeans. His presence raised hopes and returned small measures of pride. He watched groups of men shift nervously as he walked by. Some retained their inner fire, he could see it lingering in their eyes, just waiting for the opportunity to burst free. These men he collected and beckoned them follow.

Andolus and Daril Perryman were about the same business in different parts of the camp. Once each appropriated the proper amount, they returned to the command area. Long Shadow was already there, waiting with his twenty volunteers. The soldiers greeted each other while settling in to wait. None knew why they were called, especially out of thirty thousand, but the hundred men knew they'd been called for a higher task.

Field Marshal Dlorn emerged, dressed in a stained tunic and trousers. To the soldiers, he appeared less of the heroic figure he posed in armor. That didn't make him less intimidating. They jumped to their feet. He bade them relax, knowing this was no time for formality. He took time to look into each man's eyes, judging them for his own reasons.

At last he spoke. "Men, I know you're wondering why you stand before me this night. You have all been chosen for various reasons by these three men for what is most likely a fatal mission."

Aron stepped before them. Like Dlorn, he too was dressed in simple clothes.

"Tonight we are going into the enemy camp to kill the rogue general, Gulnick Baach. The darkling army is highly dangerous with a man guiding them. Cut off the head and they'll splinter. None of you have to go. The mission proceeds with or without you. We are beyond the point of worrying over life or death. Should we fail tonight, the army will be down on its last legs and in no condition to fight the Black Imelin when he arrives. Those of you who wish to, leave in an hour."

Aron, arms folded across his chest, looked at them and said, "Those who are coming, follow me. My Golden Warriors will ensure you are properly equipped."

Dlorn returned to his tent to recheck the maps and schemes. Confidence and doubt collided just outside. To his surprise, Aron reported that all but sixteen of those chosen agreed to go. A makeshift rope bridge was being constructed as the Golden Warriors outfitted the Galdeans. There would be no armor. No excessive weight to slow them. If captured, they were assured a painful, hideous death.

"Is there hope?" Dlorn asked once Aron entered the tent. He ran a tired hand through his thinning hair.

"So long as there is life, hope remains," Aron replied. Satisfied nothing else needed doing, he bade farewell and retired to his tent.

Karin was waiting for him with tear streaked face. "I don't want you to go."

He stroked her hair. "I must. We won't be safe until the Staff is destroyed. What I do tonight is for the future. I want to grow old with you, Karin. Have children and live in a quiet part of the world. Being around you has changed me more than I ever dreamed. I… I love you."

She kissed him deeply, relishing the feel of his tender embrace and the warmth of his passion. Putting a finger to her lips, the Golden Warrior slipped into the night. There was much to be done and limited time. The heavy folds of the tent flap rushed together, allowing only the slightest hints of winter to brush against her cool flesh.

"I love you, too," she whispered.

Cold wind fluttered across the knoll in the middle of the Galdean camp. Eighty-four men were clustered together. Faces and hands were painted with charcoal. Each tensed with anticipation. Short swords and daggers were strapped around waist and thigh. They stood silent, listening to Dlorn send them off.

"I thank you all for what you are about to do. It is not for me, or Commander Kryte. This is for your families, your homes, and the lives you hope to live. Fight for the future. I shall see you upon your return." Dlorn saluted and watched as they filed away.

Daril Perryman had insisted on accompanying Aron. Together, they led the file through the unnaturally silent camp. Men rose and saluted the valiant few. Some raised swords. Others smashed their fists to their chests. It was still hours before the mid of night, giving the raiders enough time to sneak across the river.

They sped through the camp and struck north to where they intended to cross. Long Shadow met them on the bank. Wrapping the end of the rope bridge around his waist, he waded into the water and crossed. Aron clenched his fists in worry. The entire plan hinged on moving with speed and secrecy. A plan that threatened to unravel if Long Shadow didn't make it to the opposite shore. Time dragged impossibly slowly until the rope went taut.

"Let's go," Aron hissed and eased into the frigid waters.

The monotonous moan of rushing waters concealed their movements while simultaneously keeping their enemies concealed. Aron, Andolus, and Perryman were the first to cross. They'd come expecting a fight, but Long Shadow had already swept the perimeter clear. A small pile of bodies, still steaming as they cooled, lay heaped beneath the boughs of a pine. The numbers of men across swelled, though painfully slowly, since only one man at a time could cross the bridge.

Aron watched as a young soldier, a boy who couldn't have been more than sixteen, slipped and fell into the waters. Perryman lunged for the bridge but Long Shadow stopped him. Together they watched, helpless, as the first casualty was carried to the river bottom. Perryman continued to struggle until the boy disappeared from sight. Brooding, he turned away and tried to focus on the task at hand. The price of victory rose yet higher. One less, the commando force moved out.

They moved in a tight wedge, with Aron and Long Shadow at the point, stalking across the frozen landscape with murderous intent. No one smiled or joked the way soldiers tended to do when matters grew extreme. The only emotion was revenge. There was a level of foolishness associated with what they were about. After all, how could a unit of less than a hundred storm through enemy picket lines, an entire sleeping army, and kill the commanding officer? Bards and drunken tavern patrons the world over would praise their deeds for decades to come, should they prove successful.

The outer picket line was caught unaware and dealt with brutal efficiency. It was only the rush of footsteps that alerted the second darkling line a fraction of a moment before they were overwhelmed. Aron exhaled through his nose. The eerie orange glow of enemy fires lit the sky like a witch's Sabbath. The darkling bivouac lay before them. Old Grim himself took a seat atop the nearest mountaintop and watched the scene develop, his icy gaze penetrating the commandos.

Aron stepped into the glow, at once holding his breath and resisting the urge to tremble. All it would take was one inadvertent darkling to stumble upon them. Not even Long Shadow was enough to beat back tens of thousands of darklings. Knowing hesitation was akin to instant death, he hurried through the camp and resisted the urge to strike down those sleeping monsters in passing.

Finding Gulnick Baach's tent wasn't difficult at all. The massive structure jutted up from the middle of camp in stark contrast to the awkwardly sleeping darklings. Aron headed directly for it. Fetid odors assaulted his senses. Slowly decaying bodies lent an obnoxious taint to the night. Cannibalistic by nature, the darklings took to eating their dead. It was a carnival-like travesty of life without bounds.

A darkling stirred, rising in front of Aron, even as the slender blade speared down to sever the spinal cord. Andolus sidestepped the corpse and ducked behind a tree to see if any others were rising. Intermittent trees and shrubs provided natural camouflage. Soon enough, he and the others were within striking distance of the command tent. The elf almost found the ease of passage disappointing. The ring of armed guards, men this time, changed that opinion.

A stationary guard was posted at each tent corner. Others roved in opposite directions. This was to be expected due to Baach's importance. Soft light pulsed through the tiny holes and tears in the fabric. Aron crouched down behind a urine soaked bush and waited. Soldiers formed up behind and around him. Perryman was in favor of a quick, immediate strike. Doing so would accomplish nothing given the amount of open ground they needed to cover just to get to the tent.

Andolus, sticking to the plan, unslung his bow and took aim. From where he stood, he had three of the four guards in sight. Using uncanny speed and efficiency, he killed all three before the first fell dead. Aron, Long Shadow, and Perryman rushed forward to slay those sleeping around the nearest fire. The fourth guard popped out from the last corner and opened his mouth to cry out. An arrow pierced his throat. He toppled face first into the flames, ropes of blood splashing across the snows.

Long Shadow struck down the roving guards, opening the way for Aron to slip inside. Instead of catching Gulnick by surprise, they found the rogue general seated behind a brace of candles, facing them. A queer look marked his face.

"I've been expecting you," he told them. "Please, come in and close the door. It's frightfully cold outside tonight."

Aron paused, sword leveled at his opponent's face. He would never know what made him comply. Taking the proffered seat, Aron eyed Gulnick as one does when playing kings, always careful to make a move for fear of what the other would do. The old general drank from a mug of steaming mulled wine. The aroma was enticing, reminding them all of better times.

"This is quite good. Would you care for some?" he asked.

"How did you know we were coming?" Aron demanded. His nerves danced with the thought of having walked, blindly, into a trap.

Gulnick sighed. "Some things in life are inevitable, young Kryte. Did you know that I knew your father? It was a very long time ago, when I was much like you are now. Wide-eyed and ready to tackle the world."

Perryman snarled. "Kill him and be done with it. This is too great a risk."

"Indeed it is. Especially when I can do more good for you alive than dead," Gulnick seconded.

Aron unexpectedly lowered his sword. He wanted to hear what Gulnick had to say.

"I thought as much," Gulnick chided. "I left the Hierarchy with the intentions of tearing them down as they did me. I was tossed aside like a broken toy. I wanted to crush them for their pompous ignorance. Imelin offered hope, promise, at least in the beginning. But I have seen things over the past few months that no living man ever should. I can't sleep, and these darklings should be cleansed from the world, rather than be embraced by it.

"Imelin is much stronger than you can possibly imagine. He will not stop until the Staff and the world are his. Even now, he sends half the army south into Valadon. Meisthelm will soon be under siege. They cannot hope to last long. Conn is off somewhere in Guerselleorn with the bulk of the army. You waste your time staying here to die."

He took another drink. Crimson stained his thin lips.

"He's playing you against each other. The old nightmares of Sadith Oom have been recreated. There he builds his keep, the heart of his fledgling empire. He will arrive soon, you know? What hope will you have then? I know now that I've been wrong, so very wrong about it all. I will do what I can to aid your efforts by righting some of the wrongs I committed."

"Why should we trust a traitor?" Perryman pressed. "My men are dead because of you. My king is dead. Why should I let you live an instant longer?"

"If you kill me now, you lose all contact with the enemy. I can hold Imelin back, turn things around and foul this army up enough that they become ineffective. It is much too late for me to return with you. When I die, it will be as a traitor. I am prepared for that. I give you my word, as a soldier, that I will do everything within my power to aid you, but know that when Imelin arrives, there will be all out war. You cannot hope to stand against that tide. Use what I have given you. Save Meisthelm from the doom he's chosen. I think you should leave now."

Aron motioned the others out. He was conflicted. A part, a very small part, wanted to believe Gulnick, while the rest wanted nothing more than to strike his head from his shoulders. Reason won out. He was fighting a war, not a battle.

"Why are you doing this?" he asked, halfway through the door.

"For the same reasons you are. One more thing, you do understand that I must summon the guards?" Gulnick said.

"Of course," Aron said. "I expect as much, perhaps even a knife in the back on my way out the door."

He left before Gulnick could reply and praying he was wrong about the knife. He couldn't help but wonder if he was doing the right thing. His mind was clouded. Too many possibilities suddenly opened, leaving him mired in confusion. Collecting a heavy cloak, he hurried back to the others. They were almost clear when the alarm was raised. The darkling army groggily awoke to raw chaos.

Aron ran as fast as the terrain allowed. Hundreds of darklings milled about. He'd already killed two. His companions were responsible for many more. His heart thumped hard. His vision blurred as sweat dripped into his eyes. The snarl-hiss of approaching darklings propelled him faster. They were almost at the edge of camp when a large body of darklings spotted them and gave chase. Aron was the last to break into the open fields. He ran for dear life, knowing the bridge crossing was going to prove their undoing unless he found a way to delay the enemy. Long Shadow spun and laid into the darklings as if in answer to Aron's concerns.

Andolus and a dozen others were already across by the time Aron arrived. The rest were impatiently waiting their turn. Knowing time was now his foe, he directed a score to turn and stand against the darklings. They quickly formed the line and waited. The darklings swarmed at them. On cue, three hundred elven archers popped up from concealment on the far riverbank and opened fire. Arrows riddled the enemy, sometimes striking two or three to a darkling. They gave the commandos the necessary time to escape.

Aron did a head count and was dismayed to find nineteen had fallen during the retreat to the river, making twenty out of the initial eighty-four. A hard toll to pay, and they weren't clear yet. Long Shadow clamped down on his shoulder, the signal the big man was crossing. Aron was alone against an army of hatred. The elves had exhausted their supply of arrows, leaving a small wall of darkling bodies blocking the river. His thrown dagger plunged into a darkling's chest and Aron clambered onto the rope bridge.

Hand over foot, he shuffled as fast as the elements allowed. Ice coated the lower rope and he slipped too many times. Exhaustion pushed into his muscles but he kept moving. He was halfway across when the first darklings jumped after him.

Andolus and Long Shadow watched, helpless in their horror, as the darklings continued to jump onto the already frayed ropes. Aron slipped and nearly fell in the river. The bridge buckled under the additional weight. The top rope snapped, sending Aron and the darklings into the water. They were swept away to the roar of the others still ashore. Raging, the river quickly washed them downstream and out of sight in the span of a few heartbeats. The darklings turned as one and went back to their camp.

Andolus shrugged out of his cloak and stepped to the water's edge. He would have plunged in if not for the bear-like strength of Perryman.

"No! You cannot save him," the Galdean said, his voice chilled with sadness. "He's near a league down river by now and probably drowned. We need to get back and inform Dlorn. I'll not have another senseless death on my conscience. Let him die a hero who saved thousands rather than a man taking his friends with him."

The elf sagged. He knew Perryman was right and resignedly agreed. Demoralized, the forty-three survivors and host of elven archers collected their meager possessions and set back to the security of their lines. The walk was much longer than it had been on the way out.

Karin closed her tent flap and almost collapsed. Tears streamed down her face. She had felt that something wasn't right, that something terrible was about to happen. She'd tried to keep him from going. To no avail. Now he was gone. Lost from her life forever. The pain of his parting threatened to tear her apart. So she sat and she cried; cried until the sun broke the frosted mountaintops far to the west.

THIRTEEN

The Hyber Pass

An uncharacteristically cool wind dragged across the sharp peaks and rolling foothills of the Grimstone Mountains. The nine-man company of dwarves and men shivered against the chill, trying their best to ignore the howl of the wind, while concentrating on the slight heat of their cook fire.

None spoke. Instead, each sulked in the memory of the life-threatening defeat suffered a day ago. The goblin attack had been as furious as it was unexpected. Friendly losses were unforgivable. Worse, Sylin became concerned that Oo Ynlon had seemingly disappeared. He knew Camden took that loss personally, knowing the journeyman could have killed the Wylin much sooner and been done with the entire ordeal.

Conversation slowly began once the morning meal finished.

"Today we must decide our course of action," Garin announced. "Do we continue east and pass within the grasp of Eleran or do we tempt death with the Hyber Pass and the dragon Tragalon?"

Marin Trailbreaker stroked his auburn beard. "I've had enough of these goblins and their trickery. They know better than to enter the pass. Fear of the dragon will keep them away."

"It has been generations since dwarves last attempted to slay a dragon," Gul said.

Sylin knew what the dwarf was thinking. "I'd just as soon forgo a crisp death. How much time will we save by using the pass?"

139

Garin shrugged in thought. "Weeks, maybe none, if we're confronted by the dragon."

"If he still lives," Camden added. "No one has seen him for as long as I've lived."

"Only a fool thinks dragons die naturally," Marin cautioned. "What is thirty years to a wyrm? They need only feed once a year. They are known for their cunning and ability to rationalize. Some say this one is the color of stone, thus blending perfectly with his surroundings. Will we be his meal for the year?"

"You worry too much," Talrn Stonebreaker looked up "There are ways around a dragon."

His brother, Garin, raised a thick eyebrow. "How exactly? We have no riches. They care little for the affairs of mortals, so there is no point in mentioning our quest. What then will you use to sway the great Tragalon?"

"First, we must decide to enter the pass," Sylin cautioned. The violent tempers of dwarves were well known and he didn't want to see a fight break out.

"Goblins own the plains from here to Eleran. Less than three leagues separate the jagged teeth of the mountains and the edge of the goblin wood. We would be passing too close to them, though if we choose the pass, they will not follow. Goblins hold to superstition. Hundreds have gone missing over the last few years. Dragon or else, something wicked guards the pass," Garin concluded.

"How far behind are the Goblins?" Camden asked.

"Hard to tell. We chipped a nice piece out of them but they'll be back. Another reason to attempt the pass."

Sylin sat in quiet thought. He wasn't overly afraid of the dragon, though the prospect of being charred or eaten left his stomach in knots, thanks in part to the magic he possessed. Magic he had yet to come to understand or control. Nine lives rested in his hands. He needed to find Elxander and get him back to Meisthelm before the Black spread his plague across the Free Lands. The impossibilities of that task robbed his strength.

"How far away is the Tower of Souls?" he asked.

"Two days ride. The tower stands atop a small island in the center of Xulan Lake. Many have said that it is where the first wizard was born. Sent down by the old gods during the wars of light and darkness. Real or not, we should make it there in under a week."

Camden already knew what the decision to this pointless debate was going to be and went to ready his horse. Sylin caught him from the corner of his eye and nodded. "We try the pass."

The dwarves immediately broke camp and readied to move. Plans already made and waiting execution fell in place. Last night, while the two men slept, they'd stayed awake and developed potential courses of action. All that was left was to move. They were mounted and heading into the mountains within the hour.

Nightfall was upon them when the now familiar eerie feeling crept into the backs of their minds. Goblins, or worse. Camden and Gul rode forward to investigate. Dwarves were keen with axe and stone, but the mountains of the Grimstone were largely unexplored. Few of their people ventured this far south without good reason.

Shadows played games with their vision, taunting them to believe things that weren't real. Camden considered himself one of the best trackers in this part of the world but there was magic alive in these forbidding mountains he found unsettling. Ghouls and wraiths were rumored to stalk the heights, tempting travelers to their demise. The Hyber Pass was yet two days ride, leaving Camden to wonder if they were going to make it.

A stream of pebbles trickled down from a small outcropping above. Man and dwarf looked up to see a wispy figure dart across the bald mountain face. Hissing laughter followed as it disappeared from sight.

Gul Killingstone shivered. "There are ill creatures at work here. I would have preferred the open plains."

"What would we get accomplished sitting in a dungeon in Eleran? Camden asked. "Either way, it is too late to back out now. The goblins are close behind and we've a dragon before us. What better sense of adventure can one have?"

"Adventure!" the dwarf sputtered. "Death is not an adventure."

Laughter mocked them. Wicked creatures watched from lofty perches secreted out of plain sight.

"I'd have thought darklings and goblins were the worst of my worries," Camden whispered in response.

"There are dark beings older than dragons at play in the hidden places of the world."

Mist formed around their ankles, growing thicker the further they rode. The clatter of hooves echoed as thunder, announcing their passage boldly. Horses strained under the steady uphill climb. Finding a natural alcove, they held up and waited for the arrival of the others.

"We could still leave these mountains," Gul said, allowing only the slightest hint of apprehension into his voice.

"How's that?" Camden asked.

The alcove turned out to be a small cave, with ample room for the horses. Camden took the mounts to the back and tethered them to a rock as the dwarf lit a fire and guarded the front entrance.

Gul said, "There are secret ways through the mountains. Old when the world was young."

The front of a large storm rolled in. A monstrosity unlike any they had ever witnessed. Camden instantly understood the source of goblin superstitions, as well as the dwarves. Winds whipped rain and sleet into the rock face. Their horses snickered in fright. Camden admitted he would have done the same, if he didn't have a burly dwarf watching him.

Gul stood firm at the storm's edge, trying to see into the darkness. "I don't like this. The others could get lost too easily. I'm going back for them."

"What if you get lost? Or fall from the trail?"

Gul strapped his axe to his back and paused. Camden was right. Leaving now wouldn't solve anything. That wicked laugh began again. Somehow louder than the storm. Electricity danced across his flesh. Camden was about to warn Gul, but the dwarf already had weapons barred. Side by side, they warded the cave entrance.

We have watched.

Yes. We have watched. The world. The world was promised us before the war. The darkness war.

"Who are you?" Camden demanded. "Show yourselves!"

Multiple voices mocked laughter. *Foolish fleshling. Yes, foolish. You ask to look upon us and know despair. Greed. Your greed keeps us here. Locked forever in this stone prison.*

"Who are you?"

A snarl trembled the ground.

We are eternal. Servants of the dark. Promised to us. Yes, promised by the gods defeated. Bane is ours to stay in these mountains men now know. We are Eldrath.

Camden shifted his stance. He'd never heard of such creatures. "What do you want with us?"

He could feel them around. The Eldrath. Hundreds of shapeless figures locked in eternal torment.

Flesh. Yes, the flesh of humans. Your flesh makes us real. You and your friends. Come. Make us real again.

Lightning struck, illuminating the canyon long enough for them to get a glimpse of their confronters. Thin, wraith-like shadows adorned the walls. Camden smelled their hunger. Felt their overpowering desire to be real again. It was like a drug coursing through his veins. Hypnotizing. Alluring. The Eldrath moved forward.

Yes. Give us flesh. We, the rightful masters of the world.

Sword and axe dropped to the ground. Both men swayed in a haze, willing to accept their new masters. The Eldrath had won.

"Heyaa!"

The cry broke the veil of silence, startling the wraiths and scattering them back to forgotten recesses deep in the Grimstone Mountains. Seven men and dwarves broke into the area and discovered their companions unconscious. Marin and Talrn dismounted and rushed to their aid. Garin rode ahead to sweep the pass, returning once he was satisfied it was clear. He slid from his pony and watched as the unconscious men were moved to the back of the cave.

"What happened?" he asked.

Sylin shook his head in bewilderment. "Hard to say. There are no external injuries. No signs of battle. I… don't know."

"Their weapons were drawn. I don't like this place. Long have my people avoided the Hyber Pass and now I see why. It makes the hairs on my back stand on end. We must maintain a tight watch tonight. There is evil at play."

Reluctant to do so, Sylin announced. "I may have a solution."

"That being?" the dwarf grunted. He was more concerned with safety than security.

"Move everyone to the back of the cave and do not interfere until I say. This is extremely delicate and I require total concentration," Sylin said.

"I don't make it a point to pry into a friend's business, but this affects me as well," Garin reasoned. "What exactly do you intend to do?"

Sylin had hoped it wouldn't come to this. Especially after the storm aboard the *Gallant*. Resignedly, he tried to explain. "I was born with a gift. A gift I shunned until leaving Meisthelm. Few people have it, at least now. The magic has been inert for most of my life. Somehow, something in this war triggered it."

"You think this wizard can help you with it?" Garin asked.

"Not only that, but the world as well."

The dwarf rubbed his beard. "I know little about magic, nor do I care to. It's been well over a thousand years since a dwarf was born with that curse. If you can save our lives, do not hesitate. Enough have already died."

Garin herded dwarf and beasts to the back of the cave. It wasn't that he didn't trust Sylin, but it was the inexperienced unfamiliarity that left him feeling ill. There was no accounting for a sharp blade and the will to fight. Magic was best left unused.

Sylin sat down and tried to find a place of sanity untainted by the madness of the day. Images of a world he'd all but given up on floated back to him. At once returning him to the innocence of his youth. Happiness flowed through him and the magic began working.

Threads of power wove together, filling him with their warmth. Their strength, coupled with his own desires worked into patterns of pale light. That light danced like water nymphs, taunting and teasing until they formed a solid web. He cast the web against the cave mouth. Tendrils snaked out, grabbing ahold of the edges and firmly securing to the rock.

Exhausted beyond measure, Sylin slumped down and sighed. There had to be an easier way to get through life.

The Eldrath came after them twice during the night. Both times they were repulsed by the magic web. Camden and Gul tossed and turned throughout the night, afflicted by some unknown illness. Their fevers ran high and despite the dwarves doing what they could, their condition remained foul.

When at last they awoke, neither recalled anything. Both were starving and racked with the debilitating effects of their illness. The dwarves were glad both were seemingly recovering and went jubilantly about preparing a meal, while discussing things to come. Camden and Gul were curiously silent.

Garin offered both plates of steaming hot food and went to sit beside the fledgling wizard.

"What were those things?" he asked. Both stared into the dismal grey morning.

"I don't know. We have so many records at Meisthelm, its next to impossible to read them all in a lifetime. Many creatures have kept themselves hidden since the wars of light and darkness. Only now are we beginning to uncover them."

The dwarf shivered. "I'd just as soon let them remain undiscovered. Gul and Camden appeared to have recovered. We should be moving soon." He rose and was walking off when he noticed Sylin hadn't moved. "Are you all right?"

"I don't know. The magic affects me each time I use it. It feels… strange."

"Well, come on now. We've a dragon to conquer and a wizard to find. What better way to start a new day than with a grand adventure?"

Garin's mood brightened the morning. Only, Sylin wasn't so sure.

FOURTEEN
Confrontation

Sadness spread throughout the Galdean army. Despair threatened to settle in. Most had never seen Aron Kryte other than in random passing but that didn't steal their emotional letdown of learning he was gone. How could they defeat the darklings with their greatest champion lost? The Golden Warriors retired to their quarters, adding further confusion to the ranks.

Karin secluded herself away. She'd known Aron for only three months. Three short months that resulted in blossoming love. Now he was gone. Stolen from her when she needed him the most. Vengeance and blind rage surged through her lithe form, threatening to overcome all the pain and sorrow consuming her. Karin resisted, knowing that to give in to animalistic urges now would only make her a monster like the Black. He may have succeeded in stealing everything else from her, but he wasn't going to take her soul.

She balled her fists so tight they cramped. Karin screamed her pain away. Amean and Andolus waited just outside, warding the tent while giving her privacy. If was close to midday before her grief overwhelmed her and she drifted off to sleep.

Field Marshal Dlorn was tired. Understanding the risks everyone was required to take, he didn't have the time to mourn Aron's death. Though a brilliant strategist and an invaluable asset, Kryte died on a mission of his own choosing. Not his or even Dlorn's own life was worth as much as the twenty-five thousand men depending on him. Each and every one looked to him and his decreased band of generals to keep them alive. To propel the Galdean army to victory. At times, the responsibility was too much to bear.

He leaned back in his aged wooden chair and puffed leisurely on the first pipe of tobacco he'd allowed himself in over a month. The luxuries of peace had no place in a combat zone. The aromatic aroma filled the tent, much to the liking of the battle leaders and commanders who began to file in.

When all were assembled, it fell on Daril Perryman to give the back brief of the prior night's operation. He filled the tent with his tale, making a few minor matters appear important and others not at all. They cringed at the telling of Kryte's demise, though one or two still held onto hope. He finished with the offered repatriation of Gulnick Baach. Debate immediately erupted.

"We are to trust this traitor?" Lestrin asked. "He has already betrayed everyone in the Hierarchy and Free Lands once. What's to stop him from doing so again?"

Calri leaned forward, adding, "He's trying to buy his life back. Baach knew he was going to die and did what he could to avoid it."

"What then shall we do with the villain?" Dlorn asked. "If he is as dangerous as we all believe, a trap is most assuredly awaiting us. However, Aron Kryte saw in him something no other did. He would not have placed his trust so easily in the hands of a man capable of killing his friends."

"I stood next to them," Perryman said. "My first impulse was to drive my blade through Baach's bowels, but Kryte stopped me. I think he made a wise decision by letting the general live."

"There are some who believe that snakes make good pets until they are bitten. Can we trust a serpent who has already sold us out?" Lestrin argued.

Long Shadow shifted uneasily in the corner.

"We are losing focus on the one factor that makes us who we are. Humanity. A man cannot be good or wholeheartedly evil in a matter of months. No matter how far gone, there is always a measure of good still within," Andolus said.

The horse commander was outraged. "I can't believe my ears! Are you saying we should embrace him as one of our own after all he's done here? I trust no man, or elf, responsible for murdering his own kind on the whims of a dark wizard."

"We waste precious time bickering over inconsequential matters. It is not a question of who believes Baach but who has to listen," Dlorn said in a calm voice. "If all he said is true, Meisthelm stands in greater peril than Galdea. Sadith Oom come back from forgotten nightmares. Gulnick Baach just may have given us what we needed to save this army.

"Long days ago, our advance scouts discovered the might of his army and it stretches far beyond the reach of the naked eye. We cannot hope to contain or defeat it. Cut in half we have but a small chance. But if what the traitor says is true, we have the opportunity to salvage the bulk of the army and escape to fight another day."

Dlorn fell silent and patiently cleaned his pipe before putting it away. He had said enough, and though fully interested in what his council had to say, had already made up his mind. Even if Baach had offered a whisper of truth, Dlorn needed to do all he could to save as many men as possible. The war promised to drag on for many months, perhaps even years. The hope of men had need for all resources, if it was to survive.

"What the General says may indeed be true," Calri stated, "but the deceiver could well be leading us to slaughter. Suppose Baach has us retreat. We already know half of his army has moved south to another campaign. We also know of their airborne capabilities."

"Your point, Captain?" Andolus asked. He was growing weary of childish fears.

"My point is what is to keep Baach from sending us into the second half of the army and trapping us between the two forces?"

"If they wanted us dead, we would not be having this conversation," the elf prince rose. "I have fought these monsters for over one hundred years. Their tactics do not change, whether led by man or beast. They remain."

A messenger burst into the tent, pallid and drained of energy. His words, when spoken, were of abject terror. "He's here! The Black Imelin is here!"

The Black Imelin glared down at Gulnick Baach with obvious disdain. "I see you have thus far managed to survive the brunt of the fighting. Tucked away in your tiny corner of security, perhaps?"

His words struck chords so deep, Gulnick struggled to maintain composure. He barely noticed the solemn form of Hurst slip from behind a tree to stand a half step back.

"Casualties thus far?" Imelin demanded.

Hurst scoffed as he picked a piece of meat from between his teeth.

"Ten, maybe fifteen thousand," Gulnick replied. "The Galdeans fight most determinedly with their backs to the wall."

"Making such a bittersweet victory. I shall enjoy destroying them. It will take close to two days to get the rest of the darklings in place and ready to attack. The scrathes will be here shortly before dawn. When I give the command, I want an all-out offensive across the river. Drive Dlorn and his rabble to the Arindl River and kill them to the man."

Gently tapping his horse's flank, the Black rode away.

Hurst leaned threateningly close and vowed, "He's going to find out about you, Baach. One way or another, you're a dead man."

Gulnick Baach stood alone amidst a host of thousands, the arid wind cracking his already dry skin. The war was well underway, but his personal torment was only just begun.

Dlorn looked into the troubled eyes of his captains and field commanders. They reflected his doubts and strengths, giving his army at least a fighting chance.

"The time for deliberations is finished," he announced. "Today we must decide our course of action. Do we stay and fight against odds the world cannot defeat or run and live to fight again?"

Again it was Perryman who took the first opportunity to voice his opinion. "I say run. We turn this war into a series of guerrilla campaigns and we stand a better chance of winning."

Long Shadow nodded agreement.

"Such a campaign would take years. Although the plague will be engaged, thus giving Meisthelm and the Hierarchy the time needed to marshal the army. We run."

Dlorn shifted his focus to the field commanders, hardened veterans forged by necessity. He purposefully passed over the Golden Warriors in doing so. They were an issue he couldn't afford to dither on. Lestrin and Calri remained uncharacteristically quiet. Dlorn took that as a good sign. With the matter out of the way, he was left with two major issues. The first was what to do with Princess Elsyn. There was no way he was going to jeopardize her safety for the sake of a madman's whim. The second, and infinitely more problematic in his eyes, was the Staff of Life. He didn't dare keep it with the army, for the token drew the Black. No other living man had the required bloodline needed to wield it, and none he knew wanted it. Dlorn silently longed for the days when the enemy and objectives were clear.

Karin slipped quietly through the tent flap. She ended beside Long Shadow. Her appearance was haggard. Unkempt hair matched the rawness in her eyes. The tears had long since dried up, leaving a heart of ice.

"I am taking the Staff on to Hyrast and then Meisthelm," she said with utter finality.

None moved to oppose her.

"Who rides with me?"

Andolus let a timid smile escape and slid in behind her, followed closely by Long Shadow. So, too, did Jou Amn and Amean Repage.

"The Golden Warriors will be honored to escort you," Amean announced.

Dlorn felt the great weight shift a little. He'd been expecting and praying for such a move. "I think it has somehow fallen into your hands regardless. You will have to leave under cover of night."

"Understood."

"I will have men tend to your mounts and pack enough provisions for one week. It should be more than enough to get you to Hyrast, or at least the town of Drim."

"Fair enough," Amean said.

As one, the tiny band filed out of the command tent. Desperate times called for desperate decisions and Dlorn had willingly parted with his greatest combat asset for the greater good. He hoped he wasn't making a mistake.

"This, gentlemen, is how I propose to deal with our enemies," he said.

All eyes fixed on him.

Elsyn wiped the tears from her eyes and tried to recall the voices outside of her tent. She was past fed up with the current turn of events. Cold, freezing actually, her body ached. The army camp lacked virtually every comfort of home. She missed the sanctuary of her life, her real life, and prayed for its swift return. Disappointment was a cold, hard fact she was now forced to endure.

"Enter," she said finally.

Elsyn wasn't surprised to see Dlorn follow her words.

"What's wrong?" she asked, upon catching the sag in his shoulders and long face.

He almost laughed. "What's wrong indeed! A more apt question would be what's right. The world seems to stand against us, Princess."

"You'll beat it. You always do."

Dlorn loved the innocence of her youth. She turned twenty in four months and was already far too mature for her age. Her parents would have been proud.

"To have your faith for one day, just a day," he sighed. "Alas, I must live with the lot I've been given."

Elsyn picked up on the distraction. "Why did you really come? I know it wasn't for a boost of morale."

"You are so much like your mother, have I ever told you that?" Her gentle smile almost made him forget his problems. "We are leaving, Princess."

Leaving? How? Why? "What of the Black? Is it possible to escape?"

He shook his head. "Escape is not my intent. The army is already preparing for the next phase in the campaign. We are going to retreat deep enough into the countryside and draw the darklings in, striking them piecemeal. By that time, the Staff should be secure in Meisthelm and the whole of the Free Lands risen up against the Black. If all goes according to plan, we'll be able to pinch his army between us and do away with the threat of this traitor for good."

Listening to his own words, Dlorn was almost impressed. He understood the inherent risks in such a maneuver and fully expected little to go his way.

"When do we leave?" Elsyn asked. She smoothed a part of her dress, catching his involuntary wince upon being asked.

"It pains me to do this, but there is little real choice. I'm sending you to Lord Felbar. It should be safe there once this storm moves on."

"No," she insisted. "I will not sit idly by while the vengeance of my father carries on."

"Elsyn, this is more than just your father's legacy. What we are doing is buying the rest of the world time. How they use it is up to them but if I die today, it will be with the knowledge that we gave the Hierarchy what it needs to prepare. My legacy will not be vengeance."

His face flushed when he realized he'd raised his voice. Dlorn offered a hasty apology.

She accepted and asked, "What of Lord Kryte and the Staff?"

"Aron Kryte died last night. You know this."

"I refuse to believe it until I see the body."

He did his best to reason with her, to tell her there was no way anyone could survive the freezing waters for more than a few minutes, but she was sharp when agitated. At times, she was too much like her mother.

"You may believe what you wish, and if those beliefs help you in dealing with the severity of the future, the better for them. However, there is no possible way any man could have lived," he said.

Dlorn hung his head, instantly regretting the harshness of his words. Decades of service to throne and crown had sharpened his tongue nearly as much as his sword.

Elsyn saw their argument quickly headed in the wrong direction and decided on a different approach. "What of the one who bears the Staff? What path do they follow?"

"They ride out before dawn. With a little luck they should arrive in a safe haven in Almarin. Our hope is they pass unnoticed, leaving the Black thinking the Staff is still with us. This is a costly game we play," he added in afterthought.

"Thank you, General. I think I am going out for a brief walk. Dinner as usual?"

He bowed ever so slightly. "Of course, Princess."

Dlorn left her, knowing what she intended. His only wish was that she went in safety. Having her anywhere near the front lines of the coming battle left him twisted. She was his greatest concern and most pressing weight. With her safely away, he could resume focus on the war.

Elsyn barely waited for the tent flap to swish shut before she began stuffing random possessions into a travel bag. Once done, she donned a grey winter travel cloak and readied to enjoy her final meal in the company of the army commanders, her commanders. Thoughts of Aron pained her, for she was already lost to the initial twinges of love. He was alive and she wasn't about to give up on him.

FIFTEEN

A World Goes to War

The tireless efforts of the Golden Warriors worked in concert with the setting sun. They stopped working just long enough to take in a last hot meal before setting out. Though a certain spirit of demise plagued them, hopes buoyed with the arrival of the elf prince and his silent friend. The duo almost made up for the death of Aron Kryte. Many of the small company took pride in the fact that their actions might prove the salvation of the rest of the world. It was a small comfort in the face of such loss.

Finishing with his bags, Andolus excused himself to bid farewell to his brethren. Traces of memory flashed as he walked. Of the happy times at Dol'ir and her eventual fall. He sorely missed all of those who'd died in the betrayal but was never in a position to avenge the wrongs committed. Until now. Andolus found the elves grouped together in a loose knot in the middle of the army. They hailed him, offering food and wine, which he graciously declined.

He found Jerns Palic warming his hands.

"Winter is particularly cruel this year, is she not?" Jerns asked, as his commander fell in beside him.

"More so than we can know. He's going to attack tomorrow."

"We know."

Andolus shuffled his feet, trying to think of how to say what he felt. "Odds are that we probably won't last much longer. I'd like to think otherwise but the host arrayed before us is quite impressive."

"Ten times that number will not be enough to make up for the loss of one of our brothers. We will fight bravely on the morrow," Jerns said.

"I wish I could be with you," Andolus admitted.

Concern sparked in Jern's eyes and then faded. "A more pressing mission perhaps?"

"Yes. Long Shadow and I are going south with the Golden Warriors. The Staff of Life must reach Meisthelm."

Jerns approved. "Elves have long stayed away from the affairs of men, though I deem this to be more important than what we attempt here. Go with the fortune of us all, Andolus. Mayhap we shall meet again."

They clasped arms and spoke a silent parting. With much pain and sorrow, Andolus, prince of the Dol'ir elves, turned his back on his people and entered a world much larger than any he'd ever witnessed.

The first units of the Galdean army began an organized retreat shortly after midnight. These were the hardest hit from earlier engagements. Wagon trains of sick and wounded, much more than Dlorn would have liked, immediately followed. Low level officers supervised the movement, while line units covered down and dug in deeper to prepare for the coming assault.

Fresh soldiers, still wide-eyed with the ways of the world, experienced levels of fear strong enough to buckle knees and burst hearts. Veterans attempted to calm their nerves but knew there was little to be done. The only way to avoid fear was to fight it away. Field commanders and generals supervised the restructuring of the army, while letting their subordinates do what needed to be done.

Catapults and heavy siege weapons were readied and moved back to cover the opposite riverbank. Dlorn organized his artillery in three ranks. The first would fire into the initial darkling assault. Once the enemy paused to reorganize, they would drop into range of the second rank. The third would be used for close support. Archers filled in fifty meters behind the already formidable ranks of pikes and swords. Ground units provided enough space for the artillery to retreat, should it come to that.

Donning his winter cloak, Dlorn made his rounds, hoping his face would inspire renewed vigor before the storm broke.

The Black Imelin sat in total darkness, mentally preparing for the wholesale slaughter about to begin. The ghosts of dead men no longer haunted him. It was much too late for that. They faded into shadow, ready to watch the collapse of life. He alone was on a level with the gods, in charge of not only his destiny but that of the entire world.

His meditations opened veiled eyes, allowing Imelin to see intricate webs of treachery and deceit. The quest was anything but simple. Each singular piece of the puzzle developed into conflicting webs. Too many people were involved. Too many chances to share his glory. Imelin frowned. He needed to eliminate the multitudes of loose ends before proceeding. Plans within plans formed. Alone in the dark, the threat of the future seemed less.

An unseasonable wind ravaged the sleepy spires of Galdarath. Fires burned in every home in the vain attempt of staving off the chill but there was a shortage of firewood and oil, thanks to the war in the east. Wood cutters were fearful of leaving the safety of the city walls. One of the largest cities in the Free Lands was brought to a standstill, one where the repercussions would be felt for many years to come.

Enshrouded by the wall of shadows coming off the main castle, three figures slinked past the guards and hired help. Their riding clothes were dusty, the color of midnight. Two were heavily laden with expensive weaponry. Two men and one woman managed to elude all the enhanced security on their way to the stables. In the coming weeks, guards would attest to the use of magic, for surely there was no other means possible. Only a select few knew that certain guards and staff had been ordered elsewhere as the trio passed. Regardless, the stealthy exit was a minor victory in an altogether separate war.

The trio mounted previously selected and prepared horses and struck out down a dark path consisting of alleys and seldom used roads to come to the base of the walls where they waited patiently.

Guards stationed atop the walls patrolled at normal intervals, unsuspecting of the goings on. Harrin Slinmyer had taken ill and was off duty for at least week. His absence allowed Jent Tariens the option of taking a final shift on the wall. He was welcomed with cheers and slaps on the back, to which he responded in kind.

Midnight saw him descending to the ground, inspecting the guards positioned at a series of bolt holes. The city designers built dozens with dual purpose. Not only could archers repel invading enemies, but they provided an exit point should the city fall. Thus far they had yet to be used, but that was no reason to ignore them.

Tariens approached the guard on duty. The man was motionless, bundled in a thick cloak with his spear in hand. Shifting eyes adjusted to his commanding officer and he tensed. Tariens offered him a mug of hot tea and began idle conversation. They spoke for a few moments before he moved on to the next bolt hole.

Scant seconds after Tariens left, the guard began to feel the effects of a drug-like state. The world spun uncontrollably. Dizziness whelmed his senses and the world went black. He struck the ground hard and was still. The half empty mug shattered on the frost covered cobblestones.

Tariens, cunningly watching from the obscurity of a column, returned to move the man to a sitting position against the wall. Disturbed with having betrayed one of his men, Tariens searched for the hidden key used to open the bolt hole. Dwarf masons often used bricks and specific stones built within their structures as keys. He shifted the ivy draping down from the parapet, running a gloved hand over the smooth surface until finding what he was looking for. Tariens gave the odd shape stone a hard push. The bolt hole opened with a constricted groan.

Three riders emerged from the darkness and halted before him. Each saluted in one fashion or another but said nothing.

Tariens looked to the lead rider and said, "Wait here until the guards change shifts. Ride the wall for a mile north and break for the tree line. No one should see you leave."

"Are you sure the forests are clear?"

Tariens stared at the crimson wrap covering most of his face before answering. "As near as we can tell. I've been sending probes out for a week and they have all come back with negative reports."

"Our tracks?"

The very tone of his voice suggested a man more lethal than any Tariens had ever encountered.

"A fresh storm is blowing in. Seems we can't escape them this year. Tracks shouldn't be a problem for too long. Besides, tired men don't look for the obvious."

And everyone on the wall was past tired. Everyone in the city, for that matter.

"Head for Prossin. There you'll find the necessary contacts to complete your missions. I'm placing heavy trust in you. Our forces have already engaged the Black on the Crimson Fields. So long as they are occupied, you have a chance at going unnoticed," Tariens said.

"We understand," the rider said sourly. He didn't appreciate being talked down to.

"May fortune favor you," Tariens said, as he stepped aside to let them pass.

His hopes and prayers rode with them. If Galdea was to have any chance of lifting the yoke of oppression shackling them, his riders must succeed. Tariens closed the bolt hole and returned to the top of the wall to finish his rounds.

From his vantage point, General Conn could view most of the Port of Grespon. Disorganized rows of tin and thatch roofed buildings twisted and curved in no discernable pattern, with the Jemman Sea in the background. The city was divided by the Simca River, providing tactical challenges he wasn't looking forward to. Fortunately, the separation was enough for him to seize half of the city at a time. Crossing the river was going to be his toughest problem.

The pirate force was dug in and expecting a heavy assault. This displeased him for two reasons. One was that his army was not equipped for a prolonged siege. The second was pirates never stayed on sight long enough to be caught. Something wasn't right. But he didn't know what.

He turned his horse back to the rest of his commanders. "I don't know what game they play at but the sight of it all mocks me."

His two gnome scouts whispered in their native tongue at his side.

Haf Forager, the stout dwarf, said, "Dug in or not, they won't prove much of a match for heavy cavalry."

"Perhaps." Conn wasn't so sure.

"It seems to me that they hold all of the advantages. The entire city stands open to their whim and mercy," Genessen, the elf, said.

Ur Oberlin fanned his gills. "They are too many to be mere pirates. I think we are being drawn away from the true objective. This is a trap."

Each gave the wylin's words deep consideration. If what he said was true, the real objective was in question.

Conn asked, "How many days ago did Meisthelm recall all units?"

"Close to thirty now," Rhea Ailwin said, somewhat caught off-guard.

"When did the pirates seize the city?"

Zin Doluth thought for a moment. "Roughly the same time."

"Coincidence or not?" Conn pressed. "I'm beginning to think there are foul hands at work here. Think on this. The High Council recalls all forces, fearing an invasion. A massive one it must be to bring the bulk of our army in. There can be no other reason for abandoning the rest of the Free Lands. At the same time, this crisis erupts, drawing away a large chunk of the army. Right when we are needed in Meisthelm the most. I think we have been tricked into coming here.

"This kidnapped heir being held for ransom?" Genessen asked.

"A ruse. This trap stinks of the Black Imelin."

Haf bolted in surprise. "How can a man halfway around the world impact us so?"

"I don't have the answers yet, but I do suggest we abandon this quest and return to the Hierarchy," Conn answered.

"What of the pirates?" Zin asked in reply. He'd never heard Conn give up so easily.

"They are not pirates. No scourge of the seas would dare think of doing what these men have. I suspect they are a well-equipped and trained military force. I'm not about to risk the lives of my men on that. We'll send a probe against them when it gets dark. If they respond like I think they will, we leave in the morning."

His decision was akin to law and his commanders knew better than to question further or argue. Elements were selected to launch the raid, the route of assault finalized, and units stood down in preparation. Conn resumed his examination of what he viewed as professional defenses once more. The mystery of it all allured him. One way or another, he was going to get to the bottom of it. Only how remained unknown.

Baron Vryce Mron circled the highest parapet of the Port of Grespon, a marginally uninspiring wall that did nothing to make him feel secure, like a predator. He was an older man, slightly overweight and balding. Despite appearances, he projected a dangerous air. Thick, black eyebrows accented his round face, turning a flaccid expression rich with evil. His arms and legs were corded with muscles. Most times, he wore loose clothing to hide his true form.

Nothing he saw inspired confidence. Both armies were evenly matched. He was trapped. Mron couldn't wait for the Hierarchy soldiers to attack, nor could he strike forth. One army was built upon the foundations of honor and duty. The other worked for the highest bidder. No honor lived among the camps of Baron Mron.

A deeply tanned man in full leather armor stood at his side. He, too, watched the enemy with intent, though for different reasons.

"They are not going to attack us. Conn's not that foolish to commit."

Mron nodded slightly. "No, but he will probe us to find out our strength. Tonight I imagine. Have the men ready."

"Yes, Baron."

Mron turned to leave but stopped short. "I have a suspicion that he's going to turn and head for Meisthelm. In that case, you already know your orders."

"Yes, Baron."

Mron left in search of the quaint ale house he'd discovered when his force first seized the city. *Several mugs of frosted, imported ale and a few wenches should ease my troubled mind.* He didn't think that would be the case, but a man could hope.

She waited and watched with the patience of a predatory cat. She knew she was going to get her opportunity. Her one chance. In massive operations with so many moving parts, there was always a window, a sliver of time in which to slip through the confusion. She double checked her riding bags. Her only possessions. Her golden hair was tied up in a tight knot and concealed under the burden of her hood. Taking precautions to remove her presence from the army, all she had to do was sit… and wait.

The Golden Warriors led their mounts on foot while they began lining up. Time was of the essence. The first darkling waves were expected shortly and they needed to be away before the battle began. As the anticipation mounted so too did the urge to depart as quickly as possible. There was no way of telling how many men had already crossed the river into Almarin.

Amean Repage inspected his men one last time. A fresh storm was brewing, threatening to delay the start of their quest. It was all he could do to stay motivated. Amean viewed the storm as more blessing than bane. Any disturbance might offer cover for their exit. Not only would it aid his mission, but it might keep the airborne threat the Black possessed grounded.

He found Jou Amn standing under the cover of an oak tree. The warrior watched the coming storm wall with clear disgust. Amean understood his torment. They'd all volunteered to leave the Saverin garrison with the intent of fighting and had done little but run. How much further was there to go? The world only went so far.

"Contemplating the joys of the past?" Amean asked, once he finished his rounds.

Jou Amn snorted and scratched his beard. "More like the problems of the moment. I want to stay."

"We have our orders."

"Exactly what orders are those?" he asked. "I don't recall getting clear instructions. Aron is dead, and with him, this quest. We left garrison to seek out and destroy an enemy, the same enemy staring down our throats right on the opposite side of that river."

"You'll die, if you stay."

Jou Amn laughed. "Seems a chance worth taking to me. I stay."

Amean knew he was losing and frankly, couldn't debate the logic of it. "Think about what you're saying. There is no way the Galdeans can defeat that host. Their one hope is to retreat and engage in a prolonged campaign of skirmishes. Head to head confrontation will result in failure."

"You almost make it sound as if you're running to save your life."

"We are escorting the Staff of Life to the Hierarchy. The High Council can use it to end this war, and the Black traitor," Amean defended. Even to him the words sounded hollow.

Jou Amn laid a strong hand on his friend's shoulder. "Bah! The order of wizards is no more. The Council has lost its way and the Black is the last with magic. This is where our fates will be decided, not in a distant golden tower where men have lost touch with the lands they rule! My decision is final. Here I make my stand."

Resignedly, Amean nodded his consent. "Fortune favor you, my friend. May we meet again in Meisthelm."

"We shall, that or the halls of our fathers."

Amean walked away, leaving the solitary warrior torn. Jou Amn watched as his dearest friends mounted their horses and began the long journey south. Soldiers offered prayers and well wishes, despite the sinking feeling of being abandoned by the Golden Warriors. It was the sad fact that wars often took on lives of their own, each one having distinct flavors no man could predict. Amean and the others needed to leave. He recognized that, admired it even, but the pull of staying with Dlorn was too strong to ignore.

His curiosity peaked as he noticed a shadow cloaked rider emerge from the dark to fall in at the rear of the golden column. Jou considered, and rejected, the idea of following to warn Amean. A cry from the front lines ripped through the camp like a clarion call. Jou turned his back on his friends and went in search of Dlorn. Battle was about to be joined.

SIXTEEN

The Crimson Fields

A legion of drums pounded out their death song. Echoes of organized mayhem chilled the blood, giving men cause to doubt their individual courage. The horrid sound began at midnight and carried on into the early morning hours, never changing beat or tempo. Dlorn and his commanders knew the only purpose was to inspire fear and demoralize the stout Galdean army. It didn't take him long to ignore the sounds and plan his next move.

The loss of the Golden Warriors, though only an understrength company, continued to eat at him. The very sight of their untarnished armor was inspiration he could ill afford to lose. Now they were gone and he was left with the skeletons of memory to hold off the darklings. Dlorn didn't harbor doubt about his men, but he did wonder if they would be able to hold out long enough to complete their proposed retreat.

The drums continued their ghastly beat as the old man finally drifted off to sleep.

The army of Galdea stood arrayed along the riverbank amidst the fury of the fresh storm. Young men and old prayed to their gods as each secretly wondered if they were going to live another day. Mouths parched, palms sweat, and hearts raced like wild horses across the open steppe. Today was the pinnacle of all their pent-up aggressions and unfulfilled oaths of revenge for the pains of weeks past.

The drums were all but forgotten. The fear they induced so quickly worn down over a long period of time. All soldiers, old and young alike, were ready to finish this. Even if they lost, the Galdeans would buy the rest of the Free Lands enough time for the Hierarchy to mount a counteroffensive. Or so they clung to.

Dlorn, geared in his finest armor, stood tall and proud on the crest of the small hill in the center of their camp. Gone were the bitter fingers of cold raking down his spine. Such notions were lost to the warmth of rushing blood and the thrill of the hunt. Age shed as he remembered the feeling of steel once more. He was intent, focused on salvaging his kingdom. He was also about to see if the information Gulnick Baach provided was true or not.

A great commotion erupted just beyond his range of vision. Fog had settled in and wasn't moving. The alliance of men and elves took refuge from this, for the enemy would not know just how few their numbers were. At last the army of the Black was upon them. Figures stalked through the fog. Scores at first, followed rapidly by hundreds.

"Catapults, stand by!"

The command echoed the newfound seriousness enveloping the army.

"Fire!"

Twenty successive thumps rang out, drowning the cacophony of darkling war cries. Flaming barrels of pitch and kindling mixed with massive boulders capable of crushing bones to dust. The flames hissed overhead. Even as the rounds impacted, scattering and killing the front ranks, another salvo was loaded and fired. The battery commander had orders to expend all ammunition. Orders he dutifully executed.

At once the darklings were cast into chaos as the brunt of their frontline forces were decimated. Burning bodies and chunks of charred flesh were whipped in every direction. Screams from the dying made many Galdeans cover their ears. Had the wounded been men, there might have been a touch of remorse, but this was total war and the enemy were monsters. Each one killed, was one less to be feared.

Unknown to Dlorn, the Black Imelin remained in his private sanctuary, unconcerned with how the initial assault played out. The beginning seldom drew as much interest as the outcome. He knew, without doubt, that the lands from Suroc Tol to the river border of Almarin would be under his control by morning. Until then, he was content with letting Gulnick lead the assault.

Acrid smoke and burnt flesh tainted the air, choking nostrils and churning stomachs. The land was inundated with body parts and massive fires. Gulnick Baach was sure if he looked up, a host of winged demons would spew forth from the bowels of the underworld. Disorganized and already reduced to a third of their initial strength, his forces drove on through the withering catapult fire until at last they came under range. Savage cheers rose from the surviving darklings as they surged forward.

Reeler Monchere watched his catapult crews with pride. Months of hard training coupled with the strong desire to go home in victory had honed them into a most effective combat team. But only twenty minutes into the fray, they had already fired half of their ammunition. The morning sun cracked the curtain of snow clouds just long enough to let the soldiers know the old gods still cared. Monchere hoped the gods would do more than send well wishes.

Late in his forties, Monchere was a career military man with a penchant for mechanics. Now he stood in the center of the defining moments of life and career, proud of the men he led and the stand they took. He caught the ruckus of the enemy's cheers and knew what must be done.

"Master gunner! Order the second battery to fire at will," he barked.

Fifteen catapults sang in one, crisp voice. Monchere grinned savagely as the impact thumps drowned out the darkling rage.

Field Marshal Dlorn had lived through hundreds of skirmishes and battles, and a dozen campaigns. Until today, he thought he'd seen it all. Visions of apocalyptic fury raged unchecked before him, tearing lives apart in the blink of an eye. This was true war. Ugly. Nasty. Desperate men doing all they could just to survive.

He watched the battle develop through his eyepiece. It lifted his spirits to see so many darklings fall, even while knowing it wasn't enough. Their mass stretched so far back, the barrage was hardly going to dent them. Shifting his gaze to his lines, he saw the green and purple standards of the late King Elian blowing in the wind. Men rallied to the memory of their murdered king. The gryphon of Galdea flew strong and proud, mocking their enemy while sparking the men with something to fight for.

The darklings broke the range of the second battery and gained the now frozen river. Dlorn suspected it was dark magic that had turned the raging waters into a solid sheet of ice. It didn't matter. The darklings were coming. They were ragged now, steadily losing their initial drive. Withering fire hurt them bad and kept doing so as they advanced. Bloodied and infuriated, the darklings finally caught sight of their enemy. Another cry went up from their ranks and they surged across the frozen Simca River. A red flag was hoisted above the front trench. Dlorn watched as the third battery opened fire.

No one bothered helping Gulnick Baach to his feet. A dozen scratches shredded his face, sending delicate streams of red down and outward in bizarre patterns. On one knee, he wiped his face and then saw what remained of his horse. The beast took the brunt of the impact, dying instantly. Another round struck directly in front of him. Shards of rock splintered out, striking his fallen horse.

Hundreds of darklings died all around him, not having the second opportunity he was given. The slaughter was incredible. Gulnick wondered if the Galdeans were capable of putting up such a fight, what would the Hierarchy do when Imelin laid siege to Meisthelm. Even through the din and roar, he caught the distinctive sounds of yet another battery of catapults open fire. The Galdeans were clearly prepared for this assault.

He took a moment to blame himself for not anticipating his foe's tactics as another round burst nearby. Gulnick caught sight of the mercenary, Hurst, sweeping ahead with a wave of darklings. He decided to make for the man. Impossible to predict where the rounds were going to fall, he gave up dodging and weaving to bore a path straight into the inferno.

Everywhere he walked, he stepped on a body or pieces of one. Had he been a new soldier, he would have been sickened by the catastrophe unfolding. But this was what war was meant to be. Before he knew it, he stood upon the riverbank. At last, he saw a thing of such great horror it turned his stomach sour.

Daril Perryman felt his heart skip a beat when the darklings regained their feet and carried on. Unlike the powers of nature, Imelin's forbidden magic had turned the river into a sheet of solid ice overnight. Each new catapult strike sent ice and stone fragments wildly on their killing paths. He saw that it wasn't enough. The darklings managed to recover far too quickly.

"Determined aren't they?" Perryman asked, in a vain attempt at levity.

A few of the younger soldiers nearby offered queer looks as they prepared for the hard fight. It was coming much faster than any wanted. The artillery barrage had been going on for an hour already. The thunder of massive chunks of stone exploding and death screams was more than enough to leave permanent scars on their psyche.

Through it all, the darklings kept coming.

"This is it, men!" he shouted. "No more probes or quick attacks. They seek to swarm us under. Will you let them? Pikemen, ready the lance!"

Hundreds of armored pikemen shouted back and lowered their deadly barbs. Visors concealed their nervous faces. Most didn't want to fight but were left with no choice. Fireballs sizzled overhead, showering them with sparks. Ranks of swordsmen filed down behind them and remained concealed. Most elven archers took elevated positions and nocked missiles. Perryman held the world in the palm of his hand. Once he dropped his arm, the battle would begin in earnest.

The darklings surged so close, the front ranks of defenders could almost feel their breath. Still the order to hold remained. The first beast jumped atop the berm, dagger drawn and already bleeding from several wounds. It howled with rage at the armored men and leapt down to attack. Perryman dropped his arm and drew his sword.

Three hundred arrows whistled, striking cold flesh. Darklings fell in masses. A wall of barbed pikes stabbed and parried with the experience of years. The lead darkling somehow managed to avoid being killed and broke through the lines of pikes. Once clear, he ran straight for Perryman. Raw hatred twisted its face.

A squad of swordsmen raced to intercept, as eager to get their blades wet as to save their charismatic commander. The darkling assassin ducked beneath a slashing blow and rolled. It stabbed up into the Galdean's groin and kept moving. Perryman appeared out of nowhere and struck the darkling's head from the shoulders. The body remained standing a moment longer before toppling over.

"Swordsmen up! Drive them back to the river!"

Leading the charge, Perryman hungrily sought his next victim.

The rider reigned to a stop close to Dlorn, his breath haggard and unwilling to come. He was a young man whose name the general couldn't place. Giving a ragged salute, the rider finally exhaled and managed his report.

"Sir, Commander Alsimmons reports we are in danger of being flanked. He requests immediate reinforcements."

Dlorn scowled. It was still much too early to give up ground. Gulnick Baach was acting up to top form today. "Tell Lestrin to attack with his heavy cavalry at once."

"Yes, sir!" he saluted again and rode off.

"Runner!" Dlorn shouted and a young soldier rushed to his side. "Get to the catapults. Tell Monchere to swing the number one battery right. Open fire as soon as emplaced. I want as much fire pouring into that flank as we can get. Those are our boys down there and I want them kept alive. Now go!"

The runner dashed off, leaving Dlorn standing alone in a sea of men and steel, wondering if the catapults would do the trick until Lestrin and his force arrived. He prayed they would be in time.

"Fall back!"

Those were the last orders Calri Alsimmons had hoped to issue so near the beginning of the battle but he was left with no choice. The darklings attacked with much more intensity than any sortie previously launched by either side. So intense the assault almost came as complete surprise. Calri and his men barely recovered.

Dozens of his men, faceless soldiers and friends alike, fell within the first moments. The rest did a commendable job at plugging the holes but the effort was much too late. Darklings were already within the perimeter and driving. He understood the importance of being on the flank and knew that if he couldn't hold the entire army was lost. Calri hefted his broadsword and plunged into the fray with a hundred fresh soldiers at his back. They would either repel the enemy or die trying. In which case, the army was doomed regardless.

"Swing about for maximum range," the master gunner bellowed just as soon as the order came down from higher command. "Open fire and do not stop until told to."

Scant minutes later, the first round rocketed toward the enemy.

Darkling confidence waivered slightly as round after round of burning oil and rock plunged into their massed lines. In doing so, they paused the attack long enough for the Galdeans to disengage and reform. The darklings were almost as fast. Calri was threatened with despair. Even with the aid of Monchere's artillery, he doubted he'd last much longer. His only hope was that Dlorn managed to receive his message and was acting on it.

"Here they come again!"

Calri tightened his grip and braced against the wall of gnarled bodies crushing against him. Steel bit flesh and the ground soon became soggy with fresh blood. Teeth and claws tore limbs and punched massive holes in the armored chests of the defenders. Screams were intense enough to make the gods cringe. Then the worst happened. Not only did the barrage wither, but rounds began to fall short, crashing into the Galdean ranks. The darklings surged again.

"No!" Calri screamed, as the first round landed in a knot of pikemen.

He ducked and darted through the missile-like debris and battling men to reach the relative safety of the signal man. The veteran frowned as he looked upon a boy who couldn't have been more than fourteen. Were things so bad that children had to fight?

He grabbed the boy by the shoulders, noticed the heartfelt fear in his eyes, and said, "Look here, boy, we need you. Soon this will all be over and you may return to your family, but not yet. Signal the firing battery. Tell them to cease fire immediately. They're killing our people."

The boy tightened down his helmet and jumped atop a large knoll. Incoming rounds soared overhead and hundreds died behind him as he spelled out the message with his flags. The barrage lifted almost at once, but the damage had been done. Calri Alsimmons knew despair. Retreat was impossible. The darklings were too intertwined with his soldiers. He had no choice but to stand and fight, but without reinforcements, they wouldn't last past midday.

Lestrin scowled. Moments after receiving word, his force was on the move. They had been prepared, while idle, since the first day and he was itching for a fight. The Golden Warrior, Jou Amn, rode at his side. Together, they headed for the pages of destiny. The cavalry commander halted his force atop the main rise running diagonally through the camp and gasped in horror. The battle being waged went far beyond his expectations. Lestrin scanned the field and developed his plan of attack. Captains immediately came to him to receive orders.

"Divide into three wedges. Keep it tight and smash their lines. I'll take center. Don't let up until we've crushed all organized resistance. As soon as you are formed, we attack."

The others left and he looked at Jou Amn. "I hope this is what you chose to stay for."

"I stayed to fight. The last I knew, there wasn't a good way to do it," he replied.

Lestrin nodded and looked over his men a final time. Both captains signaled their readiness and he exhaled sharply. Just before he dropped the visor to his helmet, he let out a single word which rumbled like thunder across the fields.

"Charge!"

Things could not have been fouler for Duoth N'nclogbar, the self-proclaimed ruler of the darklings. He stood in the middle of his once mighty army, watching hundreds of his minions die. This was not what he had in mind when he made his pact with the dark wizard. The still bodies of his warriors formed a sickly carpet of flesh across the valley floor. He was reminded of the tales passed down of the great war between darkling and elf many centuries ago. Duoth refused to repeat the past.

The darkling prince marched back toward the Black's tents. He was tired of watching his brothers die. Something must be done before the Galdeans gained the advantage and turned what was supposed to be an easy victory into a rout. The Black must be made to answer for such unforgivable sins.

"Wizard!" he hissed, throwing aside the tent flap. "Wizard! My people die in great numbers. End this or I take army back to Suroc Tol."

The Black materialized in front of Duoth. He leveled his icy gaze on the lesser creature. Duoth flinched, hand reaching for his weapon.

"Who are you to question my tactics? I have evolved beyond the laws of men and gods and you, a mere imp, would assail me with idle threats in the sanctity of my lair? I think not, worm."

"You throw away my people's lives. These men are better prepared than the white general said. Their throwing machines kill many," Duoth snarled.

Imelin swept his arms out in a grand gesture. "Enough! It is for me to decide who lives or dies. The catapults will be dealt with tonight. Keep your warriors on the offensive. Baach will know when to retreat. Now go, do as you are told."

Were it not snowing, Calri Alsimmons would have been sure a terrible thunder shook the world. He hadn't the time to worry over such things, however, for the press of darklings was fast becoming too much. Half of his men were either dead or wounded and there was no way he could hope to hold out much longer. Strength was failing as fast as hope. Weary limbs drove heavy swords, each stab or swing losing just a little of what the previous held. The darklings sensed victory and redoubled their efforts.

The rumbling grew louder, almost deafening. Out of the late morning haze burst two thousand heavy horse. His soldiers rallied at the sight, for none had ever been more in need. Spears and lances leveled as the cavalry charged through friendly lines to smash into the darkling wall. Lestrin took advantage of the confusion and was rewarded by penetrating deep enough to fold the assault in on itself. Scores of bodies fell, run through or trampled, in every direction. Bones crushed with hideous snaps and organs burst as the horses ran over the darklings without regard. Horse and rider fell as well, though not in enough numbers to stall the advance.

The darkling attack broke. All at once, they ceased fighting and turned to flee. Three wedges of armored horse charged after, unwilling to allow any to escape. The death toll continued to rise drastically as the last of Calri's infantry became disentangled. Finally, they were able to catch their breaths.

Calri watched the horses carry past with gratitude but the damage done to his command was irreversible. They would have no choice but to be removed from the front lines and disbanded. Those fit for duty would be reassigned and the others, less fortunate ones, would be evacuated in the same fashion as the first wagon train. The battered, bleeding Captain sheathed his sword and sought out his wounded.

The entire flank of the Galdean army had been decimated. Bodies lay sprawled like blades of grass, so plenty they were. The most sickening examples were among the first to die. Darklings in the rear of the strike vented their bloodlust on the corpses. Heads rolled underfoot. Severed limbs were arranged obscenely. Many had been skinned. Yet others appeared as if something hideous and previously un-encountered had burrowed deep within the body cavity and come back out.

Vapors of escaping heat pocked the battlefield. Calri struggled to retain his tears. A runner came from the center of camp with word he was to attend Dlorn's council. Though reluctant to leave the remnants of his men, he couldn't refuse. He dropped the blood-soaked bandage in the melting snow and turned to follow the runner back to a better place.

The catapults no longer fired. They didn't need to, Gulnick Baach mused from his relative solitude amidst the swarm of darklings. Thousands of the savage creatures lay sprawled in death for as far as his eye could see. Bodies were stacked like firewood on the opposite side of the river. The defeat was… impressive. The professional buried deep within loathed giving the order to retreat, but Gulnick knew it was the right thing to do.

To his surprise, and secret delight, the darklings continued to fight. It was an act that accomplished nothing. Elves continued to decimate their ranks with accurate arrow fire. Sickened at the sheer amount of carnage, Gulnick turned from the battle and stalked back to his tent. The next day needed to be planned and he was unexpectedly weary.

Guilt plagued him, despite the army he commanded being no more than savages. He wondered if the Galdeans had used his information and were in the process of saving their army. It was the least he could have done. He no longer cared if the Black knew of his transgressions. The horrors of the day would forever sear his mind far worse than anything the wizard was capable of. Lost in thought, he failed to catch the murderous glare of Hurst staring at him from behind a tree.

SEVENTEEN
Dreams Unfulfilled

Haggard and weary beyond imagination, the commanding officers in Dlorn's council slumped down into their chairs or on the ground, while struggling to remain awake. Each hurt from numerous wounds. All felt the bitter effects of exhaustion, both mental and physical. Victory was the furthest thing from their minds, but in this hour of need, the difference between citizen and soldier burned bright.

Soldiers will always do what they are told. They form the foundation of kingdoms and give power to their nobles and lords. There is associated pride which burns far deeper than the conscience, compelling righteousness. To carry on when only fumes remain. To pick up the fight, though no end is in sight. It is for these men the world should be eternally grateful, for it matters not which side they fight on. All are the children of proud mothers and should be treated with respect.

Dlorn looked from face to face, scanning to see who was going to break and who yet stood strong. The faces staring back told him what he already suspected. There was life inside the tent, one inexplicable to those who had never been under the duress of hopeless combat. Battered relentlessly for over twelve hours, his men still had heart.

"What now shall be our strategy?" he asked, with palms held out. "We cannot expect to survive another full day of carnage of this magnitude."

"We'd never make it across the river if we try an all-out retreat," Perryman said. A nasty gash ran diagonally across his forehead.

"If we scatter, we will be destroyed piecemeal," Lestrin growled. "Felbar's paltry few won't be enough to reinforce the men we lost today."

"Lord Felbar doesn't concern me now," Dlorn interjected. "Captain Alsimmons, how many units have crossed into Almarin?"

"Twenty-seven, sir. Most are down to only fifty percent effectiveness."

A grim visage stole over the old man's face. "I want that number doubled before sunrise."

"They will whelm us in one swift stroke!" Lestrin argued. "Doing this will reduce our combat strength by half."

"Commander, I am well aware of the ramifications, but I must remind you that we are not here to engage in total battle."

The cavalry commander fumed, "Food for the wolves, is it, General? I will not throw away the lives of those who ride under my command so carelessly."

"But we must! If necessary, I will take the lead of the last charge, but so long as a glimmer of hope remains, we shall retreat and fight again," Dlorn spat.

"Where lies the hope now, General?"

Dlorn thought hard on the blunt words. When he spoke it was a whisper. "In the city of Meisthelm. The world mobilizes around us and it is for them that we die."

Lost within the devouring darkness of his tent, the Black Imelin gently rubbed his temples. The insignificant flies of the Galdean army were becoming more of a nuisance than he'd anticipated. It would take weeks to root them out. Why, he failed to understand. Why were they fighting so hard, when they didn't need to?

Reports reached him that General Conn's army, the main Hierarchy force, was still bogged down deep in

Guerselleorn and no threat. Cold realization spread through his near skeletal frame. The Staff! The Galdeans must be stalling for the Staff to get as far away as possible. It had to have been taken from the field already, without his knowing.

"Barathis!"

The miscreant soldier poked his head through the heavy wool flaps almost at once.

"Summon me General Baach and that mercenary, Hurst," he commanded. "There is treachery afoot and I aim to get to the bottom of it."

Gulnick Baach stumbled his way across the frozen snow. It was the middle of the night. He was cold, hungry. What could the wizard possibly want now? He discovered the answer as soon as he entered the tent. His stomach clenched. The Black stood strong, menacing in the center, slightly overshadowing the grinning Hurst.

"Ah, my dear General. Do come in and close the door. It is frightfully cold outside. Wouldn't want my top man getting sick."

Gulnick's heart fluttered. "Can we skip the charade and cut down to it?"

An eyebrow raised. "Are you sure you can handle it?"

"Kill him now and get it over with," Hurst growled.

The Black's head snapped around. "Bite your tongue, mercenary scum. I could crush you with the blink of an eye. You are here only at my leisure. Do not tempt me on such a whim."

Hurst balked and stiffened, determined not to let the other get the better of him.

"You mentioned the word charade. Funny a man like you can throw about such so carelessly. It has come to my attention that much has been transpiring in my absence. Much I should not have found out about. Would you care to elaborate on the subject, Baach?"

Dejected, Gulnick stood firm.

"No? It was but a matter of time before I found out. Treachery has a way of staining things of this nature. How do you explain the careless tenacity with which our enemy fights? I think they have been given certain elements of information, potentially dangerous toward my forces, and goals."

He leaned forward menacingly and whispered, "I want to know everything you told the Galdeans and why."

Hurst snorted laughter.

Waves of soldiers, wounded and healthy alike, shuttled across the straining bridges away from the horrors of battle and into unknown lands. Rally points had been established. Once all units were accounted for at each, they would continue migrating south toward the final rendezvous and then south to Meisthelm. Less than ten thousand men would remain behind to fight off the next darkling assault. It was a number Dlorn could live with. He stood atop his small knoll in the center of camp and watched the bulk of his army flee east across the river. He wondered if his valiant few were going to be enough to hold out long enough. An eerie chill blew through his tired form. He'd already lost twenty pounds from the combination of stress and torment.

The train of soldiers marched away, winding deep into the night, until only the faintest of sounds could be heard on the wind. It was then Dlorn returned to his tent. He paused every few steps to search the skies for signs of the darklings' aerial threat.

The Black Imelin stepped over the slain corpse of Gulnick Baach and confronted Hurst. Killing Gulnick provided little in the way of stimulation, though he did find some advantages. One less snake to deal with, only to have another take its place. The dark wizard eyed Hurst with varying degrees of mistrust. A man who could so easily sell out one of his own once, would have no problems doing so again. *Once the battle is finished, I shall deal with him as well.*

"I want the army ready to attack in three hours. We are going to divide again. Split the remaining troops in half, put the rest on scrathes. Drop them behind Galdean lines just before dawn. Once we have their attention with a battle from behind, you send in the rest of the army. This should be enough to successfully extinguish the Galdean threat confronting us."

"And if they flee?"

Imelin snarled. "Take your part of the army and hunt them down."

"Is it safe to assume you will not be there with us on the morrow?" Hurst asked, plans already developing in his diabolical mind.

"I go south with the other half of the army. Our enemy takes the Staff to Meisthelm. I must stop them, else this war is for naught. Now go."

The mercenary slid out into the night, using natural stealth and predatory skills the Black admired. Once it was empty, Imelin faced the darkest corner of his tent. A soft hiss escaped the shadows, followed closely by a remarkably slender darkling.

"I don't trust that one. Less than the general," the darkling slurred, with rudimentary control of the common speech.

"I trust no one. Watch him, Slorix. Do not let that man out of your sight. Kill him as soon as the enemy is routed. One look in his eyes tells me the levels of treachery he can reach."

The darkling slinked back into the shadows.

"Do not fail me," Imelin said to empty air.

A hearty gust of wind blew in from the west. Guards wrapped their cloaks tighter and looked to the skies. Many had been in Galdarath during the initial darkling assault and knew full well the level of treachery yet to be unleashed here. Something wicked approached. It gnawed into their psyche, sparking untold levels of fear. Eager to be done with their shifts, the guards paced in nervous expectance of things to come.

A fresh wave of blackened storm clouds followed the wind. Daril Perryman stepped groggily into the chill night, intent on relieving his aching bladder. He finished quickly and wrapped back up in his fur cloak. Still half asleep, he was aware enough to check the sky from horizon to horizon. Grey and black clouds clashed violently into each other, losing shape and reforming effortlessly. Hidden amongst the war in the sky came a host of menacing figures.

Dragons, he thought initially. By the time they got closer, horror stained his face. Not clouds or dragons but scrathes! At last the final act of this battle had come. He watched in mute dismay as hundreds of the foul creatures swooped down through the clouds. It was as if the bowels of Suroc Tol had emptied and were come to blanket the land.

"Stand to! Stand to!" Perryman shouted, rousing those soldiers within hearing. Cloak dropping to the mud and snow, he ran to the nearest guards. "Go! Rouse the army. The enemy is upon us. If we act quickly, we might still salvage this. Go!"

Alone again, Perryman darted back into his tent to arm and then went back down the line. There was no time to don armor, or even all their weapons. The scrathes would soon be upon them. Perryman looked again to the sky. The enemy was decidedly closer and using the wind. Droves of half-asleep soldiers clustered together, their numbers growing with each passing moment. He began to think they might win out after all.

Then the first wave of scrathes were overhead and a host of airborne monsters began to fall from the sky.

Asleep for what seemed mere moments, Dlorn angrily swung his feet from the meager comforts of his cot and strapped his broadsword to his back. He had anticipated a night attack, all the while wishing it didn't come. The soldiers were already far beyond the limits of mortal endurance. Death being the only alternative, they carried on and continued the fight. No one wanted to die, especially in the frozen wastes of the Crimson Fields.

The wind immediately struck through his clothes to bite his flesh. Men and beast were already engaged in bitter acts of desperation. Elven archers were striking darklings out of the sky. Arrow riddled bodies dropped around them. Fighting on the ground was furious. The dead and wounded mounted at a frightening pace.

The sole comfort Dlorn found was in that most of his army was already across the river in Almarin and getting further away. His reflections were disturbed by a thundering crash and the harsh snap of jaws. Three darklings dropped through the worn fabric of his tent. Using what little advantage he had, Dlorn drew his sword and charged. Two of the darklings died before they were able to recover from the drop. A third and fourth slashed free of the tent fabric and charged him.

The first tackled him around the knees, driving him to the ground and knocking his sword away. The second landed on his chest. He felt ribs crack as the air was forced from his lungs. Dlorn saw his death bearing down on him and was powerless to prevent it. Hot spittle burned his cheeks. His stomach turned.

The darkling pinned his arms and laughed. His comrade sidled around with dagger exposed. Scant feet from completing his mission, the darkling hissed. Neither had heard the shrill whistle of twin arrows rocket through the frozen sky until it was too late. The first struck the darkling in the center of the chest. The force of impact drove it off Dlorn. The second arrow ripped open the vocal cords of the second with uncanny precision.

Dlorn looked up through a daze to find a lone elf salute him before moving off to find a new target. Dlorn shrugged the lifeless body aside and struggled to his feet. That brief contest took much of his energy, leaving him wondering how he was going to make it through the rest of the fight.

"Runner!" he called and waited agonizing moments for a pair of youths to appear.

"Find Captain Alsimmons and have him bring his men to the center. We make our stand here."

The younger runner took off and Dlorn turned his attentions to the second. "Get me Lestrin and his cavalry. I want this entire army ready to move. If the Black is going this far, he'll probably send another ground attack as well. Hurry, son, our lives depend on it."

Without waiting to see if he was obeyed, Dlorn ran through the confusion of battle, picking a fight when necessary and running from it at discretion. More darklings dropped in, renewing the mayhem to feverish levels. By the time he reached the heart of the defense, a third wave was incoming. Hundreds of men and darklings struggled in vain attempts at survival. Field Marshal Dlorn knew despair at last.

Reeler Monchere managed to drag himself out of his cot and dress before the screams got too close. It took more time than usual to adjust to his surroundings, which he did with a frown. Being an officer in the Galdean artillery left him unaccustomed to the ferociousness of hand to hand combat. Tonight, however, he had no choice.

Several of his catapults were already on fire, their flames somber beacons to the monsters across the river. A host of cheers erupted from the darkling camp, sparking fear in Reeler's heart. His sword felt awkward in his hands. Doubling that effect were the thousands of enemy forces ready to cross the frozen waters. He had no idea as to the status of the rest of his command. So far as he was concerned, they were cut off and doomed.

"Master gunner!"

Reeler looked frantically for his right hand advisor. He repeated the name several more times before Bernt, battered and bloody, stole through the battle to reach his side. The artillery commander breathed a sigh of relief at the sight. Dark red blood trickled down his master gunner's right arm.

"Half of the number two battery burns. Our men are holding out but if push comes to shove, we'll be overrun in a matter of minutes," Bernt announced.

Reeler nodded. "I fear things are about to get much worse. Another battle rages in the center of camp and the enemy lines the rivers. This may well be our last stand."

"I have no intention of dying this night, Commander. Everything necessary that needs to be done shall be."

Reeler wished he had his senior advisor's confidence. "Get the crews to their remaining weapons, as many as possible. Keep our defense tight and ready. Another ground attack will come before this is finished. If we die, the army dies with us."

Bernt nodded again and was gone. Lacking the desire to rush headfirst into the fight, Reeler tightened his sword grip and cautiously stalked across the land. He wasn't a hero, nor particularly brave. He was just an average soldier who'd had little else going for him before enlisting. Lost in obscure thought, he failed to see the dozen darklings drop from the sky and encircle him. Warm urine trickled down his leg.

He raised his sword to make a last stand. A dozen tiny blades slipped under his sword to tear him to shreds. The death screams of Reeler Monchere echoed like nightmares across the blood slick ground.

Daril Perryman kicked the slain darkling off his blade and sought out his next victim. Pickings were getting slim, but the damage had already been done. The darkling feint was enough to draw attention away from the catapults that had been so closely guarded. Their mass destruction reminded him of massive funeral pyres. Perryman cursed his lack of foresight.

Side by side, man and elf struggled for their lives. Perryman darted through the battle until he found a kneeling Dlorn. Tired beyond measure, Dlorn watched as his defenders managed to repulse the enemy. He delighted at seeing Perryman but it was still much too early to crack a smile. The entirety of his command was still in grave peril.

"General," Perryman called and helped Dlorn to his feet.

"I know. The catapults burn. Send Lestrin and his cavalry to reinforce."

"Yes, sir, but that's not what I'm worried about. The units on the line stand the most danger. We need to get as many troops as possible back into defensive positions. I think the Black seeks to storm us tonight."

Dlorn spied the genuine concern in Perryman's face and was instantly reenergized. *Men like that are going to save this army, and our kingdom.* He nodded. "Send as many men as you think necessary. Stop and find Monchere on the way. As soon as the remaining catapults are clear, have them open fire. I want Calri Alsimmons here. We begin a full retreat tonight."

Fear dominated the hearts of the host of defenders atop the battlements. Hordes of darklings massed threateningly, scant meters away, without worry of being struck down by catapult fire. The darkling line surged ahead, intent on ending the battle in one foul swipe, yet they paused on the riverbank and broke out in wild cheers and howls upon seeing the fires blazing behind Galdean lines.

Panic stricken by the sight, the depleted ranks of pikemen and swordsmen buckled down, expecting the worst. The sickening smell of the dead no longer bothered them like it should. Instead, they used the bodies like natural barriers. Every little bit helped, even if it was former comrades. The one solace was that their departed friends felt no pain. The cold helped decay and disease from spreading. A small boon.

The thunder of darkling drums started again. Fresh waves of fear washed into the hearts of the defenders. The drums beat out their war song for close to an hour before stopping abruptly. Shortly after, the first darkling lines marched down onto the ice and across the river.

The Black Imelin climbed atop his scrathe and comfortably strapped in. A host of concerns kept him from focusing on the battle. Most of all, was the now concealed location of the Staff. The destination was simplistic, though it might well be deep into spring before reaching Meisthelm. What route was the young lordling Aron Kryte taking? The Free Lands were a massive, sprawling expanse of kingdoms with a myriad of roads and open routes. Worse, he failed to understand how Kryte and his Golden Warriors had managed to avoid detection since entering Dreamhaven.

Burning fires from the catapults were as beacons, guiding the Black closer to his enemy. The deep cold of being airborne, forced him to use magic to keep himself warm. He was over the river when a new vision struck. Kryte wasn't going south. Not yet at any rate. Chances were he was already across the second river and marching through Almarin. The middle-northern kingdom only had one major city, so it was logical that Kryte take the Staff there first. Wicked smile adorning his face, Imelin turned his scrathe northeast and headed for the mountain city of Hyrast.

Calri Alsimmons slipped and fell on a patch of blood slickened gore. His left thigh was slashed open to the bone and he knew he'd be dead if it wasn't for the freezing temperature and the quick reaction of the man nearest him. The tourniquet was so tight, each new breath he drew threatened to render him unconscious.

The battle was nearly over, at least from his vantage point. Most of men dead were his, for his unit had stood at the center. Few darklings remained, though men stabbed each body just to be sure. Fighting had been furious. The darklings had nearly taken them all by surprise. He wished the nightmare was over.

"Captain Alsimmons?" asked a timid runner from behind.

Calri frowned upon seeing how young he was. Children didn't belong in war. "What is it, boy?"

"Sir, the Field Marshal wants to see you. He says we're to begin the retreat."

Retreat? The Galdean army had never retreated from the field of battle in the last two hundred years. Yet now, here, they were expected to abandon all the sacrifices of those brave men. It must be a mistake. The exodus had been planned, but there wasn't any mention of retreating. Surely Monchere's men had beaten back the darklings. Cut off from reinforcements, those remaining enemies couldn't hope to last much longer.

"Sir?"

The boy's voice tore him out of thought. "Tell Dlorn I'm on my way."

Taking off like a rabbit, the boy disappeared. Calri turned back to the river and inspected the gaping holes torn through the ice by the catapults. Disabled, there was no way the darklings would be able to use the river again. He began barking orders. Moments later, a fresh wave of scrathes glided close.

The battle for the river had only begun but was already in full swing. Pikemen struck and moved as best they could, for the enemy was much better prepared this time. The first trench was lost, and the second getting precariously close to falling. If not for the elves, it would have already done so.

Bernt had never heard a sweeter sound than the rumble of two thousand heavy horse. Doubts of survival erased as the first rows of riders emerged from the curtain of darkness, wild-eyed and howling for revenge. He wondered which seemed madder, the darklings or Lestrin's men. Armored horses crashed into the darklings, stealing the advantage and sending the smaller creatures scurrying for safety.

Old and beyond ready to retire, Bernt sensed this was the final act of a violent experience. "Ready the guns! Chief of batteries, I want as much fire put down on that riverbank as we've got. Expend all ammunition and fall back. Fire at will!"

Tired, knocking on death's door, the catapult crews hurried to their jobs. The first rounds erupted into the sky. It was at that time Bernt discovered Reeler's mangled corpse. The old man almost wept.

Perryman paused atop the rise to catch his breath before charging down into the battle. Surely the gods of darkness were pleased with what they saw. Pockets of the underworld rushed up to swallow the ground where proud warriors once stood. The battle was getting close to the finish and he finally saw his battered army couldn't win.

He had no choice but to retreat the troops, even with the reinforcements and lessening hail of arrows and artillery rounds. Perryman summoned his two captains and discussed his plan. They were to form a line and hold, allowing the weakened units to fall back sufficiently and do the same. This would keep going until either no darklings remained or they ran out of room to run, whichever came first.

Perryman watched events unfold. Darklings were closing in on the second trench. Pockets of defenders too slow to retreat fought valiantly but were cut off and swarmed. If any managed to survive they wouldn't be of any use in the continued campaign. When his last elements were in place, he signaled the trumpeter to sound retreat.

The bugle call reverberated across the hollows and ice hardened ground, inspiring a wide range of mixed emotions. Brave men balked at the sound, still clinging to some distant ray of hope that would never materialize. Lesser men in terms of courage, grew disheartened at the thought of running. Men broke and fled back to the east. It was all Perryman could do to prevent an all-out rout.

Thinking ahead of time saved five battalions of war-hardened infantry. A company of men were left behind Perryman's freshly formed lines. Their sole purpose was to stop the retreat and reorganize fluid defenses. The waning catapult barrage weakened considerably. Sporadic bursts of three and four rocked the ground followed by nothing. The last of the retreating soldiers darted through the spread-out line and on to potential freedom. They were meters ahead of the darklings. Perryman's troops barely had time to close the gaps and ready before the first darklings struck. The advantage was his, for the darklings were counting on a complete rout. They ground to a halt on the tip of the armor machine.

Perryman lunged at the nearest darkling, cleaving it in two. Blood and brain matter splashed across his chest armor as he dislodged his weapon and battled on. Sharpened claws raked harmlessly off his armor, at once making him grateful he remembered to don it before rushing to the front. His men fought on pure rage, making him proud to stand beside them. Many darklings lost their lives but there seemed no end to their ungodly numbers.

"Fall back!" Perryman cried, the words almost catching in his throat.

A dying darkling was thrown into him. Another leapt in synchronicity, threatening to decapitate him. Perryman stabbed up, spearing the darkling in the low belly and driving up into the throat. The weight of the dead body drove him to a knee. Hands reached for him, yanking him back to his feet.

Scrathes continued to fill the sky, illuminated now by the first timid fingers of dawn's cold light. Dlorn feared his army was lost as the new day finally afforded him the opportunity to view the carnage. The depths went far beyond anything he had ever witnessed. So many lives lost. Darklings failed to understand the meaning of the word mercy. Nor did they take prisoners.

Bodies and pieces of others lay strewn across the valley, effectively dispelling any myths of Galdean invincibility. Dlorn grew sick at the degradation being carried out on his men. Darklings continued to drop in, allowing him no time to dwell on the matter. *A dragon would do nicely, at least we might stand half a chance.* He prayed the Staff was well on the way to safety.

"General," an unfamiliar Colonel said, blood soaked and near death. "We must get you across the river. To stay any longer is mere foolishness."

"I will not leave my men!"

The Colonel shook his head. "You're not leaving them, sir. The front lines have already been pushed back substantially. The catapults have stopped firing and the darkling force on this side of the river grows. You are the heart of this army. We have already lost a king. Do not rob us of our commanding officer as well."

Dlorn thought hard on the words before breaking down and agreeing. "Fine. Full retreat. Everyone not directly engaged is to evacuate to eastern rally points and wait for us. See to it that you are with us on the other side, Colonel. I have need of strong advice in the future."

This is the most desperate hour of my life. Bernt and his men continued to battle an overpowering foe. Lestrin and his cavalry had been enough to break the initial assault, but there was no way they could have been prepared for the hundreds, if not thousands, of darklings dropping from the sky. The catapults, at least the few remaining, had stopped firing. Their crews either out of ammunition or struggling to stay alive. He could see only one way out.

It was by pure coincidence he managed to stumble into Lestrin's bleeding horse. The two haggard warriors regarded each other carefully, their blank expressions saying everything. Neither believed they were going to make it out alive.

"This is madness," Lestrin said, after drinking from his canteen and passing it to the master gunner.

Bernt agreed. "We have only one way out of here and I like the idea less than you."

The cavalry commander snarled his dislike. "Get your people moving. I'll use mine for cover. Keep going until we reach the river. The gods willing, we may yet survive this."

Both hurried off into the predawn, each clinging to the thin hopes of salvation mercilessly toying with them.

EIGHTEEN
Retreat

The night was much colder than any Amean Repage recalled since his childhood. Despite riding through the night, frost managed to cling to his face and refused to let go. The Staff of Life rode heavily at his side, plagued by the memories of losing a very close friend. Amean rode on, lost in the doldrums of self-imposed sorrow.

His thoughts took him back to a time when the fresh, young Aron Kryte first joined the Hierarchy and the Golden Warriors. Aron developed at a rate unseen in the vast history of the Order, consistently exceeding the scope of his responsibility and potential. Few men were his equal when it came to tactics, or pure intensity on the field of battle. He was definitely his father's boy.

His father had died long ago, long before the wars with rogue Aragoth and the great schism that followed. His mother took ill not long after and knowing she wouldn't be able to care for him, summoned Amean. Together with his wife, they raised Aron to manhood and watched him grow with heartfelt pride. Life had been good up until the day the bastard Imelin defected from all he held dear and turned the world on end. Then Aron died.

Three days now they had ridden on after losing Aron. Three days of whispered vengeance for the boy he had raised as a son.

"You're talking even less than I these days," Karin said, in a mild tone. "Care to tell me what's on your mind?"

She bore equal hurt, one in which the best things of her life had been violently stolen from her. Never having known love until now, she couldn't imagine living without Aron. But no matter how bad things got, she refused to believe it over. A tickle in the back of her mind told her that Aron wasn't dead. And where hope lingered, also came the will to carry on. Tender memories filled her heart, never once making her question how it was she could so utterly fall for a stranger but knowing everything was right when they were in each other's arms. The simple thought of him brought the most loving smile to her face.

"I knew him as a boy. Fought beside his father, even watched him die," Amean muttered, his voice chocked full of unexplained emotions. "I loved that boy as a son, raising him to do what was right, while growing prouder as the days wore on. It is a hard thing to watch the ones you love die needlessly."

"What if he isn't dead?"

He shifted, suddenly uncomfortable. "I saw it with my own eyes, lass. No mortal could have survived those waters."

Those were not the words she was expecting to hear.

"I admire your loyalty and applaud you for it, but you allow emotion to cloud reason. Aron is dead, leaving the legacy for us to execute," he told her.

Karin refused to let despair win. "What chance of success have we? The Red Brotherhood is gone, at least the ones we knew of. The armies of the Black rampage across the kingdoms and though I don't doubt the ability of the Galdean army, I do not think them strong enough to stand for long."

"If what Gulnick Baach said is true, half of the darkling army marches on Meisthelm. I understand what you are getting at, Karin, and the reasoning behind it. As with anything in life, there are no promises. We will do what we must, though the long road to Meisthelm be laden with dangers." Had the situation not been so dire, he would have been impressed with his words, but now was not the time to self-aggrandize.

The trail of horse and riders wound through the cool night fog blindly, for none was exactly sure where they were heading. None of the company was from Almarin and Amean had only been in the far northern kingdom once. Cold and afraid, they struggled on against nature and the threat of pursuit. No one needed to say it, for they all knew the reality that the darklings might well be ahead of them. It was a game of chances.

The blurry figures of Andolus and Long Shadow emerged from the fog. Both were near frozen and weary beyond measure, though not weak enough to show it. Strong men were needed, if for naught else than inspiration to those threatening to break. The elf lord remained a symbol of strength for others to follow.

"The road ahead is clear," Andolus told Amean. "We found a copse of ash trees maybe a half league ahead, big enough to cover the entire company. I'm concerned about pursuit, however. Any fires we light will attract the enemy. Any we don't light may result in some of us freezing to death."

They kept riding, each contemplating harsh decisions. It was a voice from behind that brought reason to them all.

"Why not light the fires and keep them burning low? One for each group of men and then double the watch. That many people on guard will alert the rest of us in time, as well as keeping the fires burning," Elsyn said, revealing herself openly for the first time since sneaking along.

Amean smiled, for he had known she was among them all along and chose to play along with her charade.

Her solutions stemmed from an unspoken love of Aron and the desperate need for acceptance. She'd been catatonic since his death and compounded with the loss of her father, the king, was on the brink of total collapse. War was never the place to develop relationships, but she couldn't help it. There was a magnetism she'd discovered, drawing her to him from the moment they met. As with her father, there were so many things left unsaid. Both men stolen from her before resolutions could be made.

Eager to get the night over and at least try to get warm, the Golden Warriors followed Andolus and his silent companion to the shelter.

Toward the middle of the night, after an hour of tossing and restless turning, Karin crawled from her bedroll and made her way to the princess. Elsyn watched her from the corner of her eye and sat up. The same tired look strained her face, bags under her eyes gave her a haunted look. Cold stole her energy in waves, taking its toll just as the siege to her kingdom had. She watched Karin with interest. The potential for establishing bonds of friendship was there.

"Couldn't sleep?" she asked.

Karin forced a smile. "Something like that. I've been thinking about a lot of different things lately and decided it was time to have a talk with you.'

"I already know what you have in mind. It's about Aron, right?"

Clever girl. "Yes. Things have happened over the last few weeks that not even I have been able to foresee. Aron and I have been together and never thought things would work out the way they did. No one envisions dying early."

Elsyn lowered her eyes to the allure of the dancing flames. She didn't want Karin to see the tears well. "You're in love with him."

"Yes. Very much so," Karin answered. Both women stared at each other as the first inkling of friendship formed. Forgotten were the present nightmares. Set aside were the facts that one had the other's father killed. Here, tonight, in the cold forested plains of Almarin, a bond stronger than all of that was forged. It gave both women the strength and courage to carry on.

"I loved him as well."

Karin ran a gentle hand over the younger princess's frozen cheek. "I know. Go to sleep now. It's still a long way to Drim and we'll have need of all the strength we can muster, especially if we hope to outrun the darklings."

"Karin, what is Meisthelm like?" Elsyn asked, the passion in her voice removed.

Taking a moment to deliberate her answers, Karin said, "Magnificent. There are golden spires reaching to the heavens where it is said the wizards once worked. Palaces and buildings as large as small towns decorate the land for leagues, each sculptured with pillars and marble floors. It is a place of great learning. The symbol of all the Free Lands hold dear."

"Are we going to make it there?"

"Yes," Karin quietly answered. "We're going to make it just fine. Go to sleep, Elsyn."

They were back on the trail at sunrise, eager to be underway and closer to the sanctuary of Drim. Scattered wind gusts blew the top layers of snow around their ankles. The day might have been bearable, if not for the wind. Shortly after breaking for a quick bite to eat, one of the horses stumbled on a hidden root and broke an ankle. The column was forced to stop as the rider transferred his bags and equipment to another and then watched as the horse was put down. It was a painful process. One each of them dreaded.

Dusk began settling as they crested a final rise. The Golden Warriors were rewarded with their first glimpse of Drim. Amean exhaled sharply, at once relieved and infuriated at reaching their initial destination. Endless questions streamed through his mind. How was he going to take care of an entire company of Golden Warriors and their mounts? They knew no one in Drim and despite quaint appearances, he was sure there was a seedy under life. Caution marking his every move, Amean Repage spurred his steed on and entered another phase of their never-ending adventure.

Field Marshal Dlorn of the Royal Galdean Army stood. He was battered and cut from head to toe. Every bone in his body ached beyond measure. He stood alone, of his own choosing, proud of his men and their determination to not only survive but find victory. The nineteen and a half thousand remaining.

They were scattered across the western region of Almarin and the northern edge of Trimlon. The bulk of the army sprawled before him, green and purple standards of Galdea billowing proudly in the wind. They waited for him. After the battle of the Crimson Fields, the army successfully disengaged and eluded the darklings. The enemy, on the other hand, appeared almost content with their half-victory. Pursuit had been minimal and easily avoided.

The last stand at the river was terrible and bloody. Darklings took advantage of the confusion and hammered the Galdeans on all sides. Losses on both sides were severe but it was the elves and their long bows who provided enough cover fire to beat the darklings back and give Dlorn enough time to retreat across the bridges.

Dlorn and his men were leagues away from the carnage now, skirting the mountain range separating Almarin and Trimlon. Dlorn's small group was hidden in a stand of pines. Guards patrolled in two sets in the event the darklings resurfaced. Dlorn paused to reflect on all that had happened, and why.

The Staff of Life was beyond his control now, as were the Golden Warriors and Princess Elsyn. He failed to understand why she'd snuck away, even while knowing he would have stopped her from trying to leave. He wished Amean and the others luck and turned his thoughts to the reorganization of his tattered army. The war had turned personal. Hoping to catch the darklings off guard, Dlorn intended on swinging south and pinch them between his men and the army of Meisthelm.

Daril Perryman appeared with an arm wrapped tight in a sling. He'd broken it during the panic and confusion of the retreat. He wore a haggard look but was still full of fire. The men, and Dlorn, garnered great respect for him. Dlorn wished he had a thousand more at his side.

"Good evening, General."

Dlorn nodded. "Commander Perryman. What news have you?"

"Everyone is accounted for and ready to march. Morale is rather high, despite our losses. Only a handful have deserted. I think we can really give the enemy a run this time." As always, Perryman's view was optimistic.

"So we shall. When dawn breaks, we strike out and recover the rest of the army while driving south to Meisthelm. The Black won't find it as easy to deal with us in the future. You should get some rest. Tomorrow we go to reclaim the lost glory of fallen Galdea."

Dlorn clasped his hands behind his back as visions of victory filled his head. A new day was coming and with it, the first legs in what promised to be a long, grueling war. But tonight, the brave soldiers of Galdea would sleep.

NINETEEN
Sadith Oom

Sadith Oom was a cursed land. All life had fled, essentially murdered during the last days of Ils Kincannon and the Knights of the Seven Manacles. Yet despite the barren plains and deep fissures, all was not tranquil. The afternoon sun withered the stamina of the thousands of laborers struggling under the whip. Man, elf, dwarf, and wylin toiled cruelly under the scrutinizing glares of their captors.

Goblin soldiers lined the masses of prisoners, kicking and slapping individuals at random as a reminder of their cruel power. Wicked creatures forged from magic, a hybrid of troll and human, stood with their massive arms folded across their chests, supervising the construction of the massive structure. Each was a giant, very much like the statues of races no longer known in the Free Lands in History's Hall in Meisthelm. Heavily muscled, with oily, hairy skin, they had curled fingers ending in claws. They'd gone unwitnessed by mortal eyes for centuries. Grohls. Monsters of the old world.

To the prisoners, the grohls were the least of their concerns. Goblins clad in leather mail warded against escapes on the back of monstrous lizards, while armed guards watched from atop stone towers. Pennants marking their cause infected the sky. Though prominently marking their territory, reconstruction of the ancient city of Morthus was of the utmost secrecy.

The architects had strategically placed the site of their fledgling empire where enemy attacks would be voided. A deep chasm ringed the plateau, plunging thousands of feet down into the dark places of the world.

Jagged spikes of fossilized rock speared up to form a natural barrier. Paths of granite, carved away centuries ago, allowed access across the abyss. Each bridge was warded by hastily constructed wooden towers high enough to give archers enough range of vision to strike down unwanted advances.

The crimson coattails of the grohl commander flowed behind him. A single curved tusk jutted up from his lower jaw. Thick veins corded his arms, straining golden torqs. He was old, his entire bitter life spent awaiting this day. The day when he could step from the caverns under the Broken Mountains and stride through the sunlight without fear of being murdered by men.

Hume Feralin growled from atop the left wing tower. Oh, how he despised the free peoples of the world. Hume dreamed of leading an army of his kind against them, crushing each race until only his remained. But the sad reality of the situation ached him in opposite directions. Grohls were fast becoming the most endangered species in the world. His people were failing to repopulate and the majority of wizards were long since turned to dust.

"Commander," a goblin snarled from behind. "We have not received this week's supplies. No word or message has come through yet.'

Hume glared. "Delays are unfortunate. How late are they?"

"Four days. This is irregular. I request permission to lead a patrol to find them."

"For what? War has not come south but the rest of the world has. Things of this nature are expected. I have had enough of this conversation," the grohl said.

"But …" the goblin protested.

Angered, Hume snatched the smaller creature by the throat. "What? Are you questioning me? What do you think will happen if I send you after the wagon train? More dead for no reason."

Hooved feet clicked impatiently on the cold stone parapet. Hume Feralin released the goblin, while thinking deeper on the proposal. If he denied the goblin's request, he would have a permanent thorn in his side. However, his malevolent eyes sparked with cunning, if he let the beast go and they discovered something of value, there was a very real chance the same might happen, thus solving a potential leadership challenge.

"Perhaps you are correct," he lied smoothly. "Take one platoon. Find out what you need and report back to me."

He walked off with a carefully concealed smile. The matter handled, it was time to feast. He clipped away, leaving the goblin wondering what his motivations were.

He watched the tens of thousands of slaves toiling. The looking glass trembled in his hands. Before the war, he was anything but a revolutionary. He was a quiet farmer doing his best to make something out of nothing in the arid heart of Eiterland. Barren Town wasn't much of a home, but it was all he knew. A raiding part of goblins ended all that. Horrific visions of the night he came home shattered any semblance of sanity he once clung to. The dreams always came at the worst time, now being one of them.

"So much blood," he whispered. He could see it flowing in small streams out of his front door and into the dirt. What awaited when he opened his front door nearly killed him. There, on the floor, lay what remained of his family.

"Sir?" asked a young student turned soldier.

He shook his head, clearing the images away. "What?"

"You said something about blood?"

Sorrow lined his eyes. "Nothing, nothing at all. By now they will have figured out something bad happened to their supply column. We need to get back to the others and prepare to attack follow on forces. After nightfall of course."

The youth eyed him in that ageless wonderment a student shows his professor upon continually being given new information. He admired this man. This haggard example of freedom who dared lead against the rising tide of oppression. It felt as if the man had been born on a battlefield.

"Over there, look."

He shifted the spy glass to where the soldier pointed and felt his stomach sour. "Close to fifty. Regular infantry by the looks. This might be a problem. Well, not exactly my idea of a good time, for it will be a task trying to sneak past so many."

Gulping his fears, the soldier admitted, "I wish I was home right now."

"Barren Town is exactly what the name suggests, barren. The goblins left nothing for us. This is all we have now. If killing these monsters is the only way home, back to a normal life, then may the gods grant strength to my steel."

"The few of us against an entire kingdom?" the soldier whispered. "We don't have a hope."

A snarl crossed the man's face. "Then we carry on without it. Think what you will but I'll not sit idly by and watch the memories of my family go to waste at the hands of despair. Now, saddle up. We've got an ambush to plan."

Stale winds blew dust aimlessly against the drab grey of the goblin infantry uniform as scores of booted feet trampled on. The sun beat down mercilessly, unimpressed with their prowess on the battlefield. The goblin force marched on, heedless of nature's disdain. Hardened professionals from a constant series of wars with their most hated enemies, dwarves, these were the survivors of decimated legions no longer active.

They growled and complained as only soldiers could while doing their jobs. All had been removed from the front lines to support the reconstruction of Morthus. The complaining stopped when given new tasks. The promise of fresh human blood drove them deeper into the Plains of Darkpool. Yet the only one interested in this mission was the goblin leader. He was convinced that no good had come to the supply column and was determined to prove Hume wrong. That determination took them far from the security of Morthus and into the wilds of Sadith Oom. Far from support or reinforcement.

The company reached the western canyons in time with the setting sun, much to the relief of the goblins. Massive iron pillars could be seen in the background. The Towers of Perdition were part of the defense against Meisthelm. Constructed to seal the evil in during the great wars between light and darkness, the Towers had long since lost their power and were reduced to silent reminders of a time long past.

Shadows played tricks on their eyes, placing enemies in the rocks above and around them. Goblins saw phantom shapes creeping around them, spying for foul masters in other parts of the world. There were greater evils loosed upon the world, greater than any threat the free peoples knew. Threats even goblins knew to fear.

"How much farther?" growled a soldier.

His brethren cheered in approval.

The cowhide whip cracked inches from his face. "Quiet, troop. We go home when the mission is done.

Any more complaints and I wring your sorry neck, understand?"

His foul speech hissed around the canyon, the echoes drawing unwarranted attention.

"Your day is coming, Galk," hissed the soldier in reply.

The goblin leader stepped between them, blade drawn. "Enough of this. I'll hear no more today. Cry when you're back in the barracks. You are both expendable. Keep moving!"

The goblin column trudged on. Galk angrily coiled his whip, contemplating his next act. The burly warrior he'd threatened leaned close in passing and snarled, "Watch your back, old one."

Galk watched him walk away, knowing there was but one solution to the problem. All he needed now was opportunity.

Morning saw them through the canyons and at last within distance of the Towers of Perdition. Galk pushed them hard, more so than he would had they been on the dwarven front. Months of being off the line had reduced their effectiveness, making them soft. It was a dangerous time to be heading into action.

"How far are we authorized to go?" he asked, as they resumed the march to the Towers.

Their leader kept up his pace. "As far as we need to. All the way to Grun, if we must. Set out pickets. We camp here."

Galk grunted and obeyed.

They stumbled upon the wreckage of the wagon train shortly after midday. Mostly ash remained, ash and the broken bodies of slain goblins. The charred timber of wagons jutted up from the sand like skeletons in the middle of nowhere. None of the human slaves were among the dead.

Buzzards and flies angrily drifted off at the intrusion of the goblin infantry. Disgusted looks twisted their faces as they sifted through the ruins in the hopes of learning what happened, all the while searching slain faces for friends or old comrades. The battle had been remarkably short. Evidence suggested ambush. Arrows and broken spears littered the bodies and surrounding ground.

There was no sign of the attackers, nor did the goblins expect any. No bodies. No blood trails. Galk had his forces spread out to secure a perimeter. Whip uncoiled, he stalked through the bodies until stumbling upon an old friend. They'd been broodmates. Angered, Galk kicked the corpse and kept moving.

"Over there!"

The grizzled veteran spun to where his soldier pointed. Galk growled, eager for vengeance. A glimmer of metal shined briefly in the sunlight. The goblins reacted. Bare steel kissed the sun, ready for the opportunity for revenge. The glimmer disappeared back into the sand and dirt.

"Where did it go?"

"Move to the target. I want blood," the leader spat, his over eagerness getting the better of him.

The goblins stalked closer, ignoring all warning signs. When next they caught the glimmer of steel, it was accompanied by the quiet whistle of an arrow. The fletched missile screamed through the air with terminal velocity until it struck the goblin leader in the heart. The advance stopped as his body struck the ground. Dust clouds kicked up as the attacker ran off.

Sensing a trap, Galk roared for the goblins to stand fast but his warning fell on deaf ears. Every goblin remaining charged after the attacker and barreled headfirst into what must be a trap. The screams began shortly after. Galk dropped down behind the wreckage of a wagon and waited.

Nightfall dropped before Galk finally mounted the courage to venture out and discover what had become of his comrades. He wasn't surprised to find them dead to the last. Their bodies were stripped of weapons and armor. The lone survivor stalked through the dead. Their deaths didn't bother him so much as the manner in which they died. There was no honor or courage involved. It was pure slaughter. He appreciated that, despite it not coming from goblin aggression. A stream of pebbles trickled down the time worn face of a small rock outcropping. Galk snapped up, searching for invisible foes.

The canyons were many leagues away but his best hope for escape and cover. Massive groupings of blanched red rocks dotted the landscape between his position and the canyons. Worried for his life, Galk clutched his sword tighter and began the long trek back to the canyons.

"What about that one?" asked a battered old dwarf as he pointed down to a spot on the valley floor.

The leader picked up the moving target and grinned. "No. it's too easy. Let him return to Morthus and warn the others. If nothing else, it should make things a little more interesting."

"This isn't a game," a gnome snapped. "If he lets the others know, there's a chance they will come in force."

Poros Pendyier, leader of the Free Rebellion in Sadith Oom, laughed. "Nonsense. They don't have the manpower or time to waste hunting us down. An operation that large would leave the keep open to assault.

No, our little goblin friend will deliver word and set this kingdom on end. Regardless, they will find out about us sooner or later."

"He goes the wrong way," a smaller than average goblin said. He'd deserted, trading in his black and grey armor for sand colored garb. He was the only survivor of the wagon train massacre. A former guard, turned traitor, who realized his life was only going to end one way. Perhaps Poros and the Rebellion would be able to change that.

Poros placed his eyepiece back to his face and watched. The goblin might just reach his intended destination, if he didn't die first. The question was where was he going?

"He might be trying to throw us off the trail," the gnome offered.

The dwarf pulled on his beard. "He's either doing that or trying to avoid being killed in those canyons."

Poros shook his head. "Too easy. He looks old enough to know better. Put a few men on him and find out where he goes."

He packed the looking glass away and took in the remainder of his band. Seventeen men, three dwarves, two gnomes, and a rogue goblin. Others were on their way to the Rebellion camp, along with the weapons and supplies from both raids. Those remaining were his most trusted.

"My friends," he said in his most statesman-like voice, "I believe it is time to return home and celebrate the victories of the week."

They eagerly agreed and followed him back to the horses and the long road home. The first blows of freedom had been struck.

TWENTY
Into the Grimstones

The Grimstone Mountains were precisely what the name suggested; grim. Save for the few scrub brushes and handful of near-dead trees, no vegetation grew throughout the immenseness of the range. Cruel winds sliced through the scarred cliff faces, echoing the wild insanity of a world gone mad. Sunlight failed to penetrate all but the tallest peaks, leaving the range cast in perpetual shadow and cold. It was an unforgiving place. Inhospitable at best.

Sylin Marth tightened his cloak and forced his horse on. He was not alone, but definitely unsuited for these conditions. Sylin almost missed the comforts of his appointment as councilor, in Meisthelm. Almost. The fools in the Hierarchy failed to see the latent dangers the Black posed to all the Free Lands. So he took it upon himself to go forth and find the one man capable of saving all. The grand, self-exiled wizard, Elxander.

Camden Hern rode at his side, his light brown skin a perfect match for the gaunt rock walls overshadowing them. The journeyman had grown to view Sylin as a comrade after their many adventures. He suddenly found himself caught up in the wily dreams of the westerner. He only hoped they didn't end in his untimely demise.

The remaining company of dwarves were in front and behind the two men. They were far from the walled city of Jerincon and all the city could spare. Thus far, they'd proven formidable companions in the face of adversity. Well-traveled, very few had ever been this deep in the mountains. Thoughts of the sleeping dragon ahead and host of goblins behind, occupied their minds as horse and pony put one foot in front of the next.

The alcove they hid in was marginally big, just large enough for all the horses and ponies, as well as a small fire. Gul Killingstone slid from his saddle and set about preparing a meal of roast fowl and stale bread. He hadn't spoken since his body had been invaded by the ghostlike Eldrath two days prior. The experience was too much, even for a dwarf of wizened years.

Garin Stonebreaker and his brother Talrn, huddled in a corner, quietly discussing events to come. The weather dominated conversation, for it had taken a decided turn for the worse. Heavy storm clouds were forming to the north and threatening to push their way. If that happened, the tiny band would be forced to find a better place to ride the storm out.

"I don't care for this," Garin murmured as Sylin walked up to them. "The storm is coming on much faster than we anticipated."

"How much longer?" Sylin asked.

The dwarf shrugged and spat in the corner of the cave. "A few hours. Nightfall by the latest."

Sylin ran a hand through his filthy hair and sighed. There was no trying to make the best of their situation. Their journey had taken a toll, leaving his preparedness to carry on uncertain at best. He was a fledgling warrior, taught by the very best swordsmen in the Free Lands. Men in battle he could handle, but this was something far different. "What is your opinion?"

Garin breathed in the aromas of fresh tobacco and roasting meat. His stomach rumbled. "There is nothing behind us. Unless we wish to deal with the Eldrath again. Which is but one of many dangers in the mountains. These peaks are old and wicked. They dislike us being here."

"We could try to wait it out," Sylin suggested.

The dwarf nodded, unconvinced. "Aye, but we'll take more than a few lumps. This cave isn't deep enough to protect us from the storm."

"What choice have we? Either we stay or press on." Sylin felt his rising hope crash upon the cold granite. "I almost wish I never started this adventure."

"Never say that. If more people like you tried to make a difference, the world might not be such a desperate place." He snorted. "I'm going to scout ahead. If the storm should hit before I return, do not attempt to find me."

Camden stopped sharpening his dagger and looked up with interest. "That is not a wise decision."

The journeyman was afraid of very few things but even this sounded of pure madness.

"I don't see that we have much of a choice," Garin argued. No matter what any of them said, his mind was decided. "It is still two days to the Hyber Pass and we have no reconnaissance. A goblin horde could be marching our way and we'd never know. I am going."

No other words were spoken as the stout tracker geared his pony up and led it out of the cave. The wind was already picking up. An ill sign. He made one last check of his weapons and tightened his thick traveler's cloak. Once again, the dwarf set out to do what he did best. After all, no one was as important as the eyes and ears of the expedition.

"Fare well," Sylin wished, just loud enough for Garin to hear. "I still need you to get us through the grasslands and then on to the wizard."

Garin barked a laugh. "I'll return sooner than you imagine. The wizard is not far off."

And then he was gone. Lost to the deepening gloom.

Sylin watched rider and pony disappear. He found the emotions he was feeling odd, especially considering he hadn't known any of the dwarves for more than a few weeks.

"Hard, isn't it?"

He looked down into Camden's cold eyes. "I suppose it isn't for you?"

Camden said, "You learn to live with the emptiness after a while. The more you see go and not return, the easier it gets. Pretty soon, you won't even remember their names. The faces all blend together and nothing stands out about any particular person. Is that what you wish to hear?"

"I'm sorry."

"You should be. Everything I just said is the exact opposite of the truth. I remember every face, every name. There are nights when the nightmares get so bad, I can't sleep. Don't criticize me because of my chosen lifestyle, Councilor."

Maric Trailbreaker gently tugged on his long, red beard. "Are you two finished? We have much to do if we wish to stay alive. Don't waste your time worrying over Garin. He's been doing this longer than the two of you have been alive. He can take care of himself."

The truth pounded through Sylin's thick skull and opened a new door. He reconsidered his statements. Perhaps he was acting too much like a parent and not enough of a leader. The only way any of them was going to survive long enough to fight the Black, was by acting like a team.

"What do we need to do?" he finally asked.

The dwarf grinned.

The storm broke just before nightfall, announced by the sharp crack of thunder careening through the mountains. High speed winds shrieked like grim demons. Pelting rains followed not long after, driving the already huddled group deeper into their narrow shelter. The gods themselves seemed to have abandoned them to die.

The animals pranced with rabid fear, attempting to break free and bolt several times. It took all the dwarves to keep them still. Both Camden and Sylin did their best to hold down the supplies and saddlebags but nature was cruel. Winds drowned out any attempt at communication. Temperatures dropped in tune with the night. Hail began slamming into the front of the cave. The wrath of the Grimstones was beyond anything they had previously endured.

Lighting struck scant meters away, charging the air with electricity and singeing the hairs on their arms. A shower of sparks cascaded down the mountain slopes. The nightmare lasted hours, as if the mountains would stop at nothing to be rid of the intruders. The battle in the skies raged unchecked, as the small band struggled just to maintain.

Sylin pulled Camden close and shouted, "We're not going to be able to take much more of this!"

"We don't have a choice! It can't last much longer. Just hold on!"

In all honesty, Sylin didn't believe he could. Not even the horrors the Black threw at them during the river passage compared to this. A pony suddenly burst free and ran screaming out into the storm. Sylin could only watch in horror, knowing the animal had gone to certain death. He briefly considered using magic, all the while knowing it wouldn't work or that he lacked the strength and depth of knowledge.

Camden dropped to a knee from exhaustion. His battle with the Eldrath had taken much out of him and he hadn't fully recovered. Perhaps his struggling friend was correct. Perhaps they weren't going to make it after all.

The thunder edged closer at a steady pace. Garin felt despair crawl forward, knowing he had no hope of outrunning the storm, though he might be able to find a shorter way out of the forsaken mountain. With a newfound sense of urgency, the dwarf pushed his pony harder. Being alone never bothered him. It was what he did best. Aside from his brother, Garin seldom spent time with others. He cared for his troops like a father would his children, but when the day ended, he often drifted off to be alone. It was the only way he maintained sanity. Garin cared little for his current position but held much compassion for his friends. It was for them he went forward. Too much was riding on the future to turn back.

His thoughts turned to what he had left behind. The war against the goblins was going badly, so bad they only managed to send a meager handful with Sylin. It was rumored that a fresh army was marching from Eleran in the south. If those rumors were true, the border city of Jerincon would be surrounded and cutoff. Dremmin Giles, general and leader of the city defense, was a cunning dwarf and had taken precautions to defeat any invading army but their numbers were few. The goblins would pay dearly, but it was unlikely to stop their war machine.

Warriors of every race flocked to the dwarven banners, but even they knew it was desperate at best. The siege would, however, give the main dwarf army time to regroup and figure out a different strategy. Add to that the sudden emergence of the Black and his demonic armies from Suroc Tol and Garin struggled with despair. The Free Lands were steadily slipping into chaos and he had no clue how to combat it.

The pony bucked against his grip, inadvertently jolting him back to reality. Garin gently pat him on the neck. "Easy friend. We've been through worse."

The march continued, apprehensions growing stronger in tune with the storm. Daylight was nearly gone, washed away through ominous portent. Haste now in his step, Garin desperately sought out shelter. He rounded a sharp corner and froze in his tracks.

The warrior before him was no more than three and a half feet tall, but as fierce looking as a battle troop of dagger trolls. He had a blade in each hand with a bow and full quiver strapped across his back. A gnome. Garin sucked in his breath. His confronter was dressed in the black-brown his people favored, with a tight skullcap and mean disposition. He was also surprised at finding a dwarf alone in the Grimstone Mountains.

The gnome hesitated, contemplating his next course of action. He was no match for a battle hardened dwarf. Distant thunder rumbled closer.

"All alone, little *gnome*?" Garin asked and hefted his axe. His eyes scanned the nearby crags for sign of more. "Step aside and I'll not kill you."

"I have no intention of dying. Move away and let me pass, *dwarf*."

The challenge was issued.

Garin snarled. Differences between the races was old, prompting current animosity toward one another. There was no way he was going to pass up the opportunity to rid the world of a gnome. They were a scourge. Opportunists who served the highest bidder. Few among the races respected them for much else.

Thunder was much closer.

"Make your choice, pest. I don't have time to waste on the likes of you," Garin grumbled.

The gnome flexed his shoulders. "Are you willing to risk your life for the sake of a blood feud neither of us created? I admit to never killing a dwarf before." Rain began falling. "Well? I have no desire to fight you. Killing you wouldn't do anything for me. I'm willing to offer you a deal."

If nothing else, Garin found the gnome amusing. "Go on."

"Neither of us has much time before this storm hits. I have a cave not far from here. It is big enough for all of us. We stay until the storm passes and then go our separate ways."

Garin Stonebreaker checked the skies. The gnome was right. They didn't have much time. A cave would provide shelter but might also be filled with gnomes looking for trophies. The rage in the skies made up his mind for him. He'd follow the gnome and either live or die.

"Deal."

TWENTY-ONE
Unsteady Alliances

The cave was deep enough to provide adequate shelter and allow a massive fire for cooking and warmth. Visibility outside was reduced to nothing, the firelight barely enough to offer any insight. It was the worst storm either of them had ever seen and both were more than willing to share the safety of the cave. Much to Garin's relief, there were no others lurking in wait. He was safe, relatively.

They sat as far apart as possible, while staying within the protective heat of the fire. Each eyed the other as if waiting for the inevitable attack that never came. Both were tired and the bad weather didn't help any. Seeing no point in staying quiet, Garin decided to liven up the mood.

"I am Garin Stonebreaker of Jerincon."

"Isic."

"What is it, Master Isic, that brings a lone gnome deep into the heart of these dread mountains? What purpose might you possibly have?"

"My business is my own," Isic shifted angrily. "To satisfy curiosity, I have been alone but for two days."

Intriguing. Why? "What of your peers?"

"Killed. All of them. Satisfied, dwarf?"

"Not especially. Gnomes are not my first concern. I've got my friends, goblins, and a dragon to worry about," Garin said.

Isic cringed at the mention of the great lizards. A thousand nightmares rushed back to him.

Garin leaned forward, beard dangling perilously close to the fire. "Scared of the wyrms?"

"You would be, too, if you'd witnessed what I went through."

Garin felt himself being pulled in. "What did you see?"

His eyes clouded over as he silently relived those dire events. "Things no one living, good or bad, should ever have to. It… it came out of nowhere. Like it was part of the mountain."

Garin's eyes sparkled in the light. "T'was the dragon? Tragalon? Speak damn you. Was it?"

"Yes. It killed three of us before we knew what struck. I hear the screams of my friends when I close my eyes."

Despite the severity of the situation, this new information was precisely what Garin needed. For the moment he forgot about his brother and companions and concentrated on the story. Every minute detail was potentially lifesaving. Isic was providing a thorough reconnaissance without knowing it.

"What part of the pass was it hiding in? This is important, Isic. I would not ask you to relive these moments if it wasn't. I need to know."

He tried to remember but certain events were hazy after the shock of the trauma set in. "Toward the beginning, if I recall."

The location made sense. From his limited knowledge, Garin figured the beginning of the pass was the widest point and the only area large enough to accommodate a dragon.

"The beast knew we were coming. It must have. There was no other way for it to gain such surprise. We didn't stand a chance. Twenty of us were sent on our mission. Only I remain."

"You alone walked away from a dragon assault?" Garin asked, with raised eyebrow. Mention of a mission peaked his curiosity.

There were reports of gnome units ranging this far south, especially ones moving north. Evil was abundant in the world and the defection of the Black from the High Council only heightened that movement. Sadith Oom was but a piece of the problem. The dwarves were threatened with being overrun, not only in Jerincon but in their mountain fastness in the Drear Hills. Somehow he needed to find out who the gnome was employed by.

A task easier said than done.

"I walked out because I'm no fool. My friends are dead because they thought they could contest a dragon. I've never been so foolish." His irritation continued to rise.

Garin saw his plan working. He needed to provoke the gnome to get him to give away his mission, knowing it was important. "You didn't stay to watch your friends perish? A dwarf would never run."

Isic scowled. "As would only a fool. I've seen many men die. Some died brave, but most died from lack of skill. The end result is all the same. They're dead and I'm alive. I could think of a lot of worse things. Why are you in the mountains, dwarf? This is far from your war."

"I, too, am on a mission," he said, leaning back against the rocks.

"Alone?"

"Don't be absurd. Do I look like a scout?"

Isic's eyes narrowed. "Where is the rest of your company? Not dead like mine or you would have already said.

"No. They are alive and well." Garin hoped. The intensity of the storm created doubt. "If you're planning to keep on after the storm, you won't make it out. Worse than a dragon awaits you."

"No doubt."

They both fell silent, each having said just enough for the time being. The crisp cackling of the fire and hollow screams from the wind were more than enough to occupy their time. Garin drifted off to sleep not long after. There remained the possibility of being stabbed in his sleep but he wasn't especially concerned. He'd been through worse over the years.

Isic contemplated killing the dwarf and being done with it, but was this the right one? He didn't know. The assassins he'd come into the mountains with were dead, along with the compliment of guards sent to protect them. All dead but him, and he was never told who the intended target was. He only knew it was a dwarf. Comfortable with the lies he'd told, Isic chewed thoughtfully on a piece of jerky and stared out into the horrible night.

Dawn broke through the remnants of the storm and the world seemed to return to normal. Isic awoke with a kick to his side. He rolled away from the attack and snapped up with dagger in hand and a snarl on his face.

"Relax, gnome. I'm not going to kill you," Garin said.

He was already leading his pony out of the cave.

"How can I be so sure?" has asked and rubbed the sore area.

"Because you're still alive. I move on and I advise you to do the same. You should turn back. My friends won't be as trusting as I."

"Go back! Into the waiting maw of that beast? You're mad."

"And you're dead either way. Even should my friends decide to spare your wretched little life, you'd still have the Eldrath to deal with, and goblins after. Consider death a mercy." Garin slung his saddlebags over the pony and walked away.

Isic's eyes widened at the mention of unknown creatures lurking ahead. "What did you say? The el…"

"Eldrath. Ghosts who steal souls and possess bodies. One of the more dangerous races I've ever seen. Luck to you, gnome. You'll need it."

Isic ran out of the cave after him. Gnomes were superstitious by nature and he suddenly lacked the courage to continue. "Wait! Perhaps we can cut a deal."

Garin smiled without letting the gnome see it. Matters were developing the way he wanted. Turning with feigned disinterest, he asked, "Another deal, gnome? I think you should cut your losses and consider yourself fortunate. Good day to you."

"You'll need my help to get past the dragon."

At last, he was thinking. "I'm listening."

"The dragon is very crafty. The way he hides in the rock and uses the shadows to lurk. I know a secret way, a path the dragon cannot enter. It will take you through the mountains and out of the pass. I only learned of it in my escape."

"Fair enough. I accept. But know this, if you try anything that will endanger my people, I will slit your throat from ear to ear and wear your skull like a trophy. Understand?"

Isic nodded.

"Good. We wait here until the others arrive."

The reluctant allies returned to the cave and waited.

Camden Hern was the first to spot the tendrils of smoke coming from the cave. The company approached with great caution, careful of another trap. It was much to their delight that they found Garin waiting for them. The dwarves stirred and went for weapons upon seeing the gnome at his side.

Talrn dismounted and the brothers embraced, both glad to have survived the storm. Hasty introductions were made before the party continued through the pass. They kept Isic at the front with Garin and Camden. Doing so would alleviate potential treachery and give advantage should they encounter the dragon.

"What do you think of this development?" Sylin asked Maric. He knew little of gnomes or the obvious animosity between the races.

Maric yawned. "Hard to say. His kind don't normally travel this far south. But you can never put anything past a gnome. He'll use us until we no longer suit his purpose and slip off into the night. I doubt he'll prove much hassle."

Sylin wasn't as positive. "This doesn't feel right. Why would he offer his services so easily, if there is hostility between you?"

"Could be he's just a coward trying to make himself look big in the eyes of strangers. Especially ones armed to the teeth and jumpy after being hounded for so long. If he is plotting, it will come out in the open soon." Maric smiled, until a new thought occurred to him. "Could be a spy for your dark wizard. We've ducked the wylin and his goblins by now."

"Or so we believe," Sylin added. "Perhaps he has employed other tactics to track our whereabouts. I do wish this was not the case."

"But it is. For good or bad, the world will never be the same again. We are on a path leading to total war.

I only hope we will be able to combat this evil before it is too late."

Maric said no more for a good while. His thoughts turned to the silence of Gul Killingstone. It was as if a poison lurked within his body, driving him closer to death. He hoped this white wizard was capable of fixing the problem. As it was, the pain was almost too much for a stout dwarven heart to bear.

He hated seeing his people suffer. Few knew the truth that he was the nephew to King Hesinar of the Drear Hills and the sole surviving heir to the throne after the king's son was killed on the plains near Lilhaven. Maric was proud of his uncle but let no one know it. The unnecessary spread of such information would instantly make him a target. The dwarf nation could ill afford to be without an heir.

The other dwarves rode with stern faces, always watching for the next attack. Some couldn't wait for the next opportunity to lock steel with the goblins and exact revenge. The spirits of their dead brethren demanded a high price and though the dwarves had thus far been able to contain the goblin threat, it was here in the midst of the Goblin Lands they stood their best chance for revenge.

"So, gnome, what special purpose brings you deep into goblin territory and through such peril?" Camden asked suddenly. He, like Sylin, knew little of gnomes but knew a sneak when he saw one. "I didn't think your people had the courage for hardships. You haven't even fielded an army since the Wars of Separation."

Isic had almost grown accustomed to the perpetual hounding over the short time they'd been together. No matter how hard the humans and dwarves tried, nothing was going to break his spirit. One of these dwarves was his target, or so he hoped.

"Why should we? Wars seldom solve anything other than population reduction. While your people die, mine pick up the profits. Let us speak of you, always preying on the weak. How many men and women have you robbed, highwayman?"

Garin arched an eyebrow. "You talk too much for a man so small. Perhaps you seek the same fate as your previous companions?"

He hissed, "Perhaps you do as well."

"Enough. As soon as we are clear of this dragon, you will be free to go. I rarely use partners and I have no use for you," Camden snapped back.

"I might surprise you," Isic said, in an effort to calm tensions and shift the course of the conversation. "I am a man of many skills and talents. If you only knew what I have accomplished, you would find yourself impressed."

"I doubt that," Camden laughed. "But if you can get us safely past this dragon, I shall change my opinion. Slightly."

Isic said nothing else. He had won his first victory.

They halted at sundown to shelter in a minor draw. The guard roster was made, for the threat of the Eldrath was still strong. Several of the dwarves believed Isic to be working for the dragon, luring them to an easy death. Oddities abounded in these grim mountains. For security purposes, they made the gnome sleep in the far corner of the draw where an axe might easily reach him.

The dwarves made a stew using water from a natural spring running off the mountain and vegetables they had brought with them. The warm food helped ease tensions. Sylin and a few others sat away from everyone else, making plans for dealing with the dragon and avoiding contact with the goblins once they cleared the pass.

"We should reach the start of the pass by tomorrow afternoon. Do we keep going or wait?" Sylin asked. Since leaving Jerincon, no one had been held responsible for making the main decisions. It was a group effort.

Garin picked a string of chewed food from his teeth. "Many centuries ago, my people sought out dragons to kill. We suffered greatly and soon saw the folly in doing so, but the lessons learned have been passed down. Dragons have an acute sense of smell. I wouldn't be surprised if the reek of our little friend will give us away."

Maric snorted. "Not that we smell any better."

His brother nodded agreement and continued. "If Tragalon decides we are an easy meal, he will make short work of us."

Camden wiped his face. He couldn't accept what he heard. All he had accomplished in his short life was about to become undone. "Is everyone here insane? Or maybe you don't realize we are about to be a fried meal for a lizard?"

"Easy now," Garin said. "Nobody is going to die if we have any say on it. Fact is, I don't plan on seeing the wyrm."

"How can we escape, if it could already know we are here?" He was confused, and rightly so. "Why isn't your little friend over here to help us plan?"

"For one, he might be leading us to our doom," Garin theorized. "I don't give trust easily, especially to his vile breed. Second, we don't know whose side this dragon is on."

Even Sylin gave a start. "Whose side it is on? I didn't know dragons took sides."

"Most don't. You see, dragons have a highly developed sense of understanding. Once they choose a course in life, they seldom change. It just might be that this one is on the side of good."

Sylin doubted there were any people in the Free Lands who knew that much about dragons. Not even the great libraries in Meisthelm had so much information.

"Enough of the dragon. What do we do next?" he asked.

"Drive on and sneak around," Garin said plainly.

"Does any of it matter? We can't run faster than a dragon flies," Camden pointed out.

No one argued.

"When morning comes, we strike out and find the gnome's tunnel as quick as possible. Hopefully, we catch the dragon asleep and ride out from under his nose," Garin said with finality.

"If it is awake?" Talrn asked.

"We try to kill it."

Breakfast was eaten and the camp broken down before the sun rose above the highest peaks. Compared to the misery of the last few days, this morning held promise. The company was underway not long after the last pony was saddled. The air about them was considerably different. The litany of perils and dangers they had already faced were reduced to minor incidents. Nothing was as dangerous as what they were about to attempt. Despite the odds, they remained in good spirits. All save Isic the gnome.

"I can smell the beast already," Camden grimaced at the raw stench choking the trail.

Isic laughed. "This? This is nothing. The mouth of the pass is littered with sun bleached bones and reeks of brimstone and death. Almost enough to void your bowels. Tragalon's lair is yet far from here. Hours, I judge."

"We are prepared enough," Sylin said, his mind retracing the precautions taken while breaking camp.

"None of it matters," Isic said. "If the dragon can smell us, we are already doomed. Do you truly think to fool a four hundred year old dragon? Or perhaps it was an accident he managed to live this long?"

Garin leaned close to the gnome. "You just worry about getting us through this tunnel. Know this, if that dragon is waiting for us, you will be the first to die."

Isic tried to repress a gulp and hide his fear.

The sun dropped faster than anticipated. Shadows were quick to swarm over the light-depleted trail, making the mountaintops appear as jagged teeth. Haunting images worked in the quasi-darkness. Deceit seemed an endearing trait of the Grimstones. They halted shortly after, understanding time was against them.

The northern entrance to the pass was much warmer than the rest of the range, for dragons required heat to survive. Sulphur choked the air, making it difficult to breathe, even with the damp clothes each placed over nose and mouth. Fires reflected off the cliff faces sporadically. Bones lay strewn about, past meals of the beast. Sylin's horse snorted in fear. The ensuring pat did little to ease either horse or rider.

Then the group heard it.

The deep, resonating rumble of the dragon's breathing. It vibrated the ground. They looked to each other for support, hoping to find strength in each other. Sylin alone felt relief.

"I don't find any reason to be happy," Camden whispered.

Sylin almost laughed, "No? The dragon sleeps."

The timid gnome led them across the mouth of the pass where the great dragon slept. Fear of death from dragon or dwarf kept him to his word. Killing one dwarf was not going to expand his life or increase his popularity. He still wasn't sure who he was working for. Any way he looked at it, he was a dead man.

It took nearly an hour to move everyone across. The slightest stir of the dragon caused much delay. Sylin was the last to leave, subconsciously taking responsibility for the band. A sudden stirring when he was halfway across the pass mouth made him abandon caution. The rumbling was much stronger now, eventually transforming into a throaty laugh, nearly knocking him to the ground.

The dwarves in the tunnel turned in horror. They urged Sylin to hurry before it was too late. Sylin was frozen. He considered attempting his magic but it would take too long to bring up. There was no doubt in his mind that the dragon was awake. Awake and watching him.

"Well, has another manling come to steal my hide and rob my life? Or do I have another meal to satisfy my hunger?"

The dragon's voice dripped venom. Sylin closed his eyes and prayed.

TWENTY-TWO
A New Threat

The glittering spires of Meisthelm, proud capital of a beleaguered realm, lay enshrouded in darkness. Cold, cruel winter had come early this year, blasting mounds of snow and freezing winds across the lands. Wagon trains filled with refugees from the north streamed through the main city. They sought to leave the wars and find shelter in the south. It was a foolish dream, for all the lands were threatened.

Matters were worse within the city proper. Rumors of a massive darkling army striking east from Suroc Tol across the plains of Galdea had reached the population. Panic threatened to set in, despite the Hierarchy's best attempts at retaining calmness. Logic on the street said it wouldn't be long before that army was at their very walls, and with the Hierarchy army engaged in the south, the city was defenseless.

The High Council, what was left of them, was stuck in the middle. They'd been torn apart when the Black defected and Shali Kolm was murdered. Sylin Marth's inexplicable resignation further plunged them into chaos. War was fast approaching and High Councilor Zye Terrio felt powerless.

Alone atop the very highest tower, a woman shuddered from the cold and drew her cloak tighter. The worst of winter was yet to come but she was from a warm kingdom and still unused to the bitter cold. Three decades in Meisthelm and she still wasn't acclimatized. She looked up at the moon again and felt relief. It was almost time.

She left the grand view of the Wizard's Tower and made her way down below. The hustle of daily life was over but the night offered a great many promises. She was near giddy with excitement as her mind wandered to the news she was about to receive. Temperatures rose the deeper into the keep she traveled. Great furnaces kept the main buildings warm, as well as heating the water for all within the walls. Life was much better here than anywhere in the Free Lands, except for perhaps the cities of the elves.

"My lady," her bodyguard said, as she slid by. Without awaiting her reply, he fell in behind her.

She loved him for his undying loyalty. He was one of the few people in all the realm she honestly trusted. An admirable quality in these troubling times.

Her journey took her down dark passages seldom trod, for she was eager to keep her business private. She had once been a simple country girl who could stand the thought of others knowing her business. In part, that led to her leaving home to join the Hierarchy. People always found a way to learn precisely what she didn't want them to know. It was the worst of civilization, especially here in Meisthelm.

She reached the forgotten meeting chamber three levels underground. Few bothered to venture down this far anymore, not since the Wars of Separation. She enjoyed the espionage of it all. The ignorance of the present Council often made things entirely too easy to slip through their fingers. Just like now. She placed her hand on the handle and pushed.

The room was dark except for a miniscule flicker of torchlight she carried with her. It was also empty, or so she believed. She sat on one of the ancient chairs, after her bodyguard dusted it off, and waited for her caller. The guard was told to wait in the hall and be alert in the event she might need assistance. She didn't foresee any issues arising he might be able to handle though.

"You are late," a deep voice growled.

She started, her heart instantly racing. The circular chamber made it impossible for her to pinpoint where his voice came from and this left her worried. She reasoned that her life wasn't in immediate danger. For if he wanted her dead, he would have already struck. She searched the shadows but found nothing.

"You won't find me like that," he said, almost disappointed.

She faked a smile. "You might be surprised at what I can do."

She took the torch and rose. Not even a man of his incredible talent could hide forever. A light wind shifted through the chamber to kiss her lips. The simple caress almost aroused her. She frowned. This was not how it was supposed to play out. Evil, however, had other ideas. The raw power affected her in strange ways, making her do things a normal woman might otherwise not.

The power left her feeling alive as it enveloped her flesh in a lover's embrace. She kept a string of pets for these special occasions. Men and women no one would miss. Where was he? The longer she stayed within his grasp, the more urgent her desires became. She needed to conduct her business and return to her private chambers.

A strong hand reached out to grab her throat from behind. She choked.

"You are getting careless, Arlyn," he growled, displeased with her performance.

His grip loosened, allowing her to turn and face him at last.

"You fail to disappoint," she replied.

The Black Imelin released her and took a seat opposite of her. His ice colored eyes searched for signs of trickery or deception in her but there was none. Satisfied, he began.

"How are matters with the Council progressing?"

She laughed. "Zye Terrio remains locked in his pompous attitudes. He refuses to believe that Meisthelm is in grave danger. A few of the others support him but the real power is shifting toward Cagic Hlorn. He poses the actual threat to us. He's being pushed to making a bid for High Councilor. If that happens, this city will be mobilized and ready for war in short order."

The Black was not pleased but expected such news. "The army, where is Conn?'

"Near the Port of Grespon last I heard, though I haven't received any new information lately. I can only assume he's waiting for our allies to make a move," Arlyn said.

Imelin frowned. "The Baron has my orders not to engage unless provoked, correct? I need him to follow Conn's army back to Valadon. Getting engaged now does not serve my plans."

"Baron Mron is a competent enough man, if nothing else," she soothed. "I trust him enough not to get killed before our armies are in place."

Our armies? She takes liberties. He reached out to grab her by the chin. "Very good. You serve the cause well, Arlyn Gert. Continue to do so and you shall be rewarded when the time is right."

A tremor ran through her body. "I live to serve."

"When next we meet, I shall be before the city gates with my host. You know what you must do in the meantime. I expect all to be ready for my arrival," he released her and rose.

She bowed her head. "It shall be as you wish."

When she lifted her head he was gone, lost to shadows. A wicked grin crossed her face. The fall of the Hierarchy was coming and she was to be a main instrument in that demise. Arlyn called for her bodyguard. He closed the door behind him after entering and watched as she shrugged off her cloak and then dress. No emotion showed as he crossed the room and took her.

TWENTY-THREE
Tragalon

Sylin stood mesmerized by the great dragon Tragalon. The dwarves remained hidden in the tunnel, while they strategized the best way to kill it. Isic, for all his duplicity, cowered behind them. It was Camden who bade them all stay in place, honoring Sylin's wishes for the time being.

Tragalon crawled down the rock face to stand before Sylin. Human eyes stared upon his magnificence for the first time in a hundred years. His scales were deceptive shades of grey-green, shifting as the wind changed the shape of his fires. Sylin was impressed and horrified simultaneously. Two horns resembling ears stretched back to reach the spikes fins on his back. His eyes were as jewels, always alert and cunning. Claws the size of a grown man clicked on the mountain pass floor.

"Better men than you have come claiming my scales, manling. What makes you think you can achieve what so many have already failed?" Tragalon demanded.

Sylin cleared his throat. "I have not come to kill you."

The dragon laughed at him. "Clever man, but you will have to do better. No one enters this pass unless they are in need. You mortals are so keen to kill each other, it makes perfect sense why one would wish to make a trophy of my kind. My hatchlings have not left the Mountains of the Fang in generations because of this.

"Look around you, manling. Those are the bones of your predecessors. All filth who sought to best me. Even those foul smelling gnomes tried my might, though they ended a little more than a snack." Tragalon sniffed the winds. "I see you brought the little worm back for me. Very kind. Bring him out and I might consider letting you go."

Isic cringed under the thoughtful glares of the Stonebreaker brothers. There was no mistaking which way they were inclined.

"I cannot do that," Sylin replied.

The dragon was unimpressed. "You gamble the lives of your group on the miserable existence of one gnome? I think you a fool."

"All life is precious."

"Is it?"

Sylin struggled to retain composure. "Yes, it is. Neither you nor I created this world and neither of us have the right to decide who should live or die."

"You have courage, manling, if misguided. What do they call you?"

At last. "I am Sylin Marth, emissary of the High Council of the Hierarchy and representative of the kingdom of Coronan."

The dragon cocked his head in thought. "Places and people mean little to me. I know the world from views you have never imagined. This Hierarchy you speak of, I know the city well. Though it is a grand sight to behold, I am afraid I will remain long after its towers crumble."

"Then you know of the dark times sweeping over the lands? No one will be safe if it is successful. I'd have thought one of your stature would show compassion for the plight of the world," Sylin urged.

"Compassion?" Tragalon fumed. "You dare ask me for compassion when all of the mortal races have come for my hide? You overestimate yourself." He reared back on his hind legs and flexed those long claws. "I tire of speaking. Now, you die."

"Wait!"

Camden and the dwarves couldn't hold back and burst into the pass in an ordered, straight line. Only Isic was too frightened to act. None of them held weapons, for the dragon's fire would have melted them in an instant.

Tragalon eyed, recalling an old hate of dwarves. That they stood side by side with men was something new for him. "Impressive. Perhaps there are redeeming qualities among the mortal races. Tell me, Sylin Marth of the Hierarchy, why do you seek passage through my domain?"

"War is coming. There are a few of us chosen to stop it. We are limited and with few resources. If we fail, the world ends. Darkness is coming. My band and I seek the white wizard, Elxander. Only he has the power to stave off what approaches."

Tragalon dropped back to all fours and sat. His eyes took in the mixed group confronting him, amusedly noticing the lack of courage the gnome displayed. "What matters any of this to me?"

Camden spoke. "Dragon! Your life hangs in the balance as well. Do you honestly think this plague will pass you by? The Black has designs for all life. Yours included."

"That name, say it again."

"The Black?"

Black fumes spewed from his nostrils. "I know that name. He has murdered one of my kind and is a sworn enemy. How is it you let this finger of evil go so far as to threaten the world? I have seen lands suffer but nothing is as evil as what he rebuilds in the dark heart of the southern kingdom. A great castle is being constructed by an army of slaves."

"Dark times," Garin added.

"Indeed."

Sylin immediately tried taking advantage of the revelation. "Will you let us pass? We must reach the white wizard as soon as possible. Each days draws us closer to the end."

"Long have I been friends with Elxander. He will not help you," Tragalon said.

Sylin reeled. "But why? Even he cannot ignore the needs of millions."

"Hmmph. Your kind have ruined any chance you might have had. He was exiled by your Hierarchy. Your arrogance may have damned us all, Sylin Marth."

The dragon leapt into the sky, his wings beating a terrible tattoo against the rock and knocking them all to the ground. "Go, if you must. Though I doubt he is the salvation you seek."

Relief washed over them as they picked themselves up. Sylin was grateful for the dragon's indifference and equally troubled by word of Elxander. Was the wizard truly that far gone? If so, who would save the world?

"Bring up the horses," he said to the dwarves.

Camden clapped him on the shoulder. "Never had to talk down a dragon before, eh?"

"I can think of easier ways to spend my nights. We'll camp when we clear the mountains. I can't wait to see green again."

"What do we do with this one?" Talrn asked.

Isic sat on the ground under armed guard. He'd been caught rifling through their gear while the others had gone out to confront the dragon.

"Kill him and get it over with. Let him rot with the rest of his friends," Maric growled.

"Thief or no, we don't have the right to kill another so," Sylin defended. He hoped the dragon was well out of earshot.

"We are not where you come from, Sylin. Survival in this kingdom is based on strength and cunning. Strike first and hope to hit the target. If you miss, your enemy will not. What you people are going through, ours have already lived." Garin spoke softly, while glaring at the gnome.

Sylin shook his head. "No. We just won a minor battle against a creature who sees only in right or wrong. I don't want to jeopardize the small gain this soon."

"What then, do you suggest? He's too dangerous to keep," Maric said. "It would remove the chance for trouble if we got rid of him now."

"I won't let you kill him, nor is it wise to let him go. We still don't know what he was doing here. As you say, these are dark times. We cannot afford to turn our backs on anyone needing assistance. If he is a pawn of the dark, he will give himself away," Sylin said.

Garin snatched Isic by the shoulders and hauled him to his feet. "The gnome comes with us. Tie him up and put him on a pony. We leave now."

The dwarves set about their tasks in silence.

Waiting until they were busy, Garin stepped to Sylin. "I hope he shows his true colors before he murders one of us in our sleep."

"He didn't kill you."

Garin scowled but said nothing.

It took three more hours to exit the Hyber Pass and then work on down to the low, flatlands. Exhaustion, now a common factor, set in among both horse and rider. Most of the journey was done in silence. The dwarves resumed their naturally taciturn natures, all while remaining on guard for another hazard. Sylin got the impression they wanted an opportunity to bare their steel.

They made camp and ate a quick meal before sundown. Guards were set up for the entirety of the night, though whether it was for the gnome or his possible nearby friends, Sylin wasn't sure. They were deep in goblin territory now and the dwarves were certain their mortal enemies were now the gravest threat.

The night passed uneventfully.

"I don't think I've slept so good since leaving Meisthelm," Sylin yawned and stretched. "Any issues last night?"

Garin said, "Nothing of notice. A few coyotes sniffing for scraps. They went away hungry."

The sun was rising higher, showing them a broad expanse of grasslands stretching all the way from the base of the Grimstone Mountains to Xulan Lake far to the south.

"What do you know about this land?" Sylin turned to Camden and asked.

"There's not much here. It's all grassland and swamps from here to the lake. Goblins don't usually come over this way. I don't know why. There used to be a lot of towns and villages on this road but now most are ruins. Rumor says people have been disappearing."

Garin added, "Doesn't speak well for your wizard, if he's letting his people disappear beneath his nose."

The statement shook Sylin's resolve for reasons he wasn't sure.

"Or he's turned against the people," Camden added. "Good men do go bad. All I need to know is if he has turned, how are we going to stop him?"

Sylin decided to ignore the issue until they reached the Tower of Souls.

"Is there any place along the way we can stop to resupply between here and the lake?" he asked.

Both dwarf and journeyman quietly conferred.

"Two, I think. To the west is the town of Drun. Goblins use it as a supply depot, kind of halfway between here and Sadith Oom. Three days directly south lies Fallon Run. Mostly outlaws and people hiding from bounty hunters reside there. We should fit in nicely," Garin said.

"I don't think we need any more run ins with goblins. The mention of the dark land opens many questions," Sylin said. "Tragalon eluded to many ill goings on happening there."

Talrn growled disappointment from behind them. "It was quiet until a few years ago. Now, on a good night, you can see the reflection of fires over the mountaintops. Evil is at work again. Some say it is Ils Kincannon returned from the grave. Mothers tell their children how his ghostly armies ride the night."

"Is that what you believe?"

The dwarf laughed. "Fairy tales and horror stories. The fires. Those are real, for I've seen them myself."

"We ride for Fallon Run."

The next few days felt much longer, despite the pleasant weather and scenery. Temperatures remained optimal, especially considering the part of the world they were in. It was all too peaceful. Almost enough for them to forget the troubles behind them. They crested a small rise at midday of their third day's ride and looked down upon Fallon Run. It was a one road town with perhaps a half a dozen houses. The town was too small for the goblins to bother with. It was also the sort of place one might easily attract unwanted attention.

"Nice place," Isic sniffed, still offended at being tied up.

Garin resisted the urge to slap him in the back of the head. "Good enough for us. There's no sense in waiting here. Let's see if we can find a hot meal and cold ale. I'm tired of being in the saddle."

The tiny company trudged on to Fallon Run.

TWENTY-FOUR
The Free Rebellion

The desert was especially chill, worse than any he could remember in recent months. He and his band of rebels slowly edged their way across the empty wastes and back to the sanctity of their camp. Poros Pendyier and his band were cold, tired, and hungry. They'd proven their worth against a formidable enemy twice since leaving camp. It was past time for respite.

Leaders of the Free Rebellion argued at great length over the sense in letting the man responsible for a rebellion go out on whim to risk life and limb as no more than a common foot soldier. He, of course, won the debate. Cowards had no place in this world, he argued and continued to lead his rebels into battle. Not only did it inspire, it filled them with confidence.

Poros was sure the main body of his rebels had already incorporated the surviving liberated slaves from the supply train and were deep in celebration. He longed to be with them, drinking his way to the bottom of a bottle, but there were urgent matters needing attention. The lone surviving goblin intrigued him nearly as much as it bothered him. There must be a way to satisfy curiosity, without getting killed.

"What troubles you so?" asked Matis, the defected goblin guard.

Poros initially ignored him, so deep in thought was he. Moments later he answered, "I want to know where that goblin is going. We shouldn't have let him escape like that."

"You made the decision," grumbled a one-eyed dwarf, Dom Scimitar. "Should have killed him right there."

"Don't you tire of killing?" Poros asked.

Dom grimaced. "As long as you've known me, and as many times as you've asked that same stupid question, have I ever changed my mind? No."

"I'll stop killing when the war is over," they said in unison.

Both laughed and took heart when two men slipped from the shadows to halt them. Poros finally relaxed. It was good to be home. The sentries let them pass with mixed smiles. The air in camp was growing brighter with the victory. Yet another mission was being planned. Only three men had been lost but Poros secured enough supplies to feed the camp for a week. Not to mention increasing their strength by one hundred. The dead would be sorely missed, but the war raged on.

Poros led them in single file down a narrow defile of pale red canyon walls. There was but one way into the camp, though several escape routes had been established. Special tunnels had been bored out to prevent a death trap should the enemy discover them. The route led down to the river and on into the open plains of Guerselleorn to the northwest.

More guards were perched in concealed positions along the trail and yet more in a pair of watch towers at the canyon mouth. The structures were built with aged lumber and creaked in the wind. Guards watched with relief as Poros led the group into the camp at last. The mission was finished.

A bald man in a deerskin vest and pants saw them approach and made his way over. His arms were raised in praise. "Ah! The great and dastardly Poros Pendyier returns at last from his quest to liberate the world!"

"Chonol," Poros nodded. "As always, your tongue bleeds lies."

Chonol Distan was as much of a mystery to him as the lone goblin now heading off into the middle of the wastes. None knew where he originated and Chonol wasn't inclined to indulge them. He was a strong man, very well built and in remarkable shape for a middle-aged man. Most guessed he was once a soldier. Others thought him a killer in hiding. Regardless, none accepted his tale of being a simple villager.

His dark eyes widened as Matis rode into view. "A prisoner. Good. Are we going to execute him in front of all?"

Matis snarled, fighting the impulse to draw his weapon. Such action would result in instant death and paint a negative image on his new-found friends. Matis remained still.

"You should watch how you speak to people," Poros scolded. "It may get you killed one day. This is Matis. He is not a prisoner but a defector from that wretched army. His insight should prove most valuable in forthcoming operations."

Chonol snorted but said no more.

Poros turned to Matis and said, "Go with Chonol. He will find you billeting and food. We will speak again later."

Matis nodded. "Thank you, Poros Pendyier. I am indebted to you."

Grinning, Poros continued deeper into the camp. There was a man who desperately needed to speak with him. *Not that I need reminding. The old man always wants to talk.* He dismounted near the back of the bowl-shaped camp, eager to stretch his legs after a long day's ride. Hundreds of men and women stared at him with nods or smiles. Against all odds, he managed to carve out a tiny spot of solitude and more importantly, hope.

Poros found the old man exactly where he figured, resting comfortably on a mound of near rotted cushions. The old man made no move to rise. Age was not kind at the end of his life.

"Success again, Hesit," Poros announced.

Hesit Carnan coughed a laugh. "Measure it against the greater view. We are still locked in a battle with no hope of ending soon. I only regret that I will not be here on that final day."

"Don't speak of such. Inviting death is a fool's choice," Poros admonished. Hesit was right, however, he didn't have much time and there was no way a war could be fought and won in a short time period.

"I'd be surprised if I live past the next moon," Hesit barked a laugh. "This world is done with me, lad. I've outlived my usefulness. You are the future. A son of a simple farmer. You and your get. Do me proud, my son."

The words hit hard, especially since Poros only vaguely remembered his real father. Hesit stepped in and inspired Poros to do good. To be greater than himself. In truth, he didn't expect to outlive the war either.

"You need wine."

"No," Hesit replied. "I gave that up long ago. Water works for me."

He rummaged through a ragged clump of personal belongings and produced a dark brown bottle. "Elvenberry wine. I picked it up in Guerselleorn long ago. Very nice people, the elves. I should like to see one again before I die."

They stayed like that for a long while, neither knowing how to console the other. Finally, Hesit cleared the tears from his eyes and said, "You should go. I'm sure the ones you brought home will want to thank you properly. Go. I just wanted to rest my eyes on you again."

"But I…"

"Go. You are only young once. Enjoy it while you can," Hesit urged.

By the time he returned to the main camp, the celebration was in full swing. A few of the freed slaves recognized him and offered their undying thanks. He smiled and shook their hands without stopping. The more interaction he had, the more he wanted to be alone and reflect upon what the old man had told him. No matter how great the victory, he didn't know if it would be enough to replace the loss of a mentor, friend, and… father.

"Excuse me, sir," asked a female voice.

He stopped and turned to face her. She was young, not much older than her early twenties and he assumed, one of the freed slaves. What drew his attention was how in shape she was, almost too good for a former slave.

"Yes?" he answered.

She gave him that look of being slightly embarrassed. "I was just wanting to thank you for saving us. None of us had any hope until your men came along. Thank you so much."

"I was only doing my job," he said, with all modesty. "Where are you from? Who are you?"

"A small town in Guerselleorn called Nonicks." Sadness filled her beautiful eyes. "I haven't been home in almost a year."

Poros frowned. "I know how you feel."

"You do?"

"Yes. My family was killed by goblins when they raided my town. That was a long time ago." He didn't know why he felt compelled to tell his story to a complete stranger. "I am Poros Pendyier."

She smiled again. "I am Sharna Del."

He liked that. The defensive walls surrounding him slowly lowered, so strong was his initial confidence in this woman. Quietly his mind rebelled, but he could see nothing outward to spark alarm.

"I am not sure how to ask," Sharna said, "But I would be interested in joining your band and getting revenge."

Caution begged him to listen, but he ignored it. Poros couldn't look away from her deep eyes. "We do not fight for revenge, Sharna. All the men and women here fight for the continuation of our way of life. No man has the right to tell another what to do, especially one of the dark ways. We fight for our survival."

Her disappointment remained concealed. "That's what I meant. I'm willing to do anything, so long as I can help."

"Why do you feel so strongly about this?" He was confused. None of the others they'd rescued was so intent.

"If I can keep another innocent girl from being abducted and sold into slavery, I might be able to save a piece of me," she replied softly.

Sharna fell quiet, dropping her gaze to the ground.

He grabbed her hand. "There's nothing to be ashamed of. If more people were as strong as you the world might not be in such a bad way."

His words inspired another smile.

"Go and get some rest. Tomorrow is a new day and we have much work yet to do."

Sharna Dal went to sleep happy for the first time in a year.

Discussion began over a hearty breakfast. There was a vast array of concerns Poros and his fellow rebels needed to pour over, greatest of which being what would happen when the goblins finally discovered their camp. Poros did his best to calm the others but they weren't as accepting of his almost laidback choices.

"We are getting away from the importance of the matter," Dom Scimitar explained. Bits of partially chewed food spewed from his mouth. "We have defenses in place in the event of an assault. It is time to look forward to another offensive strike, rather than sit back on defense."

"He's right," Libek Tug, a bright-eyed gnome with a receding hairline and good nature seconded.

Chonol Distan spat out his food. "Absurd. Every little thing we do is going to draw that much more attention. Then what? I'll not end up in a goblin slave camp."

"I bet you wouldn't," Poros said, sarcastically. "Have you ever once found something worth fighting for to the end?"

"Not in this lifetime."

Disappointed, Poros turned his attention back to the others. "The castle at Morthus is nearly complete. It won't be long before goblins garrison it. With whom, is my question."

"My people are spread thin as it is," Matis said. "Most of our resources are going to the war with the dwarves. The grohls don't have the numbers needed to wage war, but they are in charge. No one is sure who controls them, however. Nor do we know who is in charge of Sadith Oom. There is much fear among my people.

"Some nights we see large creatures fly overhead. They come at random and always at night. There is a great evil keeping all in check. Much greater than anything the world has ever seen, yet it remains hidden."

Hesit Carnan coughed. "I think our mission needs to be to find out who this source of all fears is. It might be one we cannot face."

"Harder than it seems," Poros said. "A lot of good men and women are being ground down by this Hume Feralin. We haven't gotten close enough for a clear shot either."

"It is too early to go back. They'll be expecting another move. Too dangerous," Dom seconded.

Poros finished his meal and wiped his mouth. "I want to know where that goblin went."

All conversation stopped as they looked curiously at him.

Good. I've finally gotten your attention. "He didn't head off to the garrison and he didn't head for Grun. What else is there?"

Matis offered, "There is nothing else between Morthus and Grun. It could be he's trying to circle around and draw us off his trail."

"Perhaps, but I think he's got something more going on," Poros said. "I'll take five volunteers with me. We finalize our plans upon my return."

The debate finished, Poros rose and went in search of finding a handful of brave men, or abject fools.

Valk used as much of the terrain as possible to camouflage his escape from the slaughtered column. Enemy eyes were upon him. Common sense suggested the rebels wouldn't let him go. He was a threat to their safety. Valk also knew that the grohls would not let him live after reporting his complete failure. Goblins were fond of violence and wanton carnage, but Valk was wise enough to value his neck above all else.

Which is why he struck out across sun baked plains. He was certain *they* would help him, for their love of carnage was unmatched in this part of the world. They were his secret, a force unknown by all, yet capable of storming kingdoms through their strength. His only problem lay in trying to figure out how to sway them to his side.

Blazing heat and a lack of water combined to take their toll on him. The goblin moved slower, more lethargically. His canteen had been empty for some time, though he'd made it last as long as possible. Dehydration was second place compared to the promise of a quick demise should the rebels catch him. Valk had been in the service of the goblin king for three decades. Soldiering was all he knew. He'd seen his share of comrades and brood mates slaughtered over the course of numerous campaigns, but never was he as scared for his life as now.

Valk took shelter from the blistering heat for an hour beneath a large outcropping of boulders before setting back out at sundown. His destination still lay some distance ahead. While he wasn't certain how close *they* were, Valk knew their camp lay close to the one place in the world holding more power than the mythical spires of Meisthelm far to the north. His people's sorcerers and shamans refused to step within the unmarked boundary.

Lost in the dark corners of his memory was the human tale of Ils Kincannon and his army making their final stand on what was once grass covered plains surrounding Morthus. By all accounts, it was a harsh and bitter war, beginning a thousand years ago and continuing to this day. Kincannon died for the sins of using the Staff of Life, tool of the wizard's meddling in mortal affairs. For creatures like Valk, the effects of that bitter war were always with him.

His mind wandered over these thoughts as the next five days went by. His trek had taken him halfway across Sadith Oom. Valk had grown wise and started using the cover of darkness to move through. Leagues trekked underfoot. Days blended until he at last looked upon gruesome spears of rock and stone piercing the sky. Abandoned when the world was young, this was the root of all evil. Perhaps it had been intended for good, but no more.

Sheer exhaustion forced him to his knees, even as the entirety of the nightmare before him became visible. It was a terrible sight to behold. Fear pulsated off the structure in rippling waves. Mordrun Hath. The Forge of Wizards. He'd arrived at last. Now all he needed was to find *them*.

TWENTY-FIVE
After the Pain

Karin sat before the small fire with her head buried in her hands. The winter storms raging outside were momentarily forgotten, for the pain in her heart was grievous. A week had passed since she lost the love of her life on a suicide mission into the middle of the darkling army. A week of agony unprecedented and one she never thought to experience. Her tears were nearly dried, used up over the course of the last few days. Her body ached from constant sobbing, eyes burned red with rawness. It was a small price considering what Aron Kryte had given to the Galdeans.

No doubt the Galdean army had done its part and was on the move east and south, making all of them fugitives from the Black Imelin. Exiled with a handful of friends and a company of Golden Warriors, Karin had never felt less safe. Chances of success were slim but enough to keep them in hope. The Staff of Life was a heavy burden they never should have been asked to carry, much less abscond with halfway across the face of the world in efforts to save the Free Lands. Meisthelm was so far away and there was no safe place to hide out the winter.

The tender rapping on her door jerked her from the grips of self-torment. She wiped her hands over her trousers and answered the door. "I had hoped to be alone tonight."

Amean Repage attempted a smile but it felt awkward from the start. "I don't think you should be."

His age weighed heavily on him. A lifetime spent in service to the greater good, thoughts of spending time with his grandchildren, and the loss of a man he'd treated as a son, conspired to take him to his knees.

"I'll be fine," she insisted.

"Keeping all that pain bottled inside won't do you any good. You need to be around your friends. Believe it or not, it helps," he said.

Karin almost smiled. "Perhaps. I may have gone about this all wrong, but it hurts. How can you stand being a soldier?"

"You get used to it. There will always be an empty seat at the table or a missing face in the ranks. That's part of the great game. Men are born to give battle, Karin. A sad state, but one we have always excelled at."

She doubted she would ever get used to watching men die. Yet there were elements of truth lacing his words. Being alone was the worst thing for her. She needed the camaraderie the others offered to ease the pain. Extending her arm to Amean, she invited him to take her down to the common room and the warmth of food and friends.

The sleepy town of Drim lay locked in the throes of the first winter storm. Snows had been falling since early autumn and hadn't stopped. Whispers of the dark wizard conjuring this nightmare forth ran rampant among the villagers. The war had yet to extend this far north but it was only a matter of time. The majority of the Galdean army was on the move in southern Almarin, putting the capital of Kitenurem at risk. No one in Drim was concerned with that. All that mattered was getting through the most severe winter in memory.

Snow drifts braced the aged wooden buildings, the bland white brightened by the dark pink of the setting sun. Watchers moved about Drim, setting the oil lamps on each street corner. Ten darklings went unseen in the shadows as the watchers slid past. Their haunting red eyes glared brightly in the semi-darkness. Each bore a curved dagger. They'd been sent on the trail of the Staff by the Black Imelin but were given implicit instructions not to engage their enemy.

While the two armies played a cat and mouse game in the southern part of the kingdom, the Black focused on retrieving the Staff. He trusted his commanders to carry out his war plan. The Rovers were closing in on the Unchar Pass and the Hierarchy garrison stationed on the southern side of the Lilsen Mountains. Darklings harried Field Marshal Dlorn's army as it retreated. His only unanticipated difficulty came from the reemergence of the priests of the Red Brotherhood. Their meddling had led Aron Kryte to the Staff and escape beyond.

The Black fumed, but his efforts led the darklings to Drim. A pair of Golden Warriors marched by the darklings. The lead darkling instinctively crouched into an attack position. He was snatched roughly around the throat before he could jump. The Golden Warriors continued, oblivious to the scuffle in the shadows. The darklings, brooding at inactivity, watched and waited.

The common room was normally packed with warm fires, decent food, and a pleasant atmosphere. Tonight, it was empty except for the gruff veterans of the Golden Warrior company occupying Drim. Andolus and Long Shadow sat closest to the fire. One watched the door, while the other stared at the bottom of his mug. Across from them sat the rogue princess of Galdea, Elsyn. Since allowing the others to get used to her presence, she'd done her best to integrate. Fitting in with seasoned warriors was no easy task, especially considering her father was the late king of Galdea.

A bowl of hot soup steamed in front of her. She'd lost as much as Karin, at least in her opinion, for her love for Aron was no less great. She listened to the off color banter of some of the other soldiers at different tables and while blushing at prime moments, she successfully managed to keep a grin concealed.

"Are you all right, Princess?" Andolus asked.

She nearly choked on a partially chewed piece of... beef? "Yes, why would you ask that?"

Long Shadow snorted his amusement.

"Only because your face has taken on a different color," the elf prince smiled.

"How much longer do we have to wait here?" she asked, deciding it prudent to change the subject as quickly as possible. Growing up around soldiers didn't mean she was accustomed to their mannerisms while on campaign. Back home, they were trained to show respect and etiquette. War was another animal.

The door opened and closed. Andolus was the first to react as Amean and Karin at last arrived. "Ah, fair Karin Ilth, we were beginning to wonder!"

She offered a false smile, the best she could manage. "I can't hide forever. What's for supper?"

"Warm potato soup with a mystery meat and fresh baked bread," Elsyn supplied. "All in all, it's not too bad."

"I'd love some," Karin said and sat down opposite of Elsyn.

Amean accepted a mug of hot coffee and sat on a rickety chair by the fire. As much as it pleased him to see Karin out of her shell, it was time to plan their next move. They'd been in Drim for two days. Much longer and they invited danger.

"We should leave soon," he began, grimacing at the bitter taste of the coffee.

Long Shadow nodded his agreement.

Andolus set his cup of ale down and wiped the corners of his mouth. "The Black is still lacking our precise location to give him the advantage he needs. He's not sure who has the Staff either. Right now, his forces must be spread out across half of Almarin. Each group of Dlorn's soldiers has the possibility of holding the Staff."

"Making all the more reason for us to be away, sooner rather than later," Amean added.

"Getting back on the road will draw attention. When the Black does find out we have it, there will be no safe place to hide."

Silence settled over the group.

"Rest assured my friends, there is much wisdom in leaving, but which direction? Meisthelm is our ultimate destination but there is no way we can head there directly," Andolus quickly added.

"Kitenurem is a nice city," Elsyn chimed in. Her youthful innocence was pure sham. She'd spent years learning from Dlorn and men like Jent Tariens without her father's knowledge. Still, she was young and had just enough knowledge to get her into trouble.

Amean shook his head. "Absolutely not. They'll have all the major cities marked with spies and darklings. We need to keep going east."

"To where?" Karin asked.

The old veteran sat back and thought. His chair creaked, threatening to break under the strain. "Hyrast. There is no way our foe could have gotten there ahead of us. From there we can regroup, resupply and strike south at speed."

Andolus agreed. "Hyrast is a mountain fortress virtually impervious to assault. The Black will need much to break through their walls."

Strong winds blasted the side of the inn. Shutters slammed against the wood, creating an eerie song that sent chills down their spines. It was the first time since arriving in Drim that they felt uncomfortable.

"I saw something!" the innkeeper shouted suddenly and pointed toward the nearest window.

Golden Warriors lurched to their feet, hands reaching for weapons. Andolus was the first to the window. His keen vision pierced the gloom of night but failed to notice anything out of the ordinary. Whatever the innkeeper had seen was gone.

"Anything?" Amean asked.

The elf could only shake his head.

Amean went to the innkeeper. "What did you see?"

Shock twisted his face. "I don't know. It was small and dark. Some kind of animal, I think. Only the eyes. By the gods! I've never seen anything like them. They were glowing red."

"Damnation!" Karin cursed. She drew her sword.

"What was it?" the innkeeper asked.

Andolus' expression was grave. "A very, very bad dream, my friend. Pray you never see another."

"We must kill it before more come. It will report back to the Black," Karin immediately said. The stupor of her loss shed from her shoulders as the promise of battle emerged. She deplored violence but was wise enough to know how harsh the world was.

"There is always more than one," Elsyn said.

"She's right."

Long Shadow drew both of his broadswords and kicked the front door open. His actions left the others with no choice. They followed him outside. Howling winds slashed into them, a violent change from the serenity of their warm fire. Ice crystals formed on their exposed flesh as snowflakes drifted lazily down. Temperatures dropped considerably with the setting sun. Breath came out in thick plumes.

Long Shadow stalked across the street. His every movement precise, deliberate. His eyes never stopped moving. He was lost in the hunt and was rewarded almost immediately. The darkling never saw him until it was too late. Long Shadow struck with both blades, covering the distance between them in a span of heartbeats. The severed head fell with a mushy thump. Long Shadow crouched as the body fell. Blood showered down like droplets of rain. He knew there was more darklings close. He felt them.

The others hurried over to him, barely taking time to notice the body at his feet. Once, what felt like so long ago, they'd been afraid of the squat monsters, but those times quickly fled as the war progressed. Darklings were mortal. They died as easy as a man. Contempt replaced fear. Amean and the others searched the night for more targets. Together, they'd been efficient during the battle of the Crimson Fields. The Golden Warriors were responsible for more than their share of darkling corpses on those frozen fields. But for each one killed, a hundred more streamed out of Suroc Tol. Amean prayed this night wouldn't be a repeat.

"What now?" he whispered.

Two opposing forces stalked each other. One seeking only information, the other attempting to prevent the gathering of such. It was a matter of time before one made the first mistake. Long Shadow pointed down the winding street. None doubted his instinct. The twelve of them fanned out in a tight wedge formation and advanced. Karin and Elsyn, much to their protests, were secured in the center of the wedge. Two soldiers were sent back to the inn in the event the darklings attempted to enter.

They'd barely crossed the street when a muffled cry drew their attention. Amean hoped it hadn't come from the inn. Good people didn't deserve the fate awaiting them. Andolus slipped ahead of the rest and rounded the corner of the nearest building. There he found the body of a dying city watcher. Another was backed against the far wall, fighting for his life.

The elf prince looked at how much blood the man on the ground had lost and knew it was already too late. Sword brandished, he turned his attention to the survivor. Seven darklings had him cornered. An eighth lay dead in the fresh snow. Andolus dropped to one knee, using their distraction to set down his sword and draw an arrow. He fired. A darkling arched up in pain as the arrow pierced his throat. Another fell.

Karin reloaded her crossbow, even as the Golden Warriors rushed past her to make quick work of the remaining darklings. The battle was fierce and swift. In the end, all the enemy lay dead. The wounded guard they had cornered slumped to the ground and shuddered. Andolus reached out to close his already cooling eyes.

"Secure the perimeter," Amean barked, decades of service flowing through him on instinct. "There may be more."

"The guard is dead," Andolus announced with sorrow.

Too many innocent lives had already been lost in this war, with the promise of many more yet to come.

"What now?" Elsyn asked, oddly curious about the body. She'd become no stranger to death but found queer fascination in it.

"We leave tonight. Drim is no longer safe," Karin uttered.

Elsyn was shocked. "In the middle of the night? We'll freeze! And it will be easier for them to find us. They can see in the night, we can't."

"Yes, tonight," the elf replied. "We cannot put these people at risk out of selfish reasons. There are enough deaths on our hands already. I do not want more."

Amean turned to the Golden Warriors. "Go and rouse the others. We leave in an hour."

The lone surviving darkling skulked through the night. The others were slaughtered because they refused to cull their natural bloodlust. Their actions not only saw them murdered but condemned him as well. He had no other choice but to report to the dark wizard. The Black accepted no failure from subordinates and punished them with torture or worse. The darkling considered returning to Suroc Tol and going into hiding but Duoth N'nclogbar had sold out their race by pledging allegiance to the Black.

Eventually, there was nothing left to do but return to the wizard with news of the raid and the location of the Staff of Life.

TWENTY-SIX
Hyrast

The Black Imelin, last of the order of Black wizards, slept a familiar troubled sleep. The old dreams had returned to haunt him. Failure in Galdea hammered his conscience. An ancient world reawakened through his subconscious. Images of things he had done returned to him. The promise of solitude smashed into a thousand fragments with each setback. It was that future threat which shook him to the core. He saw his castle, the fortress-keep from which he intended on ruling the world in Sadith Oom, crumble to the ground. Watched his armies get crushed on the plains of Darkpool. It was the idea that Mordrun Hath had returned to the light which disturbed him most.

The visions faded, replaced by thick fog blanketing the ground up to his knees. His room dissolved into nothing. Then came the voices.

He shames us.

Yes, very shameful.

He disgraces the elder ones.

Imelin wanted to lash out and vent his wrath upon them, but knew he was powerless until *He* appeared. The voices continued their goading. He tried ignoring them. He always tried ignoring them, but they burrowed into his mind and roosted. Magic flared through his veins. He struggled with the desire to attack. Too bad they were already dead.

At last his summoner arrived, materializing from the mists and fluxing shadows. Tall and surprisingly diminutive at the same time. Traic stared down on Imelin with clear disdain. His was an old tale. One of obscure misery. Tasked with taking the Staff of Life to be destroyed, Traic was largely ignored by history sagas. It was his master, Ils Kincannon who claimed all recognition.

Forgotten and abandoned after the last of the Knights of the Seven Manacles fell in battle, Traic spent the remainder of his sad life in exile. He died penniless, a broken wreck of a man he might have otherwise become. That longing to be more than what he was drove him. The way he was so callously discarded after years of faithful service, twisted his heart into a wicked thing. Now, in death, he was finally about to claim vengeance on the man he once idolized and the world he allowed to continue.

If only Imelin was stronger.

"We are not pleased, Imelin," Traic scolded.

Imelin feigned nonchalance. "You, who are not in the realm of men? You, who are banished to eternal suffering for your lack of vision? You are not pleased. I am not overly interested in the quality of your feelings, ghost."

The chorus of voices wailed in anger.

"You mock us as would a child. Has your ignorance risen so high? Perhaps we chose wrongly. Perhaps the young lordling Aron Kryte is more powerful than anticipated. We have looked down the wrong paths."

"Perhaps I could destroy you for good right now. I don't have time for games, banished one," Imelin said, even as he reeled in shock. The very thought of being discarded threatened to shatter his carefully built world.

"Find us the Staff of Life or you shall suffer a fate worse than that of Gulnick Baach."

"Where is it? Your Kryte has stolen it!"

Yes, from under your nose.

Shameful.

Embarrassing.

"My armies scour the kingdoms but without results. I should lead them directly to Meisthelm without the Staff and end this war in one fell swoop," Imelin snarled.

The indignity of being addressed so chafed him deeply.

Traic scoffed. "Suicide! You'll fare no better than that fool Kincannon at Sadith Oom. The Staff is the key to total domination. Without it, you cannot win. The Staff is on the way to Hyrast. You continue to fail."

"Fail!" spat Imelin. "I expect one of your nature to know intimate aspects of that word, for did you not fail your lord and master? The Red Brotherhood is destroyed, wiped from the world by my hands. No longer do the guardians of the word keep the children safe during the cold winter nights. This is the time of my ascension to godhood and a handful of vanquished souls dare proclaim me a failure?"

"Arrogance is a weakness you can ill afford. A single cell of the Brotherhood has been destroyed, nothing more. One happened to escape the wizard fire and is on the path against you. Your enemies grow stronger despite your limited success. The entire world seeks to unite against you." The ghost fell silent and began to fade.

Imelin was disturbed by the news, though he refused to show it to the ghosts. The most crucial part of his campaign was about to begin and there was no time for doubt or self-recrimination. The surreal world faded with Traic, leaving him alone to ponder the future.

They rode as hard as possible, always using the cover of darkness to keep prying eyes away. It had been days since the murder of King Elian and the battle of the Red Brotherhood beneath Galdarath's streets. Days since the three survived hardships and trials previously unexperienced. They now formed a band, a sort of fellowship, determined to keep the evil of the Black from spreading.

One was a broken, battered member of the Red Brotherhood. The sole survivor of the devastating assault that saw the Staff of Life leave Galdea. Another was a proud Galdean soldier who decided that the quest was more important than his own life. Kings came and went, but it was the duty of all when life was threatened. The third was an ancient mage from a forgotten village deep in the ruined land of Sadith Oom. Her powers kept them alive, where they might have otherwise died. For her, the quest was one of redemption.

Galdea was already far behind them. A land none thought to see again. The sorrow of leaving waned quickly, for there was a more important task to be carried out. The guardsman took leaving the hardest, for so many of his brothers had fallen under the blades of the darkling incursion. The priest of the Red Brotherhood knew that while he was the last of his cell, the order remained strong. They now rode to Meisthelm and the head of his order. So secretive was the Brotherhood, that the High Council didn't realize it thrived under their noses.

The mage saw things no other soul could and it was at her heeding they departed Galdea so quickly. The Hierarchy was the Free Lands' best chance for surviving the growing darkness. The armies of darkness had finished with the Galdeans and were now concentrating their might on Valadon and Trimlon. The High Council was blind to events transpiring around them. That was her only theory for their inactivity in the north. She prayed that ignorance was not as great as she surmised.

They rode on until the cityscape of Camerene came into view. Deep in southwestern Trimlon, they were still many days from the ultimate goal of Meisthelm.

Harrin Slinmyer was the first to notice the signs of danger all around them. Signs of massive bodies of soldiers moving through Trimlon were everywhere. Either a great battle was about to occur or one had already happened. The Lilsen Mountains were a day south and the Unchar Pass was more than wide enough for an army to pass smoothly. The invasion of Valadon was close at hand.

He insisted they consider Camerene a hostile town until they were able to discern who the soldiers belonged to. The others agreed and using discretionary magic, worked their way down to find a room for the night. They spent hours trying to think of ways to get around the massive army somewhere ahead of them. The dangers faced in Galdea were but a prelude to what the war promised to erupt into.

The ornate meeting chamber of the High Council, usually bright and full of life, the symbol of the Free Lands, stood half empty and void of cheer. Messages from across the kingdoms had been overwhelming them. High Councilor Zye Terrio, at last, knew the meaning of despair. His army was far to the south, battling brigands in the Port of Grespon. No word had come from the Golden Warrior contingent to the north and the rogue Black Imelin seemed to be having his way with multiple kingdoms, while the Hierarchy sat impotent.

"We cannot escape the reality of the situation," Cagic Hlorn growled in his rough, sailor's accent. His flame red beard and hair made him stand out in any crowd. "The Black is moving against us and we are near powerless to stop him."

Zye arched an eyebrow. "What do you propose we do? Surrender?"

"Out of the question!" spat Farill Halse, the representative from the Wilderlands. "We must fight if we expect our way of life to continue. I'll not stand by and watch as you hand over the keys of godhood to this traitor."

Arlyn Gert and Jesni Bercobin, the two surviving women on the council, conferred quietly in the far corner, much to the notice and consternation of the others.

Cagic snapped, "Anything you wish to share with the rest of us, ladies?"

Jesni shot him a false smile, while folding her arms across her stomach.

Arlyn answered for them both. "Our armies have already been recalled from Guerselleorn, correct?" Zye waved her on. "We make our stand here. The greatest city in the world with the might of Conn's full host, will be able to stand against the armies of darkness. A fitting way to end this story if you ask me."

"How many troops have already arrived from the outer provinces?" Zye asked, seeing certain wisdom in her plan, yet also the opportunity for great failure.

"No more than five thousand currently."

His eyes bulged. "That is all?"

"Our allies are already taxed beyond measure. The dwarves are locked in a bitter struggle with the goblins. That conflict threatens to spread north into the Wilderlands and south into Sadith Oom," Arlyn replied calmly. "Our war, though it may have priority above all else, is not the only one needing to be dealt with."

"The Hierarchy was established to maintain order throughout the Free Lands after the fall of the Seven Manacles. We are the ones who run this world and decide precedence of matters," Zye slammed a palm on the table.

Arlyn laughed at his inability to fathom what transpired against him. "Are we? Look around, Zye Terrio. Your precious world is crumbling and nothing we have done has so much as stalled that end. The elves, those who remain, have all but abandoned us after Dol'ir fell. Few believe in our power. We have failed the world through the negligence of our actions. How have you become so blind to this?"

"She's right," Cagic said unexpectedly. "The current problems are the result of our ignorance. We should have been able to see the Black's rising treachery and ended it before all of this but we somehow became lost in the importance of our own myth. We have but one course of action left to us."

"That being?"

Farill narrowed his gaze and quietly said, "Prepare for invasion."

Just beyond the range of archers stationed in the guard towers, stopped the column of Golden Warriors. There they donned their resplendent armor and full weaponry for the defenders of Hyrast to see. Curiously, they rode with open hands. Amean Repage decided that in doing so, they would present a professional appearance as well as leading the soldiery of the mountain fortress to believe them on official Hierarchy affairs.

Not as warm as the thick riding furs comforting them during their harried flight northeast, the armor served as a reminder to all who bore witness, that the Golden Warriors continued to maintain a sense of order through the rising darkness. They were both feared and respected in all the Free Lands.

"Commander!" called the first lookout to spy the intruders. "A column of riders approaching!"

The bearded commander of the watch made his way, grumbling about the cold, to the young scout and raised his looking glass. Surprise twisted his face, for he had never seen so many golden armored warriors in one place. It had been decades since the last delegation had arrived and then it had been as heralds for the war with Aragoth. His stomach turned.

"Open the gates. Tell the city leaders that the Golden Warriors have returned."

The steel gears groaned as they shook off layers of snow and ice. The Hierarchy's finest soldiers once again entered the mountain city of Hyrast.

Princess Elsyn stared at the multistoried buildings of the city proper with the eyes of a newborn. Built into the mountainside, each building was drab grey and massive in scale. She wasn't used to the disordered structure of being dug out of the mountainsides. Even the cobblestone roads were mottled grey and black. Everything blended with the snowcapped mountains surrounding Hyrast. The city was so unlike her beloved home of Galdarath.

The column rode up the winding main avenue akin to memories of old parades held in Meisthelm. Windows opened so all could bear witness once word of their arrival spread. Many citizens were eager for news of both the war and from the south.

Amean slowed to a halt and let the column ride on, searching out the highest-ranking man, for city soldiers now lined the roads. "You, soldier, what's your name?"

"Dreyfus Hlee, sir."

"My men need room and board. Also quality stables. Our horses are tired and in need of care," Amean instructed. Without waiting to see his orders carried out, he turned to one of his sergeants. "Have the men divide into three groups. Do standard routines before bedding down. I'll take the command group and schedule a meeting with the city council. I want all group leaders to meet at the Pincer tonight for debriefing. Take charge, sergeant."

The Golden Warrior clasped his fist to his chest and wheeled to the head of the column, barking orders along the way. Impressed with the youthful vigor, Amean felt the weight of their journey slowly bleed away.

"It appears that we were expected," Andolus said, once the veteran approached.

They looked up to see a squad of soldiers in cloaks and plumed helmets halt not far away. Each wore dark black armor with the white bird of peace emblazoned upon the breast plates. Their leader stepped forward, with a hand held up in greeting.

"Warden Ferest welcomes you to our humble city. He awaits you in the zocalo. My name is Jamez Storm, commander of the city defenses. I am your guide, so to speak, during your time in Hyrast. If you would, follow me."

"He seems pleasant enough," Karin whispered to the elf.

Andolus replied, "Almost too much. This city does not feel right. We must be cautious."

Amean grimaced. The words were not what he was looking to hear.

Warden Orlninc Ferest was seated in a flowered area at the rear of one of the common areas, quietly conferring with a scarred and hardened dwarf. He was a middle-aged man of relative good health and came from a well to do family who'd had their hands in Hyrast's political arenas for generations. He gave off the appearance of being well groomed and pompous in his mannerisms. Amean judged him the sort to hold his secrets close around. Walls went up and the Golden Warrior went on guard.

Jamez presented them and took up position by the entrance as Orlninc bade them all to sit. The half-smile on his face suggested duplicity. He introduced his companion. "This is Jalos Carb, our resident war master from the Drear Hills. He seems to have taken a liking to our little city. Not that I can blame him. This is the place where I'd wish to retire once the kingdom is done with me."

"This city has good bones," the dwarf said.

"What brings the Hierarchy here, after so many years?" Orlninc asked.

Amean accepted the mug of water and took a deep pull. "We are at war. The last of the Order of Black Wizards has turned traitor and threatens to end the world. My soldiers and I are… spreading the message across the Free Lands. The Black has already gone through Galdea and is operating in southern Trimlon and eastern Coronan. No doubt these troubles will make their way here to Hyrast."

The warden feigned shock. "Here? We have committed no offense to the Black. This kingdom hasn't been part of a conflict since the wars with Aragoth. I can see no reason for his wrath to come down on us, commander."

"You don't understand the nature of the Black," Karin said with venom in her voice. "He has already stormed through the most powerful kingdom in the Free Lands. What makes you think you can withstand him here?"

"I do love a strong woman. To the point, what makes you think he'll come here? I should think Meisthelm would be his prime target if what you say is true."

"Do not worry too much about us," Jalos said. "We have strong defenses here and are virtually invulnerable. These soldiers can hold their own."

"Dwarf-friend, we do not doubt the strength or conviction of your forces, but you will be whelmed in short order. My people warded the pass at Dol'ir for hundreds of years but even we could not stand against the might of the dark wizard and his darkling army. This city will fall," Andolus fell silent and remained so, confident he had said enough to convince the defenders of their folly. Elves and dwarves weren't always the best of friends, making any conversation potentially volatile.

"We have heard enough for one night," Orlninc intervened, upon spying the dwarf clenching his fists. "I can arrange accommodations for you within the inner city, if you wish."

"No, thank you, Warden. We have already secured billeting," Amean declined.

Orlninc stood, smoothing his cream-colored robes in the process. "Then I shall at least see you for breakfast?"

"That is acceptable. Until tomorrow."

The Warden's eyes flit left. "Jamez, please show our guests the way out."

The door closed behind them, leaving Orlninc Ferest and his guest alone. Beads of sweat trickled down his forehead. He wasn't accustomed to being debated in front of subordinates.

"What do you think?" Jalos asked. "They could be telling the truth."

Orlninc disregarded him. "I don't think so. The Hierarchy plays at something we do not know. I think they hide something important from us."

"What of the wizard?"

He laughed. "A ploy to lead us away from the truth. If you are that worried, I'll order a patrol down to Kitenurem for confirmation. Good night, Jalos."

The war master left him alone, eager to be rid of the company. Dwarves had no tolerance for the games of men. Orlninc was glad for the solitude. So much had occurred lately, he wasn't sure which way to lean. The door suddenly opened and all but one of the lights blew out. He blinked to get acquainted to the reduced light. The dark figure of a man stood before him. The smell of fear washed the area. Orlninc had never felt such.

"Do they have the Staff?"

"Th… they didn't say," Orlninc stammered.

He hadn't counted on the dark wizard returning to Hyrast so quickly.

The Black Imelin stood in silent disappointment. His spies mentioned nothing of Aron Kryte being among the Golden Warriors, though Traic was convinced he still lived. "I want them watched. Ensure they do not leave the city for at least a week. They carry an item I want. Do not let them leave."

His words curdled the Warden's blood. He knew fright and exhilaration, as waves of power pulsated off the Black. A man like that could do much to elevate his position in the kingdom and Orlninc grinned, the vacuum the new power order would leave.

He gave the wizard a political smile. "Do not worry, my lord. They will remain here or die trying to escape."

The Black slid closer, his form blurred. "I do not want them dead. You die if they do."

In the blink of an eye, the wizard disappeared, leaving Orlninc confused. The promise of persecution left once his mind began playing scenarios revolving around his rise to power. Soon, if all went right, he would hold the crown of Trimlon and perhaps the keys to the very heart of Meisthelm. He left to begin his work.

TWENTY-SEVEN
Unchar Pass

Choking columns of black smoke billowed up into the sky, fueled by dozens of raging fires as they devoured the ground below. The wreckage of homes and a multitude of barricades were reduced to charred remains and abandoned dreams. A once proud fortress lay broken to the verge of ruination. The garrison stationed here destroyed.

The attack came shortly before dawn, during those grey hours forever trapped between light and dark. It came without warning. Enemy forces swarmed the northern end of the Unchar Pass and poured through right up to garrison walls. They were in the village before the defenders had time to react. The defense, ragged as it was considering the situation, held out for nearly a day before the darkling attack from the sky broke their will to fight. Never had soldiers of the southern kingdoms battled such foe.

Three hundred Hierarchy soldiers had been garrisoned at Unchar. All lay dead. They fought bravely and died as warriors, with sword in hand, but they were overpowered by a massive army of Rovers and darklings. The Rovers burned the village, killing a fair amount of the populace before some commanders decided the violence was too much and they offered safe conduct away from the battlefield.

Their offensive stalled once they tried to storm the castle walls. There they discovered that every cook and squire had been summoned to defend. Rover forces took heavy losses before retreating into the village ruins. The invaders redoubled their efforts, this time with a column of darklings at their front. This, too, stalled. Unchar held until the scrathes arrived and dropped scores of darklings inside the castle. Hierarchy soldiers took heavy toll of their enemies but the end was never in doubt. Unchar fell, opening the road south to Meisthelm for the Black's armies.

Bodies of men, women, and children littered the snow. It was a sad testament to the atrocity of war. None were safe from the dark wizard's wrath. The ragtag army of Rovers picked through the remains, looting the peasants and burying their own. Many good men, good and evil alike, lay dead beneath the blade for reasons few, if any, understood.

Denes Dron, the half-crazed leader of rogues, strode like a king through his newly conquered territory. His past as a general of Aragoth resumed from where he had been forced to flee. The defeat suffered at Krim Salat was finally being avenged. Yet, he was only slightly impressed with the victory. Trust of the darklings was limited. They churned his stomach each time one got too close, filling his mouth with bile. Puppets of Imelin's, they were a constant reminder that his Rovers were replaceable.

"Not as organized as the Aragoth army, is it?" asked Ute Hai, as he limped up.

Denes sneered. "Too gory for you, Ute?"

He knew his senior lieutenant advocated letting the civilians go and was poised to abandon the war altogether over philosophical disagreements with Denes.

"I've been through worse."

"These darklings have spoiled what should have been a grand victory for us," Denes continued, while thinking of ways to dispose of his chief rival without rousing suspicion among the men. Given the opportunity,

Ute Hai might easily rise to be equal in power. Denes couldn't have that.

Ute placed his hands upon his hips. "We should have never sided with the dark wizard. He has done nothing but thin our ranks."

"Blasphemy will get you killed, my friend."

As much as he was displeased by the comment, Denes knew Ute was right. The Rovers had operated on their own since being branded rogues from their kingdom. That destiny was no longer theirs to control. Ute was thoroughly convinced they'd been sold into slavery, a growing sentiment among the ranks. It took little imagination to see them being slaughtered by darklings once their usefulness was outlived.

"Is it blasphemy to consider the safety of my men ahead of naïve dreams of glory?" Ute asked sharply.

Denes' frustrations were compounded by the aggressive enthusiasm the Rovers displayed upon seizing the village. Most, if not all, of his chances for success had been effectively erased. He maintained allies in the upper levels of leadership, but the balance of power was decidedly swinging against him. His one chance of removing his opponent was to wait and hope to find a crack in the armor.

"I could have you struck down for less. Have you forgotten the years of exile and suffering we've endured? This is our one chance to strike back at those Hierarchy usurpers. Don't you want to be able to go home again? To live a normal life once more?"

"I have no home. None of us do, Denes."

Denes was confused. "The Hierarchy robbed us of everything and you dare show sympathy for their citizens?"

Ute Hai spread his arms mockingly. "Look around. Is this how you want our legacy to be remembered? Puppets to a great evil and his army of demons? I find no honor in any of this."

"Honor is irrelevant, Ute," Denes stepped over a darkling corpse. "This is our last chance to erase the pain we know, to win back our lands and take control. You look around. Our fighters are long in the tooth. They grow weary of living on the run. It is time to go home."

He'd lost the edge in his voice.

"Aragoth will never be restored to past glory. The queen is dead and a ruling body friendly to the Hierarchy has taken the kingdom in different directions. We don't belong there any longer."

Denes' eyes sparkled with vehemence. "Then we go elsewhere. It doesn't matter. I grow weary of running about forests and living like an animal. Pick a kingdom. I'll speak to the Black and it will be done."

The mention of the wizard sent chills down Ute's spine, violent memories of the night they met, coming back to torment him. He could see the darklings dropping from the trees to shred one of his friends to ragged strips of flesh. This was the sort of man Denes Dron now idolized.

Laying a hand on Ute's shoulder, Denes said, "Go and have the men pitch camp. We are supposed to wait here until the other half of darkling armies arrives. Open the castle's food stores and prepare for a celebration. A great victory calls for a great feast. Tonight we live like kings!"

Both riders gingerly guided their horses to the lip of the highest point of the Unchar Pass. They were surprised to find it unguarded, but a confident army would not believe the road just traveled would hold danger. The scouts saw the smoke before they smelled it. Wafts of fresh wind brought them acrid smells of charred flesh and raw terror. They kept riding until they were awarded the sickening view of what remained of Unchar. Deplorable as it was, the scene was minor compared to the disaster of the Crimson Fields.

Using a looking glass, the scouts witnessed the full extent of the damage. The darkling-Rover army must have made short work of the diminished garrison and villagers. It was the size of the darkling army that gave the scouts pause, for they'd been expecting the majority of the army to be in the empty lands between Galdea and Trimlon.

"We should get back," the first said. "I don't like the look of this."

The second bowed his head. "They never had a chance."

With the garrison at Unchar destroyed, there was nothing to prevent the enemy from marching right into Meisthelm.

"It's nothing we didn't face a mere week ago," the first answered. "We must be away before we are discovered."

"And the army?"

He reined his horse and wheeled about. "So long as it waits here, we have a chance to get back to the Field Marshal and hope he can bring our army in time. Now, let's go."

The scouts stealthily retreated through the pass, eager to avoid darkling or Rover traps and be back on the southern plains of Trimlon and then the army beyond.

Hundreds of grey-blue tents blended with the snow-covered rock and naked trees. Tens of thousands of exhausted men, wounded and healthy alike, tried their best to find a measure of peace before the next phase of the campaign began. Each tent was allowed a small fire, for the leadership wasn't worried about being discovered. The tents were made of dense fabric capable of concealing all but the smell of smoke.

The command tent was bustling with activity, even at the late midnight hour. Fabric walls segmented the tent into three areas: the officer's mess, an operations center, and a sleeping area for the commanders when not on missions. More than a score of men, all haggard and near their breaking points, filled the operations center.

Field Marshal Dlorn, an aged man by every standard, ran a thickly veined hand through his thinning grey hair and took the opportunity to step away from the intricacies and arguments accompanying so many men with varying opinions on how to conduct the war. He'd served the throne of Galdea for four decades and never dreamed of enduring such a desperate struggle.

"How can you suggest we return to Galdarath? What are we supposed to do then, wait for the eventual end, when the Black remembers he hasn't finished us off?" fumed Calri Alsimmons. He was by far the youngest, yet highly experience, infantry commander. One of the many heroes of the battle of the Crimson Fields.

The man he addressed, the former master gunner promoted to commander of the artillery after the death of Reeler Monchere, fired a contemptuous sneer. "Why should we drive south to save the Hierarchy when our own kingdom is in jeopardy? They never came to our aid and the lone company of Golden Warriors left before battle began!"

"We must look beyond selfishness for the greater good of the Free Lands."

Bernt shook his head. "And leave an entire army free to pillage the kingdom? I understand you are you and full of youthful ignorance, but war is an ugly matter."

"Yes, it is ugly," Dlorn intervened with a long sigh. "And I seriously doubt either of you are as familiar with it as I."

Calri's cheeks flushed.

Dlorn continued. "Sit, both of you. Now is not the time for division."

He went to the map table, making quick study of previously unfamiliar territory.

"It has been a week since we managed to escape and recollected the majority of our forces. Scouts report the Black's army is stalled in a laager here, just across the river. We have a good three days on them. If we can convince Felbar to join us, we might be able to pinch them between our two forces."

"At least to the point of rendering them combat ineffective," Daril Perryman added.

Dlorn nodded. "Provided we aren't too exhausted ourselves, we should be able to pursue them all the way back to Suroc Tol and reoccupy the fortress at Dol'ir."

The elven representative stiffened at the mention of his fallen home. Elves had held the fortress for centuries before finally being overrun by darklings at the onset of winter. Now that it had fallen, Jerns Palic had no desire to return to the ghost plagued ruins.

"I would just as soon stay from there. My people will remain with you until the end of the war, but no further. We have kin in Lilhaven and are weary of mortal ways. A new age is dawning and there is no place for elves in it. We will fade quietly and let men do as they must, but we will not return to the remains of Dol'ir."

His words hung heavily on the air, no one quite believing what they had just heard. Elves had been vital to the world since the formation of the Free Lands. It was sobering to hear that they would soon be lost forever.

Dlorn stewed over the elf's words, deciding to address them later, and continued with the more pressing issues. "First, we must figure out who is going to head back to Felbar's keep and convince him to aid us. As you all recall, he failed to assist in either of the previous two campaigns. This brings up questions of loyalty. When the darklings attacked Galdarath, he did little to aid, though he knew we were going to need his five thousand swords." Dlorn kept to himself the fact that he was supposed to help protect the king but was rumored to have disappeared in the middle of the raid. Felbar was a traditional ally of the throne, but these were bitter times and the defection of the king's own minister of state set suspicions on end.

A guard burst through the main tent flap with an excited look. "Sir, the scouts have returned from Unchar."

"Have them get something to eat and see to their horses, then have them report."

"Yes, sir." The guard saluted and disappeared into the night.

Discussions of the different scenarios the scouts returned with immediately broke out. There is no certainty in war, but the only way to win a war, was to plan for every eventuality. Dlorn left them to it. Even the greatest battlefield generals needed sleep.

Dlorn returned the salute and gestured toward an empty chair. They were alone now, most of his commanders following his example and going to find their own cots. Dlorn studied the scout for signs of duplicity or worse.

"Relax, son," he said, noticing the nervousness the scout exhibited. "Start from the beginning. Tell me what you witnessed."

"The enemy has taken Unchar."

"How is that possible?" Dlorn was confused. The garrison should have been able to hold out for weeks and there was no mention of enemy forces that far south.

"As near as we can figure, their main army split in half. The ones we saw weren't the same ones we fought between the Twins, sir. There was a force of Rovers with them."

"Rovers?"

The scout nodded. "Looked like just about all of 'em, too."

Dlorn blanched. This was ill news. No one had suspected the Rovers were in league with the Black, though in hindsight, it made sense. Their inclusion in the war changed a great deal. He now had a human element to plan against. A very capable one at that.

"How bad is the damage?" he pressed.

"They've taken the pass and razed the town. Looks like they are setting up camp inside the fortress as well. We left two days past. Didn't see no survivors."

Two days. If the darkling now held the pass, they had an open road all the way to Meisthelm. If that city fell, the war was as good as lost. It also meant that the other half of the darkling army would soon come barreling toward them.

"Thank you, son. That will be all." He shook the scout's hand in thanks. "Go and get some rest. You've earned it."

Sleep still clinging to their tired eyes, Dlorn's commanders assembled in the dark hours before dawn. Tension was higher than earlier, though none knew the meaning of this summons. They didn't have to wait in speculation long. Dlorn arrived and immediately called for quiet.

"I am sorry to have rouse you this soon, but our situation has changed drastically. Our scouts have returned with grave news. The Black has fooled us all. While we were busy fighting in the north, he secretly split his army in half and force marched the second half south to the Unchar Pass. We know the first is still somewhere in Almarin, presumably looking for us."

"If they decide that the Staff of Life is more important than finding us, they will shift most of their strength north to Hyrast," Lestrin, commander of cavalry said. His men and animals needed rest more than anyone, save perhaps Calri's reduced ranks.

"Perhaps, though I doubt they would waste their time devoting an entire army to stop fifty people," Dlorn answered. He paused to check the reaction of Jou Amn, the single Golden Warrior who'd volunteered to remain with the army. Nothing. "Not when the open road to the heart of the Hierarchy lies open before them. The key to this war is Meisthelm. If it falls, the world dies. We must move quickly."

Calri looked up with red streaked eyes. "What of the Hierarchy army? Where is it during these foul days?"

Dlorn had no idea. "General Conn is a capable and confident man in command of the finest… second finest army in the Free Lands."

Chuckles rippled through the crowd.

"Whose strings are pulled by the High Council," Lestrin growled.

Dlorn frowned. "Gentlemen, you speak as if we have a choice when the path is already decided. One army lies before us while the other hurries down from behind. We have no choice but to march south and retake the pass."

"What happens if we are caught in that bottleneck?" Jerns asked.

"We die."

In the span of two short months, the world had devolved into a nightmare. Anarchy boiled over. The embattled survivors of the Galdean army were caught in the jaws of the pincer. A move too late and their war would be over. Dlorn knew, as did they all, that their backs were against the wall and they had nothing left to lose.

"Order the full mobilization as soon as dawn breaks. I have no intention of getting this army trapped like a bear in his cave. It is up to us to try and save the world until we get word of Conn's force. Tonight, gentlemen, we attempt to save the world."

They returned his salute and set about planning what would amount to Galdea's finest campaign.

TWENTY-EIGHT
The Dagger Trolls

The last thing Valk remembered was being cracked on the back of his head and the world spinning into darkness. When he awoke, he found he was bound with heavy chains, unbreakable. A quick looked showed him that he was in a dark room with no natural light or ornamentation. There was a festering stench assaulting his senses, making him gag. Once his eyes adjusted to the gloom he discerned broken skeletons and rusted chains littering the chamber.

He had no idea how long he'd been held captive. His stomach growled, threatening to cramp. He felt weak from dehydration. But were they effects of his march across Sadith Oom or from prolonged confinement? Whatever his captives had in mind he figured they needed to do it fast before his body started to consume itself.

The heavy groans of a cast iron door opening roused him from broken sleep. Pale light flooded the room and he cringed away. Large hands fell on his shoulders, hauling him to his feet before dragging him away. A burlap sack was placed over his head. He growled, tried to fight and was rewarded with a punch to the gut. The blow sent him to his knees before he was thrown over a shoulder and carried off.

"Set him down," ordered the deepest voice he'd ever heard.

The ground rushed up much faster, and harder, than he anticipated.

"Where did you find this one?"

"Snooping around the outer walls."

"Take the hood off. I want to see this miserable goblin before we eat him."

Laughter, guttural and foul.

Valk at last saw his captors. They were massive with iron skin the color of slate. Long, cruel fangs protruded from their bottom lips. All wore large hoop earrings and had savage, black hair tied off in topknots. They were monsters of men, much larger than normal trolls. These, Valk knew instantly, were the fabled Dagger Trolls. Yet another of the long lost races of the past.

"Tell me, little goblin, why have you intruded upon us?" their leader asked.

Valk struggled to a seated position. "My name is Valk and I have come to enlist your aid."

The trolls gathered around him laughed.

"Why should we help you? We kill goblins for sport."

"I can help you break free of this prison. Regain your past glory," Valk cringed as he spoke. He truly had nothing to offer.

"I am listening."

Thousands of years ago, the Dagger Trolls had complete control over all of Sadith Oom and the surrounding lands. A coalition of elves, dwarves, and wicked men beat them back, nearly rendering the clans extinct. They were reduced to a vanishing breed, without allies or interaction with others. Alone and unexpectedly, they'd turned Mordrun Hath into a home.

"Don't you wish to regain control of Sadith Oom?" Valk pressed.

Another round of laughter.

"The wizard owns these lands, little fool. Not even we are so foolish as to face him."

"Everyone dies," Valk protested.

"Including us," the troll turned to his guards. "Throw him in the pot! I want to dine on goblin tonight!"

"I can take you to the humans!"

The troll held up a staying hand. "So, there is something to you after all. I am Mard, son of kings. Perhaps we can speak after all." He looked to the one eyed troll standing to his right. "Prepare the feast. I shall hear what this thing has to say."

Mard settled back on his cut stone throne and let his mind wander to days when his kind once again were dominant.

Libek Tug watched with his naturally sharp eyes for signs of recent activity. Gnomes were especially known for their abilities of scouting and spying. Crouching beside him was the surly Dom Scimitar. The old dwarf had been sent along in the event Libek ran into more trouble than he could escape.

The rest of the ten man party was an hour behind. Their objective was to avoid enemy contact, while locating the surviving goblin and discerning his intentions. Thus far, the journey had taken them halfway across the Plains of Darkpool and out into uncomfortably open country. The flames from the Towers of Perdition turned the northern skyline pale orange, even from this great distance.

Libek wiped the sweat from his high forehead and took a sip of water. "Tracks are getting harder to pick out."

Expecting no less, Dom said, "That makes sense. He has to know he'd being tracked. What I want to know is what happened to the rest of our men. They should have reported back by now."

"Could be they all ran into a goblin column and were captured," the gnome suggested.

Dom shook his head. "No. We would have seen signs of struggle. There's nothing here, just a few tracks off on the plains. I don't think he's headed for any safe haven."

"Then where?"

The dwarf pointed to the east. "Mordrun Hath."

"That's crazy," Libek gulped. "There's no one there but… trolls."

The dwarf gave him a soured look.

"It still doesn't make any sense. Trolls don't like anyone, especially goblins. They'd kill him."

"And our men," Dom finished.

A slight wind kicked up particles of sand. Much of Sadith Oom had been reduced to a wasteland after the fall of Ils Kincannon, much like the ravaged southern expanse of Eiterland to the north.

"What do we do?" Libek asked. He didn't like the idea of men he called friend being murdered at the hands of the trolls.

Dom rose and stretched his legs. It was a difficult decision, but one he had no doubts on. "We keep moving. Keep laying a trail for Poros to follow until we can find out more. Maybe we might even be able to take down one or two before our time expires."

Libek resisted the urge to cry. "You do realize these are Dagger Trolls?"

"Yes."

"And we have no idea how many they number or where they are."

The dwarf's smile was more of a glare. "If we die, let us ensure we do not do it alone."

Hefting his axe over a shoulder, he resumed the trek across the dust choked plains of Darkpool. There was an enemy awaiting.

Poros Pendyier wasn't the one to sit back and wait while others went into harm's way. He knew from lessons taught by his father when he was a young boy, that the only way to earn respect from others, was by leading by example. It was a lesson well learned after witnessing the horrors of war firsthand. Pride and determination forced him to accompany his dearest friends as they marched into danger.

His usual group rode with him, along with the additions of Matis the traitor goblin and Sharna Dal. She remained an enigma he was determined to figure out. These were the men and women he felt most comfortable being around. Ones he knew would sacrifice their lives for his and vice versa. They had a long, hard war ahead and he needed all of them.

"What was your village like?" Sharna Dal asked, once they paused to rest the horses. She managed to get him alone.

Poros struggled with what to say, the question catching him off guard. "It was quaint as far as villages go. Easy going. The people were friendly. But that was long ago and many leagues away. There is no way I can ever go home again."

"Not even after the war?" she asked, with a pleasant smile.

He admired the way she wore her hair, pulled back just tight enough to form a long tail swishing halfway down her back. "Who is to say it will end at all?"

"Good point."

He sighed. "My home was torn apart and burned to the ground by goblins and trolls during a slaver raid. Few of us managed to escape. Those who did comprise the majority of the men and women you saw back at camp."

She cocked her head and said, "You care much for them."

"All of them. Without them, I fear I would lose who I am and become another face lost in the night. They make me who I am and I've sworn my life to keep them alive. Of course, there will be empty places at the supper table when this is done, but they won't die alone. I shall be right there with them."

"You choose death over life?"

"Freedom over slavery. I'll not surrender just to live out the last of my days in the slave pits of Morthus. We have sworn to fight the oppressors. There are but two options, victory or death." His words were filled with conviction and passion. He looked up to see timid fear spark in her eyes. "I… apologize. It is a subject I feel strongly about."

She tried to smile. "I shouldn't have pried."

"Barren Town," he said.

"Excuse me?"

"It is the name of my home, or at least what used to be my home. I lost almost everything there, but the best of what I would ever have is right here with me. I could not ask for better companions."

Sharna felt the first inklings of true passion building within. She found Poros mildly attractive but for reasons she didn't understand. It had been so long since she'd last known love, she wasn't sure how to react, or if it was love. There was certainly kinship. The surge of evil ravaging the southern kingdoms was responsible for her degradation as well.

"What about you? I'm told, it is only just that you do as well," he asked, eager to have the pressure placed on another.

"Nonicks is a simple town, not quite so small as most others in southern Guerselleorn. I was caught on my way home from the fields one evening. I think the hardest part to accept was my abductor was a man from my own village, though he'd been publicly shamed and exiled many years before."

"What did he do?" Poros asked. He was determined to unravel the mysteries surrounding her.

"He murdered an innkeeper and his family for six copper coins and two Hierarchy crowns." Sharna shuddered as past images flitted through her memory. Twisted bodies. Blood. Screams of horror.

"Why wasn't he put to death? Such a crime should not go unpunished."

"My people handle situations differently, or so I've come to understand, from the rest of the world. They figured that by sending him off into the middle of the empty lands without food or water and a means to defend himself, he would suffer a fate far worse than execution for his crimes. The suffering is key."

Poros was glad he'd never heard of her village before. The punishment described practically outweighed the crime.

"Do you remember him?"

She paused just enough for Poros to pick up on. His suspicions rose. She was hiding something but if he tried to find out what, he risked being shut out permanently. Poros suspected her of being more than the humble village girl she played at from the moment they'd met. What he needed to know was whether she was a danger to his people or not.

"I'd rather not speak of it," she replied, almost too quietly.

He switched tactics. "Don't you want to go home again? Back to your loved ones? You have to have a certain interest in the others waiting for your return."

The last bit was pushing but he didn't want her to find out he didn't trust her.

She blushed and shied away. "No. No one special enough to miss me like that."

Sudden commotion among the others ripped Poros from the conversation. Matis slid from his pony and knelt beside a hand drawn symbol drawn in the sand. Poros immediately went to the spot and rubbed his chin in thought.

"It is a sign from Dom and Libek. They have gone ahead to Mordrun Hath," Matis said after Poros asked. He was confused, however, for the last part made no sense. It was pure suicide. Not even the goblin army ventured there.

"They're going to get themselves killed. We need to catch up with them before it's too late," Poros uttered.

He hurried back to his horse. Time was fleeting.

Libek fell to the ground from a bone crushing blow by the larger of the two trolls. Dom knew that his friend was dead before he hit the dirt. The dwarf took a glancing blow from a ridiculously thin rapier. While the blade was weak, the power behind the blow was enough to drive him to his knees. Deep red blood gushed from his wounds and his entire left side was in pain. He grinned savagely, even while knowing there was no escape.

Summoning every last ounce of strength, he swung his axe in a blow that would have severed a normal body in half. His hardened steel bit deeply into the troll's thigh before getting lodged in the bone. Dom looked up a split second before a massive fist smashed into his left shoulder. Bones snapped. Dom cried out in pain and fell back.

"No! Wait!" snarled a voice from the unseen distance.

Dom blinked through the tears and was surprised to find the very same goblin they'd been tracking lurking behind the trolls. He cursed and spat but a heavy hand on his broken shoulder kept him from moving.

"We need him alive. Throw the dwarf in a sack and bring him back to the keep." Valk laughed, as the dwarf finally passed out from the pain.

"What about the gnome?" the wounded troll asked after wrenching the axe from his flesh. Black blood and chunks of ragged flesh tore away with it, though it was of minor concern.

The goblin snarled at the impish body. "Leave him. I want our enemies to see what happens if they continue to follow us."

Prisoner in tow, they headed down the short road to Mordrun Hath.

Tears welled in his eyes. For a brief moment Poros clung to the hope that the mangled heap of flesh was something other than his friend, but it was fleeting. His apprehensions were realized when he got close enough to make out the remains of Libek Tug. His heart ached as he dropped down beside his friend. Death was a constant in war, but there was no way to get used to seeing friends so carelessly slaughtered, almost as if in sport.

Poros closed the stricken gnome's horror filled eyes, while the rest of his group formed a security circle around them. There was every chance that whoever had done this was still in the area.

"We cannot stay here," Matis urged. "Bury him and let us be gone."

Sharna nearly snapped. "You insensitive bastard! This man just lost a friend and you treat it as if nothing happened. What gives you, goblin, the right?"

Matis snarled. "We may all end up like this if we stay much longer. I have no desire to die this day, not like this."

"He's right," Poros said after rising. "We all know the risks. The same could happen to you or me at any moment. Help me bury him so we can move on."

"What about Dom?" a dull eyed soldier asked.

Poros looked around. "There's no body. We must assume he is either a prisoner or still free. Now come. We need to get moving before we become victims ourselves."

A harrowing hour passed before they were able to dig out a shallow grave and lay Libek Tug to rest. His grave was unmarked and would soon be lost to the shifting sands and wind. Poros bade him farewell. Soon his ghost would join those of the thousands already wandering across Sadith Oom. The dead held sway in the nighttime hours, giving him pause to consider how many friends now wandered aimlessly for all time. Would he join them?

Saddened, the tiny band followed the trail to ancient Mordrun Hath. Matis slowed the closer he got to the forbidden area. The Forge of Wizards was an evil place, wicked and filled with hate. Rumor said it was where the Staff of Life was created, long ago in the dawning of the world. Regardless of the history, Mordrun Hath was a place filled with despair and the last of the Dagger trolls. Goblin units were instructed to stay clear of the area for leagues.

He cringed as the ruined fortress came into view. It was once considered impregnable and purposefully built a hundred leagues from everywhere. Only the main tower resembled any sort of strength, jutting into the sky well over two hundred feet. The ruins of smaller buildings, with roofs shaped like dragon spines, cluttered around the main keep. It was a dead place where only dark things were possible.

"Are you certain of this?" he asked.

Poros wasn't, but it was too late to turn away. "Yes. The trail leads here. We need to know if there has been an alliance formed. These trolls are a shadow power we won't be able to contend with."

Matis shook his head, his knees trembling. Knowing Poros had condemned them all, he continued moving. Boulders the size of small houses rose up, blocking the sky and reducing his field of vision. His skin crawled. The goblin was about to voice his concerns and urge them to turn back or find an alternate route, when a score of trolls emerged from cover to surround the group. Weapons were brandished by both groups.

Poros acted quickly, knowing that the trolls would make short work of his underprepared group. Hands empty, he raised them high to show he meant no ill will. The trolls moved quickly, disarming Poros' group and binding them. They were now prisoners of the Dagger Trolls.

Mard watched from a blackened window halfway up the main tower. The stories he'd heard of these resilient, self-proclaimed heroes were accurate, if foolhardy. He thought that leaving the gnome behind for them to discover was brash but it had been so very long since a man had last killed one of his kind. There was no risk in it. The tiny band continued crawling closer, surprisingly ignorant of any traps lying in wait. Mard was almost impressed.

He considered the dwarf languishing in a cell far underground. The dwarf had provided amusement during the torture, and he looked forward to continuing, but the promise of so many others, and of different races, made the troll leader grin. His ruminations were disturbed as he watched his warriors capture the intruders.

Valk's restless breathing as he entered the chamber disturbed him. "You continue to find ways to annoy me, mongrel. I should have you flayed and then boiled."

"They are crafty. You should be cautious," Valk gestured down.

Mard burst out with laughter. A horrid sound like boulders being crushed. "You think them a threat? Fool goblin."

"They killed many of my kind."

"Goblins are no match for trolls. Nor are humans. They will give me information or end up in the same pot as you," Mard snapped.

He returned to his vigil until the prisoners were marched inside the main keep and the gates slammed shut.

TWENTY-NINE
Alive

He couldn't recall a winter as cold as this, especially one so early. Bitter winds coming off the river were intense enough to make him want to turn away, to return to the comforts of his cottage, but he needed to fill his stomach. The prospect of going hungry another night drove him on. Like most of the others, he'd been caught short by the sudden onset of winter. He only hoped there was still some sort of game ranging the lightly forested area he called home.

He'd been out since sun up but didn't begin to feel disappointed until well into the afternoon. He hadn't come across a single track or living soul. Perhaps the next day would turn out better, or later this day. His stomach growled to emphasize a point. He had food, some, in his cottage, but not enough to last through the latest storm. Discouraged by the lack of progress, he was about to return home when his dog growled and padded toward the river. The hope of fresh food grew and he followed.

What he saw was anything but. He watched his dog paw at something lying in the snow. A man half his age lay twisted along the bank. More bodies lay up and downstream. The man wasn't a problem. He'd seen other less fortunate ones before. The river had a way of claiming the unsuspecting. It was the other bodies that bothered him. Squat, covered with hair and teeth. Clearly predators. But what kind?

Sounds of battle echoed down over the last few days, leading him to believe that the northern kingdoms were at war. Not that it bothered him. Kingdoms were always quick to settle grievances with violence. He remained away from civilization, sticking to places where life was still pure. He'd long ago given up on mankind, seeking comfort among his dogs. At least they never disappointed. Seventy-one years of life had taken a great toll on him and he was content to live out the few remaining in solitude.

Even the best plans go awry.

Setting down his bow, he reached down to turn the man over. Ice covered half of the face and hands, with clear burns from prolonged exposure evident. He figured the young man was dead for there seemed little possible way anyone could survive such. Yet, went he bent down to listen, he was rewarded with very thin breath! The young man was alive.

Ignoring the nagging feeling in his stomach warning him away, he helped the young man away from the river. The old man had no choice. He'd never killed a man nor did he wish any ill. It took an hour to construct a makeshift litter. The dog sat beside the body, as if guarding it, the entire time.

He returned to the dog when finished. "Well old friend, it seems that no matter how hard we try, we just can't avoid our own kind. This one's in bad shape. He should be dead already. I don't have a clue how he's survived this long."

The dog glanced at the pallid body with sympathy.

"Come on, let's get home before the sun sets."

The return trip lasted much longer than his foray out. Age and the added weight conspired to wear him down but he eventually returned to the warm comforts of home. For his kindness, he was rewarded with coming across a brace of rabbits too slow to outrun bow or canine. Those rabbits were now cooking nicely over his hearth as he saw to his dogs, for he had several, and brought his new charge inside.

He marveled at the lad's inner strength and will power. Never in his years had he heard of anyone surviving the frozen waters. It went against all odds. Setting a pot of fresh coffee to boil, he couldn't help but admire the feeling of authority wafting off the lad. Almost as if it held magical property. Oh, he knew all about magic, didn't he? Magic and the host of dangers that came with it. He also instinctively knew that this boy was special.

Seeing no progress, the old man ate his meal and went off to bed, somehow confident neither of them were in danger.

They went through the same routine for a week. The old man went out daily to forage for food, while the young man remained in a coma-like state. One day the old man decided he needed to venture up to where he'd heard the battle occur. Perhaps answers would be found. Instead of answers, he felt his heart burst. The living were gone, their tracks buried under fresh snowfall. Most of the dead were more of those grotesque creatures, though a hearty portion were the men of Galdea. Broken pennants and burned siege weapons littered the ground.

He wiped his tears. There was nothing he could use here. Nothing he wanted to associate with. Walking away, he knew better than to hope there were survivors. No one was meant to survive a horror so bold. He did his best to avoid looking down into the frozen faces, all of those pleading looks reaching out from the next world. The young man in his house was a mistake. He knew that. Why the gods decided to let him escape this nightmare was beyond the old man. Then again, perhaps he wasn't supposed to know. Life was often easier spent in ignorance.

He made the long trek back to his cottage, mind filled with more than he wanted or needed. So many dead. Why? He searched his memory, desperate to recall those monsters. Once, he was certain, he knew them. The familiarity was haunting, mocking him with obscurity. Confident he'd eventually remember, he knocked the snow off of his boots before entering the front door.

His mouth dropped open a moment after. All three of his beloved dogs were sitting properly on either side of his previously unconscious guest. Curiously, they allowed him to pet them. The old man repressed a frown. He was fortunate if they let him do that.

The young man cracked a weak smile. "May I please have some water?"

The old man helped him to the table, for he was still very weak and malnourished. They enjoyed a thin soup and homemade bread.

"Name's Jod Theron," the old man said. "I've been out here for years. Don't often see many others. 'Specially ones I pull out of the frozen river."

"How did I get here?"

Jod swallowed the last bite and drank deep from a mug of ale. "Found you on the banks, half dead and by all means, you should have been. I ain't never seen the like. How you lived is beyond me. There were several other bodies with you, though none human."

He got up and refilled his guest's bowl. "You are a very fortunate young man. Much more so than all of your friends upriver."

Recognition sparked in the young man. "The battle, is it over?"

"I should say so," Jod grimaced. "Been over for days now. There's a lot of dead men up there. A lot more of those monsters."

"Darklings."

Jod dropped his head. He had hoped they weren't. That he was wrong. "I thought as much. It's been a very long time since I last heard that name. Must make you important, eh?"

"I am Aron Kryte, a commander in the Golden Warriors and caretaker of the Staff of Life."

They spoke long into the night, Aron telling Jod the tale of the battle of Crimson Fields and the harrowing flight from Galdarath after the death of King Elian. He also spoke of how he was entrusted with the Staff, though he didn't know why. Compelled wasn't the right word, but Aron didn't feel any malevolence lurking beneath the surface. It felt good getting the secret off his chest, even while knowing he might pay for it later. His tale ended with the breaking of the rope bridge and his plunge into the Simca River.

That the world was in danger didn't need saying but he did anyway. Understating the importance of what the Black Imelin's defection meant served no purpose. Jod initially refused to believe it. He'd lived through the war with Aragoth, seen what men were capable of doing to one another, and couldn't see why anyone would willing instigate another, far more devastating war. He'd even been at the final battle of Krim Salat, a name that made Aron cringe. The Golden Warrior had been forced to kill former comrades that day and in doing so, invoked the wrath of a dead man's brother. Everywhere he turned, there seemed to be a man waiting with a knife for his back.

Jod laughed at the comment and slapped a palm on the table. "You seem to have an abundance of enemies for a man so young."

"It does appear that way."

"I recall a time, back before you were born, when times were happier. I was on a special envoy mission to the Isle of Illusions, deep in the heart of the Jemman Sea separating us from the rest of the world. We ran into foul weather and many travails but overcame them all at small cost. All it took was a bit of skill, and heart." His voice trailed off in fractured memory and tender dreams. "Much happier times."

Aron fought the urge to fall asleep, wanting to know more of his mysterious rescuer. He lost.

He awoke shortly after dawn, hungry and still feeling drained. His strength was steadily returning but weakness continued to grip him. Gradually, his thoughts turned toward his friends and that doubt of whether they lived or not. Closest to his heart was his newfound love, Karin. He suddenly longed just to look at her again. To smell her hair after she climbed from the bath. Just being around her enriched his previously dull life.

"I know that look," Jod said, handing Aron a cup of coffee.

"What look?"

"Love. I knew it once, long ago."

Aron asked, "What happened?"

A dog lifted his head up so the old man could rub his neck. "Now, that is a very old memory. Back before these ill wars when the monsters were locked in their dark kingdom. Even the goblins were pleasant enough for a time. She was a queen. A proud young woman from Guerselleorn. That was before the Hierarchy lost control of the kingdom, of course."

He paused to gauge Aron's reaction.

The youth did well to hide his feelings. His face remained passive, void of emotion, though his mind remained troubled. The Hierarchy was the source of all problems. Already crumbling before the Black turned traitor, the High Council was steadily losing control of the Free Lands. It was only a matter of time before the end.

"A glorious time," Jod continued. "We saw each other for three years before I was called away to another kingdom. The dwarf and goblin nations had erupted into war over petty land disputes. Isn't it always something petty? By the time I returned, I learned my one true love had died in childbirth. I was devastated. My child and great love, lost in the span of a breath. Everything I held dear was ripped away. I … I never forgave myself for leaving.

"Nor did I forgive the Hierarchy and the arrogance of the council. They stole half a year and a family from my life. I would never know happiness again. My resignation was unconditional. The Hierarchy abandoned me, so I left them. I left everything. My life, reputation, wealth. All of it, so I could come here."

"Doesn't it get lonely?" Aron asked.

"Every day."

Aron drank his coffee, thinking over Jod's sad tale. Distressed, he went to one of the three windows in the cottage and stared out into the snow. So pristine. So perfect. He thought of his own lost love. There was no telling where she was now, or if she still lived. Imelin might well be in possession of the Staff and moving south already. But if Karin was still alive, she should be on her way to Hyrast. He needed to go there. To find out for sure.

"I must leave."

Jod had already guessed as much. "I've been waiting to hear that since you awoke. Suppose it was only a matter of time. You just remember one thing, never do a thing because you have to. Do it because you want to."

"Thank you for your counsel. You are a wise man, Jod. I appreciate what you have done for me. I wish there was some way I could repay you, but you have caught me shorthanded," Aron was almost apologetic.

Jod rose. "When do we leave?"

The response threw him. Aron didn't expect the recluse to offer his aid. Nor did he wish to accept. So many had paid since his company left Saverin, what felt like years ago. What right did he have to ask another to sacrifice his life for a cause he no longer believed in? Besides, if the Hierarchy was so willing to abandon Jod, wouldn't they be willing to do the same to him?

"It is not going to be pleasant, or easy. I cannot vouch for your safety. There is a darkness rising that threatens the Free Lands and I am running straight for it. Nightmares and foul magic await me. Are you sure you really want to return to the ways of men?" Aron asked.

Jod Theron grabbed his walking stick from behind the front door and said, "I've seen the best and worst this world has to offer. What's one last adventure before my time expires?"

Aron smiled.

"Though," Jod continued, "I suggest leaving on the morning. We can't cross half the kingdom ill packed and hungry."

"We just ate."

Jod pat his stomach. "There's always room for more, my young friend."

THIRTY

It All Comes Together

"He's here!"

Denes Dron looked up from the remnants of his morning meal. Partially chewed bones and a chunk of moldy bread decorated his plate. Lips pursed, he pushed back from the bench and failed to keep his apprehension from showing. The victory his Rovers had won at Unchar Pass was confidence building but not enough for the dark wizard. Denes harbored no false illusion that his position was secure, despite reassurances given to Ute Hai over the course of many arguments.

"That didn't take long," Ute said from across the table. Fear of Imelin kept the smugness from his face.

Denes shot him a snarl. "You'd do well to mind your tongue. He's not the sort to cross with short words."

Truthfully, Ute had no intentions of speaking with the wizard at all.

"Perhaps I should remain inside," he ventured.

"I doubt the choice is yours to make," Denes replied and slipped into his wool cloak.

The Rover leader marched out into the winter day, gloom twisting his features. He found the Black riding into camp on a coal black stallion. Snow kicked up with each footstep. Plumes of cold breath marked their passing. He reined up and climbed down from the saddle a meter away and raised his cowl.

"Lord Imelin, it is an unexpected visit," Denes said.

"Why is the army laagering here?" he demanded.

Dread filled the Rover. There would be no pleasantries this day. He'd be fortunate to escape with his head still attached to his shoulders.

"We are consolidating our position in the event of a Hierarchy counterattack. This is the enemy's home territory. Columns of Golden Warriors could be anywhere."

Imelin snorted. "The Golden Warriors are few. Their ranks thinned, thanks in part to my efforts on the High Council. With the threat we represent to Meisthelm, there will be no incursions this far north."

"But my lord, we will leave an unsecured border. It wouldn't be pru…"

Imelin straightened. Waves of dark power surrounded him. "Prudent for what? This campaign must be conducted with speed and ruthlessness. Taking Unchar was but a stepping stone to opening the road south. My army does no good sitting here as winter deepens."

Denes Dron didn't know what to say. He'd hoped for at least a week to recover and refit for the push south. That idea died immediately.

Imelin continued. "How many casualties taking the fort?"

"Too many," Denes admitted, knowing the truth would cause less pain than watery deceit. "Several thousand darklings and a few hundred of my men."

"The garrison was less than three hundred," Imelin snapped.

"They fought like demons. It took multiple attempts to take the walls."

Imelin began to pace. The losses, while acceptable given his true numbers still funneling down from the north, bode ill for the coming campaign. There was no way one hundred and fifty men, even heavily defended, should have been able to kill thousands in a matter of days. He needed to rethink his strategy for taking Meisthelm. Even with Conn and the main army mired in the deep south of Guerselleorn, the city would be filled with soldiers and a handful of wizards.

Fortunately, those wizards were like poor wine, thin and half of what they should be. He knew from Arlyn Gert that several battalions of Golden Warriors had been recalled from various outposts across the Free Lands. That alone might be enough to stall this half of the army. Stalled for too long, they'd be cut off from aid and slaughtered. No. He needed to find a way to get the entirety of his army to the city before they learned of what happened in Unchar.

He stopped and looked back over his shoulder to Denes. "*You* had command of the demons, Dron. They should have been able to take the fortress with far less casualties. Perhaps your leadership lacks authority?"

"N… no of course not. My command is unquestioned."

Imelin turned to Ute Hai. "Is this true? Does Denes Dron inspire confidence among the Rovers or should I replace him with one more… capable?"

Ute knew he should have stayed in the building. Not followed Denes to this meeting. His best efforts at going unnoticed failed miserably. "Denes has been our leader since the fall of Aragoth. He's led us right thus far, wizard."

"Indeed. That war was long ago. Mostly faded from memory by the majority of the world. I fear the Rovers are a thing of antiquity and your methods outdated. Change is necessary. Change from the highest levels down."

"Master Imelin, I must protest this treatment! My men are experts at what they do."

"Your men are now mine and I will do with them what I see fit. Do not seek to question my authority, Rover. Am I understood?"

Denes balled his fists and took a defiant step forward. "If I disagree?"

Ute watched the scene with rapt fascination. While he had no desire to lead the remnants of the Rovers, he also didn't wish harm to his onetime friend and leader. He slid back and to the side as Imelin lashed out. Black bolts of raw energy sped from his fingertips. Snow and ice melted around the trio. The blast caught Denes in the chest, throwing him in the side of the building. Bone and flesh crashed upon the stone. Blood spit flew from Denes' mouth and nose. He dropped to the burned ground. Unconscious.

Satisfied his example had been made, Imelin turned back to Ute. "I want this army ready to deploy by dawn. Occupying the fortress here makes no sense. Move on Meisthelm with all speed."

"Are we to attack immediately?"

"No, encircle the city but do not attack. The rest of the army will join you within the month. We attack when I arrive."

Imelin returned to his horse without waiting for confirmation. His work in Unchar was done but there was yet much left to be done to prepare Meisthelm for his open return.

Horse saddled and bags packed with enough supplies to see him through at least a week, two if he was conservative, Ute Hai slipped through the loose picket line and back into the Unchar Pass. The confrontation with Imelin shredded any doubts he had left. His time among the Rovers was finished. They had strayed too far off course while under the maniacal influences of the wizard. Whatever road they now traveled down wasn't one he was willing to compromise all he stood for over.

He'd attended Denes after Imelin left, seeing the man to a healer and ensuring none of the injuries were mortal. The rest was easy. With so many men and darklings occupying the area, he was able to secure what he needed and disappear when everyone was otherwise occupied. He paused at the southern mouth of the pass to look back down on the men he once called friend and comrade.

He'd miss them, but he'd be alive to do so. The war against the Hierarchy was already well underway with who knew how much more before the end. How many of those friends in the valley below wouldn't be alive to see that end? How many would lie face down in a field, nameless and forgotten, while the rest of the world carried on? His conscience refused to allow him to be part of something so… final.

Life had been precarious at best since the Aragoth army turned guerrilla and declared an underground war against the Hierarchy. Ute suffered no qualms during that campaign, long as it was. It was this fight, for the wizard, that troubled his mind. So it was that he turned his back and fled. Asking others to join him was out of the question. Odds were, he would have been turned in and executed as a traitor. He very much valued his life and that of the others. If the weather held, and his luck, he'd be through the pass and heading northeast back to Aragoth without interference from marauding armies bent on destroying one another.

Ute Hai was many things, optimist not among them. A soft nudge of his boot and the horse entered the dark mouth of the Unchar Pass. He was done with the war. Done with the Rovers and done with the madness consuming everyone he knew. Life had more to offer. He just needed to find a place to settle down and enjoy it before time caught up to him and put him in the ground.

League after league sped by under hoof and foot. The soft hills of southern Galdea gradually turned to the rocky plains of northern Trimlon and again to the grasslands of Valadon. The central kingdom had yet to be buried under feet of snow like the northern half of the Free Lands. The air had grown chill but life continued normally for the thousands of citizens struggling to make a life. Normal, except for the rising tensions and the fast approaching war pushing down from the north.

Every town and village the three riders entered was awash with rumors and fear. Many families had already packed what few belongings they owned and were headed for the security of Meisthelm. It was a false promise. The hope that once was the Hierarchy had decayed beyond the point of salvation. But how could these peasants know that two massive armies of darklings were even now converging on the city?

"We should rest now. The open steppes of Valadon stretch for a hundred leagues," Halvor suggested.

Burns covered the majority of his body. His flesh was blackened, charred in more places. Pink skin began to show where Anni Sickali's magic had already began healing him, but the process was long and far from complete. The Red Brotherhood priest spoke in rasps. His eyes bore perpetual pain. Pain that could have been relieved, had he wished it. Instead, Halvor decided to keep it as reminder of his position. The last of the cell stationed in Galdarath. The fallen guardians of the Staff of Life. His cell may have been destroyed but his purpose had never been stronger.

"Our enemy will broker no delays," Anni Sickali replied. The crone idly tapped her fingertips together. "Imelin is cunning and will use our confusion and natural hesitancy to his advantage. I sense his desire."

Harrin Slinmyer frowned after swallowing a mouthful of water. "Dlorn and the army are keeping him busy on the rivers. Imelin won't reach Meisthelm before early spring."

"You overestimate the Galdean army," Anni told him. "Dlorn is capable but was never the target. Galdea was in the way. The darklings needed to break out of Suroc Tol so the Black orchestrated the fall of Dol'ir and the flooding of your kingdom. I have seen such before in my own kingdom. Many brave men will fall making a stand but the Black will have secreted thousands, if not more, of his army south, while the great army is distracted. Cunning, that one, but ultimately predictable for one who has studied the ways of magic."

"If what you say is true, the Hierarchy may well be under siege already," Harrin added after some thought. "All the more reason not to stop."

"What then shall we do when we arrive at Meisthelm, exhausted and beaten down from hard days on the road?" Halvor asked. "If the city is infested, we won't find entrance."

"It seems we are damned regardless of our decision," Harrin said.

Anni slapped her knee and crackled a laugh. "Ha ha! I haven't had an adventure like this in a lifetime!"

Harrin wasn't sure adventure was the term he'd use. He held no love for the Hierarchy, only Galdea. But if Meisthelm fell, so too, would the rest of the Free Lands. The choice was never in doubt.

"If that is the case, let us rest the horses. A few hours won't make the difference between life and death. Eat, drink, and rest. Meisthelm awaits us."

The unlikely trio pulled off the main road. It was a moment there would be little time for in the coming days. War, and the future of the Free Lands awaited.

The story continues in
The Land of Wicked Shadows:
Immortality Shattered Book III

The Land of Wicked Shadows

Immortality Shattered Book III

CHRISTIAN WARREN FREED

A New Journey

Temperatures continued to drop as the full swing of winter roared in well over a month too early. The cold was yet another devilish weapon from the Black Imelin's deadly arsenal unleashed upon the Free Lands. Under the lackadaisical rule of the Hierarchy Imelin had turned traitor, made alliances with the darkling kingdom of Suroc Tol to the northeast, and unleashed a war the likes of which hadn't been seen since the time of Ils Kincannon and the Knights of the Seven Manacles.

Aron Kryte, commander of a troop of Golden Warriors, the finest soldiers in the lands, thought long and hard on the ever growing powers of the Black. All the wizard lacked was the Staff of Life to rule. Fortunately, the Staff was well on the way to safety and away from the major fighting. Or so he prayed. There was no way to verify that until he reached the mountain city-fortress of Hyrast far to the north.

He failed to see anything short of the Staff being able to stop the Black. So much so that his mind couldn't overlook the fact even as he and Jod Theron marched across the game trails crisscrossing Almarin. Thousands had already died with the promise of so many more yet to come. To the best of Aron's knowledge his forces hadn't so much as dented the might the Black displayed. So what were they missing? The fate of the entire world was hanging in the balance and everything he needed in order to succeed remained just outside of his grasp. The dilemma hounded him with each footstep.

Old man Theron took him from the obscurity of clouded thought with a gleeful chuckle as they arrived at a lone farmhouse. Aron slipped back to the moment and scanned the area. Soldier instincts took over and he searched for hidden threats. Odd, no smoke poured from the chimney. No smell of warmth. He heard the faint creaking of rusted hinges as the front door swung too and fro with the winds.

"Friends?" he asked.

Jod nodded. "Some of the few I actually have, yes. We help each other during harsh times."

Anguish flooded him, clashing with predatory instincts. Aron sensed danger. "This is not right. I think we may have been beaten here."

Jod stopped and tried to find anything obvious out of the ordinary. His sight at distance was failing, but his senses became more in-tuned the older he became. Never a soldier, Jod was well versed in the ways of the world. What he knew remained secret, so secret not even the young lordling would find out if he didn't want him to. The dogs hunched down and sniffed the air. Their hair stood on end. Each growled in warning.

"We must be cautious," Aron whispered and drew his sword.

He was moving before Jod replied, his warrior self took over as he danced through the sparse grove of trees leading up to the farmhouse. Possibilities of what might have happened were endless. The great battle of the Crimson Fields had occurred less than a day's journey north of here and not long ago. No doubt remnants of both the darkling and Galdean armies were moving through this part of Almarin. It took little imagination to think what might have happened to the farmers.

Thankful he convinced Jod to take him back to the stretch of the icy Simca River where he'd been found,

Aron clutched his salvaged sword tighter. He shivered at the memory of plunging into those waters as darklings swarmed onto the fragile rope bridge to get to him. The rope broke and the river took them all. His last sight was of the horror on his friend's faces as he went under water.

Knowing he wasn't going to be able to keep up with a man half his age, Jod slowly made his way down the knoll toward his friend's home. For a brief moment he doubted his decision to come out of seclusion and thought of going home to wait out the end. Deep down however, he knew it was well past time to return to Meisthelm. Those responsible for the ending of his old life were long gone, but there were still amends needed to be made.

The Golden Warrior wasted no time on thought. Flanked by Jod's dogs, he was up on the porch and ready to burst inside. His senses told him whatever had happened was long past but there was danger in having a false sense of security. Aron's fingers curled around the edge of the door. He pushed and stepped inside. The dogs slinked past and fanned out.

Aron found the first body in the archway leading to the kitchen. She was very young, and very dead. Telltale signs of a darkling attack peppered the house. His sorrow for the dead rose, for they never stood a chance. Snow blew in through one of the broken windows. No doubt the monsters came during the night. Surprise was complete for the wife yet wore her cooking apron. A bowl and wooden spoon lay beside her in epitaph.

The rest of the family lay scattered around the house. He couldn't imagine being the last to die. The knowledge that all you held dear was already lost and your turn was next. Yet with that knowledge he found it odd that nothing in the house was disturbed. Nothing out of place. The house was in much the same condition as it was before the attack. This was a hunt for sport.

He finished his inspection and found Jod sitting in a rocking chair on the porch with his head in his hands. He was much too old to cry over the inevitable, no matter how tragic, though the pain of losing friends hurt deep.

"They were peaceful people. They didn't deserve this," he said without lifting his head.

"No one does," Aron answered and spat onto the snow.

"Why?"

It was a question without an easy answer. How could Aron explain that this was all part of a madman's quest to destroy the world? That without Imelin these monsters would still be trapped in Suroc Tol. Aron could only shake his head.

"There is no answer, my friend, but I can tell you this. The rest of the Free Lands will suffer similarly if my friends and I are unsuccessful. I fear this may be the final war."

Jod sniffled once. "It is sad to watch what this world has become. Is there any way we can save ourselves from this insanity?"

"There are times when I think no, but the power in our hearts holds the key to survival. The only way to win is by destroying the Staff of Life and the wizard who seeks to wield it. Then and only then will we be safe from evil's grasp."

"Everything is moving against you," Jod replied. "Not even an innocent family stands protected against a war they know nothing of. What offer of hope can you give these people when they discover you can't save them from doom?"

"What can I say?" Aron answered after a time. "I have no family of my own but my friends. I will do anything to keep them alive and end this war."

The hermit snorted. "By that logic casualties are necessary so long as they serve the greater good of the cause?"

"If it means defeating this darkness and returning the lands to the light which it needs? Yes. I would gladly sacrifice myself for that."

"Congratulations, young man. You have just learned a very valuable lesson in the ways of the world." Jod seemed oddly pleased.

"Do we bury them now?"

"No. We do not have time. Your friends are in need of you and every moment counts. I have already checked the barn. Whoever did this left the animals alone. There are a few horses and a quality wagon. We should get going as soon as possible."

"But your friends…"

Jod's smile was sad. "Are already gone. No further harm can befall them."

Whoever Jod once was, Aron came to view him as a tactical man.

Together they left the blood-stained floors of the farmhouse and saddled up the horses. The day was but half over and it would be many more before the pair reached Hyrast.

ARMIES
of the
SILVER MAGE
CHRISTIAN WARREN
FREED

Malweir was once governed by the order of Mages, bringers of peace and light. Centuries past and the lands prospered. But all was not well. Unknown to most, one mage desired power above all else. He turned his will to the banished Dark Gods and brought war to the free lands. Only a handful of mages survived the betrayal and the Silver Mage was left free to twist the darker races to his bidding. The only thing he needs to complete his plan and rule the world forever are the four shards of the crystal of Tol Shere.

Having spent most of their lives dreaming about leaving their sleepy village and travelling the world, Delin Kerny and Fennic Attleford never thought that one day they would be forced to flee their town to save their lives. Everything changes when they discover the fabled Star Silver sword and learn that there are some who want the weapon for themselves. Hunted by a ruthless mercenary, the boys run from Fel Darrins and are forced into the adventure they only dreamed about.

Ever ashamed of the horrors his kind let loose on the world the last mage, Dakeb, lives his life in shadows. The only thing keeping him alive is his quest to stop the Silver Mage from reassembling the crystal. His chance finally comes through the hearts and wills of Delin and Fennic. Dakeb bestows upon them the crystal shard, entrusting them with the one thing capable of restoring peace to Malweir.

the Dragon Hunters

CHRISTIAN WARREN FREED

The Mage Wars are a fading memory. The kingdoms of Malweir focus on rebuilding what was lost and moving beyond the vast amounts of death and devastation. For some it is easy, others far worse. Some men are made in battle. Grelic of Thrae is one. A seasoned veteran of numerous campaigns and raids, Grelic is a warrior without a war. He languishes under mugs of ale and poor choices that eventually find him locked in the dungeons of King Rentor. His only chance at redemption is an offer tantamount to suicide: travel north with a misfit band of adventurers and learn the truth of what happened in the village of Gend.

Grelic, suddenly tired of his life, reluctantly agrees and meets the only survivor of the horrible massacre: Fitch Iane. Broken, mentally and physically, Fitch babbles about demons stalking through the mists and a terrible monster prowling the skies, breathing fire and death.

What begins as a simple reconnaissance mission quickly turns into a quest to stop Sidian, the Silver Mage from accomplishing his goals in the Deadlands. The last of the dark mages seeks to recover the four shards of the crystal of Tol Shere and open the gateway to release the dark gods from their eternal prison.

Grelic and his team are sorely outnumbered and ill prepared to deal with the combined threats of a dark mage and one of the great dragons from the west. Not even the might of the Aeldruin, high elf mercenaries, and Dakeb, the last of the mages, promises to be enough to stop evil and restore peace to Thrae.

DREAMS
OF
WINTER

A FORGOTTEN GODS TALE

CHRISTIAN WARREN FREED

It is a troubled time, for the old gods are returning and they want the universe back…

Under the rigid guidance of the Conclave, the seven hundred known worlds carve out a new empire with the compassion and wisdom the gods once offered. But a terrible secret, known only to the most powerful, threatens to undo three millennia of progress. The gods are not dead at all. They merely sleep. And they are being hunted.

Senior Inquisitor Tolde Breed is sent to the planet Crimeat to investigate the escape of one of the deadliest beings in the history of the universe: Amongeratix, one of the fabled THREE, sons of the god-king. Tolde arrives on a world where heresy breeds insurrection and war is only a matter of time. Aided by Sister Abigail of the Order of Blood Witches, and a company of Prekhauten Guards, Tolde hurries to find Amongeratix and return him to Conclave custody before he can restart his reign of terror.

What he doesn't know is that the Three are already operating on Crimeat.

BIO

Christian W. Freed was born in Buffalo, N.Y. more years ago than he would like to remember. After spending more than 20 years in the active duty US Army he has turned his talents to writing. Since retiring, he has gone on to publish more than 20 science fiction and fantasy novels as well as his combat memoirs from his time in Iraq and Afghanistan. His first book, Hammers in the Wind, has been the #1 free book on Kindle 4 times and he holds a fancy certificate from the L Ron Hubbard Writers of the Future Contest.

Passionate about history, he combines his knowledge of the past with modern military tactics to create an engaging, quasi-realistic world for the readers. He graduated from Campbell University with a degree in history and a Masters of Arts degree in Digital Communications from the University of North Carolina at Chapel Hill. He currently lives outside of Raleigh, N.C. and devotes his time to writing, his family, and their two Bernese Mountain Dogs. If you drive by you might just find him on the porch with a cigar in one hand and a pen in the other. You can find out more about his work by following him on: